A DATE WITH
THE ICE PRINCESS

BY
KATE HARDY

First published in Great Britain 2013
by Mills & Boon, an imprint of Harlequin (UK) Limited.
Harlequin (UK) Limited, Eton House, 18-24 Paradise Road,
Richmond, Surrey TW9 1SR

© Pamela Brooks 2013

ISBN: 978 0 263 89905 4

Harlequin (UK) policy is to use papers that are natural, renewable and recyclable products and made from wood grown in sustainable forests. The logging and manufacturing process conform to the legal environmental regulations of the country of origin.

Printed and bound in Spain
by Blackprint CPI, Barcelona

Dear Reader

I couldn't resist going back to the emergency department at the London Victoria and catching up with everyone (you may well recognise some names!). I enjoy opposites-attract stories, and at first glance you'd think that daredevil party boy Lewis is the opposite of quiet ice princess Abigail. Except nothing's quite as it seems for these two; they both have tricky pasts and secrets to overcome, and they have a lot to teach each other.

Lewis buys a date with Abby to teach her how to relax and have fun. Except it ends up with Abby teaching Lewis to learn to trust his heart and discover what he really wants from life. And it's not what he thinks it is...

One of my favourite parts of writing is hands-on research. I didn't research the really scary stuff myself (unless you count watching Felix Baumgartner's record sky-dive on TV), but I did grill friends who've done zip-lining and ice-skating. Researching the dancing was great fun, though my husband and I are rather better at the Cha Cha Cha than we are at the Waltz (and the dance shoes Abby buys are, ahem, just like mine). The Beethoven is my favourite piece of music. And I went to the Globe with my best friend while I was writing the book (though it was a different play!). I do hope you enjoy reading this book as much as I enjoyed writing it.

With love

Kate Hardy

CHAPTER ONE

'ABIGAIL, AS YOU'VE only been with the team for a few weeks, I know it's a bit of an ask,' Max Fenton, the duty consultant, said, 'but Marina's put a lot into setting up the promise auction next weekend. So I was wondering if you might be able to donate something?'

Abigail knew that the quickest thing would be to ask her dad and his band to sign a photo and some CDs. Or offer tickets and a backstage pass to Brydon's next tour. Except she'd learned the hard way not to mention that her father was the rock guitarist and singer Keith Brydon, founder of the group that bore his surname. Or that her flat had been bought with the royalties from 'Cinnamon Baby', the song he'd written for her the day of her birth. It might be a quick win, but it'd make her life way too complicated.

She could simply say no, but that would be mean. The promise auction was raising funds to buy equipment that the department badly needed. And she did want to help.

'I, um…OK,' she said. 'What did you have in mind?'

'Max, are you pestering our poor new special reg?' Marina asked, coming to stand with them and sliding her arms round her husband's waist.

'On your behalf, yes.' He twisted around to kiss her.

The perfect couple, Abigail thought, clearly so much in love. And even though she knew she was better off on her own, she couldn't help feeling slightly wistful at the love in their expressions. What would it be like to be with someone who loved her that much?

Marina rolled her eyes. 'Ignore him, Abigail. You honestly don't have to do anything.'

Which left her on the outside, Abigail thought. Where she'd always been. Would it be so hard to be part of the team for once? 'No, I'd really like to help,' she said. 'What sort of thing do you suggest?'

'Really?' Marina looked faintly surprised, then delighted. 'Well, other people have offered things like dinner out, or cleaning for a day, or a basket of stuff.' She paused. 'Maybe you could offer some cinema tickets with popcorn and a drink thrown in, or something like that.'

'Or a date. That'd be a good one,' Max chipped in.

'Shut up, Max. You're not meant to be pressuring her. A date's not a good idea. You know what—' Marina stopped abruptly and put a hand to her mouth, looking horrified.

Abigail could guess why. And what Marina had been going to say. 'It's OK. I know people call me the ice princess,' she said dryly. 'It was the same at my last hospital.'

'People don't mean to be unkind.' Marina looked awkward. 'It's just that…well, you keep yourself to yourself. It's quite hard to get to know you.'

'Yes.' There wasn't much else Abigail could say. It was true. She did keep herself to herself. For a very good reason. Once people worked out who she was, they tried to get close to her so they could get to meet her father—not because they wanted to get to know her better. Been there, done that, worn the T-shirt to shreds. She blew out a breath. 'OK, then. I'll offer a date.'

'Please don't feel that we've pushed you into this,' Marina said. 'If you'd rather offer a basket of girly stuff or some cinema tickets, that'd be just as good.'

It was a let-out. But Abigail was convinced, whatever Marina said, that her colleagues would think even less of her if she took it. 'The date's fine,' she said.

Relief flooded Marina's expression. 'Thank you, Abigail. That's fabulous. I really appreciate it.'

And maybe, Abigail thought, this would be a new start for her. A way of making friends. Real friends for once. Something she'd always found so difficult in the past.

The alternative—that she'd just made a huge, huge mistake—was something she didn't want to think about.

Friday the following week was the night of the auction. The room was absolutely packed; all the emergency department staff who weren't on duty were there, along with people Abigail half recognised from other departments that she'd met briefly while discussing the hand-over of patients.

Max Fenton and Marco Ranieri, two of the department's consultants, had a double act going on as the auctioneers. And they hadn't spared themselves from the promise auction: they'd both put themselves up as household slaves for a day, and driven each other's price up accordingly.

Abigail bid successfully on a pair of tickets to a classical concert, and then it was her own promise up for auction.

A date.

Adrenalin prickled at the back of her neck. Why on earth hadn't she thought to ask someone to bid for her at the auction? She would've funded the cost herself, and it would've gotten her out of an awkward situation.

Still, she was the ice princess. Hardly anyone would be interested in a date with her, would they?

Except that Marco and Max seemed to be on a roll, really talking her up.

Abigail could barely breathe when the bidding reached three figures.

And then a male voice drawled, 'Five hundred pounds.'

Oh, for goodness' sake. That was a ridiculous sum. And the only reason she could think of that the man would pay that sort of money for a date with her was because he'd found out who she was.

Please, please, let her be wrong.

She held her breath, not quite daring to turn round and look at whoever was bidding. Not wanting to make eye contact.

Everyone else in the room seemed to be holding their breath, too.

And then Max said easily, 'Do we have an increase on five hundred pounds?'

Silence.

'OK, then, that's a wrap. Thank you. One date with Dr Abigail Smith, sold to Dr Lewis Gallagher.'

Lewis Gallagher?

Abigail's brain couldn't quite process it. Lewis Gallagher, special registrar in the emergency department, was the one man in the hospital who really didn't have to buy a date. Women queued up to date him because he was a challenge. Every single one of them seemed to believe that she'd be the one to make him review his 'three dates and you're out' policy. And, from what Abigail had heard, every single one of them failed.

Except her. Because when Lewis had asked her out last week, she'd said no.

And now he'd *bought* a date with her.

Oh, help. She needed some air. Time to think about how she was going to get out of this.

Except it was too late, because Lewis was standing beside her.

'Move to me, I think, Dr Smith,' he said softly, brandishing the certificate Marina had got her to sign for the auction—the promise of a date.

'Five hundred pounds is a lot of money. Thank you for supporting the auction.' She lifted her chin. 'You get a date, but don't expect me to end up in your bed.'

He laughed. 'What makes you think that's what I had in mind?'

His reputation. Colour rushed into her face. 'So why did you buy a date with me, Dr Gallagher?' *Because he knew who she was?*

He shrugged. 'Because you said no when I asked you.'

Ah. Because she'd challenged his ego. She relaxed. Just a little bit.

He held her gaze. 'And now you don't have an excuse to say no.'

'Maybe I just don't want to go out with a party boy.'

She'd recognised his type the first time she'd met him. Handsome, wonderful social skills—and shallow as a puddle.

Not her type.

At all.

Lewis gave her the most charming, heart-melting smile she'd ever seen in her life. She'd just bet he practised it in front of a mirror.

'Maybe I'm not the party boy you think I am,' he said. 'Want to know where we're going?'

'I haven't decided yet,' she said. And she almost winced at how haughty and snooty she sounded. This was ridiculous. She didn't behave like a spoiled diva. That wasn't who she was. Abigail Smith was a quiet and hard-working doctor who just got on with whatever needed to be done.

Yet Lewis Gallagher made her feel like a brat, wanting to throw a tantrum and stamp her feet when she didn't get her own way. And she couldn't understand why on earth he was affecting her like this.

'Newsflash for you, princess. I bought a date with you. So you don't get to decide where we're going.'

Shut up, Abigail. Don't answer him. Don't let him provoke you. Except her mouth wasn't listening. 'Correction. You bought a date with me. Which means I organise it and I pick up the bill.'

'Nope. It means you get to go out with me on Sunday morning.'

She was about to protest that she couldn't, because she was working, when he added, 'And you're off duty on Sunday morning. I checked.'

She was trapped.

And maybe the fear showed in her eyes because his voice softened. 'It's only a date, Abby.'

Abby? Nobody called her that. Not even her father. Well, *especially* not her father. He used her given name. The one she made sure nobody at work knew about because then it would be too easy to connect her with her father. Not that she didn't love him—Keith Brydon was the most important person in the world to her. And she was incredibly proud of him. She just wanted to be seen for who she was, not dismissed as an attention-grabbing celeb's daughter riding on her famous parent's coat-tails.

Before she could protest, Lewis continued, 'We're just going somewhere and spending a bit of time together. All we're doing is getting to know each other a little. But, just so we're very clear on this, I'm not expecting you to sleep with me. Or even,' he added, 'to kiss me.'

'Right.' Oh, great. And now her voice had to croak, making it sound as if she *wanted* him to kiss her. How pathetic was that?

'Wear jeans,' he said. 'And sensible shoes.'

'Do I look like the sort of person who clip-clops around in high heels she can barely walk in?' And then she clapped a hand to her mouth. Oh, no. She hadn't actually meant to say that out loud.

His eyes crinkled at the corners. 'No. But I think you could surprise me, Abby.'

She shivered. Oh, the pictures *that* put in her head. 'I suppose now you're going to say something cheesy about finding out if I have a temper to go with my red hair.'

'It's a cliché and I wouldn't dream of it,' he said. 'Though, on this evening's showing, I think you do.'

And, damn him, his eyes were twinkling. She almost, *almost* laughed.

'You need sensible shoes,' he said again. 'Trainers would be really good. Oh, and wear your hair tied back.'

That was a given. She always wore her hair tied back. 'So what are we doing?' Despite herself, she was curious.

'You'll find out on Sunday. I'll pick you up at your place.'

She shook her head. 'There's no need. I could meet you there.'

'Ah, but you don't know where we're going.'

Irritating man. She forced herself to sound supersweet. 'You could tell me.'

'True. But it'd be a waste of resources if we took two cars.'

'Then I'll drive.' Maybe needling him a little would make sure he agreed to it. 'Unless you're scared of letting a woman drive you?'

'No.' He laughed. 'Well, there's one exception. But she'd scare anyone.'

Ex-girlfriend? she wondered. The one that got away?

Not that it was any of her business. And not that she was interested. Because she didn't want to date Lewis Gallagher. She was only doing this because she'd made a promise to raise funds for the department.

'So are you going to make a fuss about it, or will you allow me to drive rather than direct you?'

Put like that, she didn't have much choice. She gave in. 'OK. You can drive.'

'Good. I'll pick you up at nine. Your address?'

If she didn't tell him, she was pretty sure he had the resources to find out. So she told him.

'Great. See you on Sunday.' And he was gone.

Making quite sure he had the last word, she noticed.

Abigail was really grateful for the fact that her shift on Saturday was immensely busy, with lots of people limping in with sports injuries and the like. The fact that she barely had a second to breathe also meant she didn't have to talk; the hospital grapevine had been working overtime, so everyone knew Lewis had paid a ridiculous amount of money for a date with her—and she just knew that everyone was itching to ask questions. Why would a man who could date any woman he chose pay for a date with the girl nobody wanted to go out with?

This was crazy. She wasn't his type. She wasn't a party girl or one of the women who sighed over him and thought she could reform him. And, actually, she wanted to know the real answer to that question, too. Why on earth had he paid so much money for a date with her? Was his ego really so huge that he hadn't been able to stand someone turning him down?

Though that was a bit unfair. It didn't fit in with the man she'd seen taking time to reassure a frightened child with a broken wrist earlier in the week. Or the doctor who, instead of going to get something to eat during his lunch break, had spent the time talking to the elderly man who was in for observation with stomach pains but clearly didn't have anyone to come and wait with him. Or the man who'd got a terrified yet defiant teenage girl to open up to him and tell him exactly which tablets she'd taken then had sat holding her hand and talking to her the entire way through the stomach pump that Abigail had administered.

Lewis was good with people. He gave them *time*. As a doctor, he was one of the best she'd ever worked with.

And Abigail had to admit that Lewis Gallagher was also very easy on the eye. His dark hair was cut a bit too short for her liking, but his slate-blue eyes were beautiful. And his mouth could make her feel hot all over if she allowed herself to think about it. Not to mention the dimple in his cheek when he smiled.

But she wasn't looking for a relationship, and he was wasting his time. She'd explain; she'd give him back the money he'd paid for the date, and then hopefully that would be the end of it.

Except on Sunday he turned up at her front door with a bunch of sweet-smelling white stocks. Not a flashy, over-the-top bouquet with ribbons and cellophane and glitter, but a simple bunch of summer flowers wrapped in pretty paper. The kind of thing she'd buy herself as a treat. And it disarmed her completely.

'For you,' he said, and presented the flowers to her.

'Thank you. They're lovely.' She couldn't help breathing in their scent, enjoying it. And she'd have to put the flowers in water right now or they'd droop beyond rescue. It would be rude to leave him outside while she sorted out a vase.

But this was Lewis Gallagher. In the white shirt and formal trousers he wore with a white coat at work he looked professional and she could view him as just another colleague. In faded jeans and a black T-shirt he looked younger. Approachable. *Touchable.*

How had she ever thought she could handle this? Her social skills were rubbish. They always had been. Maybe if she hadn't grown up in an all-male environment... She pushed the thought away. This wasn't about her mother—or, rather, her lack of one. She was thirty years old and she was perfectly capable of dealing with this on her own.

'Come in,' she mumbled awkwardly.

She put the flowers in water, then buried her nose in them and breathed in the scent again. 'These are glorious.'

'I'm glad you like them,' he said.

'I wasn't expecting you to bring me flowers.'

'I believe it's official first date behaviour.'

First of three, according to the grapevine. 'So today you're on your best behaviour, next time you're going to be a bad boy, and after the third date you dump me?' She shook her head. 'No, thanks. I'll pass.'

'That's a bit unfair. You don't know me.'

True, but she wasn't going to let him guilt-trip her into agreeing to anything. 'I know your reputation.'

'Don't believe everything you hear.' He held her gaze. 'Just as I don't believe everything I hear about you, princess. Even if you are starchy and standoffish at work.'

The ice princess. Touché. 'So why *did* you place that bid?'

'Because,' he said, 'you intrigue me.'

'And because I turned you down.'

'Yes,' he admitted. 'But it's nothing to do with ego.'

'No?' she scoffed.

'No. It's because I was out of ideas on how to persuade you into joining in with the team outside work.'

So this wasn't actually a date? She found herself relaxing. 'I take it this is a team thing today, then?'

'No. It's just you and me.' He shrugged. 'And a few strangers.'

'What do you mean, strangers?'

He spread his hands and gave her a mischievous little-boy smile. 'There's only one way to find out what we're doing. Let's go.'

She wasn't that surprised to discover that his car was a convertible.

'Very flashy,' she said dryly. Though she supposed that navy blue was a tad more sophisticated than red.

'Very comfortable, actually,' he corrected her, unlocking the car and pressing a button to take the roof down.

The seats were soft, white leather. This should be clichéd and cheesy and make her want to sneer at him.

But he had a point, she discovered as she climbed in. The car *was* comfortable. And driving in the sunshine with the roof down and the wind in her hair was a real treat. She hadn't done anything like this in ages; her own car was sensible, economical and easy to park, rather than a carefree convertible.

'So where are we going?' she asked.

'About three-quarters of an hour away.'

He really wasn't going to be drawn, was he?

'Feel free to choose the music,' he said.

The first radio station she tried was dance music—not her cup of tea at all. The second was playing one of her dad's songs; she left the station playing, and couldn't help humming along to the song.

Lewis smiled at her. 'I had you pegged as listening only to highbrow stuff. Classical music. Like those tickets you bid on.'

He'd noticed that?

'See, I told you that you could surprise me.'

'So you don't like this sort of stuff?' Abigail had to remind herself not to jump to her dad's defence.

'Actually, I do. This sort of stuff is great on a playlist if you're going out for a run. But I didn't think you'd be a fan of Brydon.'

Their biggest. Not that she was going to tell Lewis that. Or why.

He didn't press her to talk, and she found herself relaxing, enjoying the scenery.

Until he turned off the main road and she saw the sign.

'Urban Jungle Adventure Centre.' And it wasn't just the name. It was the photographs on the hoarding of what people were doing at the centre. 'We're going *ziplining*?'

'It's one of the biggest rushes you can get.' He gave her a sidelong look as he parked the car. 'With your clothes on, that is.'

She felt the colour stain her face. 'Are you determined to embarrass me?'

'No. I'm trying to make you laugh. I'm not trying to seduce you.'

'I don't understand you,' she said. 'I don't have a clue what makes you tick.'

'Snap. So let's go and have some fun finding out.'

Fun. Zip-lining. The idea of launching herself off a platform and whizzing through space, with only a flimsy harness holding her onto a line to stop her plummeting to the ground... No, that wasn't fun. It made her palms sweat.

He frowned. 'Are you scared of heights, Abby?'

She let the diminutive pass without correcting him. 'No.'

'But you're scared of this.'

She swallowed. 'I work in the emergency department. I see accidents all the time.'

'And you think you're going to have an accident here?' His expression softened. 'It's OK, Abby. This is safe. All the staff are trained. All the equipment is tested. Very, very regularly. Your harness isn't going to break and you're not going to fall. No broken bones, no concussion, no subdural haematoma. OK?'

How had he known what the pictures were in her head? She blew out a breath. 'OK.'

'The first time you do it, I admit, it can be a bit daunting. Hardly anyone jumps off the platform on their first time. The second time, you'll know what the adrenalin rush feels like and you'll leap off as if you've never been scared.'

She doubted it. A lot. 'So this is what makes you tick. You're an adrenalin fiend.' And that was probably why he worked in the emergency department. Because it was all about speed, about split-second decisions that made the difference between life and death. Real adrenalin stuff.

'Actually, I'm probably more of an endorphin fiend,' he corrected. 'Which is why I usually go for a run before every shift, so I feel great before I start work and I'm ready to face anything.'

She'd never thought of it that way before. 'That makes sense.'

And of course he made her climb up the ladder before him. 'Ladies first.'

'You mean, you want to look at my backside,' she grumbled.

He grinned. 'That, too. It's a very nice backside.'

She gave him what she hoped was a really withering look—no way did she want him to know just how scary she found this—and climbed up the ladder. Stubbornness got her to the top. But when it came to putting the harness on all her nerves came back. With teeth. And could she get the wretched thing on, ready for the adventure centre staff to check? Her fingers had turned into what felt like lumpy balloons.

Way to go, Abigail, she thought bitterly. How to embarrass yourself totally in front of the coolest guy in the hospital. Nothing changed, did it? She just didn't fit in.

'Let me help you,' Lewis said.

He was all ready to go, harness and wide smile both in place. Well, they *would* be, she thought crossly.

'And this isn't an excuse to touch you, by the way. Fastening the harness can be a bit tricky, and I've already gone through that learning curve.'

Now she felt like the grumpiest, most horrible person on the planet. Because Lewis was being nice, not sleazy. She'd attributed motives to him that he clearly didn't have and had thought the worst of him without any evidence to back it up. How mean was that? 'Thank you,' she muttered.

He laughed. 'That sounds more like "I want to kill you".'

'I do,' she admitted. And somehow he'd disarmed her. Somehow his smile didn't seem cocky and smug any more. He was… Shockingly, she thought, Lewis Gallagher was *nice*.

Which was dangerous. She didn't want to get close to a heartbreaker like Lewis Gallagher. She didn't want to get involved with anyone. She just wanted her nice, quiet—well, busy, she amended mentally—life as an emergency department doctor.

'OK. Step in.'

And what had seemed like an impossible web was suddenly fitting round her. Lewis's hands were brushing against her, yes, but that was only because he was checking every single buckle and every single fastening, making doubly sure that everything was done properly and she was safe. There was nothing sexual in the contact.

Which should make her feel relieved.

So why did it make her feel disappointed? Surely she wasn't so stupid as to let herself get attracted to a good-time guy like Lewis Gallagher?

'OK. Ready?' he asked.

No. Far from it. 'Yes,' she lied.

The adventure centre staff did a final check on her harness, clipped the carabiners to the zip-lines, and then she and Lewis were both standing on the very edge of the platform. Looking down over trees and a stream and—no, they didn't seriously expect her just to step off into nothingness, did they?

'You can step off or jump off,' the adventure centre guy said.

'See you at the bottom, Abby. After three,' Lewis said. 'One, two, three—whoo-hoo!'

And he jumped. He actually *jumped*.

'I hate you, Lewis Gallagher. I really, *really* hate you,' she said. Right at that moment she would've been happy to give him back the money he'd paid for their date and give double the amount to the hospital fund, as long as she didn't have to jump.

'Just step off, love. It's all right once you get going,' the adventure centre guy said. 'It's fun. Look at that ten-year-old next to you. He's enjoying it.'

So now the guy thought she was feebler than a kid? Oh, great. Her confidence dipped just a bit more.

But there was no way out of this. She had to do it.

She closed her eyes, silently cursing Lewis. Deep breath. One, two, three…

The speed shocked her into opening her eyes. It felt as if she was flying. Like a bird gliding on the air currents. Totally free, the wind rushing against her face and the sun shining.

By the time she reached the platform at the end of the zip-line, she understood exactly what Lewis had meant. This felt amazing. Like nothing she'd ever experienced.

He was there to meet her. 'OK?' he asked, his eyes filled with concern.

She blew out a breath. 'Yes.'

'Sure? You didn't look too happy when you were standing on the platform.'

'Probably because I wanted to kill you.'

'Uh-huh. And now?'

'You'll live,' she said.

He smiled, and she felt a weird sensation in her chest, as if her heart had just done a flip. Which was totally ridiculous. Number one, it wasn't physically possible and, number two, Lewis Gallagher wasn't her type. He really wasn't.

'So you enjoyed it.' He brushed her cheek gently with the backs of his fingers, and all her nerve-endings sat up and begged for more. 'Good. We get three turns. Ready for another?'

She nodded, not quite trusting her voice not to wobble and not wanting him to have any idea of how much he was affecting her.

The second time, the ladder was easier, and so was standing on the platform This time she stepped off without hesitation.

The third time, she turned to Lewis and lifted her chin. She could do this every bit as well as he could. 'After three? One, two, three.' And she jumped, yelling, 'Whoo-hoo!'

With her customary reserve broken, Abigail Smith was beautiful, Lewis realised. Her grey eyes were shining, her cheeks were rosy with pleasure, and he suddenly desperately wanted to haul her into his arms and kiss her.

Except she was already off into space, waving her arms and striking poses as she slid down the zip-line.

If someone had told him two days ago that the ice princess of the hospital would let herself go and enjoy herself this much, he would've scoffed. He'd brought her here as much to rattle her as anything else.

But he'd been hoist with his own petard, because she didn't seem rattled at all.

Unlike him. Abigail Smith had managed to rattle him, big time.

He jumped off the platform and followed her down; he was far enough behind for her to be already taking off the safety harness when he reached the landing platform.

'So are you going to admit it?' he asked when he'd removed his own harness and handed it to the assistant at the bottom of the zip-line.

'What?'

'That you enjoyed it.'

She nodded. 'If you'd told me earlier that this was where we were going, I would've made an excuse. I would've paid back your money and given the same amount to the hospital, so nobody lost out.'

'But you would've lost out.' He held her gaze. 'And I don't mean just the money.'

'Yes. You're right.'

He liked the fact that she could admit it when she was wrong. 'That's why I didn't tell you.'

'Thank you for bringing me here. I never would've thought I'd enjoy something like this. But—yes, it was fun.'

Oh, help. She had *dimples* when she smiled. Who would've thought that the serious, keep-herself-to-herself doctor would be this gorgeous when her reserve was down? He hadn't expected her to be anything like this. And he was horribly aware that Abigail Smith could really get under his skin.

'Let's go exploring,' he said. He needed to move, distract himself from her before he said something stupid. Or did something worse—like giving in to the temptation to lean over and kiss her.

CHAPTER TWO

ABIGAIL AND LEWIS spent the next couple of hours exploring every activity at the centre, including the almost vertical slides and the climbing wall. Abigail didn't even seem to mind when they got a bit wet on the water chute, though Lewis's pulse spiked as he imagined how she'd look with her skin still damp from showering with him.

'Penny for them?' she asked.

No way. If he told her, she'd either slap his face or go silent on him, and he wanted to get to know more of this playful side of her. 'Time for lunch,' he said instead.

'Only on condition you let me pay. Because you've paid for everything else today.'

'And you don't like being beholden.'

'Exactly.'

Someone had hurt her, he thought. Broken her trust. Maybe that was why she kept herself to herself so much: to protect herself from being hurt again. 'Then thank you. I would love you to buy me lunch.'

She looked faintly surprised, as if she'd expected him to argue, and then looked relieved.

'There really aren't any strings to today, Abby,' he said softly. 'This is all about having fun.'

'And I am having fun.'

Although her smile was a little bit too bright. What was she hiding?

There was no point in asking; he knew she didn't trust him enough to tell him and she'd make up some anodyne excuse or change the subject. So he simply smiled back and led her to the cafeteria.

'What would you like?' she asked.

He glanced at the board behind the counter. 'A burger, chips and a cola, please.'

'Junk food. Tut. And you a health professional,' she teased.

'Hey, I'm burning every bit of it off,' he protested.

She smiled. 'Go and find us a table and I'll queue up.'

When she joined him at the table with a tray of food, Lewis noticed that she'd chosen a jacket potato with salad and cottage cheese, and a bottle of mineral water. 'Super-healthy. Now I feel guilty for eating junk.'

She looked anxious. 'I was only teasing you.'

'Yeah. I was teasing, too.' He gave her a reassuring smile. 'Thank you. That looks good.'

He kept the conversation light during lunch, and then they went back to exploring the park.

'Do you want to do the zip-line again?' he asked.

'Can we?'

'Sure.'

And, as well as his usual adrenalin rush, Lewis got an extra kick from the fact that she was so clearly enjoying something they'd both thought was well outside her comfort zone.

'Thank you. I've had a really nice time,' she said when they got back to his car.

'The date's not over yet.'

She blinked. 'Isn't it?'

'I thought we could have dinner,' he said.

She looked down at her jeans and her T-shirt. 'I'm not really dressed for dinner.'

'You're fine as you are. I don't have a dress code.'

She frowned. 'I'm sorry, I'm not quite with you.'

'I'm cooking for us. At my place,' he explained.

This time, she laughed. '*You're* cooking?'

He shrugged. 'I can cook.'

She smiled. 'I bet you only learned to impress your girlfriends at university.'

No. He'd learned because he'd had to, when he'd been fourteen. Because the only way he and his little sisters would've had anything to eat had been if he'd cooked it. Not that he had any intention of telling Abigail about that. 'Something like that,' he said lightly, and drove them back to his flat.

'Can we stop at an off-licence or something so I can get a bottle of wine as my contribution to dinner?' she asked on the way.

'There's no need. I have wine.'

'But I haven't contributed anything.'

'You have. You bought me lunch.'

'This was supposed to be my date,' she reminded him.

'Tough. I hijacked it, and we're on my rules now,' he said with a smile. 'Just chill, and we'll have dinner.'

Something smelled good, Abigail thought when Lewis let her inside his flat. Clearly he'd planned this, and it wasn't the frozen pizza she'd been half expecting him to produce for dinner.

'It'll take five minutes for me to sort the vegetables. The bathroom's through there if you need it,' he said, indicating a door.

She washed her hands and splashed a little water on her face, then stared at herself in the mirror. She looked a total mess and her hair was all over the place, despite the fact she'd tied it back, and she didn't have a comb with her so it'd just have to stay looking like a bird's nest. Then again, this wasn't a *date* date so it really didn't matter how she looked, did it?

When she emerged from the bathroom, she could hear the clatter of crockery in the kitchen. 'Is there anything I can do to help?' she called.

'No, just take a seat,' he called back.

There was a bistro table in the living room with two chairs. The table was set nicely; he'd clearly made an effort.

There was an array of photographs on the mantelpiece, and she couldn't resist going over for a closer look. At first glance, Abigail wasn't surprised that most of them seemed to involve Lewis with his arm round someone female. One of them showed him holding a baby in a white christening gown.

His baby? Surely not. If Lewis had a child, he would've mentioned it.

But then she saw a wedding photograph with three women and Lewis. When she studied it, she could see the family likenesses: the bridesmaids were clearly the bride's sisters. And the same women were in all the photographs. One of them had the same eyes as Lewis; one had his smile; all had his dark hair.

Which meant they had to be Lewis's sisters. She

guessed that the baby belonged to one of them, and Lewis was a doting uncle-cum-godfather.

He came through to the living room, carrying two plates. 'OK?' he asked.

'Just admiring your photographs—your sister's, I presume?'

'And my niece.' He nodded. 'My best girls.'

She'd already worked out that he was close to his family. What would it be like to have a sibling who'd always be there for you, someone you could ring at stupid o'clock in the morning when the doubts hit and you wondered what the hell you were doing? Being an only child, she'd got used to dealing with everything on her own.

'They look nice,' she offered.

'They are. Most of the time. You know what it's like.'

No, she didn't. 'Yes,' she fibbed.

'Come and sit down.'

He put the plate down in front of her, and she felt her eyes widen. Oh, no. She should've said something. Right back when he'd first told her they were having dinner here. But she'd simply assumed that by 'cooking' he'd meant just throwing a frozen cheese and tomato pizza into the oven, and then she'd been distracted by the photographs.

Dinner was presented beautifully, right down to the garnish of chopped fresh herbs.

But no way could she eat it.

Maybe if she ate just the inside of the jacket potato, then hid the chicken stew under the skin?

He clearly noticed her hesitation. 'Oh, hell. I didn't think to ask. And, given what you had for lunch...' He frowned, and she could see the second he made the connection. 'You're vegetarian, aren't you?'

'Yes.' She swallowed hard. 'But don't worry about it. You've gone to so much trouble. If you don't mind, I'll just eat the jacket potato and the veg.'

'A casserole isn't much trouble. And I'm not going to make you pick at your food. Give me ten minutes.' Before she had a chance to protest, he'd whisked her plate away.

She followed him into the kitchen. 'Lewis, really— you don't have to go to any more trouble. Honestly. It's my fault. I should've said something before. Leave it. I'll just get a taxi home.'

'You will *not*,' he said crisply. 'I promised you dinner, and dinner you shall have. Are you OK with pasta?'

'I…'

'Yes or no, Abby?' His tone was absolutely implacable.

And, after all the adrenalin of their day at the adventure centre, she was hungry. She gave in. 'Yes.'

'And spinach?'

'Yes.'

'Good. I know you're OK with dairy, or you wouldn't have eaten cottage cheese. But I've already made enough wrong assumptions today, so I'm going to check. Are you OK with garlic and mascarpone?'

'Love them,' she said, squirming and feeling as if she was making a total fuss.

'Good. Dinner will be ten minutes. Go and pour yourself a glass of wine.' He was already heating oil in a pan, then squashed a clove of garlic and chopped an onion faster than she'd ever seen it done before.

So much for thinking he'd exaggerated his cooking skills. Lewis Gallagher actually knew his way around a kitchen. And he hadn't been trying to impress her—he was trying to be hospitable. Bossing her around in exactly the way he probably bossed his kid sisters around.

She went back into his living room, poured herself a glass of wine and then poured a second glass for him before returning to the kitchen with the glasses. 'I, um, thought you might like this.'

'Thank you. I would.' He smiled at her.

The spinach was wilting into the onions and the kettle was boiling, ready for the pasta. 'Sorry, I'm out of flour, or I'd make us some flatbread to go with it.'

And she'd just bet he made his bread by hand, not with a machine. Lewis Gallagher was turning out to be so much more domesticated than she'd thought. And the fact he'd noticed that she couldn't eat the food and guessed why... There was more to him than just the shallow party boy. Much more.

Which made him dangerous to her peace of mind.

She should back away, right now.

But then he started talking to her about food and bread, putting her at her ease, and she found herself relaxing with him. Ten minutes later, she carried her own plate through to the living room: pasta with a simple garlic, spinach and mascarpone sauce.

'This is really good,' she said after the first mouthful. 'Thank you.'

He inclined his head. 'I'm only sorry that I didn't ask you earlier if you were veggie. Dani would have my hide for that.'

'Dani?'

'The oldest of my girls. She's vegetarian.'

Which explained why he'd been able to whip up something without a fuss. And not pasta with the usual jar of tomato sauce with a handful of grated cheese dumped onto it, which in her experience most people seemed to think passed for good vegetarian food.

'So your sisters are all younger than you?' she asked.

He nodded. 'Dani's an actuary, Manda's a drama teacher, and Ronnie—short for Veronica—is a librarian.'

'Do they all live in London?'

'Dani does. Ronnie's in Manchester and Manda's in Cambridge. Which I guess is near enough to London for me to see her and Louise reasonably often.'

'Louise being the baby?' she guessed.

'My niece. Goddaughter.' He grinned. 'Manda named her after me, though I hope Louise is a bit better behaved than I am when she grows up.'

Abigail smiled back at him. 'Since you're the oldest, I'm surprised none of them were tempted to follow you into medicine.'

It wasn't that surprising. Lewis had been the one to follow *them* to university. Because how could he have just gone off at eighteen to follow his own dreams, leaving the girls to deal with their mother and fend for themselves? So he'd stayed. He'd waited until Ronnie was eighteen and ready to fly the nest, before applying to read medicine and explaining at the interview why his so-called gap year had actually lasted for six.

'No,' he said lightly. 'What about you? Brothers or sisters?'

She looked away. 'Neither. Just me.'

'That explains the ice princess. Daddy's girl,' he said.

* * *

Daddy's girl.

Did he *know*?

Had he made the connection with 'Cinnamon Baby', the little girl with ringlets who'd been the paparazzi's darling, smiling for the cameras on her father's shoulders? She really hoped not. Abigail didn't use her first name any more, and it had been years since the paparazzi had followed her about. Even so, the times when her identity had been leaked in the past had made her paranoid about it happening again.

And there was no guile in Lewis's face. Abigail had already leaped to a few wrong conclusions about him, and she knew she wasn't being fair to him.

'I suppose I am, a bit,' she said.

'Is your dad a doctor?' he asked.

'No. What about your parents?'

He shook his head, and for a moment she was sure she saw sadness in his eyes, though when she blinked it had gone. Maybe she'd imagined it.

Pudding turned out to be strawberries and very posh vanilla ice cream.

'Do I take it you make your own ice cream?' Abigail asked.

Lewis laughed. 'No. There's an Italian deli around the corner that sells the nicest ice cream in the world, so there's no need to make my own—though I would love an ice-cream maker.' He rolled his eyes. 'But my girls say I already have far too many gadgets.'

'Boys and their toys,' she said lightly.

'Cooking relaxes me.' He grinned. 'But I admit I like

gadgets as well. As long as they're useful, otherwise they're just clutter and a waste of space.'

Abigail glanced at her watch and was surprised to discover how late it was. 'I'd better get that taxi.'

'Absolutely not. I'm driving you home. And I only had one glass of wine, so I'm under the limit.'

It was easier not to protest. Though, with the roof up, his car seemed much more intimate. Just the two of them in an enclosed space.

He insisted on seeing her to her door.

'Would you like to come in for coffee?' she asked.

He shook his head. 'You're on an early shift tomorrow, so it wouldn't be fair. But thank you for the offer.'

'Thank you for today, Lewis. I really enjoyed it.'

'Me, too,' he said.

And this was where she unlocked the door, closed it behind her and ended everything.

Except her mouth had other ideas.

'Um, those concert tickets I bid for at the fundraiser. It's on Friday night. It probably isn't your thing, but if you'd like to, um, go with me, you're very welcome.'

He looked at her and gave her a slow smile that made her toes curl. 'Thank you. I'd like that very much.'

'Not as a date,' she added hastily, 'just because I have a spare ticket.' She didn't want him thinking she was chasing him. Because she wasn't.

Was she?

Right at that moment, she didn't have a clue what she was doing. Lewis Gallagher rattled her composure, big time. And, if she was honest with herself, she'd been lonely since she'd started her new job. Lewis was the first of her colleagues who'd really made an effort with her, and part of her wanted to make the effort back.

'As friends,' he said. 'That works for me. See you tomorrow, Abby.' He touched her cheek briefly with the backs of his fingers. 'Sleep well.'

Despite the fresh air and the exercise, Abigail didn't think she would—because her skin was tingling where Lewis had touched her. And the knowledge that he could affect her like that totally threw her. 'You, too. Goodnight,' she mumbled, and fled into the safety of her flat.

CHAPTER THREE

'JUST THE PERSON I wanted to see.' Marina Fenton smiled at Abigail. 'Are you free for lunch today?'

It was the last thing Abigail had expected. She normally had lunch on her own and hid behind a journal so nobody joined her or started a conversation with her. 'I, um…' Oh, help. Why was she so socially awkward? She was fine with her dad's crowd; then again, they'd known her for her entire life. It was just new people she wasn't so good with. And, growing up in an all-male environment, she'd never quite learned the knack of making friends with women. She didn't have a clue about girl talk. 'Well, patients permitting, I guess so,' she said cautiously.

'Good. I'll see you in the kitchen at twelve, and we can walk to the canteen together.'

'OK.' Feeling a bit like a rabbit in the headlights, Abigail took refuge in the triage notes for her next patient.

At twelve, she headed for the staff kitchen. Marina was waiting for her there, as promised, but so was Sydney Ranieri, which Abigail hadn't expected.

'I know I'm officially off duty today, but Marina said she was having lunch with you and I thought it'd be nice to join you both—if you don't mind, that is?' Sydney asked.

'I, um—no, of course not.' But it threw her. Why would the two other doctors want to have lunch with her?

'By the way, lunch is on us,' Marina said, ushering her out of the department and towards the hospital canteen. 'Because we've been feeling immensely guilty about the weekend.'

Oh. So that was what this was all about. Guilt. Well, she'd never been much good at making friends. Stupid to think that might change with a different hospital. Abigail shook her head. 'There's no need, on either count. I was happy to help with the fundraising. There's nothing to feel guilty about.'

'So it went well, then, your date with Lewis?' Sydney asked.

Yes and no. Except it hadn't really been a date. And it wouldn't be fair to Lewis to discuss it. 'It was OK.'

'OK?' Sydney and Marina shared a glance. 'Women *never* say that about a date with Lewis.'

Abigail spread her hands. 'He took me zip-lining.'

'Ah.' There was a wealth of understanding in Sydney's voice. 'That's the thing about the male doctors in this department. They all seem to like doing mad things. Marina's husband organised a sponsored abseil down the hospital tower. All two hundred and fifty feet of it.' She shuddered. 'And somehow he persuaded the whole department into doing it.'

'Mmm, I can imagine that,' Abigail said dryly. Max had persuaded her to do something well outside her comfort zone, too.

'But it had its good points. I met Marco because I got stuck,' Sydney said. 'Faced with the reality of walking backwards into nothing, I just froze.' She grimaced. 'Marco sang me down.'

'He sang you down?' Abigail couldn't help being intrigued. 'How?'

'He got me to sing with him, to distract me from the fact that I was on the edge of this huge tower, and then he talked me through every step. I was still shaking at the bottom of the tower when he abseiled down next to me.' Sydney rolled her eyes. 'And when he landed, it was as if he'd done nothing scarier than walking along the pavement towards me.'

'That sounds exactly like the sort of thing Lewis would do,' Abigail said.

'He wasn't with the department then, or he probably would have done.' Marina smiled, but her eyes held a trace of anxiety. 'Was it really that awful?'

'The first time I had to step off that platform, with nothing but a bit of webbing and a rope between me and a huge drop, I wanted to kill him,' Abigail admitted, and they all laughed. 'But then—once I'd actually done it, it was fun. The second time round was a lot better.'

'Good.' Marina rested her hand briefly on Abigail's arm. 'I've been feeling terrible all weekend, thinking that we pushed you into offering that date. I had no idea that Lewis was going to bid for you.'

'Neither did I,' Abigail said dryly.

'He's a nice guy,' Sydney said. 'As a colleague, he's totally reliable at work and he's good company on team nights out. But, um, maybe I should warn you that when it comes to his personal life, he doesn't do commitment.'

'Three dates and you're out. So I heard,' Abigail said. Though she knew that Lewis *did* do commitment, at least where his family was concerned. He was really close to his sisters and his niece. Though, now she thought of it, he hadn't had any pictures of his parents on display in his flat. Which was odd.

And why would someone who was close to his family be so wary of risking his heart? Had someone broken it, years ago?

Though it was none of her business.

They were just colleagues. Possibly starting to become friends. Though she wasn't going to tell Marina and Sydney that they were going to the concert together later in the week. She didn't want them to get the wrong idea.

Once they'd queued up at the counter and bought their lunch, they found a quiet table in the canteen.

'So are you going to see Lewis again?' Marina asked.

'Considering that we work in the same department, I'd say there's a good chance of seeing him in Resus or what have you, depending on the roster,' Abigail said lightly.

'That isn't what I meant.'

Abigail smiled. 'I know. But we're colleagues, Marina. He only bid for that date because—well, he said he was trying to persuade me to do more things with the team.'

'Helping you settle in. Fixing things.' Sydney looked thoughtful. 'Actually, Lewis is like that. He sees something that maybe could work better if it was done differently, and he fixes it.' She smiled. 'Well, I guess that's why we all chose this career. We're fixers.'

'Definitely,' Abigail said, and was relieved when the discussion turned away from Lewis. By the end of the lunch break she found herself really enjoying the company of the other two doctors. They weren't like the mean girls who'd made her life a misery at school. They were *nice*.

'I'd better get back,' she said when she'd finished her coffee.

'Me, too,' Marina said. She winked at Sydney. 'It's all right for you part-timers.'

Sydney just laughed. 'It's fun being a lady who lunches. Well, at least part time. I'd never give up work totally because I'd miss it too much. I've enjoyed today. Let's make it a regular thing,' she suggested. 'I work Tuesdays, Wednesdays and Thursdays. Which of those days is best for you, Abby?'

The same diminutive Lewis had used. Something that had never happened in previous hospitals—she'd always been Dr Smith or Abigail. But here at the London Victoria it was different. There was much more of a sense of the department members being a team. Being friends outside work. And Marina and Sydney were offering her precisely that: friendship. For her own sake, rather than because she was Keith Brydon's daughter—as people had in the past whenever her identity had leaked out.

For once in her life Abigail was actually fitting in. It felt weird; but it felt *good*. And she didn't want that feeling to stop.

'How about Wednesdays?' Abigail asked.

'Excellent. Wednesday at twelve it is, patients permitting—and if one of us is held up, the others will save a space at the table,' Marina said with a smile. 'It's a date.'

* * *

Abigail didn't see Lewis all day, even in passing. She'd been rostered in Minors for her shift and according to the departmental whiteboard he was in Resus. She wasn't sure if she was more relieved that she didn't have to face him or disappointed that she hadn't seen him. And it annoyed her that she felt so mixed up about the situation. She'd worked hard and she'd been happy to make the sacrifices in her personal life to get where she wanted to be in her professional life. So why, why, why was she even thinking about dating a man who had commitment issues and wasn't her type?

She was still brooding about it the next day. Though then it started to get busy in the department.

She picked up her next set of triage notes. Headache and temperature. Normally patients with a simple virus would be treated by the triage nurse and sent home with painkillers and advice. But this wasn't just a simple case, from the look of the notes: the nurse had written *'Query opiates'* at the bottom of the page. So the headache and temperature could be part of a reaction to whatever drug the patient had taken.

'Eddie McRae?' she called.

An ashen-faced man walked up the corridor, supported by another man.

She introduced herself swiftly. 'So you have a headache and temperature, Mr McRae?'

'Eddie,' he muttered. 'I feel terrible.'

'Have you been in contact with anyone who has a virus?' she asked.

'I don't think so.'

So it could be withdrawal or a bad reaction to the

drugs he'd taken. His breathing was fast, she noticed. 'Can I take your pulse?'

'Sure.'

His pulse was also fast, so Eddie could well be suffering from sepsis.

'Have you taken anything?' she asked gently.

This time Eddie didn't say a word, and she had a pretty good idea why. 'I'm not going to lecture you or call the police,' she reassured him. 'My job's to help you feel better than you do right now. And the more information you give me, the easier it's going to be for me to get it right first time.'

'He took something Saturday night,' his friend said. 'He's been ill today, with a headache and temperature.'

'So it could be a reaction to what you took. Did you swallow it?'

Eddie shook his head and grimaced in pain.

'Injected?' At his slight nod, she said, 'Can I see where?'

He shrugged off his cardigan. There were track marks on his arm, as she'd expected, but the redness and swelling definitely weren't what she'd expected.

'Eddie, I really need to know what you took,' she said gently.

'Heroin,' his friend said.

'OK.' She knew that the withdrawal symptoms from heroin usually peaked forty-eight to seventy-two hours after the last dose, but this didn't seem like the withdrawal cases she'd seen in the past.

'Are you sleeping OK, Eddie?' she asked.

'Yeah.'

'Do you have any pain, other than your head?'

He nodded. 'My stomach.'

'Have you been sick or had diarrhoea?'

He grimaced. 'No.'

Abigail had a funny feeling about this. Although she hadn't actually seen a case at her last hospital, there had been a departmental circular about heroin users suffering from anthrax after using contaminated supplies, and an alarm bell was ringing at the back of her head. There was no sign of black eschar, the dead tissue cast off from the surface of the skin, which was one of the big giveaways with anthrax, but she had a really strong feeling about this. Right now she could do with some advice from a more senior colleague.

'I'm going to leave you in here for a second, if that's OK,' she said. 'I have a hunch I know what's wrong, but there's something I want to check with a colleague, and then I think we'll be able to do something to help you.'

'Just make the pain stop. Please,' Eddie said.

She stepped out of the cubicle and pulled the curtain closed behind her. With any luck Max or Marco would be free—in this case, she needed a second opinion from a consultant.

But the first person she saw was Lewis.

'OK, Abby?' he asked. 'You look a bit worried.'

'I need a second opinion on a patient. Is Max or Marco around?'

'Marco's in Resus and Max is in a meeting,' he said. 'Will I do?'

Although they were officially the same grade, she knew that Lewis was older than her—which made him more experienced, her senior colleague. And really she should've asked him instead of trying to track down

Max or Marco. She grimaced. 'Sorry, I didn't mean to imply that you weren't good eno—'

'Relax, Abby,' he cut in. 'I didn't think you were saying that at all. What's the problem?'

'My patient took heroin on Saturday. He has a headache and a temperature, and what looks like soft tissue sepsis—not the normal sort of reaction at the injection site. At my last hospital, we had case notes about anthrax in heroin users. Do you know if there's anything like that happening in this area?'

'No—but you know as well as I do that if something affects one area of the city, it's going to spread to the rest, so it's only a matter of time. You think this is anthrax?'

'There's no sign of black eschar. I don't have any proof. Just a gut feeling that this is more than just withdrawal symptoms or a bad reaction.'

'I'd run with it. Do you want me to take a look to back you up? And if it is anthrax, we can split the notifications between us and save a bit of time.'

Anthrax was a notifiable disease, and the lab would also need to know of her suspicions when she sent any samples through for testing so they could take extra precautions. 'Thanks, that would be good,' she said gratefully.

Lewis walked back to the cubicle with her and she introduced him to Eddie McRae. Lewis examined him swiftly and looked at her. 'I think you're right,' he said quietly.

Abigail took a deep breath. 'I'll need to do a couple more tests to check, Eddie, but I think you have anthrax.'

'But—how? We're not terrorists or anything!' Eddie looked shocked. 'We've never had anything to do with that sort of stuff. How can I have anthrax?'

'Anthrax is a bacterium,' she explained. 'It can survive as spores in soil for years. It's not that common now in the UK, but somehow anthrax has found its way into the heroin supply chain so the drugs have been contaminated. There have been a few cases of heroin users with anthrax in mainland Europe and Scotland—and parts of London, too, because we had some in my last hospital.'

'My granddad was a farmer. His cattle got anthrax years ago and they all had to be killed. Is Eddie going to die?' Eddie's friend asked, looking anxious.

'It's treatable,' Lewis reassured him. 'We can give you broad-spectrum antibiotics to deal with the infection, but you'll also need surgery, Eddie.'

'Surgery?' Eddie looked panicky.

'The area where you injected the heroin is swollen and red, which tells me it's infected,' Abigail explained. 'This is where the anthrax spores are concentrated. If we take away the dead tissue, then that takes away the toxins and they won't spread any further into your system.'

Eddie shook his head. 'I can't lose my arm, I just can't. How can I play the guitar without my arm?'

Abigail sighed inwardly. That had happened to someone her dad knew: the young guitarist hadn't been able to cope with the amputation after the car accident and had finally taken an overdose.

'You're not going to lose your arm, Eddie. I promise. All I'm going to do is take away the damaged tissues.'

'It's going to hurt.'

'I'll give you local anaesthetic so you won't feel it, though I will be honest and admit you'll feel a bit sore afterwards.'

Eddie shook his head, wide-eyed in fear. 'I don't want you to do it.'

'If we don't take away the infected tissue,' Lewis said softly, 'the antibiotics won't be enough to deal with the anthrax. Some of those cases Dr Smith was talking about were fatal because they didn't come to the hospital in time for treatment. You've got a really good chance of getting over it right now. Plus, if you leave it, it'll hurt more.'

'I really won't feel it when you…' Eddie gulped '…use the knife?'

'You really won't,' Lewis reassured him.

Eddie swallowed hard. 'OK. I'll do it.'

Lewis patted his shoulder. 'Good for you, Eddie.'

Making sure she was using gloves, a gown and a mask, Abigail took a blood sample. With all the track marks on Eddie's arms, it was hard to find a good spot to take a sample, but she managed it. She labelled the sample as high risk, and did the same with the samples of tissue and sputum.

'Do you want me to talk to the public health lot while you talk to the lab?' Lewis asked.

'Thanks. That'd be good,' she said gratefully.

The admin side seemed to take for ever, but finally Abigail was back with Lewis in Eddie's cubicle. 'Once we've sorted out your arm, I'm going to put you on a drip with antibiotics,' she said to Eddie. 'The blood test will show if I need to put you on a different sort of antibiotics.'

He nodded, and looked anxiously at his friend. 'Is it catching? Could Mike here have anthrax because of me?'

'It doesn't spread from person to person by air droplets like a cold does, if that's what you're asking,' Lewis said. He looked at Mike. 'But if you have a tiny cut on your skin and infected body fluids get in, then it's a possibility. We can do a blood test on you now to check.'

Mike blew out a breath. 'Thanks. I don't feel ill, not like Eddie does.'

'Better to be safe,' Abigail said. 'The thing is, if you've got infected blood or sputum on your clothes, washing won't be enough to kill the spores. So I'm going to have to put you in a hospital gown, Eddie, and destroy your clothes. And you're going to be in the ward overnight so we can keep an eye on you and keep those antibiotics going.' She looked at Mike. 'Can you make sure that everyone you know is aware there's a problem with anthrax and the symptoms to look out for?'

'Yeah, I will.' Mike stared at the floor. 'I thought you'd have a go at us about taking drugs in the first place.'

'Take the lecture as read,' she said dryly. 'It's your choice and not my business, but right now you need to know there are extra risks in those choices because the supply's been contaminated.'

'I guess this is a wake-up call,' Eddie said.

'We can help you,' Abigail said. 'All you have to do is ask, and we will help you.' She sorted out a gown for Eddie and a bag for his contaminated clothes, and waited for him to change before going back into the cubicle. 'OK. Are you ready now for me to sort out your arm?'

'No, but I guess I don't have a choice. Can Mike stay?'

'Sure.' She smiled at Mike. 'Are you OK with the sight of blood? Because if you're not, just keep looking at Eddie's face and not at what Lewis and I are doing. And if you feel faint, stick your head between your knees.'

'Got it.' Mike blew out a breath. 'I think this might be a wake-up call for me as well.'

Between them, Abigail and Lewis administered the local anaesthetic and reassurance to Eddie, and she began to remove the damaged tissue.

Although Lewis had worked with Abigail before, it was the first time he'd seen her do a surgical debridement, and he was impressed. She was very neat, very quick, and she put both Eddie and Mike at their ease.

'Nice work,' he said when they left cubicles.

'Thanks. Though it wasn't just mine.' She smiled at him. 'You're the one who talked Eddie into letting me give him the proper treatment.'

'Pleasure. Shall we grab a coffee? I need to debrief you on what the health prevention agency and the hospital infection control team said.'

'Sounds good to me,' she said.

On Wednesday, the results proved that Eddie did indeed have anthrax. Abigail managed to find Lewis in the department. 'We were right. It was anthrax.'

'You were the one who noticed,' he said. 'Good call.'

'Thanks.' Funny how his praise made her feel as if she was glowing inside.

And that glow lasted during her lunch with Sydney and Marina.

'There's a team bowling evening on Friday. It was booked last month, and Jay's had to drop out, so if you want to come and make up the team it'd be good to have you,' Marina said.

No pressure, just an invite from someone who was becoming her friend. Abigail was about to say yes when she thought about the date. 'Friday? Sorry, I would've come, but I bid on tickets for a concert at the fundraiser, and the performance is on Friday.' Not that she was going to admit who she was going with.

But she didn't want to just leave it there. To be stand-offish, the way she'd always been. She needed to make an effort. Taking a risk, she added, 'But if you have a space next time, I'll be there. Even though I'm not that good at bowling.'

'It's not the result that matters—it's whether we have fun. The next department night out is going to be ice skating,' Sydney said.

'I've never done that,' Abigail said.

Another brush-off? No. She was going to make this work. She hoped that her smile didn't betray how awkward she felt. 'But I'll give it a go if there's space for me.'

'Oh, there's space. Way to go, Abby,' Sydney said, smiling at her and holding her palm up in a high-five gesture.

Still feeling that warm glow, Abigail high-fived her. If someone had told her three months ago that her

life would change totally at the London Victoria, she
would've scoffed. But here life was different.

Life was good.

CHAPTER FOUR

ABIGAIL HAD A day off on Friday. Lewis was working, but he'd arranged to meet her at her flat before the concert. She couldn't settle all day, and spent ages choosing what to wear. Which was ridiculous, because she'd already made it very clear to him that this wasn't a date. And, besides, Lewis wouldn't care in the slightest what she was wearing.

Half of her didn't want him to notice that she'd made an effort. The other half was longing for him to tell her she looked nice. And that made her really cross with herself. She was an independent woman, not a needy child. She didn't need someone to tell her what she looked like.

Crossly, she changed her outfit for the third time. And this time she made sure that her shoes were flat and sensible, and she kept her hair tied back instead of wearing it loose.

She tried doing a cryptic crossword to keep herself from looking at the clock to see how long she'd have to wait for Lewis to meet her. It worked; but when she'd finished she glanced at her watch and realised that he was late.

Or was he? Had he changed his mind, and he just

wasn't going to turn up? Or maybe he'd had a better offer and he'd make some charming excuse the next time he saw her.

Just when she was really stewing in misery, her phone beeped to signal a text message. She glanced at the screen. Lewis. She flicked into the message.

Sorry, tricky patient. Running a bit late. Meet you in foyer of concert hall instead? Sorry. L.

Working in medicine wasn't like an office job. You couldn't just tell your patient to go away and come back tomorrow, and she would've thought less of Lewis if he'd handed over his patient to someone else to deal with rather than seeing things through.

OK, see you there, she texted back.

She checked that she'd put the tickets in her handbag, headed for the concert hall and bought two programmes. She waited for Lewis in the foyer, glancing up from the programme every few seconds in case he was walking through the door. But nothing. It was getting to the point where she thought he wasn't going to make it in time when he rushed in.

'Sorry. After all that there was a delay on the Tube as well—and either your phone's switched off or you don't have a signal in here, because I did try to ring you from the station.'

'Technology, eh?' she said lightly. 'Never mind. You're here now. Let's go in. I bought you a programme.'

'Thanks.' He kissed her swiftly on the cheek.

And it was totally ridiculous that her skin tingled where his lips had touched her.

They made it to their seats by the skin of their teeth.

Lewis glanced at the programme. 'Oh, excellent. I love Beethoven.'

Abigail looked at him, faintly surprised. She'd expected him only to like the kind of pop the radio had been playing in his car. 'Beethoven's my favourite, too.' Maybe they had more in common than she'd first thought.

Two minutes after the orchestra began playing she was lost in the magic of the music. And then, during the slow movement of Beethoven's *Pathétique* sonata—a piece of music she'd always loved—Lewis reached over to hold her hand.

He didn't look at her and she didn't look at him, but it felt right to curl her fingers round his. And to let him hold her hand throughout the rest of the concert.

At the end, he loosened his hand from hers and Abigail could see in his expression that he was as surprised by what he'd just done as she was.

She could pretend it hadn't happened, retreat back into her shell and be safe.

Or she could take a risk.

At that moment, it felt as if she was at a crossroads. Which way was the right way to go?

And why was she even thinking about this anyway? She wasn't looking for a relationship. Especially with a guy who had a three-dates-and-you're-out rule.

But they'd gone to the concert together. Dinner wouldn't hurt, would it? 'Have you eaten yet?' she asked.

He shook his head. 'I didn't have time.'

Risk. She could take a risk.

'We could, um, go and get something now, if you like,' she suggested diffidently.

His eyes crinkled at the corners. 'Are you asking me out, Dr Smith?'

Panic flooded through her. Oh, help. What did she do now? 'I...um... Just as—' she began.

'A friend,' he finished, 'who realises that I've had a really long day and am absolutely starving. That would be good.'

She wasn't quite sure if he'd been teasing her about asking him out or if he'd been serious under that jokey exterior. She definitely wasn't going to be gauche enough to ask. 'Shall we go to the first place we see?' she asked.

He laughed. 'I can't see you doing a greasy spoon place.'

'If they did good eggs, I'd be OK. But you have a point. I'd rather not go to a burger bar, if you don't mind.'

Just around the corner from the concert hall there was an Italian restaurant. 'Is this OK for you?' she asked.

'Lovely.'

Once they were seated at the table, Lewis studied the menu, looking serious.

'You don't have to choose something vegetarian on my account,' she said.

He raised an eyebrow at her. 'Are you sure? I mean, it was different before I knew you were vegetarian. I don't eat meat if I go out with Dani.'

'I'm sure. I'd rather not eat meat, but I don't think that everyone else has to give it up for me—forcing my choices on someone else feels wrong. Pick what you want.'

His smile made her feel warm inside. 'Thank you.'

Abigail ordered gnocchi with sage butter and portion of garlicky spinach; Lewis ordered lasagne.

'I'm afraid this is my big weakness,' he said with a grin. 'It's my absolutely favourite comfort food—and I've had the kind of day that makes me really need it.'

'Uh-huh.' She tried not to be disappointed that her company and the music hadn't been enough to make it better.

'Except,' he said softly, 'this evening with you. That was food for the soul and made me feel a hell of a lot better.'

Was he only saying it because her disappointment had shown in her face and he was being charming?

The question must've been obvious because he said, 'I guess I'm just greedy. My favourite food and good company—that's the best way to spend a Friday night.'

They'd also ordered bread and olives to keep them going until the main course was ready, and their fingers brushed against each other as they reached for the bread at the same time. Abigail was horribly aware of his nearness, of the feel of his skin against hers—and of the possibilities blooming in her head.

'You first,' he said softly.

She hardly dared look at him as she took some bread. And she was furious when she spilled some of the oil on the table. So now he'd know that she was rattled. Not good. Luckily the napkin was paper and not linen, so she dabbed at the puddle of oil with it.

'Let me help,' he said, and cleaned up with remarkable speed and efficiency.

And now she felt hopeless as well as gauche.

'Abby,' he said softly.

She had no choice but to look at him.

'Thank you for taking me to the concert,' he said.

'My pleasure,' she mumbled. 'I had a spare ticket and it would've been a waste not to use it.' Which was only part of the truth. She'd wanted to spend time with Lewis. And that scared her.

'You've gone shy on me.' He frowned slightly. 'I thought we were becoming friends?'

She wasn't sure *what* they were becoming. And it worried her that she was starting to feel things about Lewis Gallagher that really weren't sensible.

She took refuge in asking about work. 'So what happened with your tricky patient?'

He grimaced. 'He came in because he'd blacked out at work and one of his colleagues called the ambulance. I noticed he was jaundiced; I did his LFTs and they were off the scale. He lied to me at first and said he was only a social drinker, but finally he admitted that he uses vodka to cope with stress at work and has been drinking way too much for several years.' He sighed. 'I'm hoping it's going to turn out to be hepatitis rather than cirrhosis, but he's going to need a lot of help to give up the alcohol. He'll probably need medication to support him as well as counselling.'

Which was one of the things Abigail worried about with her father. Keith Brydon drank too much and had done so for years; it went with the rock-and-roll lifestyle. And she worried constantly that she'd be called by another hospital's emergency department because he'd collapsed. Hepatitis, a heart attack, a stroke—she worried about all of them. 'Poor guy. I assume you admitted him to the main wards?'

'Yes. They're going to give him steroids to reduce the inflammation of the liver. The poor guy's got a hard road ahead of him.' Lewis looked bleak. 'Some people are too proud to ask for help when they're stressed and struggling. And they're the ones who end up in our department—if they're lucky.'

'And we can do something to help,' she said. 'You spent time talking to him tonight, didn't you?'

He nodded. 'Sorry.'

'Don't be. I would've done the same.' Especially because the situation echoed her own worst fears.

'Thanks for being understanding.' He shook himself. 'And I'll stop being maudlin.'

When their meals arrived, he looked at her plate. 'That looks gorgeous.' He sighed. 'I wish I'd ordered something vegetarian now. It isn't fair to ask you for a taste when I can't reciprocate.'

'Sure you can.'

But offering him a taste from her fork turned out to be a mistake. It felt oddly intimate. And then she managed to spill butter down his shirt because her hand was shaking. 'Sorry. I, um…I'm not usually this clumsy.'

He laughed. 'Things come in threes, so you need to spill your coffee next.'

She felt her face flame. 'Sorry.'

'Abby, I was teasing. It doesn't matter. Everyone spills things.'

Maybe, but she hated being less than perfect. 'I'll pick up the dry-cleaning bill.'

He shook his head. 'There's no need. It'll come out in the wash.'

She could offer to wash his shirt for him, but then she'd probably manage to shrink it or something. What was it about this man that made her such a klutz? She bit her lip.

'Abby. It's not a problem. Chill,' he said.

She gave him a rueful smile. 'I don't get out much. And I guess it shows.'

'Good music, good food, good company. I don't see anything wrong in that,' he said.

Was he really nice at heart, or was he a shallow player? She wasn't sure, so she just smiled back at him.

'So what made you want to be a doctor?' he asked.

'Sydney and Marina were telling me this theory over lunch that we're doctors because we like fixing things,' she said.

'They're probably right.' He raised an eyebrow. 'You had lunch with them?'

She nodded. 'I would've gone to the bowling thing tonight with them, if I hadn't had these tickets.'

He smiled. 'Good. I'm glad you're getting to know the team better. They're a nice bunch.' He paused. 'What I don't get is why you're in the emergency department. I would've put you in family medicine.'

She raised an eyebrow. 'You don't think I'm tough enough to cope with emergency medicine?'

'No, it's not that. You're good at your job. But the way you were with that guy with anthrax the other day made me think you'd be good at cradle-to-grave medicine.

You built a relationship with your patient. We don't get to do that in the emergency department—we rarely even know what happens to them once they leave us.'

Though, Lewis had spent time tonight settling a patient into the ward, and she'd just bet that he'd visit his patient over the weekend when he was on a break. 'I suppose not.'

He looked straight at her. 'So my guess is you chose emergency medicine because of your father.'

For a second Abigail forgot to breathe. Lewis had looked her up on the Internet and made the connections. He must've done. Why else would he say something like that? 'What makes you say that?' she asked carefully.

'Because playing a round of golf a couple of times a week isn't going to make up for the rest of the lifestyle.'

She went cold. So Lewis *did* know who she was. And that was why he was here with her now. Not because he'd wanted to get to know her better or because he'd wanted to help her settle into the team. He was here because, just like all the other people she'd been stupid enough to go out with or even make friends with, he was more interested in her father. 'Lifestyle?' she asked slowly.

'Sitting in an office chair all day and either grabbing the wrong kind of sandwich or going out for lunch with a client or colleagues and having all three courses. With butter spread way too thickly on the bread and a generous helping of cream on the pudding.'

She blinked at him. What was he talking about? Wasn't it obvious that her father's lifestyle meant not taking enough exercise, eating too much of the wrong kind of food at weird times and a body-clock-breaking routine? Not to mention the other stuff that came with a rock-and-roll lifestyle. Alcohol. Tobacco. Recreational drugs—well, not that her father did those nowadays. She shook her head to clear it. 'What?'

'Businessmen of your father's generation. Given that you live in a very nice part of Pimlico, I'm guessing you're from the stockbroker belt.'

Oh. So he *didn't* know who her father was. He thought her father was a stockbroker. She nearly laughed. Her father commissioned a stockbroker, but no way did Keith Brydon live the stockbroker life himself. Her worries were different ones: even though her father didn't do drugs, there were still huge risks associated with his lifestyle.

'And your family home's a mansion in the home counties,' he said.

That part was true. Her father did have a mansion in the home counties. And a swimming pool that people had driven a car into before now, in true rock-star cliché style. 'Something like that,' she said. And she needed to get the topic off herself. Fast. 'What about you? Why did you pick emergency medicine?'

'You pinned me down on that earlier. I'm an adrenalin fiend,' he said.

She shook her head. 'I don't buy that. You're good with kids—you're patient and you listen. And, given that you refer to your sisters as your girls...'

Ice trickled down Lewis's spine. He'd seen Abigail at work so he knew she thought outside the box. She was bright enough to work it out for herself. Especially because he'd shot his mouth off earlier, talking about stress and people being too proud to ask for the help they needed.

'That's because they're my little sisters,' he said lightly.

'Mmm. But you talk about them more as if...' She paused, looking thoughtful.

All he had to do now was change the topic of conversation. Talk about music. Something. *Anything*.

But the words spilled out of his mouth. 'As if what?'

'As if you were involved in bringing them up.'

His chest felt tight. Hell. This was his own fault. He'd known that Abby could be dangerous to his peace of mind. Why hadn't he just left it? Why hadn't he made up something plausible? 'My dad died when we were young,' he said. 'I was the oldest, so I helped my mum.'

Except it hadn't really been help, had it? He'd made things so much worse in the long run.

She reached across the table and squeezed his hand briefly. 'That's rough on you.'

'I didn't mind helping out.'

'No, I mean losing your dad young. That's hard. You were close to him?'

He nodded. 'My dad was the best.' Please don't let her ask about his mother. Please don't let her guess that Fay Gallagher had gone completely to pieces and her fourteen-year-old son had been the one to keep the family together.

'And I'd guess it was an accident?'

Say yes. Tell her yes. Don't let her any closer. An all-out lie would be just fine here and now.

But it was as if his mouth wasn't listening to his head. The way she'd squeezed his hand like that—it was empathy, not pity. As if she knew what it was like. 'He had leukaemia.' He looked away. 'Three weeks after he was diagnosed, he was dead.' It had been so sudden. So shockingly sudden. None of them had been able to take it in. To cope.

Except him. Because he'd had to.

'I'm sorry. For bringing back bad memories.'

He waved a dismissive hand. 'I was the one who started the conversation.'

'And you're right about the lifestyle thing.' She sighed. 'I do worry about my dad. He never listens to a word I say, and I know he's never going to give up the cigars or the brandy, but I do try talking him into eating healthily and taking some sensible exercise to help take care of his heart.'

'Is that why you're vegetarian? You're trying to set him a good example?'

She laughed. 'Dad's not one to follow anyone else's example. He says salad is rabbit food. And the only way he'll eat spinach is if it's cooked in butter with a ton of parmesan on top, which pretty much loses the point of having spinach in the first place.' She shook her head. 'When I was in my teens, I had a friend whose family owned a farm. I stayed with them, and—well, when you've fed a calf with a bottle, you just can't...' She glanced at the lasagne on his plate. 'Um. I think I'll shut up now.'

'I think,' he said softly, 'we need to change the topic of conversation. Something much, much lighter, for both of us.'

'Good idea,' she said feelingly.

They spent the rest of the evening talking about

music. Although Lewis was aware of a slight reticence on Abigail's part, he put it down to a bit of residual shyness. After all, music was hardly a contentious subject, was it?

He insisted on seeing her home to her flat in Pimlico.

She paused outside the door. 'Would you like to come in for coffee?'

Tempting. So very, very tempting.

But their conversation that evening had rattled him. He needed time to get his head together. He couldn't risk spilling any more of his guts to her. Particularly as Abigail Smith was starting to stir up feelings in him he'd buried for years and years.

'Thanks, but I need to get back.'

'OK.' She smiled at him, but it was the most fake smile he'd ever seen. Clearly she thought he was making an excuse because he didn't want to be with her.

In a way, it was true. Right now he didn't want to be with her. But it wasn't because he didn't like her—it was because he didn't trust himself. But how could he explain that without going into detail he really didn't want to share?

'Thanks for this evening. I really did enjoy it.' He brushed her cheek with the backs of his fingers. 'Even when you spilled stuff all over me.'

She blushed spectacularly, looking so adorable that Lewis temporarily lost his common sense. He leaned over and brushed his mouth against hers. The lightest, sweetest kiss he'd ever given anyone.

And then she was staring at him, all wide-eyed.

Oh, hell. He was making a real mess of this.

'I probably shouldn't have done that, Abby. I apologise.'

'Uh-huh.'

He couldn't read her expression. Was she annoyed because she thought he was trying to take advantage of her? Or did she think that he was pushing her away? Or…?

'I'm sorry,' he said again, and walked away. While he still could.

CHAPTER FIVE

ABIGAIL TOLD HERSELF not to overthink it. She should pretend that nothing had happened. Except whenever she drifted off to sleep for the next week she kept replaying the moment that Lewis's mouth had moved against hers.

Worse still, it gave her X-rated dreams. And it was a real struggle to be professional at work and act as if that kiss hadn't happened. Even though she knew he spelled trouble, Lewis had put her on a slow burn and she had no idea how to stop it.

On the Thursday evening her mobile phone beeped to signal a text message.

Are you busy on Sunday? L.

To her relief, she didn't have to lie. She'd already arranged to go and see her father. *Sorry. Doing family stuff. A.*

She thought that would be the end of it, but then her mobile phone actually rang.

She looked at the display, frowned, and answered it. 'Lewis? Why are you calling me?'

'Your social skills need some work, Abby,' he retorted. 'You're supposed to say hello and how nice it is to hear from me.'

'Hello, Lewis. How nice it is to hear from you.'

He laughed. 'And you're meant to say it with a bit of conviction. But I guess it's a start.'

'Right. What do you want?'

'OK, so you're busy on Sunday. But I also know you're off duty on Monday.'

'And?'

'And I wondered if you fancied joining me in some adrenalin-fiend stuff.'

This was her cue to make an excuse. To be sensible and stay well clear of him outside work.

But she couldn't help wanting to know what he had in mind. 'You want to go zip-lining again?'

'Better than that.'

She sighed. 'That's not enough detail for me to be able to make an informed decision, Lewis.'

He laughed. 'Tough. It's all you're getting, princess.'

'So you want me to trust you that I'll enjoy whatever this is?' Then a nasty thought hit her. 'Three dates and you're out, right?' And this would be the third.

'Technically, we're not dating,' he pointed out.

'You paid for a date with me. And then we went to the concert. This makes number three.'

'A paid-for date doesn't count. And that concert was just because you had a spare ticket.'

And he'd kissed her.

OK, so it hadn't been a full-blown smooch. But there had been something sweet and intimate about it. It hadn't been the kind of kiss you gave a colleague—or even a friend. It had been an exploratory kiss. Promising. Tempting.

Plus there was the way he'd held her hand during the concert…

'Is *this* a date?' she asked gingerly.

'No. It's part of my project to get you doing more team stuff.'

She scowled. 'I *am* doing more team stuff, I'll have you know. I have lunch with Sydney and Marina every Wednesday, and I'm going ice skating with the team next week. Plus it's really insulting to be considered somebody's project.'

He laughed. 'OK. I take that bit back. Come and do something exciting with me, Abby.'

She thought of that kiss and shivered. Right at that moment she couldn't speak.

'Abby?'

'I'm still here.'

'Come and play with me.' His voice was like melted chocolate. Sinful and tempting. Irresistible.

No. *Say no.*

But she really, really wanted to go with him. Would it be so bad just to have some uncomplicated fun, for a change? 'OK.'

'Great. I'll pick you up at half past nine.'

'Why can't I pick you up?'

'Because I'm more used to the adrenalin rush than you are, so I'll need to drive us home.' He paused. 'Unless you want to insure your car for me so I can drive you home afterwards. That'd work.'

She blew out a breath. 'I'm beginning to think I might've been a bit rash, agreeing to do whatever this is.'

'No, you haven't. I promise you'll enjoy it.'

'What if I don't?'

'Then I'll buy you an ice cream.'

She couldn't help laughing. 'Lewis, I'm thirty years old, not three.'

'You're never too old for ice cream, Abby. One last thing. Do you have asthma?'

'No. Why?'

'Just asking. See you at work tomorrow.'

'See you.'

She was still smiling when she cut the connection. Though she had a nasty feeling that she'd just agreed to a date with Lewis, even if they weren't calling it that.

Well, everyone in her life had always said she was too serious. Maybe Lewis would be good for her. He could teach her to lighten up a bit.

Her smile faded. No wonder he thought of her as his project. So, no, it wasn't a date. He had other motivations for going out with her on Monday. And part of them involved indulging himself in adrenalin-fiend stuff. She'd better remember that.

Lewis texted Abigail on the Sunday evening to tell her to wear a T-shirt, leggings and trainers—not jeans or boots. She knew there was no point in asking him why because he wouldn't tell her. And he wouldn't even tell her where they were going on Monday morning until he turned into a side road and she saw the sign for the airfield.

'Why are we going to an airfield?' She groaned. 'Please don't tell me you're one of those people who likes looking at planes.'

'As a matter of fact, I do. And steam engines.'

Was he teasing her? She couldn't be sure. He had a perfectly straight face. And he was wearing sunglasses so she couldn't see his eyes. She couldn't read him at all. 'You said we were doing something exciting.'

He grinned. 'We're not looking at planes, Abby. We're going up in one.'

'Oh.' So this was going to be a nice pleasure flight in a small plane. Well, that worked for her. She'd flown in small planes before now, in parts of the world he'd probably never even been to. Not that she could tell him that without explaining about her father, and she wasn't ready to do that. She didn't want things to change between them.

He parked the car and shepherded her to the office. 'Lewis Gallagher and Abigail Smith. We have a booking for a tandem skydive.'

Abigail was too shocked to take it in at first. But when he'd finished signing the forms and directed her to do the same, she narrowed her eyes at him. 'You said we were going up in a plane.'

'We are.'

'You didn't say we were jumping out of one!'

'Relax, Abby.' He patted her arm. 'It's a tandem skydive. You'll be strapped to a qualified instructor, so it's perfectly safe. The instructor is the one who controls the parachute and landing so all you have to do is enjoy the experience.'

It mollified her slightly. 'OK. So do we go and meet the instructor now?'

'Um, actually, you've already met him.'

She stared at him, frowning. 'When?'

He spread his hand, gave her a real mischievous little-boy grin and pointed to himself.

'What? But...you said I'd be with a qualified instructor.'

'You will be. I'm qualified.'

She couldn't take this in. 'But how? You're a doctor.'

Fair point. He knew he needed to reassure her. 'I had a gap year.' Six of them, actually, but she didn't need to know that much detail. 'I worked at a training centre— one of those outdoor places. We used to run management courses, the sort where the delegates have to do things outside their comfort zone and bond as a team. One of the activities we did was tandem skydiving. So I qualified as an instructor.'

She rolled her eyes. 'Trust an adrenalin fiend to find that kind of job for a gap year.'

Part of Lewis wanted her to keep thinking he was shallow. But part of him wanted her to know who he really was—and that was odd. He never usually wanted to let anyone get that close. He really ought to stay away from her but something about her drew him.

'Come on. We need to go to the briefing. What you need to know is that you'll be harnessed to my front. We'll jump at fifteen thousand feet and freefall for a minute, then I'll open the canopy and we'll land about five minutes later.'

Her eyes went wide. 'What if the parachute doesn't open?'

It was the question everybody asked. 'There's a reserve parachute. And there's an automatic activation device that opens it at lower altitudes if I haven't already deployed it.'

She blew out a breath. 'Do I need a mask or anything?'

'No. We're only going up to fifteen thousand feet, so there's plenty of oxygen. And even though we'll be falling at about a hundred and twenty miles an hour, the air doesn't actually enter your lungs at that speed. Though you'll have a helmet and goggles.'

'Right. And that's why you asked me about asthma.'

'Yep.' He touched her cheek with the backs of his fingers to reassure her. 'It's an amazing feeling. But it's not like going over the edge of a roller coaster. It's like floating in a swimming pool, except you can see for miles and miles and miles.'

'And you're qualified,' she checked.

'Yes. I do regular training sessions to keep my qualifications up to date. But if you'd rather go with someone else, I understand and I won't have a tantrum about it.'

She shook her head. 'Why didn't you offer something like this at the hospital auction?'

'Would you have bid for it?' he asked.

'Well—no,' she admitted.

'There's your answer, then. Ready to go?'

'I guess.'

'Good.' He squeezed her hand. 'You're going to enjoy this. I promise.'

Abigail wasn't so sure. Jumping out of a plane. It was so far outside the kind of thing she normally did.

And Lewis had surprised her. She'd had no idea that he was a qualified skydiver. Did anyone else at the hospital know? She had a feeling they probably didn't. There was a lot, lot more to Lewis than she'd thought. And she didn't understand why he kept it so quiet. Surely this would fit in with his reckless, daredevil, party-boy image?

The briefing went through all the health and safety aspects of the flight, explaining exactly what was going to happen and what she needed to do to help the instructor. Then she was kitted out with a bright orange jumpsuit, helmet, goggles and gloves—as was Lewis.

'If only your harem at the hospital could see you now,' she teased. 'Very sexy, Dr Gallagher.'

He gave her a pained look. 'First of all, I don't have a harem. Secondly, this isn't about looking good, it's about safety.' And then he knocked her completely off balance by leaning forward and kissing the tip of her nose. 'Though you happen to look really cute.'

Cute?

The only person who ever said she was cute was her father—and that was because fathers were meant to say that sort of thing. Certainly none of her previous partners had called her cute.

Except Lewis wasn't actually her partner.

And how could she look cute in something that clashed so badly with her hair?

She was only half listening when he helped her on with the harness.

'Pay attention, Dr Smith,' he said. 'What did I just say?'

'I don't have a clue,' she admitted. And she really hoped that he put it down to nerves about doing one of his adrenalin-fiend things rather than the fact that he'd put her into a flat spin by kissing the end of her nose like that.

'I said we'll attach your harness to mine when we get to the plane. Now we're going to walk to the plane. Are you OK about this?'

'I think so.' She shivered.

'Scared?'

She nodded.

He grinned. 'It's awesome. I guarantee you'll be bubbling over when we're on the ground again.'

Well, he'd been right about the zip-lining. Maybe he'd be right about this, too.

Once in the plane, they attached her harness to his. Lewis wrapped his arms round her waist and rested his chin on her shoulder, and Abigail wasn't sure what made her pulse race more: the way he was holding her or the fact that they were going to be throwing themselves out of the plane very shortly.

As they got to the landing site, the doors opened. There was a rail above the door, and Lewis held on to it. The only thing stopping Abigail falling out of the doorway and plummeting down fifteen thousand feet was the harness that held them together. A little piece of webbing.

She was going to have to trust Lewis now like she'd never trusted anyone in her life before. And that scared her more than anything else.

'Ready?' he asked.

Not in a million years. 'Yes,' she muttered.

'Let's go,' he said, and they were out in the open air. Face down and falling.

Abigail remembered what they'd said at the briefing: she bent her lower legs back and stretched her arms out.

Adrenalin sizzled through her as they fell. Lewis

was right; this wasn't like zip-lining or a roller coaster. It was just the two of them, with the earth spread out below them and a view like she'd never seen before—a total panorama with little fluffy white clouds scudding below them. She could see for miles and miles and miles, and it was breathtaking.

She loved every second of the freefall. But just as she was starting to worry about how far and how fast they were falling, she felt Lewis pull the cord and heard the parachute open. It jerked them back up in the air, and the rest of the descent was much slower. Peaceful. Like nothing she could ever have imagined.

As they neared the ground, she lifted her legs up as they'd been instructed to do, and the next thing she knew they'd landed. Not skidding along the field, as she'd half expected, but gracefully.

Once Lewis was sure that she was steady on her feet, he detached his harness from hers and she was free to move. She turned to face him.

'So did you enjoy it?' he asked.

Her smile felt as if it was a mile wide. 'I *loved* it.' Adrenalin was pumping through her veins, and she couldn't help wrapping her arms round him and lifting her face up to his.

The next thing she knew, he was kissing her. Really kissing her. Not like that tentative, skin-tingling brush against her mouth from last time: this was a full-on, no-holds-barred kiss.

Her toes curled and she felt as if her knees had melted. But he was holding her, making sure she wouldn't fall. Or was he holding on to her for dear life?

She didn't have a clue. She couldn't think straight. All she could do was feel.

And Lewis Gallagher kissed like a fallen angel.

When he finally broke the kiss, they just stared at each other. There was a slash of colour over his cheekbones, his eyes were wide, the pupils huge, and his mouth was reddened. Abigail was pretty sure she looked the same.

What now?

It felt as if they'd been frozen for ever. But then he coughed. 'I'd better sort out the parachute.'

'Can I help?'

'Thanks, but it's quicker for me to do it than to talk you through it,' he said.

Feeling a bit like a spare part, she watched him pack up the parachute then walked back to the office with him to sort out the last bit of admin.

He didn't say a word until they were both sitting in his car.

And then he turned to her, looking serious. 'Abby, what happened just now on the field—'

'Shouldn't have happened,' she cut in swiftly. Before he could say it. And no way could she look him in the eye. She didn't want him to know how much that kiss had affected her.

Abigail looked drawn. Ashen.

Oh, hell. He really shouldn't have kissed her like that. He'd been way out of line.

Then again, she'd kissed him back. And Lewis had a feeling that she was just as mixed up about it as he was. 'I know. But it did.' He paused. It was time to be honest. 'And I think it's going to happen again.'

That made her look at him. And she was all wide-eyed and beautiful. He wanted to kiss her again right at that moment, until they were both too dizzy to know where they were.

'We're colleagues,' she said.

He noticed she didn't put the word 'just' in there. Because she obviously knew they were more than that, too.

'Abby,' he said softly, 'I find you attractive. Really attractive. And I think it's mutual.'

She said nothing. He sighed inwardly. He had a pretty good idea what was bugging her: his reputation. Three dates and you're out. She'd even said it when he'd phoned her to talk her into spending today with him.

The grapevine had it wrong. He didn't date anywhere near as many women as everyone seemed to believe, and he didn't break things off that quickly, either. And he didn't promise any more than he could offer. He just wasn't looking for commitment.

He ought to be sensible about this. Back off.

But Abigail drew him. Beneath that quiet, shy exterior was a woman with as much zest for life as he had. And he wanted to know why she kept it under wraps.

'Abby, I can take you home right now,' he said. 'But I think you're going to spend the rest of the day feeling the same way that I will.'

She looked at him again. 'Which is?'

He couldn't put it into words. But he could show her. He leaned forward and kissed her stupid.

When they came up for air, she was shaking. 'Oh,

my God. I haven't been kissed in a car like that since I was a teenager. If then.'

'Guess what? I haven't kissed anyone in a car like that since I was—well, not that much older than a teenager.' Not since the girl who had broken his heart. Not that he was going to think of Jenna now. That part of his life was over. She was irrelevant.

He rubbed his thumb along Abigail's lower lip. 'So, what now, Abby? Do you want me to take you home? Or can I tempt you back to mine for lunch? I was planning asparagus and home-made hollandaise sauce.'

He could tempt her, Abigail thought. With a lot of things. And this would be the most stupid thing she'd ever done. She knew Lewis didn't do commitment, and he was the worst person she could possibly get involved with— an adrenalin fiend who wouldn't take things seriously.

'Asparagus,' she said slowly. 'With home-made hollandaise sauce.'

'Or butter and freshly shaved parmesan.' He leaned forward and stole another kiss. 'Anything you want.'

She could say no.

Or she could be brave. She could tell him what she wanted.

'Anything I want?' she checked.

He nodded. 'Tell me what you want, Abby.'

She lifted her hand to cup his cheek. 'You, Lewis. I want *you*.'

His eyes went all dark and stormy and he moved his face to press a kiss into her palm before folding her fingers around his kiss. 'If I get a speeding fine on the way home, woman, I hope you know it'll be all your fault,' he said.

She laughed, and her last doubts dissolved.

CHAPTER SIX

But Abigail's doubts came back when they became stuck in traffic, and she was silent all the way back from the traffic jam to Lewis's flat.

'This was all meant to be spontaneous,' he grumbled. 'Sorry. I should've taken a different route home.'

'It's OK.'

'You don't sound OK.' He sighed. 'Spit it out, Abby.'

'Three dates and you're out. I was just thinking—is there any point in even *starting* this?'

He rolled his eyes. 'The grapevine gets everything out of proportion. For your information, I've dated some women more than three times.'

'And some less than that, so it evens out.'

'I guess so,' he admitted. 'But I don't actually date that many women, whatever the grapevine says. And I definitely don't sleep with every woman I date.' He paused. 'Not everyone wants to settle down and get married and have a family. Just so you know, I don't.'

She thought about it. Was that what she wanted? What she'd never quite had, growing up?

And what had made Lewis wary of relationships, given that he was clearly close to his sisters and was a doting uncle? Why didn't he want a family? If she asked, she had a feeling that he'd change the subject. They really didn't know each other well enough for this kind of conversation. And it wasn't appropriate anyway—strictly speaking, they weren't even dating.

She needed to know where she stood. 'So this is a fling?' she asked.

He raked a hand through his hair. 'I don't know. I don't know what the hell it is.'

'You said I was your project.' That still stung.

He kissed her; she thought it was probably just to shut her up. Then he sighed. 'Yes. No. I have no idea.' He stared at her, his eyes stormy. 'What is it about you that puts me in a flat spin? I'm not used to this.'

That little admission of vulnerability, added to the way he looked so appealingly rumpled, widened the crack round her heart. She leaned over to kiss him.

When he broke the kiss, he said, 'Abby, you have a choice. I can take you home.'

'Or?'

'I can take you to bed.' His voice was low and gravelly and incredibly sexy.

She had a pretty good idea what he wanted her to say but she liked the fact that he was giving her the choice, rather than expecting her just to fall in with his wishes. She smiled. 'I'm really glad we had the roof up on the way back.'

He frowned. 'Why?'

'Because it'll take us less time to get from your car to your flat.'

In answer, he kissed her, putting her into the same flat spin he'd claimed she'd put him in. She barely registered that they'd left the car until he fumbled with the keys on the doorstep, dropped them and swore. 'Sorry.'

She stroked his cheek. 'I work in the emergency department. I've heard much worse than that.'

'I know. But even so, I shouldn't swear in front of you.'

Clearly he'd been brought up the old-fashioned way. With family values. So why was he turning his back on them when it came to his personal life?

'I'm sorry,' he said again.

The second he closed the door behind them he kissed her again. Her back was against the wall, his arms were wrapped round her and his mouth was moving against hers. Tiny, nibbling, teasing kisses along her lower lip, tempting and demanding and offering, all at the same time.

She opened her mouth to let him deepen the kiss, and everything around her seemed to fade. All she was aware of was Lewis and the way he was kissing her.

He broke the kiss. 'I can't wait any more, Abby. I'm burning up for you.'

To her shock, he actually scooped her up and carried her to his bedroom. Literally sweeping her off her feet. Nobody had ever done that to her before.

She was still registering that when he set her down on her feet again, making sure that her body was in full contact with his all the way and she was left in no doubt about his arousal.

'You're beautiful,' he said. Gently, he removed the elastic she used to tie her hair back. 'And your hair is amazing.' He ran his fingers through her hair. 'So soft and smooth and silky.'

'Dead straight and ginger.' It had earned her a fair bit of teasing when she'd finally gone to school. But her attempt at going blonde and curly had been a disaster. She'd ended up having her hair cut horrendously short and it had taken her two years to grow it back. Since then she'd kept it tied back and had had done nothing more than have the ends trimmed.

'Copper,' he corrected. 'And my sisters would kill to have hair that's naturally straight like this and doesn't need to be tamed with a pair of straighteners.'

He liked her hair?

The surprise must have shown in her face because he rubbed his thumb along her lower lip. 'You're beautiful. But I need to see more of you, Abby. I need you naked and in my bed, with that glorious hair spread over my pillow. Right now.'

The sheer desire in his eyes sent a thrill through her. He meant it. And he saw her for herself.

She nodded and lifted her arms up. He slid his fingers underneath the hem of her T-shirt and slowly drew the material over her head.

'Gorgeous,' he said, his voice hoarse, and traced the lacy edge of her bra, his fingertips skimming over her skin and making her feel super-heated.

'My turn.' She stripped off his T-shirt in the same way. 'Very nice,' she said, splaying her hands against his bare chest. He had perfect musculature, with a light sprinkling of hair on his chest. She let her hands slide down his abdomen. 'That's a perfect six-pack, Dr Gallagher. You take care of yourself.'

'I try.' He smiled, then dipped his head and brushed his mouth against hers. 'My turn again?'

'I—um...' She looked awkwardly at him. 'My trainers are in the way.'

'I can do something about that.' He gave her a slow, sexy smile. 'Though I have to admit I'd love to see you in high heels.'

She didn't have any. Abigail Smith wore sensible shoes and sensible clothes. She wasn't a vamp. So what on earth was she doing here, with the most eligible man in the hospital?

'Abby. Stop thinking.' He kissed her briefly. 'Right now you're everything I want. Fripperies don't matter.'

He dropped to his knees in front of her and dealt with the laces of her trainers, then peeled her leggings down. He took it maddeningly slowly, stroking her buttocks and thighs as he uncovered her skin, making her shiver.

She dragged in a breath. 'Socks. So not sexy.'

'I don't care. I've got a very nice view from here.' He looked up at her with heat in his eyes. 'But as the lady wishes.' He lifted one foot so he could remove her sock, caressing her instep as he bared it, then did the same with the other foot.

Since when had *feet* been sexy? Abigail had had no idea that feet could be an erogenous zone. But Lewis— Lewis made her feel like a siren.

'You look like one,' he said.

'What?'

'A siren. Especially with that amazing hair. I can see you as a mermaid, sitting on a rock and combing your hair in the sunshine.'

She groaned. 'Oh, no. I didn't mean to say that aloud.'

He pressed a kiss to the side of her knee, making her legs feel even weaker. 'It's cute. You're no ice princess,

Abby. The grapevine's got you totally wrong. You're all woman. Sexy as hell. And I really, really want you.'

'I want you, too,' she said shakily. 'And you're wearing way more than I am.'

He got to his feet in one lithe movement. 'Do something about it, then.'

Her hands were trembling as she slid his tracksuit bottoms over his hips. The material pooled at his feet; she knelt down to unlace his trainers and finish removing his tracksuit bottoms. Then she rocked back on her haunches and looked at him. He was glorious. Like a Michelangelo sculpture.

'I need to kiss you, Abby,' he said. He took her hands and drew her to her feet, then cupped her face and caught her lower lip between his. She couldn't help responding, letting him deepen the kiss and matching him nibble for nibble, desire for desire.

She tangled her fingers in his hair; he slid his hands down over her shoulders, pushing the straps of her bra down. He deftly undid the clasp of her bra and let her breasts spill into his hands.

'You're seriously lush,' he said. 'And I can't wait any longer.' He picked her up and carried her over to the bed, nudging the duvet aside before he laid her on the mattress.

Then she realised that his curtains were open, and froze.

'Abby?'

She swallowed hard. 'Your curtains are open.'

He smiled and stole a kiss. 'Don't worry. Nobody can see in. My neighbours opposite are out at work. And it'd be a shame to shut the sunshine out.'

How could she resist the appeal in his beautiful slate-blue eyes?

She let him kiss her worries away. He kissed his way along her collar bones then down her sternum. She arched towards him, and he smiled. 'What do you want me to do, Abby?'

'I…' She felt the colour staining her face.

'I can't read your mind,' he said softly. 'I know what I'd like to do. But it's what you'd like me to do that I'm more interested in.' He stole a kiss. 'If it pleases you, it pleases me as well.'

She swallowed hard. 'Touch me, Lewis.'

'Where?' His eyes darkened. 'Tell me, Abby.'

Her hand was shaking as she took his hand and placed it on her breast.

'Good choice,' he whispered, teasing her nipple with his thumb and forefinger. Then he dipped his head, took her nipple into his mouth and sucked.

Abigail sighed with pleasure and slid her fingers into his hair, urging him on.

She tipped her head back when he switched sides. 'More,' she whispered.

He slid one finger under the edge of her knickers and drew a fingertip along the length of her sex. When he touched her clitoris, she shivered.

'Like this?' he murmured against her ear.

It was as if he could read her mind and knew exactly how and where she liked being touched. And the way he was stroking her, teasing her, was making it impossible for her to speak a proper sentence. 'Uh.'

'Good.'

She was incoherent by the time he stopped; all she

could do was open her eyes and look at him in mute appeal.

'Condom,' he said, vaulted off the bed and stripped off his underpants.

Abigail just stared at him. Naked, he was beautiful.

And right now he was all hers.

He rummaged in the pocket of his tracksuit bottoms for his wallet and extracted a small foil packet.

'Just so you know,' he said softly, 'there really aren't many notches on my bedpost. This isn't something I do every day or even every week.'

'I can't even remember the last time I did this.'

'"All work and no play",' he quoted with a smile. 'So I think we need to do each other a favour right now. I'd hate people to think of me as dull.'

She sat up, drawing her knees up and resting her chin on them. 'They don't.' And there was the rub. 'Whereas they know I am.'

'Dull?' He shook his head. 'No. You're not. Dull women don't go zip-lining. Or throw themselves out of planes. Or kiss me in a way that scrambles my brain. And you most definitely do.'

'Only because you talked me into it.'

'Abby.' He came to sit next to her, took her hand and pressed a kiss into the palm. Then he folded her fingers around it. 'You don't have to do this. I can take you home. Well, after I've cooked you lunch.'

And now it was all going horribly wrong. She wrapped her hands round her legs, curling into a near-fetal position. 'I think you were right about me,' she said miserably. 'I need to be someone's project.'

'No. You just need to have a little faith in yourself. You know you're a good doctor, right?'

'Yes.' She wasn't worried about her professional life. She worked hard, she knew what she was doing and she knew when to ask for help.

'And you're an interesting person.'

No. She was the daughter of someone interesting. Even though she thought Lewis might understand that, she still didn't want to tell him who she really was. She made a noncommittal noise and looked away. 'Perhaps I'd better go.'

'Not yet.' To her surprise, he hauled her onto his lap. 'Right now, I think you need a cuddle.'

Since when had playboys been sensitive? 'Don't be nice to me. I might cry.'

'Shh.' He wrapped his arms round her and rested his cheek against hers.

She closed her eyes. He didn't say a word, just held her, and all her self-doubts began to melt away.

He dropped a kiss against her hair. 'Better?'

She nodded. 'Sorry. I'm being an idiot.'

'No, but I'd guess you've had a rubbish choice in men in the past,' he said dryly. 'As for the guy who made you feel you're dull—he didn't know you, Abby. Because you're *not* dull.' He took her hand and placed it against his chest so she could feel the rapid beat of his heart. 'A dull woman couldn't do that to me.'

But she could. She could make his blood heat.

'Kiss me, Lewis,' she said.

He pressed a soft, gentle kiss to the corner of her mouth.

'I mean properly.'

His eyes widened. 'You don't have to do this.'

'I want to,' she said. 'And this time I'm not going to back out. OK, so I had a bit of a wobble just now.'

'Hey. You jumped out of a plane this morning. You're allowed to have a wobble.'

God, that smile. It made her heart feel as if it had just done a backflip. Which was anatomically impossible. Lewis was impossible. This whole situation was ridiculous.

'Can we start again?' she asked.

'If you're sure you want to.'

'I am.'

This time he let her set the pace. He let her touch him, explore him, kiss her way around his body.

And when she was quivering, needing him inside her, she whispered, 'Now.'

In answer, he kissed her, ripped open the foil packet and rolled the condom onto his erect penis. Then he knelt between her thighs and eased his body into hers.

The first time it was meant to be embarrassing and awkward, second-guessing what each other liked.

But this—this felt *right*.

'OK?' he asked softly.

'Very OK.' She stroked his face. 'You're not bad at this.'

He laughed, and kissed her. 'I've hardly started.'

And then he proved it to her, by bringing her to a swift climax—then slowing down and making the tension build up and up and up, coiling inside her.

'Lewis, I can't...' This couldn't possibly happen again.

'Don't fight it, Abby. Open your eyes and look at me.'

She did, and her body tightened around his at the same time that she felt his body surge hard into hers.

This man took her breath away. He made her feel like nobody had ever made her feel before.

'Let me deal with the condom,' he said. 'And don't start thinking, Abby. I don't want a single doubt in your head when I get back here.' As if to make sure of it, he kissed her again, making her head spin.

She lay curled under the duvet, waiting for him. Lewis had been a real revelation. Sensitive, thoughtful, taking care of her needs. She really hadn't expected that.

How had he gotten a reputation as a heartbreaker? Or was that part of his defence mechanism? He'd said that he didn't want to get married and settle down. Acting like a heartbreaker was one way of making sure that his relationships didn't last that long.

'I said, don't start thinking,' he said softly, climbing back into bed beside her and drawing her into his arms.

'I'm not,' she fibbed.

'Never play poker,' he said. 'Your face is very expressive. You can't hide what you're thinking.'

Oh, yes, she could. And she'd learned how to play poker from one of the very best. Maybe, she thought, that was the way to get Lewis to tell her what was really in his head. Unpick the puzzle. She'd just bet he wouldn't be able to resist the challenge.

'Maybe,' she said, and turned her head to press a kiss into his shoulder. 'Thank you. You made me feel amazing.'

He stroked her face. 'That's because you are amazing.'

'I wasn't fishing for a compliment.'

'I know. Or I wouldn't have said it.'

She smiled at him. 'Thank you.'

He kissed her lightly. 'I promised you asparagus. Give me twelve minutes.'

'Do you want some help?'

'No. Stay there.'

'Here?' She blinked at him.

He gave her a look that made her temperature spike. 'I thought we could have lunch in bed.'

'Very decadent of you, Dr Gallagher.'

He just laughed, kissed her, and pulled on a pair of shorts. 'Butter and parmesan?'

'Yes, please.'

True to his word, he was back in twelve minutes with a tray containing a dish of dressed asparagus and a plate of good bread.

Not only was the food good, it was fun—because Lewis insisted on them feeding each other, and Abigail thoroughly enjoyed teasing him.

Though it was also messy. By the time they'd finished, they were both covered in melted butter.

'What a good excuse to have a shower with you,' Lewis said with a grin.

He proceeded to make love to her there, too. And Abigail didn't care that her hair went in rats' tails if it got wet and she didn't dry it properly. She was just enjoying being with Lewis. Pretending that the outside world didn't exist.

When they finally got dressed again, Lewis led her into his living room and pulled her onto his lap on the sofa.

'So where do we go from here?' she asked.

'I guess,' he said, 'we might be an item.'

'But?' She could hear it as clearly as if he'd said it out loud.

He sighed. 'The hospital grapevine might give us a bit of a hard time if this becomes common knowledge. I have this stupid reputation.'

She really wasn't sure whether he meant that he wanted to keep his reputation or whether he resented it. And if she asked him, she didn't think he'd tell her.

'So you want to keep it to ourselves?'

'Until we decide where this is taking us, that might be a good idea.' He kissed the tip of her nose. 'Which isn't a way of saying I'm ashamed of you. I'm not.'

'But you want to be my dirty little secret,' she said lightly.

'The ice princess dating the hospital Casanova. Yes.'

Was there a slight edge to his tone or was it her imagination? She stroked his face. 'Lewis. Why do you let people think you're something you're not?'

'It's easier that way.' He paused. 'So you don't think I'm like Casanova?'

'No, but I wouldn't mind seeing you dressed up as an eighteenth-century Venetian.' Then she looked at him. 'Tell me you didn't have a summer job as a gondolier, dressed as Casanova.'

'No. I missed a trick there, didn't I?' He smiled at her. 'I like you, Abby Smith.'

'I like you too, Lewis Gallagher.'

'Good.' He kissed her. 'So. Have you had enough of me for today or can I take you out to dinner?'

She glanced down at her T-shirt and leggings. 'You

have a really bad habit of suggesting that when I'm really not dressed for dinner.'

'We can go back to your place and you can change. Or I can cook here.'

'You cooked lunch.' She paused. She was about to take a risk. But wasn't Lewis also taking a risk in starting a relationship with her? The man who didn't do commitment had said they were an item... 'Or we could have dinner at mine. I could cook for us.'

He looked pleased, and she realised that she'd been holding her breath, waiting for his reaction.

'That'd be good. Thank you.'

Back at her flat, she made him a coffee. To her relief, he went to the bathroom and that gave her time to remove the photograph on the mantelpiece—herself and her father in the back garden. She wasn't ready to tell Lewis about that. Not yet. Not until she felt much more secure about what was happening between them and her burgeoning friendships at work.

When he joined her in the living room, she said, 'Help yourself to the television and what have you.'

'Can I do anything to help?'

'No, it's fine.'

'Territorial about your kitchen?' he asked.

''Fraid so,' she admitted.

'Then I'm going to be nosy in your bookshelves.'

Abigail spent probably too much time in the kitchen, fussing, but eventually dinner was ready and she went through to the living room to call him in. 'Sorry—I've neglected you.'

He lowered the journal he was reading and smiled

at her. 'No worries. It was nice to have the chance to catch up with some reading.'

She knew he took his work seriously, but it still surprised her that Lewis the party boy would opt for reading a serious medical journal over flicking through television channels. Then again, he'd surprised her a lot today.

'I know you're driving, but would you like a glass of wine?'

'I'll stick to a soft drink, if you don't mind.' He followed her through to the kitchen and sat at her small bistro table. 'That looks good.'

'Thank you. Though I have to admit to cheating and using a sachet of pre-cooked quinoa to stuff the peppers.'

'It's lovely,' he said when he'd tasted it. 'I'll have to pinch the recipe for Dani.'

Being with him in her kitchen felt oddly intimate. And he was still pretty much a stranger. Her shyness flooded back; trying to combat it, she said, 'Shall I put some music on?'

'Sure. Given that you knew all the words to that song, the other week, I guess you're going to choose Brydon?'

All her Brydon CDs were signed copies. And if Lewis saw Keith's flamboyant signature and took a closer look, then read the inscription to Cinnamon, it would mean way too many explanations. Ones she wasn't quite ready to give. 'I'm in the mood for classical,' she said hastily.

'Fine by me.'

Funny. Even though he'd been to the concert with her and she knew he enjoyed classical, she'd been so sure he'd prefer dance music. She chose a Bach string quartet, then came back to the table.

'Very nice. I used to study to this,' Lewis said.

Abigail looked surprised. 'There's a lot more to you than meets the eye. Why do you let people think you're someone you're not?' she asked again.

He shrugged. 'It's easier.'

'You know what you were saying about my rubbish choice of men—I think that's true for you, too.'

Yeah. The woman he'd been so sure he could spend the rest of his life with. The one he'd met when his family commitments had been starting to ease and he'd been able to see his way clear to training as a doctor. He'd proposed to Jenna. He'd even bought her a ring and asked her to wait for him to finish university. But she hadn't wanted to wait. She'd forced his hand—and she'd let him down in the worst possible way.

He shook himself. Not now. He forced himself to smile at Abigail and keep it light. 'Newsflash for you, princess. I don't date men.'

She rolled her eyes. 'You know what I mean.'

'We all make mistakes. I learned from mine.' And he didn't want to go into that now. He switched the conversation back to food, and to his relief she went with it.

When they'd finished the peppers, she brought out a bowl of mixed berries—raspberries, blueberries, cherries and strawberries. And she served it with a seriously good raspberry sorbet.

'Sorry, this is a bit lazy. I should've made a proper summer pudding,' she said.

'You weren't planning to cook me dinner, so you

didn't have enough time to make a summer pudding—
and, anyway, this is a healthier version. Much better.'

She gave him a grateful smile.

She wouldn't let him wash up after dinner. 'It won't
take me five minutes. Let's go and sit down in the living room with some coffee.'

And Lewis was quite happy to curl up on the sofa
with her and watch some old comedy re-runs. Weird.
Usually, when he dated someone, he kept the evening
short and sweet, not wanting to let her too close. But
he'd spent the whole day with Abigail and he still didn't
want to bolt.

Which should in itself be a warning.

He wasn't going to repeat the mistake he'd made
with Jenna.

But the situation was different now. His sisters were
grown up and his career was on track. His mother...
well, some things you couldn't fix.

He kissed Abigail lightly. 'I'd better go.'

'Uh-huh.'

'Abby.' He kissed her lingeringly. 'Today's been
amazing.'

'Mmm. It's not every day someone throws you out
of a plane.'

He laughed. 'No, I jumped and you happened to be
attached to me.' He traced her lower lip with the tip of
his forefinger. 'And afterwards. That wasn't supposed
to happen.'

'But I'm glad it did.'

That whispered admission warmed him. 'So am I.'
He kissed her again. 'I'll see you tomorrow.'

'At work. In professional mode.'

'Absolutely, Dr Smith.'

And he really had to go, before he broke all his personal rules and asked if he could stay.

CHAPTER SEVEN

THE NEXT DAY at work, Abigail's pulse quickened as she saw Lewis.

'Good morning, Dr Smith,' he said.

So he'd meant it about keeping their relationship away from the eyes of the hospital grapevine. He was treating her as he always did, just as part of the team. She knew they'd agreed to that but it still put a lump of disappointment into her throat that he wasn't going to acknowledge their relationship. Which was ridiculous, and she was cross with herself for being so wet and needy. Was it any wonder that men didn't usually like her for herself?

'Good morning, Dr Gallagher,' she said, keeping her voice as professional as possible.

It didn't help that they were rostered together in Resus.

Or maybe it did, because it meant they were too busy to do anything other than think about their patients. Especially when a four-year-old was brought in with suspected acute asthma.

The little girl was too breathless to talk and her pulse was fast. Her mother was panicking, her voice high with fright as she explained what had happened.

Lewis introduced them both to Mrs Jones, his voice calm and reassuring. 'I know it's scary seeing Kirsty like this, but try not to worry. We're going to make her feel better. We need to treat her to help her breathing and we'll try to talk you through what we're doing as we go, but we need to focus on Kirsty first so we might not get a chance to explain everything. Once we've started the treatment we'll have time to answer all your questions.'

'Kirsty, sweetheart, my name's Dr Abby,' Abigail said. 'I'm going to put a special mask on you to help you breathe more easily.' She gently put the mask on the little girl, talking her thorough it and reassuring her, and administered high flow oxygen.

'Has anything like this ever happened before?' Lewis asked.

'No. We were round at my friend's. Kirsty was playing with their new kitten but then she started wheezing and couldn't breathe. I thought she'd swallowed something. I didn't know what to do so my friend drove me here. It wasn't far so we thought it'd be quicker than calling an ambulance.'

'You did absolutely the right thing in bringing her in,' Lewis said, squeezing her hand.

'I think Kirsty's just had a bad asthma attack,' Abigail said gently. 'And that can be very scary to see. Does anyone in the family have asthma?'

Mrs Jones shook her head.

'How about hay fever or eczema?' Lewis asked.

'I had eczema when I was tiny,' Mrs Jones told them. 'I have to be a bit careful about the washing powder I use, doing laundry, or it makes me itch. I always use non-bio. But Kirsty never had eczema.' She shook her head. 'I don't understand why she has asthma.'

'Often if a parent has asthma, eczema or hay fever, the child will have one of the three as well. It just might not be the same allergic reaction as the parent has,' Abigail explained.

Mrs Jones looked stricken. 'So it's my fault she can't breathe?'

'It's nobody's fault. It just happens. Don't blame yourself,' Lewis said. 'The main thing is we'll get her breathing back to normal, and then you can have a chat with the paediatrician and we'll sort out some medication.'

'You mean like a puffer? One of the boys in her pre-school group has one.'

'Yes. She'll have one she takes every day to prevent attacks and one she takes if she has an attack to stop the wheezing and coughing,' Abigail said. She stroked the little girl's hand. Kirsty's breathing seemed to be easing slightly. 'Kirsty, I need to you to do something very important for me. I'd like you to blow as hard as you can into a special tube. Can you do that for me?'

The little girl nodded.

Abby removed the mask so the little girl could blow into the expiratory flow meter. Just as she'd suspected, it was less than half of what it should've been so the asthma attack was a severe one.

'Thank you, Kirsty. That's brilliant. I'm going to give you some special medicine now through the mask, and all you have to do is breathe and it works,' she said.

'The medicine's going to help open her airways and make it easier for her to breathe,' Lewis told Mrs Jones.

Abigail fitted a nebuliser to the mask and added salbutamol. 'You're being very brave, Kirsty. Can you swallow some medicine for me before I put the mask back on you?'

'Yeth,' the little girl lisped.

Quickly, Abigail gave her some oral prednisolone, then took out one of the stickers she kept in her pocket.'

Kirsty brightened at the sight of it. 'It's a star.'

'Which I only give to really brave little girls. I think you deserve this.' She gave the sticker to the little girl, who immediately took off the backing and stuck it to her T-shirt.

'And now I need to put a special machine on your finger now. It's a bit like a glove. It won't hurt, but it helps me see if the medicine is working or if I need to give you a different one. Is that all right?'

Kirsty nodded.

'It's a light beam through that goes through a sensor to measure the oxygen in her blood,' Lewis said to Mrs Jones. 'It won't hurt.'

'So is she going to be all right?' Mrs Jones asked.

'Yes. She has asthma. What happens is that when Kirsty comes into contact with something that triggers the asthma, the muscles round the wall of her airways tighten up. That makes the airways narrower and that's why it's hard for her to breathe,' Lewis said.

'What caused it?' Mrs Jones asked.

'I'd say the most likely thing that triggered today's attack would be your friend's kitten,' Abigail said.

Mrs Jones frowned. 'But she's played with the cat before and never had problems.'

'That often happens. Sometimes it takes years from

the first time you come in contact with something you're allergic to until you actually have an asthma attack,' Lewis explained. 'You might find she's sensitive to other furry animals or birds. The paediatrician will discuss this with you and set up a personal action plan to help you keep an eye on Kirsty's asthma, so you'll know what to do if you think her symptoms are getting worse.'

After a quarter of an hour Kirsty seemed to be improving. 'We're going to keep her on oxygen and the medicine in the nebuliser until the paediatrician's seen her,' Abigail said. 'But the good news is that she's responding well and I'm pretty sure you'll be able to talk to her tonight.'

The triage nurse came into the cubicle. 'Sorry to interrupt. Just to let you know that Dr Morgan's here when you're ready to see her,' she said quietly.

'Thanks. We're ready now,' Abigail said.

When the paediatrician came in, Abigail introduced Katrina Morgan to Mrs Jones and Kirsty.

'We'll leave you with Dr Morgan now,' she said. 'She'll take you up to the ward where they can keep an eye on Kirsty for a little bit longer, and she'll be able to help you with the treatment plan.' She smiled at Kirsty. 'You take care now.'

'Bye, Dr Abby.' The little girl waved shyly.

'You were very good with Kirsty's mum,' Abigail said to Lewis when they were out of earshot. 'You really calmed her down.'

'You know as well as I do that children respond better to treatment if their parents aren't panicking.' He smiled. 'And you were very good with Kirsty. I noticed you called yourself Dr Abby to her.'

'Let's just say your project's working,' she said dryly.

'Good.' He laughed. 'So you have a secret supply of shiny stickers, do you?'

'It's just from one of the stationery chains, not a special order or anything.'

He sighed. 'It's a girl thing, isn't it? My sisters can't pass stationery shops either. I bet you have one of those pens with the feathery bit on the end.'

She laughed. 'I do indeed. As you say, it's a girl thing.'

'Do you—?' he began, then shook his head. 'We'd better get on.'

What had he been about to ask her?

But she didn't get the chance to push him further, and he didn't suggest having lunch together or seeing her after work.

Maybe he'd changed his mind and he wanted to go back to being just colleagues. Well, she'd just have to deal with it. It wasn't as if she hadn't been warned that Lewis Gallagher didn't do commitment.

Lewis didn't call or text her that evening either, and Abigail didn't call him as she didn't want him to think she was clingy or pushy. He was in Resus the next day while she was on Minors so she didn't get the chance to see him at work either.

'You're quiet, Abby. Is everything OK?' Marina asked her at lunch on Wednesday.

'Yes, I'm fine,' Abigail fibbed. 'I'm looking forward to the team night out on Friday. I've never been ice skating.'

'I'm absolutely hopeless,' Sydney said. 'But my goal this time is to get round the edge of the whole rink, even if I have to hold on, and not fall over more than ten times.'

Marina laughed. 'I'm not much better, Syd. Max is surprisingly good, though.'

Abigail would just bet that Lewis was good, too. She wasn't sure whether he was going or not and didn't want to ask Marina or Sydney in case they wanted to know why she was so interested. She was happy to let the two other doctors chatter on and stayed in the background. But it was bugging her that Lewis had been practically ignoring her since they'd made love. She could see now why he drove women crazy.

He finally called her that evening. 'Hey, princess. Are you busy?'

She was tempted to say yes and put the phone down, but that would be childish. And she didn't want him to know how put out she was that he was keeping their relationship a secret at work. 'Don't call me "princess". It's annoying. And, yes, I'm busy.'

'What are you doing?'

'Watching a movie, if you must know.' And she hated the fact that she sounded so prim and snotty. That wasn't her. At all.

'If I bring a tub of posh ice cream, can I come and join you?'

'It's a rom-com. You'll hate it. Anyway, you've already missed the first half an hour, so there isn't much point in seeing the rest.'

'I don't mind.' She could almost hear the smile in his

voice. 'If I'm honest, it's just an excuse to come and lie on your sofa with you in my arms.'

'You're taking a lot for granted.'

'You really have had a bad day, haven't you?'

'No.' She sighed. 'Lewis...'

'Let me come over. I'll bring ice cream. What do you like?'

She gave in. 'Anything except chocolate.'

'You don't like chocolate?' He sounded surprised.

'I like chocolate, and I like ice cream. But I don't like chocolate ice cream,' she corrected. 'I know it's weird.'

'It is. Seriously weird. Chocolate's my favourite. OK. I'll be with you in about twenty minutes. Don't hold the film for me.'

In exactly twenty minutes Lewis rang her doorbell. 'Hey, beautiful.' He kissed her hello and handed her a tub of posh strawberry ice cream.

'Thank you.'

He narrowed his eyes. 'Right. Spit it out.'

'Spit what out?'

'I take back what I said about you having a rough day at work. You're annoyed about something.'

'What makes you say that?'

'Your eyes have a really dark ring round them.'

She raised an eyebrow. 'You're saying I've got bags under my eyes?'

He flapped a dismissive hand. 'No. I'm saying usually your irises are the soft grey of an autumn mist. But when you're upset or angry about something, there's a dark ring round the outer edge. Like storm clouds coming in.'

'Very poetic, Dr Gallagher.' But she was amazed that he'd noticed such a tiny detail.

'So what's wrong?'

She grimaced. 'It's going to sound childish.'

'Tell me anyway.'

She took a deep breath. 'OK. I feel as if you're ignoring me at work.'

He frowned. 'Of course I'm not. We work together. I think we're a pretty good team, actually.'

'But you never suggest going for coffee or lunch.'

'Ah. *That* sort of ignoring.' He stole a kiss. 'We agreed we're trying to stay under the radar of the hospital grapevine.'

'That's a mixed metaphor.'

'I don't care.' He drew her close. 'Abby. If people at work know we're together, we're just going to get hassled. Everyone's going to tell me that you're too good for me, and everyone's going to tell you that I break hearts on a daily basis.'

She sighed. 'I know.' And she could really understand now why Lewis had a reputation as a heartbreaker. She had a nasty feeling that he could break hers.

'It doesn't change things between you and me. But it means we get to explore wherever this is going without any hassle.'

'Uh-huh.' She still wasn't entirely convinced.

He kissed her. 'Trust me, this really is the best way.'

Trust. That was the rub. It was the thing she found hardest. But if this thing between them was going to work, she'd just have to try.

'Let's go and finish watching your film. We need two spoons.'

'And bowls.'

'No. It's more fun to eat straight from the tub.' He gave her a wicked grin. 'If I'm greedy and scoff more than my share, you can make me do a forfeit. I'll do anything you ask.'

Oh, the thoughts that put in her head. Totally wanton. And she blushed to the roots of her hair. That was something else new that Lewis had brought out in her. She definitely hadn't had sex on the brain before meeting him.

'I love it when you do that.'

'Do what?'

He kissed her. 'Blush. You're so cute.'

She wrinkled her nose. 'It clashes with my hair.'

'No.' He took the scrunchie out of her hair and twirled a lock of hair round his fingers. 'I love your hair. I know you're sensible and wear it up at work, but it's glorious down. Definitely the mermaid look.'

She couldn't stay annoyed with him. Not when he was being playful and sweet. She fetched two spoons and curled up on the sofa with him. Though she couldn't concentrate on the rest of the film, not with Lewis so near. She was too aware of him. Of the warmth of his body, the citrusy tang of his aftershave, the muscular feel of his arms wrapped round her.

'I'm sorry. I didn't mean to spoil your evening,' he said as the credits rolled.

'You didn't. The film wasn't as good as I thought it would be.' She shifted so she was facing him and laid her palm against his cheek. 'And you were bored, weren't you?'

'Rom-coms aren't really my thing,' he agreed. He

twisted slightly so he could kiss her palm. 'I like a good action movie.'

'Now, why doesn't that surprise me, coming from an adrenalin fiend?' she teased.

'If it walks like a duck and quacks like a duck...' he said, spreading his hands.

She laughed, and kissed him. 'Were you an adrenalin fiend when you were growing up?'

'I guess so. I used to climb trees and roller-skate too fast down slopes.' At least, until he'd been fourteen. Then he'd had to learn to be domesticated. Fast.

'What about your sisters? Are they adrenalin fiends, too?'

'No, they're girly. Well, Dani and Ronnie have fairly big nerdy streaks,' he amended. 'Manda's your typical drama teacher, with floaty scarves and lots of hats—oh, and her hair colour never stays the same two months running.'

'It must've been fun growing up in your house,' she said wistfully.

'It was.' Until his dad had died and life had turned upside down. 'Noisy, though. And sometimes it was hard to find a corner of space just for you. I guess that's part of why I like doing the outdoor stuff. It gave me space.'

'Were your parents outdoor types?'

'Dad was. He was in the local mountain rescue team. I guess that's what sparked my interest in the first place—I wanted to follow in his footsteps.'

'Did you?'

He nodded. 'I used to hang around the team and help

with the communications bit when I was smaller, then when I was old enough I did the training and I became part of the team.' Not until after his dad had died, but the team had taken pity on him and let him start a bit younger. They'd understood why he'd needed to do it.

'You miss it, don't you?'

'Yes. I did think about going back to the Peak district and working in the nearest emergency department, so I could work with the mountain rescue team again.' Which was something he'd never told anyone. Why was he spilling his guts to Abigail? He needed to shut up. Now.

'Why don't you?'

Because it was complicated. And he wasn't ready to explain about his mother. 'I like living in London,' he said simply. 'And I can still do outdoor stuff here.'

'Like zip-lining and skydiving.'

'You enjoyed it, too,' he pointed out.

She smiled. 'Yes. But I don't think I could keep up with your pace.'

'Hey. We're having a quiet evening in front of the television, are we not?'

'And you're bored.'

'I'm not bored with your company,' he said softly. And he spent the next half an hour proving it, to their mutual satisfaction.

Friday night was the team ice-skating night. Abigail discovered that, just as Marina had said, Max was good at skating. Marco was on duty, or no doubt he would've been doing a double act with Max, but Sydney spent more time falling over than skating—and so did Abigail. And Lewis, just as she'd suspected, turned out to be brilliant.

'OK, you two. I can't stand by and see you do this any more. I'm going to teach you to skate. Sydney, you first,' Lewis directed. 'You're not going to fall because I won't let you, so stop over-thinking it.'

He proceeded to coax her round the edge of the rink, holding her hand and directing her movements. Abigail watched them and could see Sydney relaxing, becoming more confident and skating more smoothly as Lewis coached her.

Right at that moment she could see why Lewis had taken a gap-year job with a training company. He was a natural teacher, using the same skills he used as a doctor: calmness, patience and precision.

'Marco's never going to believe this,' Sydney said as she came to a halt by Abigail.

'I'll vouch for you if he asks. Sorry, I should've thought to film you on my phone. It looked pretty good from here.'

'I can skate. I can actually *skate*.' Sydney beamed at her. 'Abby, you have to let him teach you next. It's amazing.'

Lewis held out his hand. 'Your turn, then, Abby. And stop panicking. You saw Sydney do it. I'm not going to let you fall either.'

'Trust you, you're a doctor?' Abigail asked wryly.

He laughed. 'Something like that. Come on.' He lowered his voice as they moved away from the others in the team. 'And it's a great excuse for me to hold your hand in public without anyone asking questions.'

She couldn't help it. She blushed to the roots of her hair.

He smiled. 'If half the emergency department wasn't on the rink, I'd kiss you. Because you look adorable. But that'll have to wait until later.' He drew her just a little bit closer. 'And I'm really going to enjoy paying up on that particular promise.'

He slowly guided her round the rink, praising her as her confidence grew and correcting her technique without being bossy. And then she was skating. Gliding across the ice—holding Lewis's hand, admittedly, but not clutching the handrail, almost too terrified to move.

'I feel like a swan. Or a mermaid.'

'Mermaid on ice. That's a new one.' He smiled. 'We'll have to come to the rink again. Just the two of us.'

'I'd like that.'

'Look at you two,' Marina said as she skated up to them. 'You look like the perfect couple.'

Abigail felt the panic seep through her. Did Marina know, or was she just teasing? Abigail couldn't really read her friend's expression. 'I'm just his project,' she said. 'And did you see him teach Syd to skate?'

Marina smiled. 'He's a real Sir Galahad at heart, our Lewis.'

Lewis, predictably, did a twirl on the ice and then bowed. 'Thank you, kind madam.'

'Oh, you.' Marina laughed, and skated back to Max, greeting him with a kiss.

'You were brilliant. And I filmed you skating so you can see for yourself,' Sydney said when they returned to where they'd left her. She handed over her mobile phone. 'Take a look.'

Their heads were actually touching as they reviewed the footage. And Abigail had a nasty feeling that Marina hadn't been teasing. Because they *did* look like a couple. The way they smiled at each other, exchanged little glances—the tender expression on Lewis's face. Oh, help. How was Lewis, Mr Three-Dates-and-You're-Out, going to see all this?

Lewis wasn't prepared for the footage. The way Abigail looked at him, her expression all soft and trusting instead of the slightly wary look the doctor he'd first met had worn. Marina had been teasing—of course she had—but at the same time she had a point. They *did* look like a couple. Which was crazy, because they both had issues and neither of them wanted to settle down.

What if...?

He shook himself mentally. 'Ten out of ten for effort, Abby. You, too, Syd,' he said.

'I don't think we should tell you how good you are, Lewis, or your head will swell so much you'll never get through the doorway,' Sydney teased back.

He just laughed. 'So did you both enjoy it?'

'Definitely,' Abigail said. 'If anyone had told me last week that I'd be skating in the middle of the rink, I would never have believed them. I'm way too clumsy.'

'All it takes is practice,' Lewis said.

When their slot at the rink was over, the team headed for the pizza parlour, where Marina had booked their table. Somehow Lewis managed to sit next to Abigail;

he held her hand briefly under the table, making her feel warm all over. When their pizzas arrived, he pinched two of the artichoke hearts off her pizza.

'It's payment for teaching you to skate,' he claimed at her pained look.

'You haven't taken anything from Sydney's pizza,' she pointed out.

'That's because she's sitting at the other end of the table.' He winked at her. 'But I can tell you that her secret chocolate stash is going to be under major threat next week. I know where she keeps it.'

'You're impossible,' Abigail said, rolling her eyes.

But she absolutely loved the team evening out. For the first time she could remember she actually felt part of things. Valued for who she was. It was a weird feeling, but one she wanted to get used to.

At the end of the meal, Lewis said, 'Abby, you're on the same Tube line as me, aren't you? I'll walk you to the station.'

Nobody batted an eyelid or seemed to take his words as anything other than a colleague being gallant, so she smiled. 'Thanks.'

He didn't hold her hand or kiss her after they left the restaurant, and Abigail guessed why—in case someone came out into the street and saw them. But as soon as they were on the train and were sure they didn't know anyone else in the carriage, Lewis hauled her onto his lap.

'Lewis, you can't do this sort of thing on the Tu—' she began.

He kissed her words away. 'Yes, we can. I've been

dying to hold you properly all night, and I can't wait
any longer.'

It was the same for her, so she could hardly protest.

And he held her hand all the way from the Tube station to her flat.

'Do you want to come in for coffee?' she asked.

'Decaf, please,' he said.

She bustled about the kitchen, making coffee. 'I had
a wonderful evening. Thanks for teaching me to skate.'

He smiled. 'Pleasure.'

'Is there anything you're not good at?'

He pretended to think about it. 'Well, I can't knit
or crochet.'

She cuffed his arm lightly. 'You know what I mean.
You're good at everything.'

'Everything? Why, thank you, ma'am,' he drawled.
Her blush made his grin broaden. 'But I could always
do with some practice…'

He started kissing her, and the coffee was forgotten
as he carried her to her bed.

Afterwards, Abigail was half tempted to ask him
to stay the night, but she knew he'd back away. Given
his commitment phobia, no doubt he had a few mental adjustments to make about their fling, too. Maybe
it would be better to just enjoy this while it lasted and
not expect too much.

'I have to go,' he said, pulling his clothes back on.
'Stay there. You look comfortable. I can see myself out.'

She nodded. 'See you at work.'

He leaned over to kiss her. 'Sweet dreams.'

'You, too.' She kissed him back.

Was she doing the right thing, having a fling with

Lewis? she wondered as she heard the front door close behind him. She'd had such a good time tonight, really feeling part of the crowd. And she knew she had Lewis to thank for that. Knowing he was there had given her confidence and helped her feel comfortable in a group setting.

Their fling didn't have a stated time limit, though she knew it would end between them because Lewis had made it clear that he didn't want to be tied down. But fear bubbled through her at the idea of it ending.

Lewis was the one who was responsible for her fitting in on the team night out. How would she manage without that safety net? And, given that Lewis was a party boy who'd never miss a team night out, what would that mean for her if things got awkward after their break-up and she had to avoid him? Would she end up back in her old lonely life, trapped by her lack of social skills?

Worse still was the fear that her feelings were already starting to run away with her where Lewis was concerned. Somehow she was going to have to get them back under control. Lewis wouldn't change, and she couldn't let herself hope for more than he was able to offer. That wouldn't be fair to either of them.

She groaned and rolled over in bed. On the side that was still warm from Lewis's body heat. 'Cinnamon Abigail Brydon Smith, you really need to stop over-analysing this and get a grip,' she told herself crossly. 'It's a fling. Probably for more than just three dates, but still only a fling. Just enjoy it for what it is and don't be so sad and needy.'

Which was easier said than done.

CHAPTER EIGHT

OVER THE NEXT few weeks Abigail got used to her double life, being just colleagues with Lewis at work and lovers outside. She enjoyed spending time with him, a mix of doing the adrenalin-fiend stuff he loved and the gentler, quieter stuff she was used to doing in her spare time. And they were quietly synchronising their off-duty days so they could spend more of their days off together. Nobody in the department had commented, so they were definitely getting away with it, Abigail thought.

'So where exactly are we going?' Lewis asked when he met her at her flat on the Thursday morning.

'Somewhere I really like. You might find it boring—or you might not. And we can walk there from here,' she said.

'An art gallery?' he asked when they arrived, sounding surprised.

'Keep an open mind,' she said.

Inside, she led him through the maze of rooms to the one containing her favourite paintings. 'This is where I like to come on a wet afternoon. I love these paintings and the colours.'

'They're very bright, considering they must be a hundred years old.'

'A hundred and fifty,' she corrected him. 'That's because they used to paint on a wet white background, a bit like the old fresco painters.'

Lewis smiled. 'Your nerdy streak's coming out, princess.'

She closed her eyes. 'Sorry. I'm being boring. I'll shut up now.'

'No—you're all animated when you talk about the paintings, and I like seeing you like this.' He wandered round with her, hand in hand, examining the paintings.

'It's not like seeing a print or a postcard. The real things are totally different. Take this one.' She pointed out a painting by Millais. 'A print makes the model's clothes look flat and a bit boring. But if you look at the real thing up close, you can see they're actually iridescent.'

He peered at it. 'You're right. How do you know this sort of thing?'

'Because I always had my head in a book when I was a kid—probably while you were outside climbing trees,' she added wryly.

'Probably,' he agreed. 'My sisters would like you.'

Maybe, she thought, but you haven't asked me to meet them. Then again, she hadn't asked him to meet her father either, so she wasn't in a position to complain.

They walked over to look at the next painting. 'Now, this one reminds me of you,' he said.

'Rossetti's *Lady Lilith*?' she asked, surprised.

'Uh-huh. Combing your glorious hair in a bower of roses.'

She raised an eyebrow. 'Considering my hair's dead straight and the model has curls...' Like she'd had years ago. Cinnamon baby. As she'd grown older, her hair had straightened. Dull and boring, like she was herself.

'It's a similar colour, like copper in sunlight. And a similar length.' He stood behind her with his arms wrapped round her waist and rested his cheek against her hair. 'And your hair smells of roses. I rest my case.'

If anyone had said to Lewis that he'd enjoy wandering around an art gallery, he would've scoffed; he'd always thought them a bit dull and he would much rather have been doing something active. But with Abigail he really enjoyed it. She made him look at things differently.

Which in itself was scary. He'd promised himself that he wouldn't get involved with her, wouldn't let himself get too close, because he knew from experience that you just couldn't have it all. The trouble was, Abigail Smith made him want to take that risk.

He shook himself, not wanting to spoil his day with her, and concentrated on the paintings. They took a break for coffee and cake, then browsed in the shop. He saw a fridge magnet of the painting that reminded him of her and couldn't resist buying it.

'So now we get to do some adrenalin-fiend stuff?' he asked.

She shook her head. 'It's still my day. We're doing staid, quiet, nerdy stuff.'

'You're not even going to give a clue about what we're going to do?' he grumbled.

'You mean, like you did when you planned to chuck me out of a plane?'

But there was a sparkle in her eyes, so he knew she

wasn't really cross about it. 'That was a controlled descent, princess, and you were strapped to me.'

'OK. What we're doing is on the other side of the Thames.'

Which told him next to nothing. He didn't manage to kiss any more information out of her either.

But when they reached the station at Blackfriars and she shepherded him across the Millennium footbridge, he had a pretty good idea of what she had in mind. 'Another art gallery,' he said, looking up at the enormous chimney of the brick building in front of them. And this time it was modern art. Which he really didn't get. He only hoped that she didn't want to spend the rest of the afternoon doing something so tedious, because he'd get seriously itchy feet.

She laughed. 'Don't look so worried. I realise I've art-galleried you out for today. No, I have something else in mind. We're heading this way.'

As soon as he saw the white, timber-framed, polygonal building with its thatched roof, he knew. 'Shakespeare,' he said with a smile. 'Now we're back on more normal territory for me.'

'Oh, of course—your sister's a drama teacher. I take it you've been here with her?' she asked.

'I've been a few times, yes. Enough to know to rent a cushion to sit on.' He smiled at her. 'I assume we have seats? I can't quite see you doing the groundling thing and standing in the yard.'

'And getting either too hot or too wet? No. I'd rather sit under cover. And me, too, on the cushions. I learned that one the hard way, too. Literally, on those benches,' she said with a smile.

The matinée performance turned out to be *Much Ado About Nothing*.

'The original rom-com,' she said with an arch look.

'Ah, but I like this one. And it has some action scenes as well as the mushy stuff, so I'm happy,' he said, squeezing her shoulders briefly and kissing the top of her head.

He held her hand through the whole performance. And he couldn't help tightening his fingers round hers when Benedick said to Beatrice, 'I do love nothing in the world so well as you. Is that not strange?'

Was he beginning to fall in love with Abigail?

He shook himself. Of course not. He was way too sensible to let his heart get involved. He was just letting the romance of the play get to him—especially as they were seeing it only a few hundred yards away from where Shakespeare's company had performed the play, in a building that was as near as you could get to the original.

They walked along the bank of the Thames afterwards, enjoying the late afternoon sunshine, and eventually found a small Moroccan restaurant. This time he joined her in choosing a rich vegetable tagine and then cinnamon-spiced oranges served with tiny almond-studded biscuits.

Sitting on a low cushion opposite him, with the tiny tealight candles making her hair seem all shades of bronze and copper, she looked utterly beautiful. Funny, a day of doing quiet things should've left him with itchy feet, desperate to go and do something so he didn't have to think or let any emotions run riot in his head. But, weirdly, he could be quiet with Abigail. And he found himself lingering over the meal. Just being with her was enough.

Back at Abigail's flat, Lewis kissed her goodnight on the doorstep. He was tempted to ask if he could stay, and that scared him. He hadn't felt like that about anyone in years.

'You're on an early shift tomorrow, aren't you?' he asked.

She nodded.

'Then I'd better go and let you get some sleep.'

She looked faintly disappointed, as if she'd been about to ask him in for coffee.

'But thank you for today,' he said hastily. 'I really enjoyed it.'

'Even though it wasn't adrenalin-fiend stuff?'

'Actually, yes.' He had to be honest. 'I couldn't have done a second art gallery, but I enjoyed the play. And dinner.' And being with her. 'I'll see you later.' He kissed her again, and left.

But he couldn't settle, back at his flat. That feeling, earlier, that he might be falling in love with Abigail… It couldn't happen. Long term didn't work for him; he'd been a total mess after Jenna. Of course he knew that Abigail wasn't like Jenna, but he still wasn't prepared to take any risks. His life was on an even keel now and he wanted it to stay that way. Light and fun and not having to think about anything emotional.

He ended up putting his running shoes on and going out. It didn't matter that it had started to drizzle. He needed to move, to get the adrenalin and endorphins flowing. To drown out everything that was in his head.

* * *

It took Lewis a week to risk seeing Abigail again outside work. 'Can you swap with someone so you're off on Tuesday?' he asked.

'Probably. Why?'

'Because I want to take you somewhere.'

'And wear sensible shoes?' she asked wryly.

'I don't say that all the time.'

She laughed. 'Yes, you do. Even though you know I don't own anything apart from sensible shoes.'

He let that pass. 'Do you have such a thing as a floaty dress?'

'I'm not *that* ungirly, Lewis.'

He leaned forward and kissed her. 'You're girly enough for me.' Oh, now, why had he said that? Hinting at a promise he knew full well he wouldn't be able to keep. It wasn't fair to either of them. He should just stay away from her.

But he couldn't. She drew him like nobody else ever had. And he couldn't work out why. Why was he drawn to a quiet, shy, clever woman who had no confidence in herself? Why was he drawn to someone who was the complete opposite of the party-loving women he usually dated?

'Wear your dress next Tuesday,' he said. 'I'll meet you at your flat at eleven.'

Her black and white floaty dress was perfect for what he had in mind. But the shoes weren't. They were low-heeled and black, reminding him of ballet pumps. And for this she needed heels. And, he thought, some colour.

'Are all your shoes low-heeled and black?' he asked.

'Yes.' She lifted her chin. 'Is there a problem?'

'Nothing I can't fix.'

She frowned. 'What are we doing?'

'It's a surprise. And, no, it doesn't involve skydiving, zip-lining or swimming with sharks.'

Her eyes widened. 'I hope that last bit was a joke and you're not planning that at some point in the future.'

'Why? Wouldn't you like to swim with sharks?'

'I'll pass on that one, I think. Dolphins, maybe—but not sharks. Too many teeth.'

'Chicken.' He laughed. 'Come on. Let's go.' He took her to Covent Garden.

'Oh, are we having lunch?' Her face cleared. 'So that's why you wanted me to wear a floaty dress. To look girly for once.'

'Nope. We can stop for a sandwich if we're quick, but we're here to go shopping.'

'For what?'

He was going to have to tell her now. 'To get you some dancing shoes.'

'Dancing shoes?' she repeated. 'Why?'

'Because we're going dancing.'

'But—how? The nightclubs aren't open in the afternoon.'

'I didn't say we were going clubbing. We're going *dancing*.'

Abigail had no idea where Lewis was planning to take her dancing, especially at this time of day. But she'd enjoyed the other mad activities he'd introduced her to, so she decided to go with it.

'I would've liked to have done this as a surprise,' he

said, 'but you really can't buy someone a pair of shoes as a surprise. Not if you want them to fit properly.'

She remembered what he'd once said about wanting to see her wearing nothing but a pair of high heels and went hot all over. To cover the fact that she was flustered, she said, 'But I can't dance.'

'You don't need to,' he said with a smile. 'Just let me lead.'

She gave him a speaking look, and he laughed. 'You really have problems trusting people, don't you?'

She lifted her chin and told an outright fib. 'No.'

'It's going to be fun. I promise.' He led her into a shop. 'As you said yourself, you don't totter around on high heels every day, so it'll be easier for you to get a pair with a medium heel.'

'Why do my shoes need a heel at all?'

'Because it makes it easier for you to dance in. And, no, the shoes you're wearing aren't going to work as dancing shoes.'

She couldn't resist a pair of purple satin shoes with diamante buckles, but she refused to let him buy them for her. 'I'm perfectly capable of buying my own shoes.'

'There weren't any strings attached, princess,' he said softly. 'I just wanted to do something nice for you.'

And then she felt mean. How did Lewis manage to wrong-foot her so often?

'Don't go prickly on me, Abby. We're going to have fun. Really.'

'I know. I'm sorry.'

He stroked her cheek. 'You really have been dating the wrong sort of men.'

'Mmm.' She didn't want to think about that.

He took her to a hotel in the West End. She looked at him, puzzled, as they stood outside. 'I thought you said we were going dancing?'

'We are, and this used to be one of the most popular venues in London for dances years ago. They have regular tea dances here.'

'Tea dances?'

'Ballroom dancing and cups of tea,' he explained. 'In very nice porcelain cups.'

This was absolutely the last thing she'd expected. She shook her head in bemusement. 'You never fail to surprise me, Lewis. Where did you learn to dance?'

He shrugged. 'It doesn't matter.'

'Is this something to do with the training company you worked for?'

'No.'

'A way to get the girls at med school?'

He laughed. 'No. All right, if you really want to know, I had a patient who broke her hip. I spent some time with her while we were waiting for a slot in Theatre.'

In other words, she thought, the old lady didn't have anyone to wait with her, and Lewis had given up his break to wait with her and make sure that she wasn't frightened and alone. Abigail was coming to recognise that he did that sort of thing a lot. Without any fuss, without drawing attention to himself, he just saw something that needed to be fixed and did it.

'And she liked dancing?'

'When she was younger, yes—she told me a lot about it. And she said I reminded her of her son.' He grimaced. 'It turned out her son was a soldier, and he'd been killed on duty. Her husband had died years before so she was completely alone. And I promised her that, when her hip was fixed, I'd take her dancing.'

Abigail had a pretty good idea that Lewis had done a lot more than that. That he'd visited the old lady and that he'd made sure she was being looked after properly. 'So you took lessons?'

He nodded. 'I promised her a waltz. We came here because she used to dance here with her husband. We were going to make it a regular thing and come here once a month.'

'But?' she asked softly.

'She caught pneumonia before we could come again. And, she, um, didn't make it back here with me.'

She held him close. 'I'm sorry.'

'Me, too. But I did manage to bring back some good memories for her. And I discovered I liked this kind of dancing.'

'I take it Marina doesn't know about this or she would've got you to offer a dancing lesson for the auction.'

'No. It was at my last hospital. I was still a wet-behind-the-ears, very junior doctor.'

She sighed. 'I really don't get why you let people think you're a selfish heartbreaker, Lewis. You're a good man.'

He shrugged, and kissed her.

Which told her that he really didn't want to talk about it. She was definitely going to have to resort to that poker game to get him to open up to her.

'You need to change your shoes here and check your

bag into the cloakroom,' he said, and waited for her to do it.

It felt odd wearing such girly shoes; and here, at the hotel, they looked much brighter than they had in the shop. She wished that she'd bought something more invisible. Something to let her fade into the background like she normally did.

'Don't look so worried. I promise not to stand on your toes.'

'I'm not worried about that.'

He took her hand and squeezed it. 'This doesn't have to be complicated. We can make it as simple and easy as you want. The idea is just to have fun.'

Fun. That was what made Lewis tick.

But she was pretty sure there was more to it than that. She had a feeling that Lewis kept himself busy doing physical things that needed concentration and meant that you didn't have time to think.

'Oh, and wear your hair down.'

She wrinkled her nose. 'It gets in the way.'

'I love your hair,' he said simply, reaching out to twirl the ends round his fingers.

She gave in and let him remove the hair band, then walked with him into the room where the tea dance was being held.

It was amazing. The roof was curved glass, letting so much light into the room. There were tables dotted round the outside, waiters and waitresses in traditional black and white uniforms carrying trays of tea and cakes, and more palm trees than she'd ever seen before in her life. And the floor was packed, she noticed, with couples of all ages.

'The tea dances are pretty popular,' Lewis said, as if reading her mind.

People were practising before the music started. She watched them, fascinated. 'Lewis, I hope you realise I don't have a clue how to do that sort of thing.'

'Have you ever been to an aerobics class?' he asked.

'Yes.'

'So you can follow a small routine.'

'Well, once I've learned the steps.'

'OK. Here's the cha cha cha.' He stood facing her. 'Your left hand goes here…' he put it in position on his arm '…and you hold my right hand.'

So far, so good, she thought.

'Now, your right foot goes back.' He moved forward with his right foot, and she found herself stepping back automatically.

'Good. Now, keep your weight on the back foot, then shift the weight forward again.' The pressure of his palm on her back led her to copy his movements.

'And now it's the cha cha cha bit—you take a small step to the side with your right foot, bring your left to join it, and a small step to the right again.' Again, he led her through it.

'And that's it?'

'Then we do it back the other way. Think of it as rock, rock, side to side.' He led her through it. 'And we can add some twirly bits onto it when you're confident with that. We'll take it at your pace, no rush.'

The band struck up the first number.

'This is a quickstep, so it's probably not fair to start you on this. Let's sit this one out and watch.' He found a chair and settled her on his lap as he sat down.

She felt her eyes widen. 'Lewis, we can't do this.'

'Nobody's watching us. They're either watching the dancers or they're too busy dancing to notice what anyone else is doing,' he soothed. 'Be with me and just enjoy it.'

Something about his nearness calmed her, and she found herself enjoying the music—even though it wasn't the kind of thing she usually listened to and definitely wasn't the sort of thing she thought Lewis would like.

Then the band played a different song and he gently moved her off his lap and led her on to the dance floor. 'Time to cha cha cha, princess.'

She was expecting to be stumbling all over the place but Lewis kept her close, pointing her in the right direction all the time. Having seen what other people were doing, she had the confidence to let him talk her through a twirly bit—and then realised that she was really enjoying herself.

'See?' He leant over and stole a kiss. 'It's fun.'

'Yes, it is.' She smiled at him. 'I've never done anything like this before. I tended to avoid the dances at university.'

'If yours were like the ones I went to, they weren't exactly dances—just people moving awkwardly about, out of time with the music, and spotty teenage students hoping that someone might let them grope them in the dark.'

'I can't imagine you being a spotty teenage student,' she teased.

For a moment she thought she saw a flash of panic in his eyes.

Then he laughed. 'Are you saying I'm vain?'

'No, I just don't think you would've ever been one of the desperate ones.'

'I'll take that as a compliment, even though I think there's an edge to it.'

'No edge,' she said. 'But you have to know you're beautiful, Lewis. Women look at you all the time.'

He shrugged. 'I'm just me.'

She laughed. 'You're blushing.'

He kissed her—a move she was beginning to realise he used to stop a conversation that made him feel uncomfortable. So much like Benedick, in the play they'd seen together. *'I'll stop your mouth...'* Lewis had held her hand particularly tightly during that line. And another, which half made her wonder...

The song ended and the next one began. She recognised the timing as a three-four beat—the sort her father used when he wrote a ballad.

'This is a waltz,' Lewis said. 'We're not going to do anything flashy with it today, just the basic steps. I'll teach you the twirly bits another time.'

'OK.'

'Just go where I lead you. Try and remember it's alternate legs, and it goes back, side, together then forward, side, together.'

He was asking a lot, she thought. And his idea of fun definitely meant that you didn't have time to do anything except concentrate on your physical movements.

But then he started dancing with her, and it turned out to be a lot easier than she'd expected. He talked her through the steps as they went round the room, but at the same time he was guiding her so she didn't go wrong. She let herself relax and enjoy it.

The first few numbers were instrumental, but then a woman with a smoky jazz-style voice came to join the orchestra. Abigail thoroughly enjoyed doing the fast cha cha chas with him and then slowing it down again for the waltz, held close in his arms all the time. Now she knew why he'd asked her to wear a floaty dress. And he was right about the shoes, too.

At that moment she actually felt like the princess he teased her about being. Except she wasn't made of ice. With Lewis, she was all flame.

The afternoon seemed to just vanish, and she was disappointed when the orchestra had played their last number.

'Thank you—I really enjoyed this,' she said. She kissed him impulsively. 'Can we do it again?'

'They hold tea dances once a month. I can get us tickets for the next one, if you like.'

'That'd be great. It's my turn to pay, though.'

He raised an eyebrow. 'If you insist.'

'I do.'

She retrieved her bag from the cloakroom, changed her shoes, and they caught the Tube back to his flat.

'I forgot to tell you—you look lovely in that dress.' He kissed her lightly. 'Dance with me again?'

How could she resist? She changed into her dancing shoes while he put some music on. And although she'd enjoyed the faster dance, she was glad that he chose a waltz, where he could hold her closer.

Somehow they ended up dancing down the corridor from the living room to Lewis's bedroom. And somehow he managed to peel off her dress while they were dancing, leaving her in just her underwear and the dance shoes.

He dragged in a breath. 'Abigail Smith, you're the most gorgeous woman I've ever seen. Do you have any idea what you do to me?'

Shyness flooded through her but he held her hands. 'Don't cover yourself up, princess. I meant it. You're gorgeous.' He lifted one hand above her head, and she found herself doing the pirouette he'd taught her on the dance floor. 'Every inch of you is lovely,' he said softly. 'Every inch of you makes me want to touch you and taste you. And those shoes make your legs look as if they go on for ever.'

The intensity of his gaze told her that he wasn't just spinning her a line. He really was that attracted to her.

A slow burn of desire fizzled through her as he kissed her and finished undressing her.

Finally, he knelt at her feet and removed her shoes.

He looked up at her then, and that smile was just for her. A smile that made her heart feel as if it had done a backflip. A feeling she'd had about nobody else.

She realised then that she'd just broken every single rule and fallen for Lewis. A man who'd pushed her way out of her comfort zone and made her realise that she could do so much more than she thought she could. A man who'd taught her to trust again, even though he didn't do commitment and had made no promises for the future to her.

Totally crazy. This could only end in tears, and she should back off.

But then she stopped thinking as he stripped off his own clothing then scooped her up and laid her back against his pillows. And as he eased into her body, she couldn't help feeling that there had to be a way to make this turn out all right. They were good together. They had fun—and yet there was more to it than that. A connection like she'd never felt with anyone else.

If she just could get him to open up to her, if they could be honest about who they were—then maybe, just maybe, this would turn out all right. For both of them.

CHAPTER NINE

ABIGAIL WAS ROSTERED in Resus the next morning, while Lewis was in Minors. Her second patient of the morning was a serious one.

Biddy, one of the paramedics, came in to do the handover. 'This is Matthew. He's fifty-five. He's been diagnosed with flu by his family doctor and he hasn't been able to get his temperature down for a couple of days—at the moment it's thirty-nine degrees C but he's still feeling cold.'

Abigail had noticed the violent shivering. And it wasn't a good sign.

'He tried to get out of bed this morning to get himself a drink, but he thought he was going to pass out. He called his wife, who was at work,' Biddy said. 'She called us and she's on her way in now.'

'Thanks, Biddy. What are his obs?' Abigail asked.

'His heartbeat and respiration are both a bit too fast for my liking, and he's been a bit confused on the way in.'

It *could* be flu, Abigail thought. But when she laid her hand on Matthew's to give it a reassuring squeeze, she noticed his skin was cold, clammy and pale. No, this wasn't a simple case of flu. This had progressed a stage further.

'Thanks for your help, Biddy,' she said.

'No worries. But my gut tells me it's not just flu.'

'I agree.' She looked at Dawn, the nurse who'd been rostered with her. 'I think we're looking at sepsis—the flu's making his body shut down. I want to put him on antibiotics straight away.'

The paramedic team had already put a line in so Abigail gave Matthew some high-flow oxygen while Dawn took blood samples and then gave him some broad-spectrum antibiotics and put him on a drip to help with dehydration.

'We need to monitor his urine output,' she said to Dawn.

The nurse nodded. 'I'll get the catheter kit.'

Abigail had just finished inserting the catheter and making Matthew comfortable when an anxious-looking woman came in with the triage nurse. 'I think my husband's here? Matthew?'

'Yes. I'm Abby Smith and I'm looking after him today.'

'I'm Bella.' The woman bit her lip. 'What's happening? I thought he had flu, and I left him in bed—but then he rang me and said he felt really ill and thought he was going to pass out. I called the ambulance.'

'Which was exactly the right thing to do,' Abigail reassured her.

'So is it not flu, then?'

'Sometimes the body's immune system overreacts to an illness like flu and causes sepsis,' Abigail explained, 'and that's what Matthew's symptoms are telling me.'

'Sepsis?' Bella frowned. 'Is that like blood poisoning?'

'It used to be called that, yes. Basically the body deals with infection by producing white blood cells, which cause inflammation around the infection and stops it spreading. With sepsis, the inflammation spreads throughout the body. That's why Matthew's got a temperature and his heartbeat and breathing are a bit on the fast side.'

'Is he going to be all right?' Bella asked.

Abigail's heart sank. She knew that with cases of sepsis a third to a half of patients didn't make it. Had they started treatment in time for Matthew to get through it? 'We're doing our best,' she said gently. 'At the moment we're giving him antibiotics and keeping a very close eye on him. But if the infection starts to affect his organs, we might need to send him to Intensive Care so his breathing and circulation can be supported while we treat the infection.'

Bella looked terrified. 'Can I stay with him?'

'Of course you can, and if you've got any questions just ask me. I'm not too busy and it doesn't matter if you think the questions are little and unimportant—you need to know what's going on.'

However, over the next couple of hours Matthew's condition worsened.

Abigail sat down with Matthew's wife. 'Bella, I'm going to send him up to Intensive Care. I know even the department name is scary, but the staff are great and they can look after him better than we can down here,' she said.

She went up to Intensive Care with Bella and Matthew so she could do the handover, introduce Bella to the staff and help them settle in. And she spent her lunch break there, too. She knew Bella wouldn't want to leave Matthew's side so she brought up some cheese sandwiches and a bottle of water.

Bella's eyes filled with tears. 'That's so kind. Thank you.'

'It's the least I can do. I know how I'd feel in your shoes.' If she was at her father's bedside, she'd be frantic and not want to leave for a second. 'I can get you a hot drink, too—just let me know what you'd like.'

'No, this is fine.'

'Make sure you eat them,' Abigail said. 'I know you're worried about Matthew, but you need to look after yourself, too.'

Throughout the day Abigail wondered how Matthew was doing. But then, an hour before the end of her shift, Bella came down to see her. 'Abby? I just wanted to let you know that Matthew...' her breath hitched '...passed away.' She swallowed hard. 'And I wanted to say thank you, because you were so kind earlier.'

Abigail blew out a breath. He hadn't made it. 'I'm so sorry.'

'I've got to tell the kids. I sent them a text to say their dad wasn't well so go to their grandmother's after school and I'll collect them later.' She shook her head. 'I can't believe he's gone.'

At a loss for words, Abigail hugged her. Bella gave a small sob then straightened her back. 'I'd better go and call the kids. But thank you for what you did. I know you did your best for Matthew.'

Yes, but it wasn't good enough, was it? Abigail thought. Not nearly good enough.

Dully, she watched Bella leave the department, then headed to find Dawn to let her know before going to the staff kitchen and putting the kettle on. Right now she needed some hot, sweet tea. And she felt sick. She'd just lost somebody's dad. She knew it was ridiculous to be superstitious, but she couldn't help thinking that what goes around comes around. Please don't let there be karma and let her lose her father, too.

Unable to settle even after drinking half the tea, she called him. 'Dad?'

'Hello, darling. I thought you were at work. Is everything all right?'

'I, um, just lost a patient. Sorry, I'm being horribly wet. I just wanted to—well—talk to you.' Her voice gave a treacherous wobble.

'Cinnamon, stay right where you are and I'll come and get you.'

'No, don't do that. I've still got a bit of my shift to go. It's not fair on the others if I just walk out.' She sniffed. 'I know I'm being stupid. But I just wanted to tell you I love you.'

'I love you, too, darling.' He sighed. 'I wish I could wave a magic wand for you.'

'Right now I could really do with one of those. I might've been able to save my patient.'

'It wasn't your fault. You did your best, and nobody could ask any more of you.'

Keith was the one person in her life who'd always, always believed in her. Who'd been there for her—unlike her mother. 'Sorry, Dad. I know you're probably busy. I'm sorry if I just took stuff out of your head.'

'My person from Porlock, you mean?' He laughed.

'I'm never too busy for you, Cinnamon, and don't you ever think I will be, because I won't.'

'I know, Dad.' He'd always made time for her. Even when it hadn't really been convenient for him. 'I'd better get back to work. I'll call you tomorrow.'

'Better than that, I'll take you out for dinner. I'll book somewhere and I'll meet you at your flat at, what, seven?'

She smiled. 'I'd like that. See you tomorrow.'

'Love you.'

'Love you, too.'

When she ended the call, she realised that Lewis had walked into the kitchen.

'I take it that was your dad?' he asked.

She frowned. 'Why do you think that?'

'Because, according to Dawn, you just lost a middle-aged male patient you'd been trying to save all morning. And you're crying.' He wiped her tears away with the pad of his thumb. 'So I'm guessing that set you worrying about your dad, and you just wanted to check he was OK.'

She swallowed. 'I was being wet.'

'No. You clearly love him very much. He's a lucky man.'

Did Lewis think her dad was lucky because she loved him? Or because her dad was loved?

And she knew that Lewis had lost his own father. 'Sorry. That wasn't tactful of me, considering...' She stopped. She had no idea if the grapevine knew about Lewis's father, and she didn't want to be the one to spill the story.

'It's OK.' He clearly guessed what she was thinking. 'Has that tea got sugar in it?'

She nodded. 'It's vile.'

'Good for shock.'

'Here.' She passed the mug to him.

He took a mouthful. 'You're right. It's vile. And it doesn't make it better.' He sighed. 'Some days this job really sucks.'

'Today's one of those days,' she agreed.

He gave her a hug. 'Hang in there. I'll shout you a pizza after work. And you can choose all the toppings.'

'Oh, now that sounds interesting.' Eve, the charge nurse, came in to the staff kitchen. 'Date night, is it?'

'Not unless I was the last man on earth,' Lewis said lightly. 'Remember, Abby's already turned me down. Actually, Eve, you're just the person we need.'

'Me? Why?' Eve asked.

'Tough day.' He tipped his head to one side, indicating Abigail. 'Abby just lost a patient. Right now she needs hugs and carbs, but the carbs'll have to wait until after our shift ends. And your hugs are better than mine.' He patted Abigail's shoulder. 'I'll leave you in Eve's capable hands. But I'll shout you that pizza later. As I'd do for anyone in your shoes, and I'm sure you'd do it for me.'

'Thanks.'

Eve gave her a hug. 'It's always hard when you lose a patient.'

'The first one I've lost here.' Abigail grimaced. 'I'll never get used to this side of the job. I hate it.'

'You're only human, love.'

Abigail sighed. 'I guess I'd better get back to work. We have patients waiting.'

Eve patted her shoulder. 'Tomorrow will be a better day.'

Lewis was waiting for Abigail at the end of her shift.

'There's a nice pizzeria around the corner from me. We'll pick up a takeaway and I'll drive you home afterwards. What would you like me to order for you?' he asked.

She shook her head. 'It's really sweet of you, but I don't really think I want anything.'

'You have to eat something, Abby. Look, I'll order for both of us.' He made a quick call. 'OK. It'll be ready for us by the time we get there.'

Back at his flat, Abigail discovered that Lewis had ordered a vegetarian special with artichokes, mushrooms and peppers. He also whipped up a quick rocket and baby plum tomato salad and sprinkled shaved parmesan over the top.

She couldn't face eating but choked down a couple of mouthfuls to be polite. After all, Lewis had made the effort for her.

He looked at her and sighed. 'Oh, Abby.' He came round to her side of the table, scooped her out of the chair and settled her on his lap, then just held her, stroking her hair. 'Remember, we can't fix everyone. We do the best we can and that's enough.'

'It isn't, though. Right now there's a family who's missing their—' She stopped. Husband and father. Not the most tactful thing to say. Lewis's family had been in the same situation as Matthew's once. And, even though it was a long time ago, she was pretty sure that Lewis still missed his father.

'Maybe if he'd come to hospital sooner, we could've helped him more. What was it?'

'His family doctor diagnosed him with flu. It turned to sepsis.' She sighed. 'I had to send him up to ICU.'

'The sepsis was that bad?' He whistled. 'Abby, you know as well as I do that once it gets to that stage there's only a fifty-fifty chance of pulling through.'

'I know. But it still feels bad.'

'I don't know how to make you feel better.' He held her close. 'But I do think you shouldn't be alone tonight. Stay here with me. We'll get up early and I'll see you home in the morning.'

'I...'

'Stay,' he repeated softly. 'I can put your clothes through the washing machine and they'll be dry before morning.'

'Thank you.' She leaned against his shoulder. 'I'm sorry I'm being so wet. I don't often lose patients. And I'm afraid I don't deal with it very well.'

'Princess, nobody does. It's the downside of our job. Sometimes our patients are too ill for even the most experienced doctors to save them.'

'How do you deal with it when you lose a patient?' she asked.

'Go for a run. Push myself that bit harder, and do something physically demanding that I have to concentrate on so I don't have the time or the energy to think about what's happened.'

That was how he dealt with everything emotional, she thought. Except tonight. Tonight he was holding her.

'Come on. I'm not that hungry either. I'll run you a bath.'

Part of her wanted to protest that she was fine, that she could look after herself. But, just for once, it was good to let someone else take charge. To lean on someone and trust that they could support her.

'I don't have any girly bubble bath,' he warned. 'I do citrus and that's it. Nothing pink, nothing flowery.'

'Citrus is lovely,' she said.

And he'd left her a soft, fluffy bath robe next to the towels; she assumed it belonged to one of his sisters.

When she emerged from the bath, Lewis made her a mug of hot chocolate. Such a small thing, but it made her feel cherished.

Loved.

They curled up together on the sofa, watching re-runs of an old comedy series, with Lewis's arms wrapped tightly round her. He hadn't said the words but his actions tonight had told Abigail just how much he cared about her. The fact that he'd asked her to stay tonight, offered to share his space with her instead of driving her home—from Lewis that really meant something.

So maybe this relationship was more than just for fun. More than a fling.

Maybe it was time they opened up to each other.

Maybe it was time she told him the truth about herself.

Maybe tomorrow.

Finally she fell asleep, wrapped in his arms.

The next morning, Lewis woke up first. It felt odd, having someone asleep beside him. He'd made it a rule never to spend the night with a partner, not since Jenna.

But last night Abigail had been vulnerable. Upset. She'd needed him to comfort her.

He propped himself up on one elbow and watched her sleep. In repose, she was beautiful. She made him ache. And she scared him at the same time—because he wanted to do this again.

He really ought to back off a bit before both of them got hurt.

But then she woke up. Her smile was so sweet and so trusting it made his heart turn over.

'Thank you for last night, Lewis.' She cuddled into him. 'Sorry I was being so wet.'

'You weren't being wet. You'd had a rough day.' He just about stopped himself from saying, 'I'm glad I could be there for you.' Instead, he said, 'We're both on an early shift. Get dressed, and I'll drive you home.'

'There's no need, honestly.' She pressed a kiss against his shoulder. 'But you're right, I'd better get my skates on.'

'Your clothes are dry. I checked them last night. Feel free to use whatever you need in the bathroom.'

'Thank you. For everything,' she said softly.

And he had to really hold himself back from telling her that he wanted to give her more. That he wanted to wake up with her in the mornings and not have to rush back to his flat or for her to have to rush back to hers. That he wanted to move this thing between them on to the next step. That he wanted to try commitment.

He needed his head examined. Relationships didn't

work for him. He couldn't have it all. He'd learned that the hard way.

So he just kissed her, smiled, and let her get dressed and walk out of the door.

Abigail didn't see Lewis that evening because she was seeing her dad, and their shifts clashed for the next couple of days, but they arranged to see each other on Saturday night.

'A quiet night in might be nice,' she said, inwardly planning nothing of the kind. 'There's a really good Chinese takeaway near me.'

'Sounds good,' Lewis said. 'Enjoy this evening with your dad.'

'I will.'

Was it her imagination or did he look slightly disappointed that she hadn't asked him to join them? Then again, she still hadn't told Lewis who her dad was.

And that could wait until Saturday.

Her father enveloped her in a warm hug as soon as she opened the door to him.

'Did you have a better day today?' he asked.

'Yes, and seeing you makes it even better.' Abigail hugged him.

He ruffled her hair. 'I love you. Let's go out and eat. I've found a really good place.'

'Where's your car?' she asked.

'Taxi tonight,' he said.

'All the way out to Surrey?'

'No, I'm staying over with Joe in Putney. And I don't want to drink and drive.' He gave her a hug. 'I'll take the lecture as read, darling.'

'Sorry. I know I'm dull. But I worry about you. And Joe, for that matter. He's practically my uncle.'

Keith smiled. 'I'll tell him that. He thinks a lot of you.'

Once the taxi had taken them to a plush restaurant in Mayfair and they'd settled at their table, Keith gave her a searching look. 'There's something different about you.'

'How do you mean?' she asked.

'For a start, you seem happier than you were at your last hospital.'

She nodded. 'The team's really nice. I've made friends.'

'Good.' He looked at her. 'And would one of those be a special friend?'

'No. I mean yes. I've met someone. But it's early days,' she said swiftly.

'And you don't want him to meet me yet.' He hid the hurt quickly, but Abigail had seen it in his expression. She reached over and squeezed his hand. 'I love you, Dad, and I'm so proud of you—but, no, I'm not ready for him to meet you yet. I don't think he'd be thrown by who you are, and I happen to know he likes your music, but...' How could she put this? 'He finds commitment hard,' she finished.

Keith sighed. 'You've fallen for a heartbreaker.'

'No. He's a good man. Honourable.'

'So you've fallen for him.'

She smiled. 'Dad, don't look so worried.'

'It's part of the job description—if you're a dad, you always worry about your daughter. Especially when it comes to this sort of thing.' He frowned. 'I might be pushing sixty now, but I can still pack a mean punch, even if he is about your age.'

She laughed. 'Don't go all alpha male on me. You're not going to need to punch him.'

'So are you going to tell me anything about him?'

'He's a doctor.'

'And?'

'He's a good man. You'd like him.' She rolled her eyes. 'He's an adrenalin fiend. I think he could be a bad influence on you. So let's make it clear right now—no swimming with sharks, no throwing yourself out of planes, and no ridiculous thrill rides at the amusement park, OK?'

Keith laughed. 'Isn't that meant to be my line?'

She laughed back. 'Actually, he's already done one of those with me. We went skydiving. And it was amazing. And, because you're over forty, you'd need a doctor's certificate before you'd be allowed in the plane, let alone anything else, so don't even think about it.'

'Noted, though I could point out that I'm not an old man yet.' He paused. 'As long as he's good to you. That's all I ask.'

'He's good to me.' She smiled. 'He was great yesterday, when I had my bad day.'

'Good. All right, I'll back off. For now,' Keith said.

He had her laughing with all sorts of scurrilous tales, and it was late when he finally saw her back to her flat.

'Thanks, Dad. I had a really good time tonight,' Abigail said.

'My pleasure.' He hugged her. 'You take care. And, um, let me know when you're ready for me to meet the man who swims with sharks and throws himself out of planes.'

'I will. And it'll be soon,' she promised. Because she was going to tell Lewis the truth about herself this weekend.

CHAPTER TEN

ON SATURDAY NIGHT, when they'd cleared away their plates and the cartons from the Chinese takeaway, Abigail brought out a brand-new pack of playing cards, still in the wrapper.

'What's this?' Lewis asked.

She tapped the cards. 'I seem to remember someone challenging me to a game of poker.'

He laughed. 'I think it was more like telling you never to play poker because your face is too expressive.'

'We'll see, shall we?'

'So what are the stakes?' he asked

She gave him a cheeky grin. 'I was thinking strip poker.'

'Are you quite sure about this, princess? Because I should warn you now that I had a misspent youth and I'm reasonably good at poker.'

'That's fine.' She smiled at him and handed him the playing cards. 'Shuffle and deal, Dr Gallagher.'

She lost the first three games. Deliberately. Two socks and her cardigan went onto the discard pile.

And then, just when Lewis was looking confident, she won five games straight. Enough to take him down to just his underpants.

'Well, well. And I thought you said you were reasonably good at this, Dr Gallagher,' she teased.

He narrowed his eyes at her. 'Why do I get the feeling that you just hustled me?'

She shrugged. 'It could be beginner's luck.' She stretched and leaned back against the sofa. 'Let's change the rules. Instead of losing a piece of clothing, we could answer a question instead.'

'Answer a question?'

She nodded. 'And we have to be totally honest with our answers.'

'Honest. Hmm. Are you quite sure you're not hustling me?'

In answer, she just smiled.

And she won the next game.

He blew out a breath. 'OK. Your question, princess.'

'I looked up how long it takes to qualify as a skydiving instructor,' she said. 'So how long exactly did you work for that training company?'

'I worked there part time before I took my A levels,' he said.

'That's too vague, Lewis. And we agreed honesty. How long?'

He sighed. 'Two years, while I was doing my A levels.'

'And then you took time out before university, didn't you?' she asked softly.

He closed his eyes. 'Yes.'

'Would I be right in thinking it was more than one gap year?'

'That's another question.'

She spread her hands. 'You and I both know I'll win the next game. Do you really want to drag it out?'

He opened his eyes and sighed. 'OK. I took six years out.'

'Six years?' She frowned. 'That's quite unusual. Why so many?'

'Where did you learn to play poker?' he countered.

'From a friend of my dad's. And you haven't finished answering the question.'

'Strictly speaking, it would be a new question and you haven't won a game.' His lips thinned. 'But you're a hustler. OK. Since you're asking. And I'm not going to insult you by asking that you keep this to yourself,' he said. 'It's something I don't talk about.' He looked at the floor.

'I told you my dad died when I was fourteen. My mum fell apart afterwards. It was as if she'd just frozen. She couldn't cope with anything. She just about managed to get up in the morning, but that was it. She sat in a chair all day long. She barely spoke to any of us. Obviously I knew later it was a mixture of grief and because she was reacting badly to anti-depressants—back then, family doctors used to hand them out without really thinking about whether it was the best option. But at the time I didn't have a clue what to do.'

Abigail stared at him, utterly shocked and unsure what to say. She'd had no idea.

'Then I overheard one of the neighbours saying we'd get taken into care and be split up if my mum wasn't careful.' He swallowed hard. 'I'd already lost my dad. I didn't want to lose my mum and my sisters, too. If we got taken away from her, no family would take the four of us on. Especially the ages we were. I knew we'd be split up and I might never see any of them again. So I thought that if I took over looking after us, we'd be able to stick together.'

Abigail couldn't quite take it in. 'You looked after your mum and your three sisters from when you were *fourteen*?'

'It was that or risk losing them,' he said simply. 'I wanted to keep my family together. And it was what Dad would've wanted me to do, too. Be the man of the house.'

'But you were only fourteen, Lewis. You were still a child.'

'I was old enough to learn how to cook and clean.' He shrugged. 'OK, so I burned a few things, and there was the time I didn't cook the chicken properly and we all had food poisoning the next day, but we managed.'

'That's pretty incredible. And I feel horrible now.' She blew out a breath. 'I accused you of learning to cook so you could score with girls.'

He spread his hands and gave her the fakest smile she'd ever seen in her life. 'Well, that worked pretty well for me at university.'

'I'm sorry.'

He shook his head. 'Don't pity me, Abby. It was my choice.'

'I'm not pitying you. But I'm sorry you had to grow up so early.' And sorry she'd pushed him into telling her all this. 'I see a very different man from the one the hospital grapevine sees.'

His face became set. 'Which is precisely why they don't know about it.'

'Now I know why you call your sisters your girls. You were pretty much a parent to them.'

He shrugged. 'Mum couldn't cope. There wasn't any-one else to step in. So that left me. And it was easy to get a part-time job at the training centre when I was six-teen, fitting it round my A levels—Dani was fourteen, by then, so she could take over some of the cooking and what have you. And that meant we had enough money to put food on the table and pay the bills.'

'How old's your youngest sister?' Abigail asked.

'Ronnie's the same age as you. Six years younger than me.'

She worked it out. 'So basically you stayed at home until the girls had all finished their A levels and left for university?'

'How could I walk away at eighteen and leave them to deal with Mum? They were still kids, Abby. Ronnie was only eight when Dad died. She was only halfway through primary school. She'd been at high school for a year when I finished my A levels. She needed stabil-ity. They all did. I couldn't just go and do whatever I wanted and leave them to sink.'

Abigail blew out a breath. 'Why didn't your mother get help?'

Lewis shrugged. 'I guess she was too proud.'

'Like your patient with alcoholic hepatitis,' she said, remembering. 'Too stressed and too proud to ask for help.'

'Or maybe she was too scared, in case the doc-tor called social services. She'd lost her husband. She needed to keep the rest of her family. If they'd seen how she was, that neighbour would've been right. Back then, the way social services were run, they would've taken us from her and put us into foster-care. Separately.'

'Why didn't any of your family or her friends do something to help?'

'She didn't give them the chance,' he said softly. 'She just closed off. Shut everyone out. Even the girls and me.' He wrinkled his nose. 'Anyway, it worked out OK. The girls all did well at school and went to university. And when Ronnie went to university, so did I.'

'You,' Abigail said, 'are a really good man.'

'I wish I was.' He shook his head. 'But I screwed up. Big time.'

She waited.

Eventually, he gave in and told her. 'A week after Ronnie and I went to university, my mum took an over-dose. She couldn't cope with being on her own.'

'And you blame yourself for it? That's not fair, Lewis. It wasn't your fault.'

'I should've got her more support before I left, instead of just pulling the rug from under her. Or maybe I could've done it differently.'

It still shocked her that he blamed himself. 'You'd already put your own life on hold for six years, until your sisters had all finished school. It wouldn't be fair to expect you to put your life on hold forever.'

'Maybe. But I could've found a place to study nearer home, somewhere that I could commute, so I could keep an eye on Mum.'

She bit her lip. There wasn't a tactful way of asking this, but she needed to know. 'Did your mum…?'

He shook his head. 'They found her in time. And

then she finally got the help she needed. Help I really should've made sure she got ten years before.'

'You were fourteen. You couldn't take responsibility for her crumbling, and you weren't to know what antidepressants do to people. If anything, that was your family doctor's responsibility. They should've kept a better eye on her instead of just writing out script after script.'

'It's how things were back then.' He sighed. 'I still feel I should've done more for her.'

'You kept the family together from when you were only fourteen years old, still a child yourself. You paid the bills and you made sure everyone was fed, and you deferred your own dreams of university for six years— which is long enough for quite a few of them to have refused to admission. There aren't many people who would've done anywhere near that much, Lewis.'

He looked at her. 'You don't get it, do you?'

What more he could have done? No. But she understood something else now. No wonder he was an adrenalin fiend—he was making up now for the fun he'd missed out on for most of his teens, when he'd taken on responsibilities that had been way in advance of his years. 'I get now why you don't want to get married and settle down.' Because he'd already had the responsibility of bringing up a family.

'Good,' Lewis said.

She had a feeling there might be more to it than that, but she'd already pushed him into telling her an awful lot. Difficult stuff, too. Things he normally kept buried. Right now, she thought, he needed a break.

She let him win the next game.

'You let me win,' he accused. And he looked annoyed about it.

'I wasn't patronising you.'

'No? It feels like it, princess.' This time, there was an edge to his voice.

She shook her head. 'That wasn't my intention, Lewis. Really.'

'I can't believe I told you never to play poker because you're easy to read.' He blew out a breath. 'You're a shark.'

'I played absolutely fairly,' she pointed out.

'And you normally play to win. The fact that you lost...'

She rolled her eyes. 'OK, so I threw the game. But it wasn't to patronise you. You've just told me a lot of really difficult stuff. I figured that you could do with some breathing space. So which item of clothing do you want me to remove?' She paused. 'Unless you want to remove it for me.'

'Nope. We're playing by your new rules now.' He looked her straight in the eye. 'So who exactly taught you poker, Abby?'

'I already told you that. One of my dad's colleagues.' On the tour bus. Keith had kept her clear of the crazy side of the rock 'n roll lifestyle, so going on tour for her had meant long, tedious hours spent with grownups who hadn't had much in common with her. But her dad's best friend and drummer had spent time with her while Keith had been writing, and he'd taught her how to play cards.

'That's not an exact answer, though, is it? Vague as anything. I want more than that, Abby. I want a *name*.'

She'd planned all along to tell him the truth about her background tonight, but now the time had come she felt sick with nerves. She wasn't ready yet. Maybe the name of her father's friend would pass him by. After all, Keith was the star of Brydon. Most people knew the name of the lead singer in a band and the lead guitarist, but the bass player and drummer tended to fade into the background. 'His name's Joe MacKenzie.'

Lewis's eyes narrowed. 'The same name as the drummer in Brydon.'

She squirmed. She should've guessed he'd know that. Lewis had a lot of music and he knew his stuff. 'It's a common enough name.'

'Not that common. And when you say he's your dad's colleague, I'm putting two and two together.'

'And coming up with more than four.'

'Am I?' He looked her straight in the eyes. 'Is your name really Smith?'

'Yes, it is. My turn to deal.'

He won. This time, not because she let him but because she couldn't concentrate.

'Right, Abby. What's your full name?'

Oh, help. This wasn't the way for him to find out. She had a feeling that he wasn't going to take it well.

But maybe she had to trust him. After all, he'd told her something important—something he was trusting her to keep to herself. She took a deep breath and threw his words back at him. 'OK. I'm not going to insult you by asking you to keep this to yourself. I know you won't rush to spill the beans to the hospital grapevine.'

'Uh-huh.'

'I was going to tell you anyway, but I hadn't worked

out the right way to do it yet.' She lifted her chin. 'My full name's Cinnamon Abigail Brydon Smith.'

She saw the second the penny dropped. 'You're Keith Brydon's daughter. "Cinnamon Baby". That's you.'

'Yes. He wrote that song for me the day I was born. And the royalties over the years paid for this flat.' She dragged in a breath. 'That's why I go by my middle name. People are more likely to take me seriously. I mean, would you want to be treated by a doctor with a flaky name like Cinnamon?'

'Where does the Smith come from? Or is that your dad's real name?'

'It's my mum's.' She paused. 'She didn't marry my dad.' Or keep Abigail. Adeline Smith had left them both for a new love when Abigail had been four. So Keith had been forced to make a choice: give up his job to look after his daughter or take her on the road with him and employ a nanny-cum-governess. And Adeline hadn't been interested enough to see her daughter since.

His face was stony. 'You said your dad was a stock-broker.'

'No, *you* said he was a stockbroker. I just didn't correct you.'

'Abby, your dad's a famous rock star.'

'Yes, and I hate people seeing me as just the child of a famous person, not for who I am. I had years of it when I was small. Dad did his best to keep me out of the limelight, but the paparazzi loved the whole "Cinnamon Baby" story and they found ways of getting their shots.' She sighed. 'So I suppose you want to meet my dad now.'

He raised an eyebrow. 'Why do you say that?'

'Because my dad's Keith Brydon.'

'And?'

'Like you said. He's a rock star. Famous.'

'That doesn't have anything to do with you and me.'

'Doesn't it?'

Lewis frowned. 'Is that why you don't date? Because you think once people find out who you are, they'll stop being interested in you and want to hang out with your dad?'

'It happens.' Her voice was expressionless.

'I like your dad's music, yes, and it might be nice to meet him some time. But that'll be because he's *your* dad, not because he's Keith Brydon.'

Exactly what she'd told her father. But right now she was having a tough time believing it. Believing that Lewis really was different from the people she'd thought were her friends or partners in the past.

'Abby...' He leaned forward and kissed her lightly on the mouth. 'You really have had lousy taste in men.'

'Not just men. It was all the way through.'

Now she'd started talking, her tongue was running away with her. This wasn't supposed to happen. She tried to stop it, but Lewis was a trained doctor, too, and he knew the same waiting trick that she did. And the words just kept spilling out.

'My mum left us for someone else when I was four.'

Lewis frowned. 'Why didn't she take you with her?'

Abigail sighed. 'Dad would never say. But I think it's because I would've cramped her style and the other guy didn't want a brat hanging round.' She shrugged. 'At least Dad wanted me. He got custody of me officially and kept me with him. I was home-schooled until I was fourteen, and I used to travel with him when he was on tour. Then he realised that it wasn't much fun for me—you wouldn't believe how tedious it is, being on a tour bus. Day after day after day, moving from one town to another, never getting time to actually see anything of whatever country you're touring in because you have a rigid schedule, so all you see is the inside of the bus and the inside of the hotel.

'That's why Joe taught me to play cards. I ran out of books on one tour and he noticed how bored I was.' She grimaced. 'And Dad knew I wanted to be a doctor when I grew up. So he said after that he'd just tour in the school holidays so I could go to a proper school and do my exams, and we settled in Surrey.'

'But?' Lewis asked softly.

'But I never fitted in at school.' She shrugged. 'I'd spent all my life hanging around adults so I wasn't used to being around kids, and I didn't have a clue how to make friends. I wasn't used to the way the pack works. How to be popular, how to make people like me. And I'd spent all my time with guys—the band, the roadies. Even my tutor was male. I didn't know how to connect with girls, be part of a group.'

She stared at the floor. 'Sometimes I wonder if things would've been different if my mum had stuck around. If she would've taught me how to do the girly stuff.' She looked at Lewis. 'But even if she'd taken me with her, I don't think she would've loved me as much as Dad does.'

'Do you miss her?'

Abigail shook her head. 'I don't really remember much about her. I suppose you can't really miss what you've never had. Yes, sometimes I wish I had a mum to talk to. There are some things I'd rather not discuss with Dad.' She shrugged again. 'I'm just not good with other people. And I got a fair bit of hassle at school because of my name. You wouldn't believe how many stupid little names they made up for me. Every spice they could think of, every nickname for someone with red hair, every word that started with "sin". On and on and on. It was relentless.

'One of the teachers found me crying after school one day, and she suggested to Dad that maybe I should use my middle name instead. Because it was a bit more— well, normal.'

'But it wasn't enough to stop the other kids teasing you?'

She swallowed miserably. 'I thought I was starting to make friends after that. Then I overheard some of them talking. They said the only reason they were hanging around with me was because they hoped I'd invite them to a party at my place, and they'd meet all these pop stars. Which is ironic, because Dad didn't hang out with the kind of bands they liked. They wouldn't have recognised any of the musicians he knew.' She gave a mirthless laugh. 'I really wasn't happy at that school. Dad moved me to a different school, and from then on I was known as Abigail Smith. It was better after that.'

'I'm glad.'

And, damn him, he waited. As if he knew that there was more. The words bubbled to the surface. 'But the guy I met when I was seventeen...I really thought he loved me. It turned out he was only interested because he knew who my dad was, and hoped Dad would get him a recording contract.'

'And you found that out the same way as the girls at school, because you overheard him talking to someone?'

'No.' She bit her lip. 'We had a fight when I said I wouldn't sleep with him until I was eighteen. He called me a stupid kid and lost his temper. That's when he told me he wasn't interested in me anyway—he'd only been with me because he wanted to get close to my dad. I had no idea he'd even known who my dad was—especially as everyone knew me as Abigail Smith by then, rather than Cinnamon Brydon. I guess I must've confided in someone at some point, and it leaked out. That, or someone had seen us together and worked it out.'

Lewis stroked her hair. 'Not everyone's out for what they can get.'

'I know. But university wasn't much better. It was the same thing—I never really fit in. I was always on the outside, and the only time I was ever invited in was when they found out who I was. Every man I dated…as soon as they found out who Dad was, things changed. And not for the better. I guess that's when I started keeping myself separate so I didn't get hurt anymore.'

'It doesn't have to be like that.' He paused. 'Newsflash for you, princess. People in the emergency department at the London Victoria like you for who you are. Now you've started opening up and letting people close, you've given them the chance to like you. And they do like you, Abby.'

'Sydney and Marina—they've been kind.'

'It's called being your friend.' He paused. 'But you're scared it'll change if they find out who you are.'

'It always does,' she said bleakly.

'Is that why you left your last hospital?'

'No. I wanted the special reg job, so I applied to the London Victoria. That's why I moved.'

'And you work in emergency medicine because of your dad.'

She nodded. 'It's like you said—a couple of rounds of golf in the week doesn't make up for a sedentary lifestyle. Sure, when Dad's touring, he's active—but when he's writing music or just practising at home, he doesn't do any real exercise, not much more than a couple of rounds of golf in the week. He eats the wrong stuff and he doesn't eat regular meals—sometimes he even forgets to eat. His hours are nothing like a normal person's hours, and he drinks way too much. He doesn't do drugs, so I guess that's one thing I don't have to worry about—but I do worry about him having a heart attack or a stroke or ending up with a fatty liver.'

She blew out a breath. 'I guess if I can keep saving someone's dad in Resus, I feel that what goes around comes around. And if my dad ever ends up in Resus then someone will save him. I know it's stupid and superstitious, but I can't help it.'

'That's why you rang him when you lost your patient.'

'Yes. I just needed to be sure that he was OK.' She sighed. 'I wish he'd find someone who makes him happy. Someone who'll love him and look after him and do all the wifely nagging stuff to make him eat properly and do a bit of gentle exercise.'

'Why hasn't he found someone else? Is he still in love with your mum?'

'I don't think so. But it probably didn't help, being a single dad—I remember him having a couple of girl-friends when I was younger, but he overheard one being rude to me about the colour of my hair. I never saw her again after that day, so I guess he dumped her.'

'Good for him. You should always put your kids first.'

Something, she thought, that his own mother hadn't done for him. Lewis's mother had opted out, leaving him to pick up the pieces and look after his sisters.

It must've shown in her expression because he said, 'Don't judge my mother.'

She flushed. 'Lewis, she let you deal with everything when you were still a child.'

'She really loved my dad. He was her whole world. Losing him totally devastated her. And not everyone's strong enough to cope with something like that.' He looked grim. 'She's never been involved with anyone since because she says nobody can ever match up to him. I can understand why she crumbled. The loss was just too great.'

'But she's OK now?'

He nodded. 'She went through the mill a bit, coming off the anti-depressants. She'd been on them for way too long. And at the moment things aren't great between us. She feels so guilty about not being there for us when we were kids and for dumping her responsibilities on me. I've told her it doesn't matter, but she just can't get past the guilt—and she shuts us all out.

'Manda was hoping that Louise being born would help break the ice a bit, but it hasn't. Mum doesn't trust herself not to let us all down again so she's pretty much a hands-off grandma. It's pretty awkward when we do see each other. So right now I email her once a week, just to say hello and see how she is. Just keeping the lines of communication open.' He grimaced. 'It's better than calling her. At least in an email there aren't any long, difficult silences. You can sound bright and breezy—you know, smile from the wrists up.'

'That's hard for you.'

He waved a dismissive hand. 'I cope.'

By doing all the adrenalin-fiend stuff. It meant he didn't have time to think or feel. Now she was really beginning to understand him.

He looked at her. 'I never would've thought you were the child of a wild rock star. Didn't you ever want to be a singer or play guitar?'

'No. I probably take after my mother—not that I know for definite, as we're not in touch. I did try to get in contact with her when I was eighteen but she wasn't interested: she had a new life.' Somewhere else she didn't fit in. 'I suppose, seeing all the rock-star lifestyle, I just went the other way,' she said dryly.

'I didn't join in and do the parties and the late nights and the smashing up of hotel rooms. I guess it's like someone who runs away from the circus to be a book-keeper—swapping all the chaos for something secure. And it was chaos, when it wasn't endless travelling. I love my dad, but I really can't live the way he does.' She blew out a breath. 'This wasn't how tonight was meant to go.'

'Baring souls, you mean?'

'I was just hoping you'd open up to me a little bit. Let me understand you a bit more.'

'But you didn't bargain on that lot,' he said wryly.

'No. And I didn't mean to dump all that lot on you either.'

He raked a hand through his hair. 'I feel pretty wiped.'

'So do I,' she admitted. 'Lewis—let's just go to bed.'

His eyes widened. 'You want sex *now*?'

'No.' She looked at him, shocked. 'I just want to hold you. And for you to hold me. Like you did the other night. Maybe we can give each other some comfort. Maybe everything will look a bit better in the morning.'

'Maybe.'

Except it wasn't. Eventually Abigail fell asleep, but Lewis couldn't. Every time he began to drift off, he woke up with a start, panic seeping through his veins. He felt as if he were stuck to the bed, pinned down by a cold, heavy weight.

Responsibility.

Commitment.

This was a mess. Part of him wanted to stay; part of him wanted to run. And he knew what the problem was. What was making him panic so much.

He was in love with Abigail Smith.

Given his track record, it was all going to go wrong. Both of them would end up hurt.

He already knew that Abigail had been hurt in the past. The feeling of never fitting in. The feeling of people only seeing her as Keith Brydon's daughter, not for herself. The people in her past who'd used her to further their own careers and social ambitions, not caring that they were trampling on her.

She deserved better.

A lot better.

And she needed someone who could commit to her. Someone who'd put her first in his life, someone who'd love her and cherish her.

Much as Lewis wanted it to be him, he knew he couldn't do it. He just couldn't handle commitment.

So there was only one thing he could do. The right thing. Even though it was going to hurt like hell, it was much better to do it now than to let it drag on and hurt them both even more.

Quietly, carefully he wriggled out of bed. Abigail stirred and Lewis froze, willing her to go back to sleep. Her breathing became even again and he grabbed his clothes. It took only a few moments to put them all on once he'd left the bedroom.

Part of him knew that he ought to leave a note, but he didn't have a clue what to say, and he didn't want to wait around while he thought about it in case she woke.

Hating himself for being so unfair to her but not knowing what else to do, he let himself quietly out of her flat and headed for home.

CHAPTER ELEVEN

ABIGAIL'S ALARM SHRILLED; she groped for the clock on her bedside table, hit the snooze button and rolled over towards Lewis.

Except his side of the bed was empty.

And, given that the sheet was cold, it had obviously been empty for quite some time. Maybe he hadn't been able to sleep and had got up to make himself a coffee without disturbing her; maybe he was reading a journal on the sofa while he waited for her to wake up.

But when she padded into the kitchen, it was empty and the kettle was cold. The living room was equally empty.

Which meant he'd left.

Without even leaving a note.

So much for thinking that everything would be better this morning. What an idiot she was. She'd pushed him way too far last night. She was pretty sure he was going to break up with her now; the worst thing was, there was absolutely nothing she could do about it.

She wished she hadn't made him talk to her, wished she hadn't spilled out her own insecurities. Of course he wasn't going to want to know her now. How could she have been such a fool?

She was glad she was on duty that morning and he wasn't. It would give them both a bit of space and would mean that she didn't have time to brood about the way he'd left without even saying goodbye. She was as bad as he was, she thought wryly, using work in the same way that he used his adrenalin-fiend stuff. But it helped.

All the same, she was disappointed not to find a text from him or anything when she left the hospital and checked her phone. Maybe he was doing family stuff with his sisters. A chill ran through her. Or maybe he was just working out the right way to end it with her.

Lewis couldn't settle to anything. Not while this whole thing of letting Abigail down gently was hanging over him. He was off duty, and he knew that Abigail was working. He thought about texting her, but he knew that this was something he had to do face to face: it was the only fair way. He wasn't going to be a coward about it, even though he didn't like what he was about to do.

How did you break up with someone?

It had always been easy enough for him in the past. But the difference was those women hadn't mattered. Abigail did.

'It's not you. It's me.'

That was true enough. But it sounded weak. As if he was making excuses.

He brooded about it all day. He went for a run in the late afternoon, but the exercise didn't clear his head and make him feel better, the way it usually did.

He had to see her. Chances were she'd go straight home from her shift. Though he'd left it too late to buy her flowers or anything; the only places left open would be corner shops and garage forecourts, and they'd hardly have something special. He shook himself. Flowers probably weren't appropriate anyway. Goodbye, and here's a bunch of roses? Hardly.

No. He needed to do this like you'd take off a sticking plaster—firm, fast and final.

Lewis ended up driving over to Abigail's flat. He called her on his mobile phone when he'd parked the car.

'Lewis?'

He really hated himself for the sound of the hope in her voice. Hope that he was about to stamp over in hobnailed boots. 'We need to talk. Can I come and see you?' he asked.

'When?'

'Now. I'm outside,' he explained.

'Oh.' She sounded wary now. 'You'd better come up, then.'

He practised the words all the way up to her flat, under his breath.

Abigail answered the door, looking tired and unhappy, and he felt even guiltier. 'Do you want a coffee?' she asked.

'No, thanks.'

She closed the door behind him and ushered him into the living room, but he didn't sit down.

'You didn't leave a note,' she said.

He could see the hurt in her face, and hated himself for it. 'Sorry.' He shook his head. 'I didn't know what to write.'

'Uh-huh. So what did you want to talk about?' she asked.

He took a deep breath. 'I've been thinking. You and

I—we want different things out of life. It's really not going to work between us, so I think the best thing we can do is to go back to being just colleagues.'

She said nothing.

He raked a hand through his hair. 'Abby, it was always going to be nothing more than a fling between us. I told you right from the start that I don't want to get married and settle down to have kids. I never promised you a happy ending.'

'I guess I should be grateful that I lasted more than three dates.'

That hurt—she knew he was more than the image he projected at the hospital—but he guessed he deserved it. Because he knew he'd just hurt her, really badly. 'I'm sorry. I hope you find—'

'Don't,' she cut in. 'Just don't. OK. You've said what you want to say. End of story. Please, just go.'

'Abby—'

'No.' Without saying another word, she marched to the front door, opened it and waited for him to leave.

He walked through the door, knowing there was no way back, and feeling like the meanest bastard under the sun.

But he'd done the right thing.

He *had*.

Abigail closed the door and sank down to the floor, her back sliding against the wall. She wrapped her arms round her legs and rested her chin on her knees.

She'd guessed this was coming. But she hadn't expected it to hurt so much.

It was her own fault. How stupid she'd been to hustle Lewis at cards, to push him into talking before he was really ready for it. And then she'd dumped all her own insecurities onto him. No wonder he'd run a mile. It had all been too much, too soon.

And now it was over.

So much for thinking that they had something special. That they could move their relationship on to the next step. The whole thing had just blown up in her face.

And there was nobody she could talk to about it. How ironic that he'd asked her if she missed her mother. Right then Abigail could really do with a mother figure to talk to, to help her make sense of all this mess. But there was nobody. If she confided in her friends at work, it would make things awkward in the department. She didn't want her dad to worry about her. The only other person she could maybe talk to was Joe, but then she knew he'd tell her dad, so that was a no-no as well.

Which left…

Nobody.

Well, she'd just have to deal with it on her own. She was used to being on her own. What was the difference now?

Abigail slept badly, and ended up using way too much concealer to disguise the dark shadows under her eyes before she went to work the next morning. Luckily she and Lewis were rostered in different sections of the department so she didn't actually have to work with him, and it was easy enough to give an anodyne smile when she had to. Everyone knew she was quiet and shy so they didn't expect much from her; for once, she was really grateful for her ice princess reputation.

She concentrated on her patients during her shifts at the hospital and tried to drown out her memories after work by studying hard. Give it enough time, and the physical ache of missing Lewis would go.

It had to.

Seeing Abigail at work was hard. She was quiet, barely smiled, and she'd gone right back into her shell—and Lewis knew that it was all his fault.

What he hadn't expected was how miserable he felt without Abigail. How much he missed her quiet common sense, her shy smile, that sweet, wide-eyed look when he'd kissed her until she'd been dizzy.

Had he just made the biggest mistake of his life?

He knew he could trust her. Abigail hadn't said a thing about his family or his background to anyone. No way would the hospital grapevine pass up such juicy material.

And she wasn't like Jenna. She'd never made any demands on him. She didn't expect him to choose between her and his family, and she never would—that wasn't Abigail's style.

He tried to talk to her a couple of times, but she pretty much blanked him. Which he knew he deserved.

He was going to have to do something really spectacular to get her to talk to him. He needed to think about it, but for now he wasn't going to make a fuss at the hospital. The last thing either of them needed was to be the topic of gossip. But somehow he was going to persuade her to talk to him. And maybe, just maybe, she might forgive him for being an idiot and give him another chance.

* * *

On Wednesday, Abigail ducked out of lunch with Marina and Sydney, claiming that she was caught up with a patient.

But at the end of what should've been her lunch break they found her in the office where she was doing paperwork and closed the door behind them.

She looked up at them and forced a smile. 'Sorry I didn't make lunch.'

'But you had a patient you couldn't leave,' Sydney said.

'And then all the paperwork,' Abigail confirmed. 'You know what it's like.'

'I've used enough avoidance tactics in my time to know when other people are using them, Abby,' Marina said gently. 'Have you even had a sandwich at your desk?'

'I…' She couldn't lie. 'No,' she said dully. She hadn't felt much like eating.

'I thought not. So we brought you these from the cafeteria.' Marina handed her a latte and a raspberry muffin.

'Not just the sweet stuff. And we remembered that you're vegetarian.' Sydney placed a brie and tomato baguette in front of her.

'I…' There was a lump in Abigail's throat. 'That's really kind of you.'

'No, it's not kind. It's because you're our friend and we can tell you're upset about something. We're worried about you,' Sydney said.

The lump in Abigail's throat got even bigger.

'What's happened, Abby?' Marina asked.

She sighed. She wasn't going to get away with this,

was she? But maybe they'd be satisfied with the barest of details. 'I was seeing someone. We, um, split up on the weekend.'

'He's an idiot,' Sydney said immediately. 'Why would he break up with someone as lovely as you?'

Abigail wasn't going to break Lewis's confidences by explaining. 'It just didn't work out.'

'And you were in love with him?'

'Yes.' She bit her lip. 'Sorry, I'd rather not talk about it.' And she really didn't want them to guess who she'd been seeing. Thank God she and Lewis had kept their relationship quiet or the hospital grapevine would be unbearable.

'Girly night out required, I think,' Marina said. 'Tonight we'll go and see a really girly rom-com and then eat our combined body weight in ice cream. And no excuses, Abby. You need to go out and do something to take your mind off him. And just remember the guy's an idiot.'

'How do you know it's not my fault?'

'Because you're nice. You're not high-maintenance or difficult,' Sydney said with a smile, and patted her shoulder. 'Let's meet outside Leicester Square station at half past six.'

The film was good, but Abigail found it hard to concentrate. She kept thinking of the night when Lewis had brought ice cream over to her flat and suffered the second half of a film he'd loathed, just so he could hold her.

It wasn't going to happen again.

And in future she wasn't going to make the mistake of losing her heart to anyone. Lewis had it right. Three dates and you're out. That was the way to protect yourself.

* * *

Working in the same department for the next week was almost unbearable. They'd gone back to the formal Dr Smith and Dr Gallagher. It was worse even than when Abigail had first met Lewis and had thought him charming and as shallow as a puddle. Because now she knew the real man—and he was so far from what the hospital grapevine said about him it was untrue.

Several times he tried to talk to her, but she couldn't just pretend they were friends—not just yet. It was still too raw. She needed some distance. Changing her job was out of the question, her promotion was far too recent. So she'd just have to grit her teeth and get on with it.

At the end of the week Abigail was rostered in Resus with Lewis. She'd known that she'd have to face this situation at some point, and she managed to cope just fine, being cool and professional and acting as if they barely knew each other.

Until the last patient on their shift.

Biddy, the paramedic, did the handover. 'This is Jack. He's fifty-eight and was complaining of chest pains. He said it felt like an elephant was sitting on his chest.'

Abigail went cold. She knew that was a classic symptom of a heart attack.

'We gave him GTN spray under his tongue, but it didn't have any effect.'

Abigail went colder still. If the pain didn't ease with glyceryl trinatrate, that was a bad sign.

'And the trace we ran off shows signs of an MI.'

Myocardial infarction. The thing Abigail worried

about more than anything else with her dad—and this man was exactly the same age as her dad.

'We've given him oxygen and aspirin, and cannulated him,' Biddy finished.

'Thank you,' Abigail said quietly.

'Have you given him an anti-emetic yet?' Lewis asked

'No,' Biddy said.

'OK. I'm on it. Thanks, Biddy.' Lewis administered the anti-emetic swiftly and had the leads of an ECG in place so they could monitor the activity in Jack's heart.

Abigail was about to give Jack some more drugs when the monitor changed.

'He's in VT,' Lewis said.

Ventricular tachycardia was where the lower chamber of the heart beat too fast; the abnormal rhythm of the heart could be life-threatening.

'Crash team, ready. Can you take the upper layers of Jack's clothing off, ready for the paddles?' she asked. She knew that really Lewis ought to be leading, as he was her senior colleague, but this case was important to her. She needed to feel that she was the one making the difference. He caught her eye, and she knew from his expression that he understood how she felt and would let her carry on.

She put the paddles in place. 'Charging to two hundred and clear,' she said.

Everyone stood back with their hands off the patient.

'Shocking now,' she said.

'Still in VT,' Lewis reported.

'Charging to two hundred again,' she said, 'and clear. Shocking now.'

Still there was no response.

Come on, come on, she willed Jack. You have to get through this. Keep the karma going, so if the worst happens to Dad someone will be able to save him.

'Charging to three-sixty. And clear,' she said.

Thank God, the monitor showed the rhythm she was looking for: normal sinus waves. It was going to be all right.

'No pulse,' Lewis said.

No. No. *No.* This couldn't be happening. It meant Jack's heart wasn't pumping blood round his body, and she knew the odds were rapidly stacking up against them.

Life support algorhythm. Now. 'Can you bag while I do the compressions?' she asked Lewis.

'Are you sure you don't want me to do the compressions?'

'I'm sure.'

She administered the drugs she hoped would make Jack's heart respond and went through the basic sequence of life support. Ten repetitions, checking for a pulse between each one.

No pulse.

No change on the monitor.

Please, please, respond, she begged inwardly.

'Giving more epinephrine,' she said, and continued with the chest compressions, fifteen to two of Lewis's bagged breaths.

Still nothing

'We'll keep going,' she said.

Dawn, the triage nurse, came in. 'His family's here.'

Abigail shook her head. 'I don't want them to see

this. It's not fair on them. Can you take them off to a side room, please?'

'Sure.'

After another twenty minutes, Lewis placed his hand on her wrist. 'He's been without oxygen too long now, Abby. He's gone.'

'No.'

'We need to call it.'

'No.' She knew he was right, but she couldn't do it. Fear flared up inside her, making her cold.

'Abby, if I have to pull rank, I will. Call it,' he said grimly.

She closed her eyes. 'Everyone agreed?' she whispered.

One by one, everyone agreed.

She looked at the clock. 'Time of death, sixteen thirty-four.'

'Do you want me to talk to the family?' he asked.

'No. I'll do it.' She couldn't face the concern on his face either, and walked out of the room before he said something that cracked her composure completely.

Jack's wife and daughter were waiting in the office where Dawn had put them. They looked up hopefully as Abigail opened the door.

'I'm so sorry,' she said, and their faces crumpled.

Jack's daughter looked to be about her own age. Heavily pregnant, too, so he hadn't even had the chance to meet his grandchild. It felt as if someone had reached into Abigail's chest and was squeezing her heart.

If it had been her own father, there would only be one person in the room, waiting to hear the news. Her. And that thought was unbearable.

She sat with Jack's family for a while, answering their questions and being as kind as she could. Then she went back into the office, on autopilot. It was near the end of the working day, but there was just enough time for her to call the coroner and get in touch with Jack's GP.

She put the phone down and leaned back in the chair, closing her eyes. Today was definitely the worst day she'd spent at the London Victoria.

'OK, princess?' a voice asked softly.

Oh, no.

Lewis.

She kept her eyes closed. 'What are you doing here?'

'Checking up on you.'

'I'm fine,' she lied.

'Abby. I was there the last time you lost a patient.'

He'd cradled her and cherished her, made her feel loved—and, only a few days later, he'd dumped her. She gulped down the sob that threatened to escape. 'And?' she drawled, aiming to sound completely unbothered by his presence.

'And I know why this case is going to upset you even more. Jack was the same age as your dad.'

Trust him to go right to the heart of it. Tortured, she opened her eyes and looked at him. 'And I didn't save him.'

'Neither did I. Nor did anyone else on the team. You know the odds, Abby. Nobody could've done more. Nobody could've saved him.'

And then he did the one thing that made her crack.

He stood there in front of her with his arms open. All she had to do was stand up, walk into them and he'd hold her close. Make her feel warm again. Make the bad feelings go away.

Right now she was just too miserable and it was way, way too tempting. She stood up and walked into his arms.

He cradled her, just as he had the night she'd lost Matthew, resting his cheek against her hair and stroking her back.

But this was all wrong. They weren't together any more. And it hurt too much for her to stay here in his arms.

She pulled away. 'I can't do this. Leave me alone, Lewis.'

'Abby, it doesn't have to be like this,' he began.

'Yes, it does.'

'Abby.' He took a step towards her.

She couldn't handle this. And the only thing she could think of to do was to rush out of the office to the nearest toilet and lock herself in. Unless Lewis was going to make a scene—and, given how much he hated the hospital grapevine, she was pretty sure that wasn't going to happen—he'd have to give up and leave her alone.

Lewis stared at the locked door in exasperation.

OK. She'd won this round.

But she was going to have to go home tonight, and he had every intention of being there on her doorstep. And he'd wait for as long as it took.

CHAPTER TWELVE

ABIGAIL WALKED HOME from the hospital with a heavy heart. Her legs felt like lead and it was a real effort to put one foot in front of the other. Her dad was in the studio, so his mobile phone was switched to voicemail; not wanting him to worry, she hadn't left him a message. Maybe she could ring Sydney or Marina—they'd been there for her earlier in the week. But if she spoke to them she'd have to explain about Lewis, and then it would get complicated in the department.

Which left nobody to talk to about the situation.

Right then, Abigail felt more isolated and alone than she'd ever felt in her entire life.

Where had she gone so wrong?

When she reached the corner of her road, she saw someone sitting on the step at the entrance to her block. She frowned. Why would anyone be waiting there? Had someone forgotten their key? As she drew nearer, she realised it was Lewis.

Oh, no. She really wasn't in the mood for a confrontation. And she'd made it pretty clear at the hospital that she wanted him to leave her alone. Why was he sitting there, waiting for her?

Gritting her teeth, she walked up to him. 'What do you want?'

'To talk to you.'

'I don't think there's anything to say.'

'I do.'

She shook her head. 'Leave me be, Lewis.'

'Abigail, please. Just give me five minutes. When I've said what I've got to say, if you still want me to go, I promise I'll go.'

'I'll give you two minutes,' she said. And that was more than he deserved.

'Two minutes,' he agreed.

She let him into the block and he followed her up the stairs to her first-floor flat in silence. Taking a deep breath, she opened her front door and let him in.

She knew the courteous thing would be to offer him a drink, but right at that moment she wasn't feeling particularly polite. 'So what do you want, Lewis?' She knew it sounded grumpy and ungracious, but she didn't care.

'To apologise, for starters—and to explain.' He sighed. 'I don't know where to start. I could've brought you half a florist's to say sorry. I could've hired a skywriter and had it written in huge letters in the sky. Or I could've sent you up in a plane and written you a message on the beach that was big enough for you to read from the plane. But, with your background, big showy gestures like that...'

The type he'd normally rely on, she thought.

He shrugged. 'Well, they don't really mean anything.'

'They don't,' she said. 'They're just an ego-boost for

the person making the gesture, or something a publicist has dreamt up. There's no real heart in it.'

'Exactly. So what you're getting is me. No flowers, no fancy trappings—just me, talking from the heart.'

She gave a mirthless laugh. 'You're over-egging it, Lewis.'

'Probably,' he agreed with a grimace. 'I don't mean to. I'm not good at this sort of thing. So I'll cut to the chase. I'm sorry I hurt you, Abby.'

She shrugged. 'I'm a big girl. I'll get over it.'

'I was wrong. I've been an idiot.' He shook his head in apparent frustration. 'I've thrown away something very special, just because I was scared.'

This was the man who threw himself off zip-lining platforms and out of planes and thought nothing of it. He didn't have a fearful bone in his body. 'There's actually something an adrenalin fiend is scared of?' she asked, her tone a shade more caustic than she intended.

'Yes. Lots of things.' He paused. 'Bottom line—because I realise I'm running out of time here—will you give me another chance?'

She looked at him. 'Do you have any idea how miserable I've been this week?'

'If it's anything like the way I've been feeling, yes. And I'm sorry. I wish I could take it all back.'

'You can't change the past.'

'But you can learn from it—and I realise now that I've spent half my life being wrong. Keeping people at a distance.' He held her gaze. 'Just like you do.'

She narrowed her eyes at him. 'I don't treat people the way you do. Three dates and you're out.'

'You don't even give them one,' he pointed out. 'You don't let them close.'

'And you do all the adrenalin-fiend stuff so you don't have to face anything emotional,' she countered.

'Running away from my feelings? Yes, you're right. I do. It's easier.' He paused. 'Just so you know, it scared the hell out of me when I asked you to stay with me that night. I never let anyone stay with me, and I never stay overnight with anyone. When I woke up in the morning next to you, I knew I wanted to do it again. And that scared me even more.'

She frowned. 'Why didn't you tell me? I thought you couldn't wait to get rid of me.'

'Because I was scared it was all going to go wrong.' He spread his hands. 'OK, fine. I've used up my two minutes. I'll get out of your hair.'

She could let him walk away.

Or she could let him talk. Tell her why he was so scared of commitment.

And maybe—just maybe—they could find a way forward through this.

'You said,' she reminded him, 'that it was my decision whether or not to kick you out after you'd had your two minutes' say.'

He winced. 'I didn't put it quite like that but, yes. If you want me to go, I'll go.'

She needed to be clear about where this was heading. 'You really want me to give you another chance? You want me back?'

'Yes.'

'You're quite sure about that?'

He looked her straight in the eye. 'More sure than I've been about anything in my entire life.'

'Then I need to understand why you dumped me.'

He winced. 'Because I thought it would be better to end it now than let us get even closer and have it all go wrong—when it would hurt us both more.'

She frowned. 'Why did you think it would go wrong in the first place?'

She really wasn't going to make it easy for him, was she? Then again, he didn't deserve an easy ride. He'd hurt her.

'I guess I owe you an explanation.' But telling her... The words stuck in his throat. 'I've never told anyone this before. Not even the girls.' Especially not them. He hadn't wanted his sisters to think that he'd sacrificed his happiness and his future for them. Piling on the guilt like that wasn't fair.

'I'm listening,' Abigail said.

'I met Jenna when I was twenty-three. She was a client at the training centre. She gave me her number at the end of her course and asked me to call her.' He blew out a breath. 'We started dating. I fell head over heels in love with her. And I asked her to marry me. I even bought her a ring. It wasn't an expensive one—I was supporting Mum and the girls, so I didn't exactly have much spare cash—but I always planned to buy her a better one later, when I could afford it.'

And then it had all gone wrong. 'She asked me to move in with her.' He looked away. 'I told her I couldn't even think about it until the girls were settled. OK, so Dani was doing her finals and Manda was in her first year at university, but Ronnie was still only seventeen, and I was applying to university to read medicine. I asked Jenna to wait for me.' He dragged in a breath. 'She wasn't happy about it. I guess she wanted me to stay, put her before my family and my dreams of being a doctor.'

Abigail frowned. 'If she'd really loved you, she would've understood the situation and waited. You weren't exactly old. You had plenty of time.'

'That was my thinking. But she didn't want to wait four years for me to finish university and then another two more years for me to qualify.' He knew he was going to have to tell Abigail the rest of it. The bit he never talked about.

'Then she told me she was pregnant. She was on the pill, but she claimed she'd forgotten to take it.' He grimaced. 'And I was horrible. I thought she'd done it on purpose. I felt trapped—just when I thought my life was going to start, it was all over and I was saddled with responsibilities again.' He blew out a breath. 'But of course I was going to stand by her. I wouldn't abandon her.'

'So you got married and had the baby?' Abigail asked.

He shook his head. 'It turned out that she wasn't pregnant at all. She'd just said that because she knew I'd do the right thing by her, and it was the only way she could think of to stop me leaving my job and going to university.' He rubbed a hand across his face. 'I only know because she fell out with her best friend over it—and her best friend thought I deserved to know the truth.'

'What did you do?'

'Asked her straight out.' He sighed. 'She admitted it. And I broke it off with her. I couldn't be with someone who'd lie to me over something that big. I know you should put your partner first, but she wasn't prepared to see that I had needs, too. She wasn't prepared to compromise.' He sighed. 'I learned the hard way that you couldn't have it all.'

'I'm not Jenna,' Abigail said.

'I know that.'

'I'd never ask you to choose between me and your family or your dreams. Just as I know you wouldn't ask me to choose between you and my dad.'

'Of course I wouldn't.'

'And I'd never lie about being pregnant. That isn't fair on anyone.'

'I know.'

'But that's why you don't do commitment?'

'Yes. Because, in my experience, it's going to blow up in my face. And you have issues, too,' he pointed out. 'You worry about not fitting in.'

'That's because I *don't* fit in.'

'Maybe that was true in your last hospital, and at schools that—well, you were home-schooled for so long. Of course school wasn't going to work for you. But you do fit in at the London Victoria. Everyone in the department likes you.' He paused. This was a risk. The biggest one he'd taken yet with her. 'And I love you, Abby.'

She gave a mirthless laugh. 'If you love me, Lewis, why did you hurt me like that? Why did you dump me?'

'Because I'm an idiot. Because I was scared. And it was the worst decision I've ever made. I'm miserable without you. The world feels as if nothing's in the right place and nothing fits. I've never had that feeling before. When it ended with Jenna—yes, I was miserable, but I was sure I was doing the right thing. Since the day I broke up with you, I've been trying to convince myself that I made the right decision, and I know full well I didn't. I want you back, Abby.'

'If I say yes—' and she was giving him absolutely no clue about whether she was going to say yes or no '—how do I know you're not going to get cold feet and break up with me again?'

'I guess,' he said, 'I'm asking you to trust that I won't. I love you, and if you'll give me another chance then I'll learn to get over this ridiculous fear. With you by my side, I know I can do that.' He blew out a breath. 'I'll be honest, Abby. This scares me stupid. I want to do anything but sit here spilling my guts to you. I'd be happy to climb a mountain, walk over hot coals, swim through shark-infested waters. For me, talking about how I feel is harder and scarier than all of that put together.' He lifted his chin. 'So that's me done. What about you?'

'Me?' Abigail stared at him, not comprehending.

'How do you feel about me?' he asked. 'Because I really don't have a clue.'

Now he was challenging her to meet him halfway. To tell him how she felt.

To risk being rejected again.

'I thought,' she said carefully, 'that things were working out between us. I know I'm not particularly brave. I'm dull and quiet and the only interesting thing about me is that I'm Keith Brydon's daughter. But I thought you liked me for who I was.'

'I do,' he said softly.

'And I thought…with you, I could be brave. I thought I could risk telling you who I was. That it wouldn't matter and you'd still see me for who I am.'

He reached out and took her hand. 'I do see you, Abby. I see the woman who's quiet and serious and shy, but who's brave enough to go way out of her comfort zone whenever I've asked her to. I see the woman whose eyes have stormy circles round them when she's angry and whose cheeks have dimples when she's happy. I see,' he said, 'the woman who makes me see things in a different way. With you, I don't need the adrenalin stuff. You make my world feel complete. I love you, Abby.'

Abigail swallowed hard. 'Saying this isn't easy.'

He waited. And the hope in his eyes was enough to give her the courage she needed.

'I love you, Lewis,' she said.

'Even though I somctimes make stupid decisions?'

'Even though you sometimes make *very* stupid decisions,' she agreed. 'I see a man,' she said softly, 'who's more committed than anyone I've ever met. Who put his life on hold to keep his family together, and who even now tries to build bridges. I see a man who makes out that he's as shallow as a puddle and doesn't care, but he spends time with patients who've got nobody and he looks out for the vulnerable ones, having a quiet word with the right people to make sure they get the help and support they need. I see,' she said, 'the man I want to take a risk with.'

'I want to take a risk with you, too,' he said. 'I want

commitment. I want you back, Abby. For now and for always. And I want the world to know that you're mine.'

'So you're suggesting we go public about the fact we're seeing each other?'

He shook his head. 'More than that. I want the whole deal. Marriage. A family.'

Everything she wanted.

Everything he'd said he didn't.

'But—I thought you didn't want marriage and a family? You said you felt trapped when you thought Jenna was pregnant.'

'Because I was twenty-three and ready to start my life. I'm older now. Settled in my career. And,' he pointed out, 'you're not Jenna.'

'And you've already sort of done it, bringing your sisters up.'

'That was different, and I don't regret what I did— if I could rewind time and do it all over again, I'd still take those gap years and stick by my family. I wouldn't change that.' He wrinkled his nose. 'Except I'd do it with the benefit of hindsight and get my mum some proper help a lot earlier than she got it.'

He was really close to his sisters. And Abigail's old fears of not fitting in rose up to choke her. 'What if your family doesn't like me?'

'They will. You're nerdy enough for Dani and Ronnie to adore you, and Manda will love the fact that you take me to art galleries and Shakespeare. They'll love you,' he said simply. 'I can't make any guarantees about my mum. She might give you the cold shoulder. But don't take it personally—she's like that with everyone.' He looked thoughtfully at her. 'But I've seen

20% OFF*

with code
THANKSJUL

Visit www.millsandboon.co.uk today to get this exclusive offer!

Ordering online is easy:

- 1000s of stories converted to eBook
- Big savings on titles you may have missed in store

Visit today and enter the code **THANKSJUL** at the checkout today to receive **20% OFF** your next purchase of books and eBooks*. You could be settling down with your favourite authors in no time!

MILLS
BOON

JUL13

you get through to the most uncommunicative patient at work. I have a feeling you might just be able to get through to her.'

'I can try,' Abigail said.

'What if your dad doesn't like me?' he asked.

She coughed. 'I've already talked to him about you.'

Lewis blew out a breath. 'If he knows how much I've hurt you, he'll want to take me apart. Which is pretty much how I feel about anyone who ever hurts you. Or our children.'

'He doesn't know that. And he doesn't need to know. He'll take you for who you are. If anything, I think you'll be horribly bad influences on each other and egg each other on to do mad things.' She stroked his face. 'You say you want children. What if we can't have them?'

'Then we can adopt. Or foster.' His eyes glittered. 'Actually, I know that foster-care is a lot better now than it was when I was a kid. And I'd quite like to be part of that.'

'Taking risks?'

He nodded. 'Teaching kids who've had a rough deal that life doesn't have to be that way. That everyone deserves a second chance.'

She could understand that. 'That works for me. I'll go with you on that.'

He smiled. 'Part of me wants to do this in a much more spectacular place, but you've taught me that I don't need all the trappings.' He dropped to one knee. 'Cinnamon Abigail Brydon Smith, I love you and I want to spend the rest of my life with you. Will you marry me?'

She could see in his eyes that he meant it. He really did want the whole thing with her. Marriage, a family, forever.

'Yes.'

He whooped, then in one single move stood up and scooped her up, whirling her round in the middle of her living room. And then he let her slide down his body until her feet touched the floor; he held her close, lowered his face to hers and kissed her. What started out slow and sweet and soft quickly turned heated; he kissed her as if he were starved for her.

When he broke the kiss, he was shaking. 'I love you, Abby.'

'I love you, too.'

'And I can't wait to get married to you.'

There was a suspicious gleam in his eyes, which made her back away. 'Lewis, don't get any bright ideas about skydiving with me to the wedding reception.'

He laughed. 'You wouldn't be allowed to jump out of a plane in your wedding dress. Unless, of course,' he said thoughtfully, 'you wear an orange jumpsuit as your wedding outfit. That would work.'

'No.' She laughed. 'I think I'd rather wear something that doesn't clash with my hair.'

'You looked cute. But I guess on our wedding day you'd rather have a tiara than a safety helmet.' He kissed her lingeringly. 'Besides, I don't need the adrenalin stuff with you.'

'I'm not going to stop you doing it,' she said. 'I might choose to watch you from the ground rather than join in with you every time, but I won't stop you doing something that makes you happy.'

'You make me happy,' he said softly. 'And I intend to do the same for you. For the rest of our days.'

* * * * *

THE REBEL
WHO LOVED HER

BY
JENNIFER TAYLOR

First published in Great Britain 2013
by Mills & Boon, an imprint of Harlequin (UK) Limited.
Harlequin (UK) Limited, Eton House, 18-24 Paradise Road,
Richmond, Surrey TW9 1SR

© Jennifer Taylor 2013

ISBN: 978 0 263 89905 4

Harlequin (UK) policy is to use papers that are natural, renewable and recyclable products and made from wood grown in sustainable forests. The logging and manufacturing process conform to the legal environmental regulations of the country of origin.

Printed and bound in Spain
by Blackprint CPI, Barcelona

Dear Reader

Can love overcome all obstacles?

That's the question that Becky and Ewan have to find the answer to in this final book of my *Bride's Bay Surgery* series. Eight years ago they were deeply attracted to one another but Becky realised that they wanted very different things out of life and married someone else. When she meets Ewan again she is shocked to discover that the old feelings she had for him are still very much alive. The fact that Ewan feels the same fills her with dread. She has nothing to offer Ewan these days.

Helping Becky and Ewan to find a way through their problems was a real joy, although I have to confess that I shed the odd tear when it looked as if they would never reach a solution! They are such a lovely couple that they deserved a happy ending, and I hope you will agree that I have given them that.

So...*do* I believe that love can overcome all obstacles? Yes, I do. I wouldn't be writing romance novels if I didn't believe it!

Love to you all

Jennifer

**These books are also available in eBook format
from www.millsandboon.co.uk**

DEDICATION

Good friends are scarcer than hens' teeth and I am very
lucky to have some of the very best friends possible.

So a huge thank you to Barbara, Charlotte and Ted,
Jeremy, and John.

Life wouldn't be half as much fun without you all.

CHAPTER ONE

'BECKY! HEY, BECKY…wait!'

Becky Williams stopped when she heard someone calling her name. Turning around, she peered at the faces of the other passengers gathered in the baggage hall of Heathrow Airport. The flight had been long and arduous despite the fact that her parents had insisted on upgrading her and Millie to business class. Twenty-plus hours non-stop from New Zealand would have been hard enough on her own, but it had been little short of gruelling with a small child in tow.

Becky sighed when Millie started to whimper. She cuddled her close, hoping it wouldn't be too long before their pushchair appeared on the carousel. At fourteen months, Millie was getting quite heavy and Becky's arms were aching from the long hours spent holding her as they had flown across the globe.

'I thought it was you!'

All of a sudden a man was standing in front of her and Becky jumped. She stared at him in confusion. He was tall, several inches taller than her own not inconsiderable height, in fact, with dark brown hair and the most wonderful deep blue eyes. Although his face wasn't classically handsome, there was something very

appealing about those craggy features and the upward
curve of his mouth that hinted at a well-developed sense
of humour....

'Don't tell me you don't recognise me. I'm gutted!'
He grinned at her, his face lighting up in a way that was
all too familiar, and Becky gasped.

'Ewan! Is it really you?'

'It is indeed.' He gave her a quick hug, his strong
arms closing around her for the briefest of moments before he drew back. His blue eyes sparkled with laughter as he stared down at her. 'Or at least I *think* it's me.
After all those hours in the air I'm not sure if I'm actually here or not!'

He laughed, mercifully missing her reaction. Becky
sucked in her breath as she took a firmer hold of Millie. She was tired, that was all, tired and stressed after
the long hours spent travelling. It was little wonder that
it had felt so good to have Ewan hold her but it didn't
mean anything. She may have had a massive crush on
Ewan MacLeod at one point but that was all in the past.
An awful lot had happened since then.

The thought of what had happened in the past year
was never far from her mind, but Becky pushed it aside,
knowing that she couldn't cope with all the soul searching right then. The baggage carousel began to move
and people stepped forward to look for their luggage.
Becky spotted their pushchair and tried to force her
way through the crowd but with Millie in her arms, it
wasn't easy.

'Is that yours?' Ewan gently moved her aside when
she nodded. Leaning over, he lifted the pushchair off
the carousel and set it down in front of her. He quickly
opened it so she could place Millie in the seat then

crouched down before Becky could do so and fastened the safety harness, smiling at the little girl as he did so. 'There you go, poppet. You can have a little nap now.'

He ruffled Millie's honey-gold curls and Becky did her best to hide her surprise when Millie laughed. Normally, Millie was wary of strangers. Maybe it was all the upset of the past twelve months but Millie's usual response when she was approached by someone she didn't know was to cry. However, there was no sign of tears now, just the opposite, in fact.

Ewan straightened up and Becky hurriedly smoothed her face into a suitably noncommittal expression. Maybe Millie had responded unusually favourably but it meant no more than her own reaction had. They were both exhausted and the sooner they were home in Bride's Bay the better. She glanced at the carousel, willing her suitcase to appear. Cases were being claimed from all sides but she couldn't see any sign of her bag.

Ewan reached over and grabbed a battered old holdall and dropped it on the floor by his feet. 'That's mine sorted. There's just yours to come now. Shout out when you spot it.'

He seemed to have taken it for granted that he should help her and Becky wasn't sure what to do. It didn't seem fair to make use of him, especially not after the way they had parted all those years ago. The guilt that had become such a large part of her life of late rose up inside her and she shook her head.

'Don't worry about us, Ewan. We can manage. You've got your bag so you get on off home.'

'And leave you to struggle on your own?' His dark brows rose. 'I can just imagine what my mother would say if she found out. She'd have my guts for garters!'

Becky summoned a smile. 'I think you're a bit too old to worry what your mother will say.'

'True.' His smile faded and he looked at her with a seriousness that made a shiver pass through her. 'However, I'd never forgive myself if I abandoned you, Becky. Mum wrote and told me what had happened to Steve. I'm really sorry. Losing your husband like that must have been horrendous. You've had a really rough time and I'd like to help any way I can, even if it's only by seeing to your luggage.'

Becky felt a lump come to her throat when she heard genuine concern in his voice and looked away. She was afraid that she would do something silly if she wasn't careful, and cry. She had learned to hold back her tears in the past year for Millie's sake. It hadn't seemed fair to upset her daughter so what little crying she'd done had been done in private. Maybe it was tiredness or the fact that she'd been caught unawares by seeing Ewan again, but she knew it would take very little to make her break down.

'Thank you,' she said quietly. 'You're very kind.'

'It's my pleasure.' He touched her hand then turned towards the carousel, thankfully missing the start she gave.

Becky took a deep breath as she focused on the cases travelling along the conveyor belt. She *was* tired, so it was little wonder that she seemed to be overreacting. The fact that her pulse had started racing when Ewan had touched her wasn't an indication of anything else.

She finally spotted her case and pointed to it. 'That's my case—the red one with the yellow tag on it.'

'Okey-dokey.' Ewan elbowed his way through the crowd and lifted the case off the belt with an ease that belied its weight. Setting it down on the floor, he looked at her. 'I take it that you're being met?'

'Yes.' Becky sighed. 'Mum and Dad insisted on coming to meet us. I tried to talk them out of it but they were adamant.'

'Of course they were.' Ewan frowned as he released the handle of her suitcase and turned it towards the exit. 'You've just flown right across the globe, Becky. Anyone would be tired after a journey like that—I know I am. Plus you've had the added stress of looking after your daughter. What's the point of making your life even more difficult by refusing to let your parents collect you?'

Becky bit her lip. What Ewan had said made sense but she still felt bad about her parents making the long drive from Devon. They had been through enough in the past year thanks to her and she was determined that she wasn't going to put them under any more pressure. Once again the thought that she might be making a mistake by returning to England rose to her mind.

She'd thought long and hard before she had made her decision but, in the end, she had accepted that she didn't have a choice. She needed to work to provide for herself and Millie, and the cost of full-time childcare would have been exorbitant. There simply wouldn't have been enough money left over each month to pay all the other bills. Her parents had not only offered her and Millie a home, but her mother had offered to look after Millie while Becky went out to work. Becky knew that she should be grateful for their kindness, and she was, but it wasn't easy to sacrifice her independence. She would be right back where she'd been eight years ago, living with her parents and dreaming about Ewan.

The thought slid into her mind so fast that she didn't have time to stop it. Becky shook her head, determined to dislodge it as she followed Ewan towards the exit. There was no chance of history repeating itself. Maybe she had fallen under Ewan's spell once upon a time but it was Steve she had married and Steve she had loved....

Hadn't she?

Becky felt her breath catch as her eyes rested on Ewan's broad back. All of a sudden she wasn't sure what was true any more. Had she loved Steve, *really* loved him, or had he merely fitted her idea of the perfect husband? Steve had appeared so calm and dependable, so focused on what he wanted from life. They'd held similar views, shared the same objectives—marriage, a home and a family—that she had believed she had found her soulmate. Ewan, however, had been very, very different.

Ewan had been charming, funny, exciting, sexy—everything Steve hadn't. Although he'd had numerous girlfriends, he'd made no secret of the fact that he didn't plan on settling down. As he'd stated on many occasions there was a great big world waiting to be explored and he was going to do his level best to see as much of it as possible. Even though she had been deeply attracted to him, and had known he'd felt the same about her, Becky had realised it wouldn't work. They had wanted such different things out of life that any kind of relationship had been doomed from the outset.

In the end she had chosen to stay with Steve, sure in her own mind that it was the right decision. Steve had offered her the security she'd wanted, the chance to create a marriage exactly like her parents'—stable and enduring. It was only now, looking back, that she found herself wondering if she had made the biggest mistake of her life. Who knew what might have happened if she had chosen Ewan?

Ewan could feel a knot of tension twisting his guts. He took a deep breath, forcing the oxygen through his lungs. Seeing Becky at Christchurch Airport had been a shock admittedly, but he'd had hours to get over it. As he had sat in the cramped confines of the aircraft, he had, quite deliberately, gone over everything that had happened eight years ago.

He'd been doing his rotations and Becky had been in her final year, training as a nurse, when they had met at the hospital where they were both seconded. Although they both came from the Bride's Bay area, he was a few years older than her so she'd not been part of his set. It had been a while since he'd seen her, in fact, and Ewan had been surprised by how attractive she was. Not only was she extremely pretty but she had a lively and engaging mind.

He'd got into the habit of stopping by the ward she was on, timing his visits to coincide with her breaks. They'd chatted about this and that over coffee, but each knew the conversation was merely a cover for their real feelings. If he was attracted to her then it was obvious that Becky felt the same about him. Although he knew that she was seeing someone—a definite no-no in his book as he made a point of never encroaching on another man's territory—he asked her out and she accepted.

They went for dinner at a little bistro down by the river recommended by one of his friends. Candlelight, soft music, discreetly attentive waiters—it was so self-consciously *romantic* that it would have been laughable if Ewan hadn't been mortified in case Becky thought he was trying to seduce her. However, when he apologised, she simply laughed. And it was then that he realised he could very easily fall in love with her.

He drove her home afterwards with his head in a spin. He had always ruled out the possibility of falling in love just yet. He wanted to see something of the world before he settled down and making a commitment like that would make that impossible. However, meeting Becky had changed everything; he was no longer certain what he wanted any more. And when he kissed her, right there in the street, he was less certain than ever. Maybe he had found something even more wonderful than anything the world had to offer?

In other circumstances he might have asked her if he could spend the night with her but what had happened was just too profound. He drove himself home in a state of turmoil, aware that he needed to decide what he was going to do. However, before he could work it out, Becky came to see him. She told him that she and Steve were getting engaged and that in the circumstances she didn't think they should see each other again. Whilst Ewan was stunned by the announcement, he was also relieved. Now he could carry on with his plans, do everything he wanted to do. There was nothing and no one to hold him back, although if Becky hadn't called a halt, he wasn't sure if he could have done so…

Ewan cursed under his breath as they reached the arrivals hall. He was acting like an idiot by thinking about all that. It was over and done with and they had both moved on. Turning, he smiled at Becky, seeing the dark circles that exhaustion had painted under her eyes.

His hands clenched because it was all he could do not to reach out and smooth them away.

'Where did your parents say they'd meet you?'

'They said they'd be waiting when I came through Customs...' She broke off, a smile lighting her face. 'There they are!'

Ewan turned, glad of the excuse not to look at her. When she smiled like that she looked like the old Becky, the one he had found so beguiling, and it wasn't easy to reconcile the mix of emotions that thought aroused. There had been umpteen women in his life since Becky. Admittedly, none of them had made much of an impression on him, but he hadn't wanted them to. He'd been happy to play the field and enjoy his life as a bachelor. Maybe he had decided it was time he settled down, but he wasn't in a rush. He would wait until he found the right woman...

If he hadn't found her already.

Ewan felt alarm scud through him. Was Becky that woman? Was it possible that he was still attracted to her? He didn't want to believe it but he couldn't pretend that he didn't feel anything. Maybe it was only sympathy because of what she'd been through, but, there again, maybe it was something more.

He groaned. Once again it felt as though all his plans were up in the air. And once again it was all down to Becky!

CHAPTER TWO

'Darling, it's so wonderful to see you!'

Becky smiled as her mother enveloped her in a hug. She hugged her back, surprised by the feeling of relief that swept over her. Maybe she did have reservations about coming back to England, but she couldn't deny that it was good to know she wasn't on her own anymore. She kissed her mother's cheek then turned to her father.

'Hello, Dad. How are you?'

'All the better for seeing you, sweetheart.' Simon Harper gave her a bear hug then bent down and chucked Millie under the chin. 'And for seeing you, too, poppet.'

Becky felt a lump come to her throat when she saw tears in his eyes. Her parents had been marvellous and she knew that she wouldn't have coped without their support. No matter how difficult it was, she was going to make sure their new living arrangements worked for all of them. Perhaps it would be like stepping back in time, but that didn't necessarily mean it was a bad thing. A lot of good things had happened in the past, like her friendship with Ewan.

Heat rushed through her as she glanced at him. He was standing to one side, obviously giving them the chance to say their hellos in private. It was so typically considerate of him that Becky's heartstrings twanged. Despite his playboy image, Ewan had always been incredibly thoughtful. It was one of the reasons why she'd been attracted to him, that plus the fact that he'd been so exciting and sexy, of course. She had never felt bored when she was with Ewan but wonderfully, vibrantly alive.

She blanked out the thought as she turned to her mother again. She wouldn't allow herself to be seduced by memories. She'd had her fill of relationships and she didn't intend to make the mistake of getting involved again. 'Ewan very kindly helped me with my luggage.'

'Ewan?' Ros Harper repeated uncertainly as she glanced at him. Her face suddenly cleared and she smiled in delight. 'Ewan! What a wonderful surprise.'

'It's good to see you too, Mrs Harper.' Ewan stepped forward and shook hands with Ros then turned to Simon. 'And you, too, sir.'

Simon smiled warmly as he shook the younger man's hand. 'Make that Simon, eh? I heard via the grapevine that you were coming back to England, although I thought you'd been working in Australia, not New Zealand.'

'I was,' Ewan agreed. 'I did a twelve-month stint at a hospital in Sydney.' He shrugged. 'I did consider staying on there but in the end the lure of home was too strong. I popped over to New Zealand on my way back to visit my sister. Shona's third child is due any day and I was hoping it would arrive while I was there, but no such luck.'

'Another grandchild for your parents!' Ros exclaimed. 'How many is that now?'

'Eight…or is it nine?'. Ewan grinned. 'I've lost track. We MacLeods tend to be highly productive in the baby-making department.'

Everyone laughed at the comment, Becky included, although there was a hollow ache inside her. She bent down, tucking a lightweight blanket around Millie so that nobody would notice how much it hurt. She still found it hard to accept that she would never have another child. She loved children and had planned to have at least four, but the accident that had cost Steve his life had robbed her of that chance. She stood up, feeling her heart lurch when she caught Ewan's eyes and saw the concern they held. Surely, he hadn't realised something was wrong?

'Right, let's get you two home.'

Her father's voice broke into her thoughts. Becky quickly settled her bag on her shoulder then took a deep breath before turning to Ewan. Maybe he did suspect that something wasn't right but that was all it would ever be—a suspicion. She wasn't going to tell Ewan the truth about the accident, wasn't going to tell anyone, in fact. It was hard enough having to live with the guilt without everyone knowing what she had done.

'Thank you again for all your help, Ewan. It really was kind of you.'

'My pleasure.'

He smiled but his deep blue eyes were searching as they rested on her. Becky shifted uncomfortably. Maybe she didn't plan on telling people the truth but if anyone could get it out of her, it would be Ewan. She had told Ewan things that she'd told no one else, not even Steve. Definitely not Steve.

He looked away and she breathed a sigh of relief,

which was short-lived when she heard her father ask
him if he wanted a lift. Although she knew it was selfish, she couldn't face the thought of having to travel
all the way back to Devon with Ewan in the car in her
present frame of mind.

'Thank you, but I'm staying in London with my
brother until I can sort out my accommodation. Ryan
and I plan to down a few beers and catch up on what's
been happening.' He laughed. 'Always assuming I manage to stay awake long enough, of course!'

He smiled at them, his gaze lingering a fraction longer on Becky, but she didn't respond. Maybe he would
think she was being churlish but it was better than allowing herself to be drawn into making a confession.
When he bade them farewell, she didn't make a fuss,
certainly didn't make any attempt to arrange to see
him again. Meeting him like this had been a chance
encounter. It wasn't an excuse to resume their former
relationship.

Becky knew she was doing the right thing, yet it
didn't explain the sense of loss she felt as she watched
him wending his way through the crowd. Even though
she knew it was foolish, she was going to miss him.

Ewan took a taxi to his brother's flat and let himself
in, using the key Ryan had left with a neighbour. He
dumped his bag on the living room floor and flopped
down onto a chair with a sigh that stemmed partly from
weariness but mainly from frustration. What was wrong
with Becky? Why had she behaved so warily towards
him?

Closing his eyes, he tried to conjure up her image,
surprised by how easy it was. He'd not thought about

her in ages and yet—hey, presto!—there she was in his head: honey-gold hair, hazel eyes, that pert little nose. She had changed, of course, but she was still incredibly pretty. Although she was a shade too thin in his opinion, she had a very feminine figure with curves in all the right places....

He groaned as his body responded with predictable enthusiasm to that thought. He might be bone-tired but his libido was in fine fettle! Not that it should be a surprise because Becky had always had this effect on him. In fact, he couldn't think of a single woman he'd dated in the past eight years who had aroused him the way Becky had done.

The thought was too near the knuckle. Ewan got up and went into the kitchen. Ryan had told him to make himself at home so he took him at his word as he set to and made himself a fry-up. Eggs, bacon, sausages— the plate was heaving by the time he finished. He sat down at the table and tucked in, but after a couple of mouthfuls was forced to admit defeat. He didn't want food. He wanted answers. He wanted to know what was wrong with Becky and he wouldn't rest until he found out, although he refused to delve too deeply into the reason why. Suffice it to say that Becky had meant a lot to him at one point. Even though that was all in the past, he hoped they could be friends.

He got up and scraped the uneaten food into the bin, trying to ignore the mocking little voice in his head. Friendship was all he wanted from her. Nothing more!

It was several days before Becky got over her jet-lag. Fortunately, Millie didn't seem to be affected by it and soon settled down in their new home. Her parents had

had her old room redecorated so it felt less like stepping back in time than it could have done. They'd also turned her brother's room into a bright and cheerful nursery, complete with lots of colourful posters of Millie's favourite cartoon characters.

Becky could tell they'd gone to a great deal of trouble to make her and Millie feel welcome and she was grateful, but it still felt odd to be living under their roof again. She made up her mind that she would find a place of her own as soon as she could, and that meant finding a job. Although she scoured the local papers each day, there were very few jobs available. As a highly qualified nurse practitioner, she had a lot to offer, but cutbacks in the health service meant there were few posts being advertised. All she could hope was that something would turn up eventually.

She was washing the breakfast dishes a week after she'd returned when her father poked his head round the kitchen door. Millie was helping her and the floor was awash with soap suds. 'Mind you don't slip,' she warned him. 'This little lady gets as much water on the floor as she gets on the dishes.'

'I wonder who she takes after,' Simon said, drolly. He stepped over the puddles and dropped a kiss on his granddaughter's head. 'You are doing a wonderful job helping Mummy, poppet.'

Millie smiled beatifically as she beat her small hands up and down in the water and Becky groaned. 'It'll be like Noah's flood in here soon. We'll need our very own ark!'

Simon laughed. 'It's only water, sweetheart. It will soon mop up. Anyway, seeing as Millie is happily occupied, can I have a word?'

'Of course.' Becky dried her hands on a towel, wondering what he wanted to speak to her about. 'Nothing's wrong, is there?'

'No, no, not at all,' Simon assured her. 'It's just that I have a proposition for you but before I tell you what it is, I want you to promise me that you'll say no if you don't like the idea.'

'That sounds very mysterious,' Becky said, laughing.

Simon smiled. 'I suppose it does. It's just that I don't want you to feel that you're under any sort of...well, obligation.'

'Curiouser and curiouser. Come on, Dad, tell me what's going on.'

'All right. You know that Brenda Roberts took over as practice nurse at the surgery when Emily left to get married?'

'Yes. Brenda came out of retirement so she could help you.'

'That's right.' Simon sighed. 'I was really grateful to her, too. Although we had plenty of interest when we advertised the post, we didn't find anyone who we felt would fit in.'

'It's difficult to find the right person,' Becky observed.

'Exactly. Anyway, Brenda's just informed me that she would like to leave at the end of the month. Apparently, her husband, Fred, is taking early retirement and they've decided to go and live in their apartment in Spain.'

'What a shame!' Becky exclaimed. 'Not for Brenda and Fred of course, but it's going to make life difficult for you and the rest of the team.'

'It is. It will mean us having to advertise again and

that will take time. That's why I was wondering if you'd consider helping out?'

'You want me to cover until you find someone?'

'Yes. Or, better still, maybe consider taking the job on a permanent basis,' Simon said quietly. 'With all the changes we're having to make now that we've been awarded health centre status, I need staff I can rely on. You fit the bill perfectly, darling, although I'll understand if you feel it's too much, living and working with your father.'

'I'd never thought about it,' Becky said slowly. 'But it does make sense. I mean, I need a job and if I'm working here at the surgery then I'll be on hand for Millie. I have to admit that I was worried about leaving her for long stretches, even if she was with Mum.'

'So you'll think about it?' Simon said hopefully.

Becky smiled. 'There's nothing to think about. I'd be delighted to take the job if you think I'm suitable.'

'Great!' Simon gave her a hug then glanced at his watch. He grimaced. 'I know this is a bit of cheek, but is there any chance that you could start right away? We're overrun with patients needing BP checks this morning and it would really help to take the pressure off us if you would give Brenda a hand.'

'Slave driver!' Becky laughed. 'Of course I can start immediately, so long as Mum will look after Millie.'

'Oh, there's no problem about that. Your mother is longing to have this little one all to herself for a couple of hours,' Simon assured her. 'I'll just let her know what's happening.'

Becky cleared up after her father left, feeling her spirits lift when it struck her that she'd taken her first step towards regaining her independence. Once she was earning regular money, she could look for a place of her own, somewhere she could turn into a proper home for her and Millie. Millie needed stability after all the recent upsets and Becky was determined she was going to give her that.

A shadow darkened her face as she lifted the little girl down from the chair and dried her hands. What had Steve said during their last fateful conversation, that he wished they'd never had a child? Her mouth compressed. No way was Millie ever going to find out that her father had wished she hadn't been born! It had been a terrible thing to say even in the heat of anger. She couldn't imagine Ewan even thinking such a thing, let alone saying it.

She sighed as once again she found herself thinking about Ewan. Although she had tried to blot out all thoughts of him, she hadn't succeeded. Their chance encounter had affected her far more than it should have done and she could only thank her lucky stars that it was unlikely they would meet again. Their paths certainly wouldn't cross when Ewan was working in London and she was living and working here.

'Mrs Rose? I'm Ewan MacLeod, one of the registrars. I believe you took a bit of a tumble this morning.'

Ewan smiled at the elderly lady lying on the bed. It was midday and he hadn't stopped since he'd arrived at six that morning. The emergency department of Pinscombe General Hospital was a very busy place. It served the communities of three major towns plus a number of smaller ones like Bride's Bay.

His heart gave that all-too-familiar jolt it had started doing every time Bride's Bay was mentioned, and he swallowed a sigh. He really was a sad case if the mere mention of the place where Becky lived had this effect on him. Drawing up a chair, he sat down beside the bed. It was time to concentrate on his patient.

'Can you tell me what happened, Mrs Rose?'

'It was so silly, really,' the old lady replied. 'I was carrying my washing out to peg it on the line when I tripped over Mog.'

'Mog? Who's that, then? Your dog?'

'No, my cat, of course,' Edith Rose said sharply, treating him to a frosty glare.

Ewan grimaced. 'My mistake. Sorry.' He frowned. 'But why on earth did you call your cat Mog? I thought moggies were mice.'

'Hmm, it all depends which part of the country you come from,' Mrs Rose informed him tartly. 'Where I come from, young man, a moggy is a cat.'

'I stand corrected.' Ewan laughed, pleased to see that there was nothing wrong with her mental faculties. He had a feeling that Mrs Rose wouldn't appreciate the usual questions used to determine an elderly patient's mental prowess, such as the date and the name of the current prime minister. He put a tick in the relevant box on the patient's history and heard the old lady sniff.

'Convinced you that I'm compos mentis, have I?'

'Absolutely.' Ewan put the clipboard down and folded his arms. 'There's nothing wrong with your mind, Mrs Rose.'

'I wish you'd tell that to my son. He seems to think I'm going gaga. No doubt he'll try to use this as an excuse to put me into a nursing home.'

Ewan frowned when he heard the tremor in the old lady's voice. 'I take it that it isn't what you want?'

'Certainly not. I've lived on my own for almost forty years now since my husband died. I couldn't bear the thought of having to live with a group of strangers.'

'There's no reason why you should have to leave your home because of this accident,' Ewan assured her. He picked up the tablet computer and showed her the X-ray she'd had done on admission. 'There's no sign of a fracture. Granted, your leg is badly bruised and the cut will need dressing to make sure it heals properly, but you'll be back on your feet in no time.'

'Are you sure?' Relief washed over the old lady's face when he nodded. 'Thank heavens. Geoffrey has been going on and on about me moving into a home and I was sure this would be the excuse he needed to have me admitted.'

Ewan shook his head. 'No. So long as you feel that you can manage on your own, that's fine. And even if you do have problems, there's help available. Your GP should be able to put you in touch with social services and they can assess the level of help you need.'

'That's a weight off my mind, I can tell you.' Edith Rose smiled at him. 'Thank you, young man. You've made an old lady very happy.'

'Good.' Ewan laughed as he stood up. 'I'm just going to phone your GP and let him know what's happened. As I said, your leg will need dressing so we need to arrange for it to be done at the surgery.'

'Old flesh doesn't heal as fast as young does,' Mrs Rose observed wryly and he grinned.

'I'm afraid not.'

He went to the desk to make the call, unsurprised to discover that Mrs Rose was registered with Bride's Bay Surgery. A lot of the people he'd seen since he'd

started at Pinscombe General had been registered with
the practice, which meant it must be a very busy place
to work. He asked to speak to the practice nurse when
the receptionist answered, shaking his head when one
of the nurses came over to see if he could look at a patient for her.

'I'm tied up at the moment,' he began then stopped
when a voice came over the line, a voice that was all
too familiar.

'Sister Williams speaking. How may I help you?'

Ewan turned to face the wall, not wanting anything
to distract him. The one thing he had never anticipated
was that Becky would answer his call. He took a deep
breath, deliberately ironing all trace of emotion from
his voice. Maybe it did feel as though his head was
being whirled around inside a washing machine on the
spin cycle but he wasn't going to let Becky know that.

'Becky, it's Ewan MacLeod.' He gave a short laugh,
praying that it sounded less forced to her than it did to
him. 'This is a surprise. Again!'

CHAPTER THREE

'EWAN!'

Becky felt shock race through her when she recognised Ewan's voice. It was all she could do to concentrate as he continued in the same teasing tone.

'Of all the surgeries in all the world.... I had no idea you were working there.'

'I...um...it came as a surprise to me too, actually.' She finally managed to gather her addled wits, relieved to hear that she sounded almost normal. Maybe it had been a surprise to hear Ewan's voice but did it really explain why it had sent her into such a spin? She blanked out the thought, not wanting to set off down a route that was guaranteed to lead to more questions. 'Dad needed a practice nurse for the surgery and asked me if I'd consider taking the job, and I agreed.'

'Sounds ideal to me. Not only are you able to earn your living but you're on hand if Millie needs you.'

'Exactly,' Becky agreed, wondering how he always managed to hit on the salient point. Ewan possessed the rare ability to cut through all the dross and see the bigger picture. It was something else she had admired about him, she realised, his ability to get to the heart of a matter with so little fuss. Steve had been the exact opposite, sadly. He'd got so caught up in the details that he had often failed to appreciate the real crux of an issue. Whenever that had happened, he had blamed everyone else, too, rather than himself. It was one of the things she had disliked most about him, in fact.

The thought made her feel incredibly guilty. It didn't seem right that she should compare the two men, especially when she had found her late husband lacking. She hurried on, wanting to get the conversation onto a more solid footing. 'Anyway, I take it that this isn't a social call?'

'No. I have one of your patients with me, a Mrs Edith Rose.' Ewan was all business as he explained what had happened. 'The cut on her leg is quite deep and it will need dressing. I was hoping I could arrange for her to be seen at the surgery.'

'Of course.' Becky opened the diary, relieved to turn her attention to other matters. Ewan was Ewan and Steve had been Steve; she mustn't make the mistake of weighing one against the other. 'I'll book her in for Wednesday morning at eleven. If the dressing's only been done today, it would be better not to disturb it, although tell her to contact me if she has any problems, won't you?'

'I shall. She's a feisty old lady, very alert and determined, although she does seem worried that her son may try to use the accident as an excuse to have her admitted to a nursing home.'

'I see.' Becky frowned. 'You don't believe that's necessary, obviously.'

'Definitely not,' he said firmly. 'In my opinion, Mrs Rose is more than capable of looking after herself, although perhaps she could do with a bit of help.'

'Would you like me to have word with her about what social services can offer?' Becky suggested.

'Are you a mind reader? That's exactly what I was going to ask you to do!'

Becky felt her breath catch when she heard him laugh. He really did have the most attractive laugh, she thought, so soft and deep and so very, very sexy. She took a quick breath, forcing some much-needed air into her lungs. 'Great minds think alike, or so they say?'

'They certainly do.'

There it was again, that delicious, toe-tingling rumble coming down the line, and Becky's lungs went into spasm once more. She was glad that Ewan didn't seem to expect a reply as he explained that he would fax through a copy of Mrs Rose's notes. By the time he'd finished, she was able to speak again, although she kept it brief, wary of pushing things too far.

'I'll make sure the information is entered on her file.'

'Thanks. Right, I won't keep you any longer. Good to speak to you, Becky. Maybe we'll run into one another again at some point.'

'Maybe.'

Becky hung up then went to the window, needing a few minutes to herself before she called in her next patient. So Ewan wasn't working in London as she'd thought. He was right here in Devon, just a few miles away. Even though it shouldn't make a scrap of difference, she knew that it did. Did she want to see him again? If anyone had suggested it a week ago, her answer would have been a resounding no, but she was no longer sure. Talking to Ewan had aroused feelings inside her she had never expected to feel again after what had happened with Steve.

Discovering that Steve had had an affair with one of his colleagues had turned her off sex. Even though she had tried to overcome her distaste and make a go of their marriage for Millie's sake, making love had become a penance rather than a pleasure. The fact that Steve had used it to excuse his own behaviour had only made matters worse. He'd called her frigid, told her that it was little wonder he'd had to seek comfort in another woman's arms. Although Becky had known it wasn't true, part of her had wondered if she was to blame in some way. Now, after talking to Ewan, she realised how unjust the accusation had been.

She wasn't frigid—far from it! She could and did respond to a man. However, the fact that it was Ewan who pushed all the right buttons was what worried her. Ewan wasn't interested in settling down. He enjoyed playing the field and one woman would never be enough for him, not that she was in the market for another relationship. She had tried her best to make her marriage work and failed, and she wasn't going to put herself through that heartache again, especially when there was even less chance now of a relationship working. Maybe Ewan was happily single at the moment but the time might come when he decided to settle down and start a family, and a family was the one thing she couldn't give him or any other man.

She sighed. It would be far better if she steered well clear of Ewan in future.

Ewan found it impossible to stop thinking about Becky. At odd moments throughout the week, thoughts of her would pop into his head. He couldn't rid himself of the thought that there was something troubling her and it only served to pique his interest even more. When his mother phoned and invited him to lunch on Sunday, he found himself agreeing even though he had planned to start redecorating the flat he was renting. The previous tenant had had a penchant for red and after a couple of weeks of waking up to pulsating scarlet walls, he desperately needed to do something about it. However, the décor could wait. Finding out what was worrying Becky seemed far more important.

He set off early on Sunday morning and made good time. It was the beginning of April and the main bulk of tourists hadn't arrived yet so the roads were clear. His parents lived in Denton's Cove but he bypassed the turning to their house and headed into Bride's Bay. It was just gone ten when he drew up outside the surgery, which was attached to Becky's parents' home, and he frowned when he saw all the building work that had been taking place. He'd heard that the practice had been awarded health centre status and it was obvious that a lot of changes were being made.

He made his way to the back door and lifted his hand to knock when he heard voices coming from the garden. Turning, he peered over the hedge and felt his heart lift when he saw Becky. She was pushing Millie on a pint-sized swing attached to a bough of the old apple tree. She was wearing jeans and a white sweater, her honey-gold hair pulled up into a ponytail. She looked so young and so lovely that Ewan felt his senses swim. Eight years may have passed but he was still attracted to her. It was only when Millie let out a shriek of laughter that he pulled himself together.

'It sounds as though you two are having fun,' he called, adopting a deliberately upbeat tone. He wasn't going to make the mistake of harking back to the past. Becky had chosen Steve and it had been the right decision for all of them. Maybe he would like to help her if he could but it was purely out of friendship. He wasn't planning to get back with her, not that Becky would be interested even if he was.

'Ewan!'

Ewan heard the dismay in her voice and grimaced. It was obvious that his arrival was less of a pleasant surprise than it could have been. He summoned a smile, not wanting her to suspect how much the idea stung. 'I thought I'd pop in to see how you were doing. I'm having lunch with my parents so I was heading this way.'

'Oh, I see.'

She dredged up a smile but it was such a poor effort that Ewan found himself wishing he hadn't bothered. Even if there was something troubling her, why would she choose to tell him?

'I should have phoned first.' He shrugged dismissively. Although he wasn't vain, most of the women he knew would have been more than happy to have him turn up on their doorsteps unannounced. 'I've been working in Australia for too long. I'd forgotten how much more formal life is here in England. Sorry.'

'It's fine, really. I…erm…it's nice to see you.'

Ewan's teeth snapped together. *Nice!* Quite frankly, she couldn't have said anything more guaranteed to offend him. The first prickle of anger ran through his veins and he smiled sardonically. 'There's no need to be polite, Becky. I can tell you're not exactly overjoyed to see me. Not to worry, I'm not stopping. Enjoy your day.'

He headed back up the path, his temper hovering just below boiling point. So Becky wasn't interested in seeing him; so what? It wasn't going to make any difference to his life.

'Ewan, wait!'

Ewan stopped reluctantly. He turned around, feeling his heart jolt when he saw her hurrying after him. She was carrying Millie in her arms and the picture they made was one he knew would stay with him for a long time to come. His pulse was racing when Becky came to a halt in front of him, the blood pounding through his veins in a way that made him feel both dizzy and yet wonderfully clear-headed.

This was what he wanted from life, he realised with sudden, startling clarity. He didn't need riches to be happy or professional acclaim. He just wanted someone to love and their child, and he would have everything he could possibly desire. The only thing wrong with the scenario was that it was Becky who featured in it, Becky who had made it abundantly clear that she didn't want anything to do with him!

Becky could feel herself trembling as she put Millie down. Even though she knew she was probably making a mistake, she couldn't let Ewan leave like this. He had come with the express intention of checking she was all right and all she'd done was throw his kindness back in his face.

'Don't go,' she said, her voice catching. 'I know I wasn't exactly welcoming, but please don't leave like this.'

'There's no point my staying if you don't want me here.' His tone was cool and she shivered. Ewan sighed softly. 'It's all right, Becky. I understand, really I do.'

'Do you?' It was impossible to keep the anxiety out of her voice and he grimaced.

'Yes. You're worried in case I want to pick up where we left off.' He didn't give her chance to reply as he continued flatly. 'Well, there's no need. That's all in the past and I just thought it would be good if we could be friends.'

'Friends?' she echoed uncertainly. Was he right? Was she worried in case he tried to resurrect their relationship, or was it more complicated than that?

'Yes.' He smiled. 'I could be wrong, but I've a feeling you could do with a friend right now.'

Becky felt a surge of emotion well up inside her when she heard the sympathy in his voice. She swallowed hard, desperately trying to hold back her tears. Ewan obviously realised her predicament because he bent down and smiled at Millie.

'How about another go on the swing, poppet?'

Becky watched as he led Millie back into the garden. How had he known that she didn't want Millie to see her crying? she wondered. He had accused her of being a mind-reader the other day, but he appeared to be equally skilled in the art.

It was a worrying thought in view of the fact that there was a lot she didn't want him to know. Becky took her time, wanting to be sure that she had herself under control before she went to join him and Millie. The little girl was having the time of her life, kicking her legs up and down as Ewan pushed the swing.

''Gain! 'Gain!' she shouted each time the swing slowed down.

'That's high enough, sweetie. We don't want you flying right up into the sky, do we?' Ewan said, laughing. He glanced at Becky and raised his brows. 'All right?'

'Fine.' She shrugged, embarrassed about what had

happened. Normally, she kept a rein on her emotions but she didn't seem able to do that when Ewan was around. 'Things just get on top of me at times, that's all.'

'It's only to be expected after everything you've been through.'

The kindness in his voice brought more tears to her eyes and she blinked them away. 'Perhaps. But I try to hold it together for Millie's sake.'

'I can understand that, but you can't be brave all the time. It won't do you any good in the long run.'

He touched her hand, his fingers lingering for just a moment before he turned to push the swing once more, but Becky felt a frisson of awareness race from her hand and travel through her entire body. It felt as though every cell was suddenly on fire, creating an immense amount of heat inside her. It had been ages since she had felt this way, she realised. Not since those first heady days when she had met Ewan at the hospital had a touch aroused her so swiftly, so completely. She had never felt this way with Steve, not even when they had made love.

The thought was too unsettling to deal with. Becky summoned a smile, refusing to dwell on it. 'Do you fancy a cup of coffee?'

'I'd love one, but don't go to any trouble on my account,' Ewan said flatly. 'I didn't mean to intrude, Becky. I just wanted to check you were all right.'

'I know.' She looked into his eyes, feeling warmth envelop her again when she saw the concern they held. Despite the less than effusive reception he'd received, it was obvious that Ewan genuinely cared about her. She sighed, knowing that she owed him an apology. 'I really do appreciate you coming here, Ewan, even if it didn't seem like it.'

'It doesn't matter. So long as you're all right, that's the main thing.'

He smiled at her, his face breaking into a heart-melting smile, and Becky's heart did what was expected and melted. She turned away, afraid that if she didn't put some distance between them she would do something really stupid. Hurrying into the kitchen, she filled the kettle, her mind racing. Tempting though it was, it wouldn't be fair to pour out the whole story to Ewan and expect him to absolve her of any guilt. Maybe he wanted them to be friends, but how would he feel if he found out the truth about the accident and her part in it? Would he still want to be her friend then?

Pain lanced her heart as she watched him pushing the swing. She wouldn't blame him if he didn't want anything to do with her when he found out that she was responsible for Steve's death.

CHAPTER FOUR

'THAT'S GREAT. Thank you.'

Ewan spooned sugar into the mug of coffee that Becky had placed in front of him, wondering what on earth he was doing. What was the point of dragging this out when it was obvious that she had mixed feelings about him being here? He should have taken his leave when he'd had the chance, once he was sure she was all right.

He sighed as he watched her carry Millie into the house for her morning nap. Seeing Becky cry like that had been so damned hard. He had ached to take her in his arms and comfort her, but what comfort could he have offered when she was grieving for the man she loved? His heart spasmed with a pain that surprised him. It shouldn't matter how Becky felt about her late husband, but he'd be lying if he said that he didn't care.

'She went out like a light. She'll probably sleep till lunchtime by the look of her.'

Becky came back and sat down. Ewan summoned a smile, determined that he wasn't going to let her know how ambivalent he felt. Maybe he was still attracted to her but that was all it was; he'd get over it. 'She seems happy enough, I must say. I take it that she's adapted to living here.'

'She has.'

Becky picked up her mug and blew gently on her coffee to cool it. Ewan looked away when he felt his stomach muscles clench. The sight of her beautiful lips puckering that way was playing havoc with his self-control. He had to force himself to concentrate as she continued in a no-nonsense tone that immediately demolished any half-baked ideas he'd been harbouring about her doing it deliberately. Becky definitely wasn't trying to be provocative!

'I was really worried that the move would unsettle her but Millie's taken it in her stride. She seems really happy living here with my parents.'

'It must be a relief,' Ewan observed, doing his best to match her tone. He had to accept that Becky wasn't interested in him *that* way. Maybe she had been interested once but it was a long time ago.

'It is.' She took a sip of coffee then put the mug down with a sigh. 'Although it wasn't just Millie I was worried about, if I'm honest. I wasn't sure if moving back here was the right thing for me either.'

'Because it was a wrench to leave the life you and Steve had created for yourselves?' he suggested, although it felt a little like rubbing salt into a wound. However, he couldn't ignore the fact that she had been married even if he wanted to.

'It was more the thought of having to move back in with my parents, actually,' she admitted, then flushed when he looked at her in surprise.

'Really?' Ewan found it impossible to keep the astonishment out of his voice.

'Yes, really.' Her tone was defensive. 'Steve and I hadn't lived in Christchurch for very long. We moved around quite a bit so that Steve could further his career.' She shrugged. 'I expect that's why it didn't seem such a wrench to leave—I hadn't had time to put down any roots.'

'I see.' It made sense, yet Ewan had a feeling that it wasn't the real explanation. He frowned as he weighed up what he'd heard. Had Becky's marriage not been as happy as he'd thought, or was he merely putting his own interpretation on what she'd said? He realised that he needed to find out, although he wasn't prepared to examine his reasons too closely. Suffice it to say that he needed to know all he could if he was to help her.

'So you moved to Christchurch because Steve got a job there?'

'That's right. I would have preferred to stay in the country for Millie's sake, but Steve was offered a consultant's post so we moved to the city. He didn't want to be too far from the hospital in case he was called in after hours,' she added hastily.

'I thought he worked in orthopaedics,' Ewan said, frowning. In his experience it was rare for a consultant in that field to be called into work. Normally, one of the registrars would be expected to cover, unless it was some sort of life-threatening emergency, and they didn't happen very often.

'That's right.' She took another sip of her coffee and he sensed that she was playing for time. 'Steve was... well, he was very committed. He never minded being called back into work.'

'Highly commendable,' Ewan observed, wondering why he didn't believe her. Why on earth would Becky make such a claim if it weren't true? After all, it didn't matter to him how Steve had conducted his life. However, the fact that she had felt it necessary to lie piqued his interest. 'Did he get called in a lot?'

'Quite a bit.' She grimaced. 'You know what it's like—something crops up and the staff don't want to take responsibility so they call in the boss.'

It was so far removed from his own experiences that Ewan was stuck for an answer. Mercifully, he was saved from having to reply when Becky's parents appeared. They had another couple with them plus a little boy, slightly older than Millie, and they greeted him in delight.

'Ewan! How lovely to see you.' Ros kissed him on the cheek. 'Becky didn't mention you were coming. I wish she had done. Simon and I wouldn't have gone for our weekly constitutional if we'd known you were planning to visit. It would have been the perfect excuse to enjoy a lazy Sunday morning!'

Ewan laughed as he stood up. 'Becky had no idea, I'm afraid. I'm having lunch with my parents so I decided to drop in on my way over there.'

'Well, I'm very glad that you did.' Ros turned to the other couple. 'You won't have met Ewan. His family live in Denton's Cove so he and Becky have known each other for years. He's a doctor too, although he's been working overseas for the past few years. Ewan, I'd like you to meet Tom and Hannah. They both work at the surgery. Oh, and this little fellow is Charlie.'

'Good to meet you.' Ewan shook hands, taking an immediate liking to the other couple. He smiled at Charlie, taking note of the braces on his feet. He'd seen them before and guessed the little boy had been born with club feet. 'And you too, Charlie.'

The child solemnly shook his hand then hurried away, heading straight for the apple tree. Hannah laughed as she dropped her bag onto the table. 'I wondered how long it would be before he made for the swing. He loves it!'

Everyone laughed as she raced after him. Ewan remained standing as the others sat down. 'It's time I was on my way. Good to see you all again, and to meet you and Hannah,' he added, smiling at Tom.

'Ditto,' Tom said, returning his smile. 'I don't know if Becky has mentioned it, but Charlie is being christened next Sunday. We're having everyone back to ours for lunch afterwards and it would be great if you could join us, Ewan.'

'Oh, but…'

'I don't think…' Ewan stopped when he and Becky both spoke at once. He shrugged when he saw the surprise on Tom's face. 'What we're trying to say is that Becky and I aren't an item, if that's what you thought.'

'Sorry.' Tom laughed. 'My mistake. Still, it makes no difference. I know Hannah would love you to come along if you're free.'

'Thanks. I'm not sure what hours I'm working next week but I appreciate it.'

It wasn't strictly true. Ewan had seen the coming week's roster and although he couldn't remember all his hours, he knew that he had Sunday off. However, it seemed politic not to accept the invitation when he sensed that Becky wouldn't approve. He adopted a deliberately neutral expression as he turned to her. Maybe they would be friends and maybe they wouldn't, but one thing was certain—they would never be lovers.

The thought was far too unsettling. Ewan blocked it from his mind as he smiled at her. 'Thanks again for the coffee, Becky. I'll see you around.'

'I expect so.'

She returned his smile but there was no real warmth in it. Ewan guessed that she was merely going through the motions because the others were watching. He sighed as he headed up the path and got into his car. He may as well accept that Becky wasn't interested in him and stop worrying about it.

The next week flew past. Although Becky had agreed to work only mornings while Brenda was still there, she found herself doing extra hours most days. A couple of practices in the area had closed in the past few years and their patients had transferred to Bride's Bay's list. It meant that everyone was under a lot of pressure but Becky was glad, even if it did mean her spending less time than she would have liked with Millie. At least while she was working, she wasn't thinking about Ewan, and that had to be a blessing.

She had found it increasingly difficult to put him out of her mind since Sunday morning. Although she knew it was stupid, she couldn't help wishing that she hadn't lied to him about Steve's reasons for living in the city. She felt guilty about what she'd done and confused as to why she'd felt it necessary. After all, what difference would it make to Ewan if he found out that her marriage had been less than perfect?

By the time Friday arrived, Becky was worn out from worrying about it. When Mrs Rose arrived to have her dressing changed, she had to make a determined effort to appear upbeat.

'Come in, Mrs Rose,' she said, ushering the old lady over to a chair. 'How are you today?'

'Fine, thank you, dear.' Edith Rose winced as she sank down onto the seat and Becky frowned.

'Is your leg troubling you?'

'No, no, it's fine. I just get the odd twinge in my hip from time to time.' Mrs Rose adjusted her position and smiled. 'There. That's better.'

'Good.' Becky went to fetch the tray she'd prepared, making a mental note to ask her father to take a look at Mrs Rose. Although the old lady had made light of it, she suspected that her hip was causing her some discomfort. She carried the tray over to the desk and then donned a pair of gloves. 'I'll just remove the old dressing and see how the cut is doing. It may be a little uncomfortable, I'm afraid.'

'You just do what you have to, my dear,' Mrs Rose told her, stoically.

Becky peeled away the dressing, pleased to see that there was no sign of infection. Although the cut was deep, it was already starting to heal. 'That looks fine. Using a non-adherent dressing means that the new tissue that's formed hasn't been disturbed.'

'That nice young doctor I saw at the hospital insisted the nurse should use one of those special dressings,' Mrs Rose told her. 'She was going to put a gauze pad on my leg but he told her to fetch something else.'

'He was quite right,' Becky agreed, feeling a small rush of pleasure run through her. Although she knew it was silly, it was good to hear Ewan receiving praise. 'The last thing we want is delicate new tissue being disturbed because the wrong type of dressing has been used.'

'That's what he said.' The old lady laughed. 'You two would get on very well, my dear. You obviously have a lot in common!'

Becky smiled although she didn't say anything. It was unsettling to realise that she and Ewan held such similar views. She gently cleaned the area around the cut and then placed a fresh dressing over it.

'There, that's all done. If it carries on healing as well as it's been doing then it won't be long before you don't need any more dressings.' She straightened Mrs Rose's skirt then helped her to her feet, frowning when she heard the old lady suck in her breath. 'Is your hip bothering you again?'

'Just another twinge,' Mrs Rose assured her. However, Becky could tell that she was making light of how painful it really was.

'Would you like me to ask one of the doctors to take a look at it, seeing as you're here?' she suggested.

Mrs Rose shook her head. 'Oh, no, dear. There's no need. It's just a twinge, as I said.' The old lady smiled brightly. 'It's all part and parcel of getting old, I'm afraid.'

Becky laughed dutifully although she couldn't help feeling concerned as she saw Mrs Rose out. She found herself wondering if Mrs Rose's reluctance to have her hip examined had something to do with what Ewan had told her. If the old lady was worried that her son would have her admitted to a nursing home if he could prove she couldn't manage on her own, then she would be wary of admitting that she had a problem.

Becky decided that she would mention her concerns

to the rest of the team. They held a weekly team meeting each Monday when everyone had the chance to talk over any problems that had arisen. She made a note to bring it up the following Monday, thinking idly that it would have been even better if she could have discussed it with Ewan. He always had such a clear view of any problems and she was sure that he would have come up with a solution.

She sighed. That was the *fourth* time she'd thought about Ewan in under half an hour. He seemed to be taking over her life and it had to stop. Ewan was history; whatever might have been between them was over and done with. If she said it often enough, hopefully her brain would get the message.

Although Ewan was used to hard work, he had to admit that he had never worked as hard as he did at Pinscombe General. The fact that they were carrying several vacancies meant there was extra pressure on the staff. He arrived early and left late, usually so exhausted that he could barely summon the energy to make himself a drink let alone a meal when he got home.

As for his social life, it was non-existent. Although several of the nurses had made it clear that they would welcome his attentions, he was far too busy to think about dating, or that's what he told himself. It was easier than admitting that he wasn't interested in them now that he'd met Becky again.

Saturday rolled around and he was working the two-to-ten shift. The other registrar had called in sick on Friday so Ewan made a point of arriving early. He was glad that he had when he saw the queue in Reception.

'What's happened?' he asked, looping his stethoscope around his neck. 'Has war been declared in Devon or something?'

'It seems like it.' Cathy Morrison, the senior sister, rolled her eyes. 'It's been non-stop ever since I got here at six this morning.' She plonked a case file on the counter. 'Can you take a look at this one first? She's been here almost three hours now and you know what'll happen if the bean-counters flag up that we've kept a patient waiting for that length of time.'

'We'll be marched outside and shot at dawn?' Ewan suggested, drolly.

'Worse. We'll be sent on a time management course!'

'Fate worse than death,' Ewan concurred, grinning. He headed to the cubicles and didn't leave them again for the next six hours. Cuts, bruises, fractures, burns: he dealt with the lot. By the time he was able to snatch a break, he had lost track of the cases he'd seen. As he made his way to the canteen, he found himself thinking that it was a good job he hadn't accepted Tom's invitation to the christening. After an evening like this, all he wanted to do tomorrow was sleep!

His heart gave an unruly little hiccup as he found himself tagging on a codicil. All he wanted to do was sleep...with Becky.

Becky took Millie to the beach on Saturday afternoon. Although it was rather dull and cloudy, at least it was dry. She helped Millie make some sand pies and then they went looking for crabs. There were several other families there and Becky couldn't help feeling a little wistful as she watched them. Although she intended to do everything possible to make sure Millie enjoyed a happy childhood, the fact was that she was a single

mother and it would never be the same as Millie having two parents to love and care for her.

The thought immediately made her think about Ewan
for some reason and she sighed because it was stupid to
place Ewan in this context. Ewan had never made any
secret of the fact that he wasn't interested in settling
down. At least he'd known what he'd wanted, unlike
Steve. Although Steve had professed to want a family,
he hadn't been a good father. He'd been too self-cen-
tred, put his own needs before anyone else's, including
Millie's. Even if the accident hadn't happened, it was
doubtful if he would have stayed around long enough
to watch Millie growing up.

In a strange way, Becky felt better for having faced
the truth at last. In the past year, she had skirted around
it, mainly because she'd known how upset her parents
would be if they found out that her marriage had been
a disaster. Although she still didn't intend to tell them,
at least she had come to terms with it and that had to be
a good thing. If only she could get over her guilt about
the accident, maybe she could move on.

She took Millie home, feeling more at ease than she
had felt for a while. Her parents were going out to dinner that night so she made Millie's tea. Although it
was the little girl's favourite, she didn't eat very much
and she refused the yoghurt that Becky offered her for
dessert. She seemed tired and rather listless so Becky
decided to put her to bed as soon as she'd had her bath.

She settled Millie in her cot, leaving the door ajar so
she could hear her if she woke, then went downstairs
and made herself some supper. As soon as she'd finished, she ran upstairs to check on the little girl, her
heart turning over when she saw Millie lying stiff and

rigid in the cot. Millie's lips were rimmed with blue, her breathing was laboured and when Becky felt her forehead, it was burning hot. Millie had suffered a febrile convulsion the previous year and Becky realised in horror that she was having another one.

Becky ran downstairs and tried to phone her father but the call went straight to voice mail. She bit her lip, wondering who she could ask for help. She needed to get Millie to hospital and she couldn't drive as well as look after her. After a moment's thought, she phoned Tom and Hannah. Hannah answered.

'Hannah, it's Becky.' Becky didn't waste time on pleasantries. 'Millie's having a febrile convulsion. Mum and Dad are out and I need someone to run us to the hospital. It will be faster than calling an ambulance.'

'I'll be straight there,' Hannah said immediately. 'Try to keep her cool in the meantime. You know the drill.'

'Will do.'

Becky left the door on the latch then ran upstairs, grabbing a facecloth off the rack in the bathroom on the way. She soaked it in lukewarm water then went into the nursery and sponged Millie's hands and face. The little girl was wearing only a cotton sleep suit but Becky slid it off and sponged her body as well. By the time Hannah arrived, Millie felt a little cooler and the rigidity in her limbs was starting to ease.

'How long has she been like this?' Hannah asked, slipping a thermometer under the child's arm.

'Ten, possibly fifteen minutes.' Becky bit her lip. 'It's all my fault. She seemed very listless when I put her to bed. I should have stayed and checked if anything was wrong with her.'

'You weren't to know this would happen,' Hannah

said soothingly. She checked Millie's temperature and frowned. 'It's still very high. We need to bring her temperature down and as we can't administer any drugs orally, it will have to be done via an IV drip. Can you wet a sheet and wrap her in it? That will help to keep her cool while we get her to hospital.'

Becky soaked a sheet in warm water and wrapped Millie in it. Hannah had the engine running when she carried the little girl outside. The drive to the hospital seemed endless even though Becky knew that Hannah was going as fast as she could. Millie kept drifting in and out of consciousness although, thankfully, she didn't suffer another convulsion.

Hannah drew up outside ED. 'You take her in while I park the car. I'll be with you as soon as I can.'

Becky slid out of the car and ran inside. She looked round, trying to get her bearings. Reception. Triage. Treatment rooms…

'Becky? What is it? What's happened?'

All of a sudden Ewan was there and Becky felt a rush of relief hit her. 'It's Millie. She's had a convulsion,' she began then couldn't go on as the shock of what had happened caught up with her.

Ewan put his hand under her elbow. 'Through here.' He steered her into a treatment room, gently taking Millie off her and laying her on the couch. Pressing the bell, he summoned one of the nurses. 'I need a fan in here, please, and a fine bore cannula.'

He rattled off a list of what he needed, his tone so calm and controlled that Becky felt some of her fear start to ease. Drawing up a chair beside the bed, he sat her down next to Millie. 'She's going to be fine, Becky. I promise you.'

He squeezed her shoulder, his fingers biting gently into her flesh, and she shuddered. 'I was so scared, Ewan.'

'I know.' Bending, he looked into her eyes. 'I know you're scared but I won't let anything bad happen to her. Trust me.'

He straightened up as the nurse came back with a fan and the rest of the items he'd requested. Becky took a deep breath as she watched him. Cannulating veins as tiny as Millie's wasn't easy, as she knew from experience, but Ewan didn't hesitate; within seconds the line was in and Millie was receiving the drugs she needed to lower her temperature. Ewan knew what he was doing and she trusted him to do everything necessary to help Millie. He would be exactly the same with any other child but she knew this was different. Ewan would do everything possible to help Millie because he cared about her. And he cared about Millie because Millie was *her* daughter.

Becky's heart filled with warmth. Knowing that Ewan cared made such a difference.

CHAPTER FIVE

EWAN CHECKED THE monitor, nodding when he saw that Millie's temperature had dropped. Although it certainly wasn't the first time he had treated a child who had suffered a febrile convulsion, there was no point pretending that he hadn't been worried.

He sighed. Although he knew it was ridiculous to feel personally involved, he couldn't help it. Millie was Becky's daughter and that made a world of difference. Turning, he smiled at her, his heart aching when he saw the worry on her face. Becky had been through enough without having to contend with this as well.

'Her temperature's falling. Give it another half-hour and it should be back to normal.'

'Thank heavens.' Becky looked up, her hazel eyes shadowed. 'It's all my fault. I knew Millie wasn't herself and I should have kept a closer watch over her.'

'Now you're being silly.' Ewan drew up a chair and sat down. Taking her hand, he gently squeezed it, trying to ignore the rush of sensations that flooded his body. There was a time and a place for feelings like those, and this was neither. 'You're not psychic, Becky. You weren't to know that her temperature would shoot up like that.'

'No...' It was obvious that she didn't believe him and his hand tightened. He hated to think that she was beating herself up when there was no need.

'No,' he repeated firmly. He leant forward and looked into her eyes. 'You know as well as I do that a child can be perfectly fine one minute and running a fever the next. It could have happened to any child and it's just unfortunate that Millie's brain couldn't handle the rapid rise in her temperature.'

'The first time it happened, they told me that she'd grow out of it,' she said, obviously seeking reassurance.

'That's right.' Ewan managed to curb the urge to put his arms around her. Millie was his patient and Becky was her mother; he had to behave with professional decorum. 'Once the temperature-lowering mechanism in her brain has matured, it will be able to deal with any sudden rise in her temperature.'

He released her hand and stood up, determined that he wasn't going to let her know how difficult it was to maintain his distance. Becky didn't need any more pressure on her tonight.

'But until it matures, it can happen again,' she said anxiously. 'I'd rather you told me the truth, Ewan, please.'

'Then, yes, it could.' He sighed inwardly, realising that no amount of reassurance would fully erase her fear. 'That's why we advise parents to be proactive. At the first sign of fever, you need to give Millie liquid paracetamol and repeat the dose every four to six hours as necessary. Sponging her with lukewarm water and removing her clothing—as you did tonight—will also help.'

'That's what I was told the last time,' she said in a

wobbly little voice. 'Which proves that what I said was true. If I'd been more vigilant, this might never have happened.'

'You can't watch her every minute of the day,' Ewan said sternly. He shook his head when she went to speak. 'I mean it, Becky. It won't do you or Millie any good if you start being overly protective.'

He looked round when the door opened, summoning a smile when he saw Hannah. Maybe he was wrong to take such a hard line but he hated to hear Becky berating herself when there was no need.

'Millie's temperature is dropping. It shouldn't be long before it's back to normal,' he told the other woman, wondering if *he* was in danger of committing the same error. After all, Becky was a grown woman and she didn't need him looking out for her.

'That's great news!' Hannah turned to Becky and smiled. 'You must be so relieved. I know I would be if it happened to Charlie.'

'I am.' Becky managed to smile but it was a poor effort.

Ewan shrugged when Hannah looked at him. The thought that he was becoming far too involved had touched a nerve. He and Becky weren't a couple and it would be a mistake to imagine that she needed his protection. 'Becky thinks it was her fault this happened. I've told her it wasn't, but she isn't convinced.'

'A mother's angst,' Hannah said lightly, giving Becky a hug. 'If I had a pound for every time I've blamed myself when something has happened to Charlie, I'd be a rich woman!'

Becky laughed shakily. 'So it's not just me who feels guilty all the time?'

'Nope. It comes with the territory, love.' Hannah straightened up and glanced at her watch. 'I just need to phone Tom and let him know what's happening. Will you be sending Millie home once her temperature's back to normal or do you intend to keep her in?'

'I'd prefer to keep her here for a while longer just to be on the safe side,' Ewan explained. He hurried on when he saw Becky blanch. 'Not that I'm expecting anything to go wrong. However, I prefer to err on the side of caution when I'm dealing with a child.'

'Quite right,' Hannah said firmly. 'I'll let Tom know that I'll be a while yet.'

'You don't need to stay,' Becky protested. 'We'll be fine, honestly.'

'I can keep an eye on them,' Ewan assured her. He didn't look at Becky mainly because he didn't want to see that his offer wasn't welcome. He cleared his throat, calling himself every kind of fool for allowing the thought to upset him. 'I'm here till ten, probably longer if no agency staff turn up, so I'll be on hand if Becky needs anything.'

'Well, if you're sure?' Hannah looked from him to Becky.

'You go,' Becky said firmly. 'It's the christening tomorrow and you must have loads to do.'

'That's true, although I'm happy to stay if you want me to,' Hannah demurred.

'I'll be fine.' She turned to Ewan and he felt his heart jerk when he saw the expression in her eyes. Far from disliking the idea of him being around, she actually seemed to welcome it. It was hard to contain his delight as she continued, 'Ewan will take good care of us.'

'I'm sure he will,' Hannah agreed, and there was

something in her voice that would have made Ewan blush if he'd been the blushing sort.

He quickly excused himself and went to see what other cases were lined up for him, trying not to read anything into what had happened, but it was impossible. Becky hadn't wanted to get rid of him, amazingly enough. On the contrary, she had seemed pleased that he would be sticking around. Did it mean that she was having second thoughts about him? But second thoughts about what, exactly? About him becoming more than just a friend? Was that what *he* wanted?

He grimaced. Maybe he was very attracted to Becky, but he'd been in this position before. And when push had come to shove she had chosen to stay with Steve. If he was honest, he knew it had been the right decision too. Although he had felt things for Becky he had never felt for any woman before or since, he hadn't been ready to settle down. Becky had understood that, which was why she had decided to stay with Steve and it had been the right decision for her too. She had married Steve and been perfectly happy… Hadn't she?

Ewan sighed. He had no right to speculate on the state of Becky's marriage. Maybe he was looking for flaws because it was so hard to accept that she had loved Steve and was still grieving for him. He should take it as a warning, in fact, and not get any more involved than he already was. There was no point setting his sights on Becky when she was still in love with her late husband.

Becky checked her watch, frowning when she discovered that it was almost midnight. Leaning over, she laid the back of her hand on Millie's forehead. Although she could see from the monitor that Millie's temperature was normal, motherly instinct had her testing it the old-fashioned way. A smile curved her lips when she felt the coolness of her daughter's skin. It seemed that tonight's little drama had been successfully concluded thanks to Ewan.

As though thinking about him had conjured him up, he suddenly appeared. He smiled when he saw what she was doing. 'Don't you trust the monitor?'

'Yes, but I just like to check for myself that she's all right.' Becky returned his smile, wondering if he realised that her attitude towards him had changed. Ewan had always been extremely perceptive and it wouldn't surprise her if he had noticed that she had softened towards him. How did she feel about that? she wondered, then realised that she was far too tired to worry about it.

'Well, if you want my professional opinion then I'd say she's fine. Her temperature's been steady for over an hour now and I can't see it rising again.' He made a note on Millie's chart, stifling a yawn as he put it back in the holder. 'Excuse me! I'm afraid all the late nights are catching up with me.'

What sort of late nights? Becky wondered. Did he mean that he'd been working late or that he'd been out enjoying himself? That thought immediately led to the next one; who he'd been enjoying himself with. It was surprising how unsettling she found the idea. She cleared her throat, not wanting to go down the route of imagining Ewan and some woman out on the tiles or, worse still, spending cosy nights in together. What Ewan did in his private life wasn't any of her business.

'So you think it's safe to take her home?' she asked, focusing on Millie.

'Perfectly safe.' He smiled understandingly. 'You're

bound to feel anxious, Becky. It's only natural, but she's fine. Believe me.'

'I do believe you.'

She gave him a quick smile, afraid that she might give too much away. Maybe she did feel differently about him, less wary and more open to having him around, but she mustn't be silly. They weren't going to get back together, neither did she want them to. There were too many reasons why it could never happen, starting with the most important one of all, the fact that Ewan would probably want children some day, and children were the one thing she couldn't give him.

'You've been absolutely brilliant tonight,' she said sincerely, her heart aching at the thought of never being able to bear another child. If she was guilty of causing Steve's death then surely she'd been punished for it? 'I'm really grateful for everything you've done for Millie.'

'I was only doing my job,' he said lightly, but they both knew it had been far more than that.

Becky felt heat rush through her when she saw the warmth in his eyes. There wasn't a doubt in her mind that Ewan genuinely cared about her and even if it was only the sort of concern one felt for a friend, she found it incredibly comforting. It was on the tip of her tongue to say something when one of the nurses poked her head round the door.

'There's a phone call for you, Mrs Williams. It's your father.'

'Oh, right. Thank you.' Becky stood up then glanced uncertainly at Millie.

'I'll stay with her while you go and speak to him,' Ewan offered. He stifled another huge yawn then grinned at her. 'I am officially off duty at last so I won't be called away.'

'Oh, right, thank you,' Becky said gratefully. She made her way to the desk and picked up the phone. 'Dad, it's me. I'm sorry. I know I should have called you but I'm in ED and I had to switch off my phone. However, the good news is that Millie's fine.'

Becky couldn't help feeling guilty when she heard the relief in her father's voice as he relayed the news to her mother. She quickly filled him in about what had happened. 'As I said, Millie is fine,' she repeated. 'In fact, I'll be bringing her home shortly. Ewan's happy for her to leave so that's good enough for me.'

'Ewan? So he's there with you, is he? Ah, good. Good.'

Becky felt her cheeks bloom with colour when she heard him repeat that to her mother. She didn't have to try too hard to imagine how her parents would interpret it and wished she had made it clearer that Ewan was there purely in a professional capacity. She glanced round when she heard footsteps and felt her heart leap when she saw Ewan coming towards her. He was carrying Millie, snugly wrapped in a blanket. The little girl's head was resting trustingly on his broad shoulder, her small hand gripping tight hold of his shirt collar. They looked so *right* together that Becky felt a rush of emotions hit her.

This was what she might have had if she hadn't chosen to stay with Steve. She had turned her back on the wild attraction and excitement that Ewan had brought to her life and opted for a relationship that had appeared to be rock-solid. It hadn't taken her long to realise how wrong she had been.

Although Steve had projected an air of calm and control, it had been all on the surface. Underneath, he'd been a mass of insecurities. He had blamed others for his failings, unable or unwilling to accept responsibility when things went wrong. Living with him had been a strain; it had felt as though she was permanently on a knife-edge, waiting for the next outburst. She had done her best to hold it all together for Millie's sake, but after she'd found out about his affair, something inside her had died. She had felt like a shell of her real self—empty, hollow.

Now, however, as she watched Ewan coming towards her with her daughter in his arms, she realised that she didn't feel empty anymore. She felt alive for the first time in ages, filled with expectation, and it scared her because she knew it wasn't right. That it wasn't fair. She had nothing to offer Ewan. Nothing at all that he truly needed.

'Becky? Are you still there?'

Becky roused herself when she heard her father calling her. No matter how she felt, she had to make sure that Ewan didn't get hurt. 'Yes, I'm here, Dad. Sorry. As I said, I'll be bringing Millie home soon.'

'I wish we could drive over there and collect you but your mother and I had a bottle of wine with dinner,' Simon apologised.

'Don't worry. I'll get a taxi,' she assured him. She ended the call then turned to take Millie from Ewan, somewhat surprised when the little girl clung to him.

'She's exhausted,' Ewan said easily, settling the child more comfortably against his shoulder. He smoothed back her soft fair curls with a gentle hand. 'You're ready for bed, aren't you, poppet?'

Millie nodded, her thumb slipping into her mouth the way it always did just before she drifted off to sleep, and Becky sighed. 'You're right. She's worn out after all the excitement. The sooner she's tucked up in her cot, the better. I don't suppose you know the number of a local taxi firm, do you?'

'You're hoping to find a taxi to take you home?' Ewan said in surprise, and she shrugged.

'I don't have a choice. Mum and Dad went out for dinner tonight and had a drink so they can't drive over here to collect us.'

'We must have some phone numbers somewhere,' Ewan said slowly, then grimaced. 'Although I don't rate your chances of finding a driver who's prepared to drive all the way out to Bride's Bay at this time of the night. It's Saturday, don't forget, and all the cabs will be busy ferrying folk home from the local clubs and pubs.'

'I never thought about that,' Becky admitted worriedly. 'I don't know what I'm going to do if I can't find a cab, though.'

'I can always run you home.'

'Oh, no. It wouldn't be fair to expect you to do that, Ewan. You've been working all night and you're worn out.'

'In that case, why don't you stay at my flat tonight?' He shrugged when she didn't answer. 'It's just five minutes away from here so it would be the ideal solution. You can have Millie tucked up in bed in no time at all.'

CHAPTER SIX

'AND THIS IS the bedroom. You're in luck because I changed the sheets this morning. They might not be ironed but they are clean!'

Ewan drummed up a laugh. Inviting Becky to stay the night had seemed like the right thing to do but he couldn't help wondering if it had been wise. He was already far more involved than he wanted to be and surely this would only make matters worse. He drove the thought from his mind as he opened the wardrobe and took out a couple of pillows. He'd be a poor sort of friend if he hadn't offered Becky somewhere to stay in her hour of need.

'You can use these to stop Millie rolling off the bed.' He laid the pillows along the edge of the bed to form a barrier. 'That should work all right, I think, don't you?'

'It's fine. Thank you.'

Becky sounded a little breathless, but that could have been his imagination, Ewan decided as he watched her look around the room. He followed her gaze, inwardly sighing because there wasn't much to see. He'd been travelling for so long that he hadn't had a chance to acquire many possessions. A selection of clothes, a few books, the odd photograph of him taking part in some mildly risky adventure like bungee jumping. It didn't seem a lot to show for the past eight years, especially not when he compared it to what Becky had achieved. She had been married and produced a child. That seemed like a far more valuable use of the time.

It wasn't like him to wonder if he should have set himself different goals. Ewan had always known what he'd wanted to do and to suddenly find himself questioning his decision was unsettling. Anyway, it was pointless trying to rewrite history. Becky had chosen Steve, not him, and that was the end of the matter. He cleared his throat, ignoring the little stab of pain that thought engendered.

'The bathroom's on your right and the kitchen is straight ahead, through the living room. I doubt you'll get lost as the place is so small but give me a shout if you need anything and can't find it.'

'I will. Thank you,' she repeated in the same breathy little voice that was starting to do funny things to his libido.

Ewan forced it back into its box because this wasn't the time for it to make an all-singing, all-dancing appearance. 'That's it then…oh, you'll need something to wear.'

He opened the wardrobe again and snagged a T-shirt off the shelf. It was faded from many washings, its original deep blue colour mellowed to a smoky grey, like the sky just before dawn. He tossed it onto the bed, trying not to imagine how Becky would look wearing it, the soft, pale fabric clinging to her body. That way lay madness, or so the saying went!

'You're sure you don't mind, Ewan?'

He was almost out of the door when she spoke and he

paused reluctantly, not wanting to put himself through any more tests that night. He'd managed pretty well so far, but he wasn't sure how long he could hold out. Maybe it was the fact that he was bone-tired or perhaps it was having her here in his home, but it was proving an effort to keep his hands to himself and away from her.

'Of course I don't mind.' A quick glance back, an even quicker smile, then another step towards safety, and he began to breathe a little easier.

'It's such an imposition, though. Especially after… well, after what happened between us all those years ago.'

Ewan took a deep breath. He could feel it filling his lungs right enough but it achieved very little else. It certainly didn't erase those pictures in his head, the ones of Becky modelling his ratty old T-shirt, neither did it screw down the lid on the box his libido was trying to climb out of. If he was honest, the extra oxygen simply enhanced all the bad things he was thinking and did nothing for the worthy, like the fact that he was playing the good Samaritan by inviting her into his home.

'That's all over with, Becky. We've both moved on since then, so let's forget about it, shall we?' He feigned a yawn, wanting to bring the conversation to a speedy conclusion. The last thing he needed right now was them going back over old ground. 'Right, that's me done for the night. I'll see you in the morning. Sleep tight.'

He closed the door, leaning against it for a moment while he gathered his strength. It would be the work of seconds to go back and discuss what had happened but what was the point? The past was the past and there was nothing to be achieved by dwelling on what might have happened, definitely no point wishing that the child who was sleeping in his bed tonight was theirs. Millie was another man's daughter, not his. She never would be his, either.

The pain of that thought stung but he ignored it. Going into the living room, he shoved the coffee table aside and set about converting the sofa into a bed. He'd forgotten to get himself a pillow or a blanket but it was too risky to go back for them. There was no point pushing himself beyond all sensible limits.

'I thought you'd need these.'

Ewan jumped when Becky appeared with a pillow and a blanket in her arms. She dropped them onto the sofa and grimaced. 'That doesn't look very comfortable.'

'It'll be fine,' he assured her, picking up the blanket. He draped it over the sofa then smiled with as much cheer as he could muster. 'I'll be as snug as a bug in a rug, as my gran used to say.'

'I hope so.' She went to go then stopped. 'I know you said to forget what happened but I can't. I never meant to lead you on, Ewan, and I'm sorry if I did.'

'You didn't lead me on,' he said flatly, sitting down on the edge of the sofa. There was a broken spring digging into his backside but he welcomed the discomfort because it gave him something to focus on apart from his own turbulent emotions. 'The attraction was mutual.'

'Yes, it was.' She bit her lip. 'It took me completely by surprise, if I'm honest.'

'These things happen, Becky.' He shrugged. 'And at the end of the day you made the right decision by choosing to stay with Steve.'

'I wish I could agree with you.'

Ewan's eyes flew to her face in shock. 'I beg your pardon?'

'Nothing. I shouldn't have said that.'

She turned to go but there was no way that he was letting her leave after saying that. He shot to his feet and caught hold of her arm.

'Maybe not, but you did say it and I want to know what you meant. Weren't you and Steve happy?'

'Our marriage was like everyone else's—we had good times and we had bad ones too.'

Ewan could tell that she was fudging the issue and even though he knew it was a mistake, he was determined to get at the truth. 'More bad times than good from the sound of it.'

'A lot of marriages go through rocky patches,' she said defensively.

'And that's what you went through, is it, rocky patches?'

'Yes. Steve...well, he set himself very high goals.'

'There's nothing wrong with that,' Ewan replied, not wanting it to appear as though he was criticising the other man.

'No.'

She bit her lip. Ewan could tell that she wanted to say something else and held his breath. It had to be her decision whether or not she confided in him, although whether he would want to hear what she had to say was another matter. For some reason he couldn't explain, it would be incredibly painful to discover that Becky had been unhappy in her marriage.

'Steve and I should never have got married,' she said at last. 'That's the long and the short of it.' She looked up and her eyes were very clear as they met his, clear

and so devoid of emotion that Ewan felt as though his
heart was cracking wide open. To know that Becky had
been hurt so badly was almost more than he could bear.
'I wasn't right for him, you see, not supportive enough,
not interesting enough, definitely not *sexy* enough.'

She gave a bitter little laugh that cut him to the quick.
It was all he could do not to beg her to stop, only that
would have been cowardly. She needed to get this off
her chest and he had to listen, no matter how agonising he found it.

'So what happened?'

'What you'd expect, basically. Steve had an affair.'
She shrugged. 'That was why he was so keen to move
to the city. All those times he was supposedly called
back into work, he was actually seeing her.'

'How did you find out?' Ewan asked, sickened by the
thought of Becky being treated so shoddily.

'It was common knowledge in the hospital so it was
simply a matter of time before I got to hear about it.'

'What did you do then?'

'We had a massive row and I threatened to leave,
but Steve begged me not to for Millie's sake. He said
he didn't want her growing up without both her parents present.'

'And you agreed with him, I take it?' Ewan said
flatly, doing his best not to show how disgusted he felt
about the other man's behaviour.

'Yes. I couldn't bear to think of Millie suffering, so
I agreed to give our marriage another go on condition
that Steve never saw the woman again.' She shrugged.
'He swore their affair was over but the night he was
killed, I found an earring in the car and it wasn't mine.'

Ewan cursed under his breath. 'What did you do?'

'Asked him who it belonged to. Oh, he tried to explain it away but it was obvious he was lying and in the end he admitted that he was still seeing her. That's what we were arguing about when the accident happened. If we hadn't been, he might have seen the truck in time to avoid it. So, in a way, it's my fault that he's dead.'

Becky took a deep breath. She felt strangely removed, as though it hadn't been her speaking, but someone else. Ewan didn't say a word, although that didn't surprise her. What could he say? Even if he tried to tell her that she wasn't to blame, she wouldn't believe him. He hadn't been there, hadn't heard the terrible things she and Steve had said to one another.

'That has to be the craziest thing I've ever heard!'

The anger in his voice shocked her. Becky stared at him in surprise. 'Crazy?'

'Yes.' He turned her round to face him, his eyes blazing into hers in a way that made heat flow through her numb veins. 'You weren't responsible for his death, Becky. It was an accident. One of those awful things that simply happen.'

'You weren't there,' she said, shaking her head. 'You've no idea what we said.'

'Maybe I can't repeat it verbatim but I can guess.' He gave her a shake, not hard or roughly, just enough to emphasise the point he was making. 'Your husband had just admitted he was still seeing another woman so you were hardly going to smile and agree that it was perfectly all right, were you?'

'No '

'No.' Another tiny shake, another blast from those searingly hot eyes, and the heat inside her turned into a flood. 'You're only human, Becky. You were bound to feel hurt and angry. It was only natural that you wanted to lash out.'

'I kept thinking about what it would mean for Millie,' she murmured.

'That she wouldn't have her daddy around while she was growing up?' Ewan said softly, and she nodded.

'Yes. The only reason I'd agreed to try and make a go of our marriage was because I didn't want Millie to miss out on having a proper family.'

'A lot of kids grow up without one parent or the other,' he pointed out. 'They manage fine, too. Anyway, I'm sure you and Steve would have reached some sort of an understanding with regard to Millie. I can't imagine that you'd have stopped him seeing her.'

'I wouldn't if it had been what he'd wanted. However, he made it clear that night that he wasn't interested in seeing her.'

'What! Are you sure?'

Becky nodded. 'Quite sure. As Steve put it, he was sorry that we'd ever had a child and if I thought he was going to spend the next umpteen years putting his life on hold while she grew up, I could think again.' She laughed harshly. 'Using Millie as the reason for us to stay together had just been an excuse. It turned out that the woman he was involved with was the wife of one of the members of the hospital board. It wouldn't have done his career any good if she'd been cited in divorce proceedings.'

'I don't know what to say.' He tailed off, an expression of pain crossing his face as he let her go.

'There's nothing to say, Ewan. Maybe Steve only said it because he was angry—who knows? But it isn't easy to forget it.'

'I can understand that.'

He sat down on the sofa, looking so shaken that Becky found herself wishing that she hadn't told him. Maybe it had helped to get it off her chest but it wasn't fair to have upset him in the process. She laid her hand on his shoulder, feeling the heat from his body seeping into her palm in a way that was all too familiar. Ewan had always generated a lot of heat, she suddenly recalled. In fact they'd used to joke about it. She had accused him of being hot-blooded and he had claimed that it only happened when he was with her.

She removed her hand, unable to deal with the memory. It hurt to know that she had given up all they'd had for what she had believed would be a secure and stable life. 'It's time I let you go to bed. Thank you again for letting us stay. I appreciate it.'

'It isn't a problem.' He summoned a smile but she could tell it was an effort. Her story had affected him even more than she had expected but it was too late to take it back.

Becky wished him goodnight and went into the bedroom. Millie was fast asleep. She felt her forehead but it was cool to the touch with no hint of fever, not that she'd expected there would be. Ewan would never have allowed her to take Millie home if there'd been a chance of her suffering another convulsion.

She sighed as she slipped off her clothes and picked up the T-shirt he had lent her. The cotton felt cool against her bare skin and, she felt her nipples peak as it slithered over her body and shuddered. It had been a long time since she'd felt any sexual stirrings but all of a sudden she was aware of her body in a way that surprised her.

Climbing into bed, she made herself comfortable but sleep proved elusive. Although the sheets and pillow-cases were freshly laundered, she could still smell Ewan on them, that spicy, masculine aroma that was his alone. When she finally drifted off to sleep, her dreams were filled with pictures of them together but not as they used to be. These pictures were of a time that hadn't hap-pened, of a time that must never happen. Maybe there was some vestige left of the old attraction they had felt for one another but it wasn't enough; it never would be enough to make up for the fact that she had nothing to offer him. She could never ever give him a child.

Ewan let himself back into the flat, taking care not to make any noise. It was just gone seven but he'd been awake for hours. If truth be told, he hadn't slept, merely lain awake thinking about everything Becky had told him. He still found it hard to take it all in but Becky hadn't been lying. She had told him the truth, every painful word of it, and it hurt to know how she had suf-fered and not been able to do anything about it.

He made his way to the kitchen, stopping dead when he found her sitting at the table. She was nursing a cup of tea and he got the impression that she'd been sitting there, nursing it, for some time, too. 'What are you doing up so early?' he asked, plonking the carrier bags he was holding onto the worktop.

'I couldn't sleep.'

She gave him a quick smile but Ewan was aware that she avoided looking directly at him. Was she sorry that she had told him about her marriage? he wondered as he began decanting the contents of the first bag. Wor-ried in case he told someone else? His mouth thinned at the thought that she didn't trust him to keep her confidences.

'If you're worried that I'm going to tell anyone about what you said last night, there's no need.' He ripped open a packet of coffee and spooned some into the cafetière, trying not to let his disappointment show. Becky had no reason to trust any man after what had happened, not even him. 'I have no intention of repeating what you told me, Becky.'

'I know that.' She met his gaze for a second before she looked away. 'It isn't your style to gossip, Ewan.'

'Oh. Right.' Ewan wasn't sure what to say. If it hadn't been that keeping her awake then what had it been? He finished unpacking the first bag and started on the second.

'Are you expecting an army for breakfast?'

There was a hint of laughter in her voice and he felt his heart lighten. Glancing at the array of goodies he'd piled on the counter, he chuckled. 'I wasn't sure what you and Millie might fancy so I thought I'd better cover all bases.'

'So I can see.' Becky got up and came over to the counter. 'Croissants, bacon, cereal, yoghurt, fruit, eggs… Hmm, the only thing missing is steak.'

'Steak,' he repeated rather hoarsely, suddenly finding it difficult to breathe. Becky was wearing his T-shirt and he had to admit that it had never looked better than it did at that moment, the full swell of her breasts adding an extra allure to the washed-thin fabric.

'To go with the eggs, of course.' She gave a tiny giggle that made the hair all over his body stand to attention. 'You always claimed that steak and eggs was the perfect breakfast. It gives you a double hit of protein plus umpteen other benefits, or so you maintained.'

'Probably end up giving you a coronary as well if you indulged too often,' he said wryly because he could *do* wry even if he couldn't do much else. He added a pot of jam—to go with the croissants—to the pile then started on bag number three. Nappies, wet wipes and a packet of bibs emerged and Becky gasped.

'You really have thought of everything!' She picked up a Cellophane pack containing two little cotton sleep suits with butterflies embroidered on them and shook her head. 'You shouldn't have gone to all this trouble, Ewan.'

'It was no trouble. Anyway, they're all things that Millie will need this morning.' He rolled the bag into a ball and stuffed it under the sink, his heart turning over when he straightened up and saw the tears in her eyes. 'What's the matter? Have I bought the wrong size or something?'

'No. They're perfect.' She gave a noisy sniff. 'I just didn't expect this…any of it.'

Tears began to pour down her face as she swept a hand towards the worktop and Ewan did the only thing he could think of. Drawing her into his arms, he held her while she cried, feeling the shudders that racked her body. He had a feeling that it had been a long time since she had given in to her emotions and was suddenly glad that he'd been around when she needed comforting. If Becky needed a shoulder to cry on, she could have his. Willingly.

'It's okay, sweetheart. You have a good cry,' he murmured, stroking her hair. A few silky tendrils snagged against the rough skin on his fingers and he gently

freed them before letting his hand slide down her spine.
Whether he'd intended to urge her closer, he wasn't sure,
but she took a tiny step towards him, just enough to
bring her body into intimate contact with his, and Ewan
felt his own emotions suddenly run riot. He could feel
the soft swell of her breasts pressing against the wall
of his chest, feel to the very second when her nipples
hardened, and his heart ran wild. A lot of water might
have flowed under the bridge but there were still feelings between them—that was obvious!

He didn't pause to think as he bent and kissed her,
didn't give himself time to wonder if he was making a
mistake. He just wanted to kiss her, just needed to feel
the softness of her mouth under his once more. The
years seemed to fade away as they stood there, their
mouths joined, their bodies entwined.

Becky was kissing him back and that was all that
mattered, the fact that she wanted this as much as he
did. What happened next was in the lap of the gods,
although Ewan was under no illusions that it was the
start of something. He wasn't even sure that he wanted
it to be. All he wanted was to hold Becky in his arms
and kiss her, comfort her and, if he was honest, comfort
himself too because what she had told him last night
had put a dent in his own heart.

His mouth opened over hers, inviting her to respond,
and desire surged through him when she did so. He
guessed that Becky had no more idea than he had where
this was leading but it didn't matter to her either. At
this precise moment in time, this kiss was enough for
both of them!

CHAPTER SEVEN

BECKY COULD FEEL her heart pounding, a fierce, wild rhythm that made her cling to Ewan. His mouth was so hot, so urgent and yet so tender as it plundered hers. Even in the throes of passion, Ewan was aware of her needs, put her first. He always had done.

Tears stung her eyes once more and she heard him murmur in concern. However, when he went to pull back, she refused to let him go. Wrapping her arms around his neck, she drew his head down, taking the lead this time as she let her tongue slide between his lips. She didn't want the kiss to end just yet. She felt safe in Ewan's arms, safe and wonderfully alive. After the emotional wasteland she'd existed in these past few years, it was a marvellous feeling.

'Becky, please.' His hands gently gripped her shoulders as he set her away from him. 'I think we should stop.'

His voice was firm, but she could hear the desire it held and smiled. 'If it's what you really want.'

He groaned as he pulled her back into his arms and kissed her hungrily. 'Of course it isn't what I want! But I don't want us to do something we'll regret either.'

A chill ran down her spine. Tilting her head, she stared into his face. 'You're sorry this happened?'

'I don't know how I feel, if you want the truth.' He stepped back, his hand trembling as he raked back his hair. 'I didn't plan on kissing you. It was the last thing I intended, in fact.'

'And now you're having second thoughts,' she said as calmly as she could. It hurt to know that he regretted what they'd done, hurt far more than it had any right to do. She drummed up a laugh, loath to let him see how vulnerable she felt. 'I understand, Ewan, really I do.'

'Then I wish you'd explain it to me.' He sighed. 'I want us to be friends, Becky. I want us to meet up for coffee, maybe go out for dinner occasionally, do all the things that friends do. We had our chance and I'm under no illusion that we can be more than friends these days. Yet when I kissed you just now, it wasn't friendship I was feeling, believe me.'

'Maybe it was because of how we once felt,' she suggested, wondering if it explained why she had felt so aroused. It was years since she had wanted anyone the way she had wanted Ewan just now, so was it familiarity that had rekindled her desire?

'It was a blast from the past—is that what you're saying?'

His tone was sceptical but Becky didn't want anything to ruin her theory. Maybe the kiss had been wonderful but she'd be crazy to imagine it could lead anywhere. Ewan had his own life to lead, a future that would probably entail a wife and a family at some point, and she wouldn't do anything that might hold him back.

'Yes.' She shrugged, refusing to dwell on the thought of what the future held in store for him. She had no right to feel jealous of the woman he would eventually choose to be his wife and the mother of his children. 'Let's face it, Ewan, we were very attracted to one another, weren't we?' She gave a light laugh. 'I had a real crush on you, if I'm honest!'

'And like most crushes, it didn't last.' He laughed sardonically. 'Hmm, I think we should leave it there. I don't think my ego can take a battering this early in the day!'

Becky laughed as well, although her heart was heavy as she excused herself and went to get dressed. It was doubtful if Ewan's ego took a pounding very often. From what she had seen in the past, he was far too successful with women to suffer many setbacks. He could have his pick, in fact, so it was little wonder that he didn't want to get involved with her. After all, why should Ewan be interested in a single mother like her?

It was a sobering thought. Becky found it difficult to shake it off as she woke Millie and changed her. She carried her into the kitchen and sat her down on a chair. Ewan glanced round, holding up the pot of coffee.

'Want some?'

'Please.' Becky opened a packet of cereal then found a bowl and poured some into it. She added milk from the jug then went to get up to fetch a spoon.

'Here you go.' Ewan handed her a teaspoon, grinning when Millie began to bounce up and down in excitement. 'Someone's eager for her breakfast.'

'She loves cereal and this just happens to be her favourite,' Becky explained, helping the little girl spoon some into her mouth. She shook her head when Millie tried to take the spoon off her. 'No, let me help you, darling, otherwise it will end up all over the place.'

'Don't worry about making a mess.' Ewan handed

Millie a spoon, laughing when she plunged it into the bowl, showering milk all over the table. 'It's not as though she can spoil the décor.'

Becky smiled as he shot a wry look around the room. 'You mean to say, this particular shade of red isn't to your taste?'

'I can't imagine it being to many people's taste,' he retorted. 'It's like living in a nightmare—there's pulsating red walls everywhere you look.'

Becky chuckled. 'I take it that you're planning to redecorate.'

'As soon as I find the time.' He took the croissants out of the oven and brought them over to the table. 'We're short-staffed at the moment so I've been working extra shifts. Hopefully, things will ease off soon, though.'

So he hadn't been out on the town; he'd been working. Becky hurriedly squashed the feeling of relief that thought aroused. She concentrated on helping Millie, smiling when the little girl finished her cereal in record time. 'You must have been hungry, sweetheart. Would you like a banana?'

''Nana,' Millie repeated.

'I'll get it.' Ewan reached over and took a banana out of the fruit bowl. Becky looked away when the hem of his polo shirt lifted an inch or two, affording her a tantalising glimpse of taut, tanned midriff.

'Thanks,' she murmured, willing her racing pulse to slow down. It was just a glimpse of bare skin, she told herself sternly. Nothing to get worked up about. However, it was surprising how difficult she found it to follow the advice. Whichever way she looked at it, Ewan still possessed the power to disturb her.

They ate their breakfast, chatting easily about this and that. Becky leant back in her chair when she finished. 'That was delicious! I'm afraid I made a bit of a pig of myself. Sorry.'

'There's no need to apologise.' Ewan grinned at her. 'I'm just in awe of the fact that you managed to eat *three* croissants. It takes a dedicated eater to manage that little lot.'

'Make me feel better, why don't you?' Becky retorted, and he laughed.

'I'm just teasing. Anyway, you could do with putting on a few extra pounds.'

It was the sort of throwaway comment that anyone might make; however, the fact that it was Ewan making it put a whole different spin on it. Becky couldn't help wondering if he found her new, slimline figure less attractive than her previous curves before she realised what she was doing. Whether or not Ewan found her attractive wasn't important, was it?

'If I keep on eating like this, it won't be long before I'll need to think about dieting,' she said lightly. She peeled a wet wipe out of the packet and wiped Millie's hands. 'Right, I'm going to get this little lady washed and dressed in one of those lovely new sleep suits you bought her.'

'You do that.' Ewan stood up and started clearing the table. 'Give me a shout when you're ready to leave.'

Was that a hint that she had outstayed her welcome? Becky wondered as she lifted Millie down from the table. Not that she blamed him if it was. After all, he had done everything possible to make her feel welcome. Maybe that kiss hadn't been part of his plan, but she could hardly object when she had been as eager for it as him.

She sighed as she carried Millie into the bathroom. It wouldn't happen again. Ewan had made it perfectly clear that he only wanted them to be friends and she should be pleased he felt that way. There was less risk of getting hurt if they stuck to friendship.

It was the right decision, the sensible one, yet Becky couldn't help feeling downhearted. Deep down, she knew that if the situation had been different she would have wanted more than friendship from him.

Ewan took his time as he drove Becky back to Bride's Bay. The roads were a lot busier than they'd been the previous week. This part of the coast was a tourist magnet and soon all the roads would be thronged with cars and caravans and trailers.

'Looks like the early summer rush is starting,' he observed, slowing down when the driver in front stopped to check a signpost.

'Give it a few more weeks and the roads will be packed,' Becky agreed. She grimaced when the car ahead indicated right and then turned left. 'People's driving doesn't get any better, does it?'

'They're wearing their holiday heads,' Ewan said lightly. 'The rules of the road take second place to the need to reach their destination.'

'They'll be lucky if they make it in one piece if that's the way they drive,' she said tartly, and he laughed.

'Good job we locals know to give the tourists a wide berth.'

'A very wide one in some cases,' she said sharply.

Ewan glanced at her. 'Are you nervous about being driven after the accident?'

'A bit.' She sighed. 'I kept getting flashbacks in the beginning, although they've stopped now, thankfully. It's just at odd times that I feel a bit…well, anxious, I suppose.'

'I expect I'd feel the same.' He picked up speed, although he was careful not to go too fast in view of what she had said. 'Mum told me that you were quite badly injured in the crash.'

'That's right.'

She glanced out of the window but not quickly enough to hide the sadness on her face. Ewan couldn't help wondering what was behind it but short of asking her there was no way of knowing, and he wasn't sure if he should go down that route. They had already crossed boundaries he hadn't planned on crossing with that kiss and it would be too risky to cross any more that day.

They reached Bride's Bay and drove straight to the surgery. Ewan parked the car then lifted Millie out of the back. She chuckled when he buzzed her cheek with a kiss.

'Who's been a good girl, then?' he said, tossing her into the air.

Millie squealed in delight. ''Gain, 'gain!'

Ewan laughed as he tossed her up again. 'So you're a little daredevil, are you?' He settled her in his arms then looked round when Becky joined them. 'She obviously enjoys a bit of rough and tumble.'

'Oh, she does. She adores it when Dad plays with her. He picks her up and swings her round, and she screams with laughter.'

'Men play differently with a child,' he observed wryly. 'We tend to be a lot more physical.'

'Which is what Millie loves.' She sighed. 'She's missed out on such a lot in the past year. It's a real shame.'

'She doesn't seem to have taken any harm from it,' he said firmly, not wanting her to feel guilty when there was no need. 'Anyway, now she has your father to play with her, she'll soon make up for lost time.'

'Yes, although I'm not sure how long we'll be living with my parents.'

She led the way up the path and Ewan followed her, his heart sinking. It had never occurred to him that she might not stay in Bride's Bay and he found the idea strangely unpalatable.

'So you're thinking of moving?' he said as she let them into the kitchen.

'As soon as I can save enough money for a deposit, yes.' She took Millie from him and set her down on the floor. 'I'll have to rent, of course—I certainly can't afford to buy with property prices being so high. But my plan is to get a place of my own as soon as I can.'

'Here, in Bride's Bay, or further afield?' he asked, determined not to let her know how much he hated the idea of her moving away.

'Oh, here, or somewhere close by at any rate.' She filled the kettle and set it to boil. 'I love working at the surgery and I don't want to have to give it up, plus it will be so much easier if Mum helps me with Millie. Millie will be starting nursery soon but she'll only be doing half-days to begin with so I'll need someone to look after her for the rest of the time. Mum has very kindly offered to do it.'

Thank heavens for that! Ewan thought in relief, although he took care not to show it. 'It sounds like a good plan to me.'

'It's the best I can think of in the circumstances,' Becky said flatly.

Ewan bit back a sigh. It was obvious that Becky had never expected her life to turn out this way but it wasn't her fault she had ended up as a single parent. He was on the point of telling her that when Ros Harper appeared. She smiled broadly when she saw them.

'Ah, so you're back, are you? Good.' She bent down and picked up her granddaughter. 'And how are you this morning, poppet? You certainly gave your poor old granny and grandpa a fright.'

'She's as right as rain,' Ewan assured her. 'I know it must have been worrying for you, but, as I explained to Becky, Millie will grow out of the convulsions in time.'

'I'm sure she will.' Ros kissed her granddaughter's cheek. 'I'm just glad you were around, Ewan. Simon and I felt a lot happier once we knew you were there, looking after them both.'

Ewan wasn't deaf to the nuances in Ros's voice; neither was Becky, he suspected. It was obvious that it would suit Ros if he and Becky got together but it wasn't going to happen. He smiled politely, feeling that he should set matters straight.

'It was lucky that I was on duty last night and able to help. After all, Becky and I have been friends for some time.'

'Of course you have.' Ros seemed undeterred as she turned and smiled at her daughter. 'Do you want me to get Millie ready while you get changed? Tom and Hannah are expecting us around noon.'

'Oh, I'd forgotten about the christening party!' Becky exclaimed. She glanced at Ewan. 'Are you coming? I know Tom invited you and seeing as you're already here...'

She tailed off, leaving him to make the final decision. Should he go? he wondered. Or would it only make the situation more complicated? If he turned up with Becky, it wouldn't be only Ros expecting great things of them.

He shook his head. 'I think I'd better shoot off home. I've got loads to do after working all those extra shifts last week.'

'Oh, surely you can spare an hour?' Ros put in before Becky could say anything. 'Tom and Hannah will be so disappointed if you miss the party. They both said how much they'd enjoyed meeting you.'

'I enjoyed meeting them too but I really do have an awful lot to do,' Ewan countered.

'An hour isn't going to make much difference, though, is it?' Ros glanced at her watch. 'It's gone eleven already, so why not pop along and have some lunch and then go home? I mean, you'll have to eat whatever you're doing, won't you?'

Ewan knew when he was beaten and gave in as gracefully as he could. 'All right. I'll drop in to say hello and then shoot off.' He hurried on when Ros went to interrupt. 'Becky and I had a massive breakfast, as it happens. I'm not sure if I can manage lunch as well.'

'Oh, well, never mind. I'm sure Tom and Hannah will be thrilled to see you.' Ros smiled contentedly as she picked up her granddaughter and left.

Ewan sighed. 'Ever had the feeling that you've been outmanoeuvred?'

'Frequently. Mum's a master at it.' Becky's tone was

wry. 'She does it so nicely, too, that it's hard to take offence.'

Ewan laughed. 'Don't I know it!' He sobered abruptly. 'You do realise that she thinks we're going to get together?'

'Yes. Don't worry, Ewan—I'll set her straight. There's no point her getting her hopes up about something that's never going to happen.' She glanced at the kitchen clock and grimaced. 'I'd better get changed. Make yourself a cup of coffee, won't you?'

She left the kitchen and a moment later Ewan heard her running up the stairs. He found himself a mug and spooned some instant coffee into it. The sugar was in a jar by the kettle so he added a spoonful to the mug, sighing as he realised that he needed to make it clear to everyone that he and Becky weren't romantically involved. Maybe people were hoping it would happen but it wasn't what either of them wanted....

Was it?

His heart seemed to leap into his throat. Did he want to be more than a friend to Becky? He knew that his answer should be a resounding no and the fact that it wasn't worried him. He didn't *want* to fall in love with her, certainly didn't *intend* to run the risk of getting hurt. Maybe her marriage hadn't been all it should have been but she must have loved Steve, otherwise she wouldn't have married him. She probably still had feelings for him, so it would be crazy to get involved with her. However, despite all that, he couldn't in all conscience put his hand on his heart and swear it wouldn't happen.

CHAPTER EIGHT

'BECKY, HI! How lovely to see you. And this must be your little girl—Millie, isn't it?'

Becky smiled as Emily came over to them. Emily had been the practice nurse at the surgery before she'd got married and moved to Paris. 'Hello, Emily. Lovely to see you too. Yes, this is Millie. Say hello to Auntie Emily, darling.'

Emily laughed when Millie promptly hid her face in Becky's neck. 'She's going through the shy stage, is she? Theo was exactly the same at her age.'

'I'm hoping that she'll grow out of it when she goes to nursery,' Becky explained ruefully. She looked up when a tall, dark-haired man came to join them. He had a little boy with him and the resemblance between them was unmistakable. 'No need to ask who you two are,' she said, smiling at them.

Emily laughed. 'As you so rightly guessed, this is my husband, Ben, and our son, Theo. They're like two peas in the proverbial pod, aren't they?'

Emily shot an adoring look at her husband and Becky bit back a sigh. She couldn't help feeling wistful when everywhere she looked there seemed to be couples madly in love with each other. Her gaze slid over Tom and Hannah, who were holding hands, and moved on to her parents, who even after thirty years of marriage had that special glow about them. Would she ever feel like that? Did she want to?

Her gaze alighted on Ewan, who was chatting to Lizzie, the receptionist at the surgery, and her heart jerked. Suddenly, all she could think about was that kiss and how wonderful it had been....

'Becky?'

Becky jumped when Emily jogged her arm. Colour rushed to her face as she realised that she'd missed what the other woman had said. 'Sorry. I was miles away. What did you say?'

'I was just asking if you were enjoying working at the surgery,' Emily explained, then grinned as she glanced over at Ewan. 'I take it that's Ewan. Ros told me he was here with you.'

'I...erm...yes, that's right. Mum persuaded him to pop in and say hello,' Becky said quickly. She took a deep breath and hurried on. Maybe that kiss had been wonderful, but there wasn't going to be a repeat. 'Millie had a febrile convulsion last night. I took her to the hospital—Hannah drove us there—and Ewan happened to be on duty and treated her. He very kindly drove us home again this morning.'

'They kept her in overnight?' Ben queried, frowning.

Becky groaned. Obviously, Ben was wondering what she was doing, bringing Millie to the party if the little girl had been ill enough to be admitted to hospital. 'No. She was well enough to be sent home, thankfully. It was rather late by then, though, and I couldn't get a taxi, so we stayed at Ewan's.'

'Ah, I see,' Ben said, smiling. He brushed Millie's

cheek with his finger. 'It is good to know that you are feeling better, *ma petite*.'

They exchanged a few more pleasantries before Emily and Ben went to say hello to Mitch Johnson, the landlord of The Ship Inn, and his wife. Becky took Millie over to the sandpit. Charlie, Tom and Hannah's son, was making sand pies and Millie eagerly joined in.

'Looks as though someone's having fun.'

Becky didn't glance round; she didn't need to. She would recognise Ewan's voice anywhere, she realised, her heart sinking because it was yet another example of how deeply he had infiltrated her thoughts of late.

'Millie loves making sand pies,' she said lightly, doing her best to behave as though everything was fine, which in a way it was. After all, they had both agreed they weren't looking for more than friendship. Maybe that kiss had been unexpected but it had been a one-off and it wouldn't happen again. 'If Millie had her way, we'd spend every day at the beach.'

'Can't say I blame her. I'm a bit of a sand-pie freak myself.'

He crouched down and helped the children fill their buckets. When Charlie begged him to help them make a sand castle, he set to work with gusto. In a very short time they had constructed several turrets and were busily forming the base of the wall that surrounded them.

'You missed your vocation,' Becky told him, laughing. 'You should have been an architect, not a doctor.'

He grinned. 'I'm not sure I'd have been much good at it. The test of a good building is its stability and I think my designs may be somewhat lacking in that respect.'

The words were prophetic because just then one of the turrets gave way. Millie let out a loud wail as one side sheared off. Ewan swung her up into his arms. 'It doesn't matter, sweetheart. We can do it again. Don't cry.'

He tossed her up in the air and successfully distracted her. She was all smiles as she demanded that he do it again. Becky noticed several people watching them and smiling, and realised that they were putting two and two together and coming up with the wrong answer. However, short of announcing that she and Ewan weren't an item and that they had no intention of becoming one, either, there was little she could do. It was a relief when Tom clapped his hands and called for silence.

'I'm not going to bore you all by making a speech,' he began.

'That's a relief,' someone shouted, and everyone laughed.

Tom grinned. 'Exactly. I just want to thank you all for coming. Hannah and I really appreciate you taking the time to help us celebrate this very special day.'

There was a round of applause. Tom waited until it died down. Becky frowned when she realised how nervous he looked. From what she had learned of Tom, he wasn't the sort of person who suffered from nerves. Something was obviously going on.

'If I could beg a few more minutes of your time, folks, there's something rather important I'd like to do.' He turned to Hannah and held out his hand. 'Would you come over here for a second, darling?'

'What's going on?' Hannah demanded as she took Tom's hand. 'You're up to something, Tom Bradbury. I can tell!'

'I am indeed.' He suddenly dropped to one knee.

'Hannah Morris, will you do me the great honour of becoming my wife?'

A collective gasp broke out from all the guests. Without even thinking about it, Becky reached for Ewan's hand as she waited to hear what Hannah would say. She heard a phone ring and glanced round in time to see her father take his mobile out of his pocket but she was more concerned about Hannah's answer than anything else.

'Of course I'll marry you.' Hannah sounded indignant. 'I can't believe you thought I wouldn't!'

A huge cheer erupted as Tom swept Hannah into his arms and kissed her. Becky cheered as well, thrilled to have been witness to such a happy event.

Ewan laughed. 'There's nothing like a spot of old-fashioned romance to cheer everyone up.'

'There certainly isn't.' Becky turned and hugged him then realised what she was doing. 'Oh, I'm sorry…'

'Don't apologise. It's a time for hugs, I'd say.'

He hugged her back, making it appear so natural that any doubts she had fled. After all, friends often hugged one another and that was what she and Ewan were, friends. It was only when she caught her mother's eye and saw the smile that Ros bestowed on them that she realised how other people might interpret it. It was a relief when her father appeared and she and Ewan broke apart.

'That was Ambulance Control on the phone,' Simon announced. 'There's been an incident at Bride's Bay Manor—a coach carrying a party of holidaymakers has collided with a car. There's several dozen people injured apparently and Ambulance Control has asked if we can attend until the ambulances get there.'

'Do we know what sort of injuries they've sustained?' Ewan asked immediately.

'No. Details are sketchy, I'm afraid. We'll have to wait until we arrive to see what's happened.' He looked round when Tom and Hannah came to join them. Emily and Ben had followed them and they all listened intently while Simon recounted what had happened.

'Typical,' Hannah snorted. 'Put a whole load of medics together and it's guaranteed there'll be some sort of emergency!'

'At least it saves us having to make umpteen phone calls to rally the troops,' Ewan pointed out, grinning.

Tom laughed. 'Good point. So how do you want to play this, Simon?' He glanced at the others. 'Hannah and I can give Ben and Emily a lift—that's assuming you're both coming.' He carried on when the other couple nodded. 'Which means there's room for Becky and Ewan in your car even if you need to bring extra supplies.'

In a very short time everything was arranged. Ros and Lizzie had offered to look after the children, and Marie and Mitch Johnson had insisted on taking care of the buffet so that lunch could go ahead. All the guests then lined up outside and waved them off.

Becky shook her head as they drove back to the surgery. 'It's such a shame that Tom and Hannah's day has been ruined.'

'I doubt this will have spoiled it,' Ewan said. He was sitting in the front and he turned to look at her. 'From the looks on their faces, it will take more than a call-out to take the shine off today. I don't think I've ever seen a couple who looked so happy, have you?'

'No.' Becky summoned a smile but Ewan's words

had merely highlighted her earlier thoughts. Tom and Hannah were happy together, as were Emily and Ben. They'd each found the person they loved and their lives were all the richer for it.

She bit her lip as Ewan turned to face the front again. She'd thought she had found that sort of happiness with Steve but she had been wrong. Now she was in no position to look for that kind of a relationship when she had so little to offer anyone. She was a single mother who couldn't have any more children; what man would be interested in her?

Her eyes rested on the back of Ewan's head as sadness swept over her. Ewan certainly wasn't.

'Lady on the coach complaining of severe pain in her right leg. I think it may be a fractured femur.'

'I'll take a look.'

Ewan followed Becky over to the coach. The accident had happened close to the entrance to Bride's Bay Manor, a beautiful Tudor manor house that had been gifted to the nation by its former owners. Most of the passengers had been brought into the grounds for safety and everywhere he looked there were people sitting or lying on the grass. Although it appeared rather chaotic, it was, in fact, all very organised.

Becky and Emily had been performing triage ever since they'd arrived, sorting out the most seriously injured so they could be seen first. Thankfully, there didn't appear to be anything life-threatening. Cuts, bruises, a couple of fractures—much as could be expected from this type of incident. Ewan was confident that once he had dealt with this patient, he'd be able to start on the walking wounded.

He climbed aboard the coach and knelt down beside the woman and smiled at her. 'Hello, there. My name's Ewan and I'm a doctor. Becky tells me that your leg is hurting. May I take a look?'

'Sandra Fielding.'

The woman offered him her hand which he shook. She was very pale and her skin felt cold and clammy. Ewan glanced at Becky. 'Can you put in a line, please, Becky? Sandra could do with some extra fluids.'

Becky nodded, immediately understanding. Ewan set about examining the woman, pleased that he hadn't needed to elaborate. Sandra was exhibiting all the classic signs of shock, which could mean that she was bleeding internally. The fluid would help to compensate for what she was losing but it did mean that time was of the essence. The sooner she was transferred to hospital, the better.

He gently examined Sandra's thigh, unsurprised when he discovered that it was very swollen. It was obviously extremely painful, too, because Sandra winced even though he applied minimum pressure. With a fractured femoral shaft, like this, there was often extensive blood loss from the bone so he was relieved when Becky quietly informed him that the line was set up.

'Thanks.' He smiled at her, thinking how pretty she looked. She was still wearing the dress she had worn for the party, a soft green cotton overprinted with a pattern of vivid pink roses. Her hair was caught up into a loose knot, a few honey-gold strands falling around her face as she knelt down to check their patient's pulse. She looked so lovely that Ewan felt his heart surge before he determinedly brought it under control. They were here to do a job, not so he could indulge in his own little fantasies.

'It looks like your femur is fractured, Sandra,' he explained, adopting his most professional tone so that his attention would be less likely to wander again. Opening his backpack, he took out a vial of morphine. 'That's why you're in so much pain. I'm going to give you something to make you more comfortable. Have you had morphine before? It can make you feel rather sick but I can give you another drug that should help with that.'

'I've never had it before,' Sandra said anxiously.

'In that case we won't take any chances.' He added metoclopramide—an antiemetic—to the syringe. Becky swabbed Sandra's arm and he slid in the needle. 'You'll feel a lot more comfortable in a few moments,' he assured her, putting the used syringe into the sharps box.

'What will happen about my leg?' Sandra asked. 'Will they put a plaster on it when I get to the hospital?'

'Obviously, it will need to be X-rayed but once the doctors know what they're dealing with, they'll decide on the best course of treatment,' Ewan said gently. He knew from past experience that people often reacted badly when they were told they might need an operation so he decided not to go down that route. However, it appeared that Sandra wanted to know exactly what she might have to face.

'So what will the treatment entail?' she demanded.

'The usual way to repair a fracture like this is to re-align the ends of the bone and pin them together. It's done under a general anaesthetic so it isn't as painful as it sounds. Sometimes surgery isn't necessary and the bone can be manipulated into place and supported with a splint. The leg is then put in traction to make sure the bone heals correctly.'

'But that will take weeks!' Sandra exclaimed. 'I could end up stuck in hospital for ages.'

Ewan frowned when he realised how upset she sounded. Although nobody liked the idea of being hospitalised, her reaction seemed way over the top. He glanced at Becky and raised his brows, wondering if she could shed any light on the problem.

'You'll only be kept in for as long as is necessary,' Becky said soothingly.

'I know. I'm just being silly.' Tears welled in Sandra's eyes and Ewan saw Becky reach over and pat her hand.

'Of course you're not being silly. No one wants to end up in hospital.'

She gave the older woman a warm smile and Ewan looked away when he felt his heart give that crazy little lurch it had started doing recently. He couldn't believe how aware he was of Becky, how responsive he was to her every look, her every smile. He'd dated his fair share of women over the years but not one of them had had this effect on him.

It was a disquieting thought, all the more so in view of the fact that they'd agreed they weren't looking for romance. Even if he had wanted to get together with Becky—which he didn't!—she wouldn't welcome his advances...

Although she hadn't exactly pushed him away when he'd kissed her, had she? a small voice whispered mischievously in his ear.

Ewan ground his teeth as he put the sharps box into the bag. He and Becky weren't going to rekindle their relationship. End of story. 'I'm sure you won't be kept in hospital for longer than is absolutely necessary,' he said firmly. 'If there's a problem about you being away from home then the social work team should be able to help. They can make arrangements if there's someone dependent on you for their care, or even a pet that needs looking after.'

'It's not that. I live on my own and I don't have any pets,' Sandra informed him.

Ewan smiled encouragingly. Despite what Sandra had said, he could tell there was something troubling her. 'So what's the problem? It would be better if you got it off your chest and then you'll be able to concentrate on getting better.'

'You two young people will probably think I'm being very silly but I have a date next week, you see, and now I won't be able to go.'

'A date?' Ewan repeated, nonplussed.

'Yes. I'm a widow and it's the first time I'll have been out with a man since my husband died. Edward—that's the gentleman I'm supposed to be meeting—is an old friend from way back. He and I used to work together. We got on really well, but Edward was engaged to his late wife at the time, so nothing ever came of it...'

She tailed off, leaving them to fill in the gaps, which Ewan did only too easily. He glanced at Becky and could tell from her expression that she was very aware of how the situation mirrored their own.

'And now the two of you have met again?' Ewan said gently.

'Yes. Edward contacted my daughter. He sent Louise an email. He'd been trying to find me for a while, apparently. Anyway, it was Louise who persuaded me to meet him. I wasn't sure, but she insisted, so we arranged to meet on Monday night for dinner.' Sandra sighed. 'Edward wanted it to be sooner but I'd booked this holiday and I didn't want to cancel it and lose the money. Now I won't be able to go.'

'Why not phone Edward and explain what's happened?' Becky suggested. 'I'm sure he'll understand and you can arrange to meet some other time.'

'That's the problem, though. Edward lives in Canada now and he's due to fly home on Tuesday. There won't be another time.'

Sandra fell silent, obviously upset at the thought of them not being able to renew their friendship. The first of the ambulances had started to arrive so Ewan went outside and flagged one down. He knew the crew and quickly explained what treatment the patient had received then helped them fit an inflatable splint to Sandra's leg in readiness for the journey. In a very short time Sandra was being driven away.

Becky sighed as she watched the ambulance disappear. 'I feel so sorry for her, don't you? She was obviously upset at the thought of not seeing this Edward again.'

'Yes. There but for the grace of God, eh?' Ewan replied, picking up his backpack.

'Sorry?' Becky looked quizzically at him.

'I simply meant that if I hadn't spotted you at the airport then we might never have met again.'

'No, I don't suppose we would,' she agreed quietly. 'It's funny how these things turn out, isn't it?'

'It is indeed.' He summoned a smile, aware that the conversation was in danger of becoming a shade too heavy. Although there was little doubt that his mother would have informed him that Becky was back in

Bride's Bay, he couldn't help wondering if he would
have followed up the information.

Would he have sought her out? he asked himself as
they headed over to the next casualty. Or would he have
played safe and stuck to the status quo? He had been
caught off guard when he'd seen Becky in Christchurch
and hadn't stopped to weigh up the consequences of
his actions. He'd been determined to speak to her and
he had, but had it been the right thing to do? Had it
been wise?

He sighed. Only time would tell, but it was unsettling to realise that one impulsive decision could affect
the rest of his life.

CHAPTER NINE

MOST OF THE guests had left by the time they returned to Tom and Hannah's house. There were just Becky's mother and Lizzie left, looking after the children, plus Mitch and Marie, from The Ship Inn, who had stayed behind to clear up the remains of the lunch. Becky plopped down onto a deck chair, feeling completely exhausted. She and Ewan had treated at least a dozen people and the pace was starting to tell on her.

'I don't know about you but I'm shattered.' Ewan flopped down onto the grass beside her and groaned. 'And here was I thinking I'd have a nice, relaxing day off. Remind me not to count my proverbial chickens next time, will you?'

Becky chuckled. 'Stop complaining. You know you enjoyed every moment.'

'Hmm, I'd argue the toss with you about that if I could summon up enough energy.'

He gave her a lazy grin and Becky felt her heart squeeze in an extra beat. Ewan had always had a particularly sexy smile, the sort of smile that was guaranteed to make any woman's knees go weak, and hers were no exception. She struggled to her feet, not wanting to go down that route when it would only lead to a dead end. There was no mileage in recalling all the things she found so attractive about him.

'I'd better go and rescue Mum and Lizzie. They must be frazzled after having to look after the little horrors all afternoon.'

'I bet they've enjoyed every second,' Ewan countered. 'If your mum is anything like mine, she probably adores being a hands-on granny.'

'She does but even so...' Becky shrugged, not wanting to explain that it was more for her own peace of mind that she needed to get away. She had enjoyed working with Ewan, enjoyed it far too much. His skill as a doctor had never been in doubt and today he had demonstrated so many other qualities as well.

She sighed as she went to find her mother. Ewan had been kindness itself as he had dealt with the casualties. He had listened to what they'd had to say and shown no hint of impatience as each had repeated how shocked they'd been when the accident had happened. She knew that it would have helped them enormously to tell him about their experiences and couldn't help wishing that she'd been able to do the same after her own accident. If only she'd had Ewan there offering reassurance, maybe she would have dealt with the aftermath far better than she had done.

The thought troubled her as she collected Millie. Maybe it would have helped to talk about the accident but it wouldn't have changed the outcome. No amount of reassurances could make up for the fact that she would never be able to have another child. She cuddled Millie close as she carried her outside, knowing how selfish it was to feel this way. So many women were unable to have a child of their own and she was one of the lucky ones, but she couldn't help it. She had always hoped to have more children, although, now that she thought about it, she doubted if Steve would have agreed. Steve had found it taxing enough to cope with just one child. How on earth had she ever thought he was ideal husband material?

Her gaze rested on Ewan, who was lying spread-eagled on the grass, as a wave of regret washed over her. Her life could have turned out very differently if she'd chosen Ewan.

Ewan closed his eyes, enjoying the warmth of the sun playing over his body. This latest incident coming on top of an already busy week had left him feeling drained. He was looking forward to going home and putting his feet up but first he needed to check how Becky and Millie were getting home.

A shadow fell over him and he opened his eyes, squinting against the sun's glare. Becky was standing beside him and his heart gave its customary little hiccup. Even though there was no chance of them getting back together, he couldn't help responding to her. It was as though he was genetically programmed to react; Becky was around so it was all systems go.

He rolled to his feet, suddenly impatient with himself. He was acting like an idiot and it had to stop. 'I take it your mum and Lizzie survived?' he said drolly, reaching out to tickle Millie under her chin.

'Just.' Becky treated him to a smile and off it went again, his pesky heart and its hiccups. Ewan just managed to suppress the curse that tried to escape, calling himself every kind of a fool instead. He and Becky were friends—period.

'Looking after a bunch of under-fives takes some doing, although your mother must be well versed in the art seeing as you and your brother are twins. I have to take my hat off to her. Coping with two little ones must be a major feat.'

'I'm sure you're right.'

Becky gave him another smile but some of the shine seemed to have gone out of it and he frowned. He had a feeling that his comment had touched a nerve although he had no idea why. However, before he could attempt to find out, Tom and Hannah appeared.

'There you are. We were hoping you hadn't left yet.' Tom said, grinning at them.

'I was just thinking about making tracks, actually,' Ewan admitted, relieved that he hadn't had the chance to say anything. He needed to remain detached if he was to stick to their plan of being friends. Something warned him that it wouldn't work if he got too involved in Becky's affairs.

'Oh, can't you hang on a bit longer?' Hannah implored him. She glanced at Tom and Ewan felt his heart ache when he saw the love in her eyes.

'It sounds as though you two are up to something,' he said jovially, avoiding looking at Becky. It wouldn't help to recall the way Becky had used to look at him all those years ago.

'We just thought that it would be nice to celebrate our engagement properly.' Hannah laughed. 'Tom had it all planned, apparently—champagne, toasts, the ring— but everything got hijacked when we were called out.'

'So what were you thinking of doing?' Becky asked and Ewan knew—he just knew!—that she'd been thinking the same thing.

His heart began to pound so that he missed what Hannah said. It was only when he realised that she and Tom were looking expectantly at him that he rallied. So what if Becky *had* been remembering how they'd felt about one another? It wouldn't change what had happened, certainly wouldn't alter the fact that she had chosen another man and not him.

'Sorry, I missed that. It must be my age. I can't stand the pace any more and tend to drift off at the least opportunity.'

'Less your age than the fact that you're worn out after having your day off ruined,' Tom said ruefully. 'I don't blame you if you think twice about accepting another of our invitations, although I do hope you'll come tonight. It will be all very casual—just dinner and drinks at The Ship—nothing fancy. And I promise on my honour that no matter what disaster befalls the town tonight, you are excused!'

Ewan laughed. 'Can I have that in triplicate, please?'

'If it means you'll come then yes.' Hannah grinned. 'Everyone's coming: Ros and Simon, Emily and Ben, Lizzie and her husband. It would be such a shame if you and Becky weren't there.'

'I'm afraid it's out of the question,' Becky put in quickly. She shrugged when they all looked at her, Ewan included. Although he had his suspicions about why she didn't want to go, he needed them confirmed. It might help him deal with this situation a bit better if he kept on reminding himself that Becky wasn't keen to spend any time with him.

'If Mum and Dad are going, there'll be no one to look after Millie,' she explained.

'Can't you take her along?' Ewan heard himself say,

and blinked in surprise. Where had that come from? Surely he should be backing her up rather than making suggestions if he intended to keep his distance. He opened his mouth to backpedal but Hannah beat him to it.

'Of course you must bring her. We're taking Charlie and I know for a fact that Emily and Ben are intending to bring Theo along. Millie won't be on her own. She'll have a couple of cohorts there to help her create chaos!'

Tom and Hannah went off to speak to Mitch and Marie, who were about to leave. They seemed to have taken it for granted that everything was sorted out and short of making a fuss, Ewan realised, there was nothing they could do about it. He glanced at Becky and grimaced. 'Sorry. I wasn't much help, was I? It sort of…well, crept out.'

'It doesn't matter,' Becky said shortly. She settled a sleepy-looking Millie onto her hip and glanced round. 'I'd better go and find my parents. Millie will need a nap if I'm taking her out tonight.'

'I can run you home if they're not ready to leave yet,' Ewan offered, but she shook her head.

'No. It's fine. Thank you.'

She gave him a tight little smile and his heart ached when he saw how strained it was. It was obvious that Becky didn't relish the idea of them spending any more time together and he couldn't blame her. She'd made her feelings clear and he didn't need it spelt out. She wasn't interested in him in any way apart from as a friend and even that wasn't guaranteed.

It should have been a relief to know that but as he said his goodbyes, Ewan's heart was heavy. Becky had been an important part of his life and it was hard to accept that he had been such a minor part of hers.

Becky settled Millie in her cot for a nap then went to lie down, hoping that a rest would help her relax. She would have preferred not to go to the engagement party but she simply couldn't think of an excuse not to attend. Even if Ewan hadn't suggested she should take Millie along, Hannah would have done, so there was no point blaming him. In fact, Ewan wasn't to blame for any of the things that had been plaguing her recently.

She sighed. Choosing to stay with Steve rather than allow her relationship with Ewan to develop had been her decision. She had opted for security, sure in her own mind that it had been the right decision, but look how it had turned out. Her marriage had been a disaster and she couldn't help wondering how different her life would have been if she had followed her heart rather than her head. She had been on the point of falling in love with Ewan, had known that he had felt the same about her, and she'd panicked.

Ewan hadn't been good husband material. He'd wanted to travel, see the world and explore what it had to offer. It had been so different from what she had always wanted—marriage, a home and a family—and she had been scared. It had seemed safer to stick to her plans even though it had hurt unbearably to let Ewan go. She could only imagine how hurt and angry he must have felt too, yet he hadn't tried to take it out on her when she had told him her decision. He had treated her with kindness and understanding—all those wonderful qualities that made him the man he was. Ewan stood head and shoulders above other men. He always had done.

It was painful to face up to the fact that she had made a terrible mistake. Becky was relieved when her mother tapped on the door.

'Are you asleep, darling?' Ros called quietly.

'No. Come in, Mum.' Becky sat up, smiling when she saw that Ros was carrying a tray of tea. 'Tea! How lovely. I'm gasping.'

'I thought you would be.' Ros put the tray on the window seat and poured two mugs of tea. 'There's some homemade biscuits as well. I thought you might be hungry seeing as you missed lunch.'

'I am.' Becky took a couple of ginger biscuits off the plate. 'I don't know how you find the time to bake along with everything else you do.'

'Years of practice,' Ros assured her as she sat down on the bed. 'Millie's flat out. I just popped in to check on her and she's fast asleep.'

'Probably worn out after all the excitement of last night and today.' Becky dunked her biscuit in her tea, grinning when her mother tutted. 'Sorry, but they taste even better when you dunk them.'

'So your father keeps telling me,' Ros said dryly. She sipped her tea then looked at Becky. 'You and Ewan seem to be getting on extremely well. Several people remarked on how happy you looked together.'

Becky bit back a groan. So this was to be an interrogation, was it? Although she knew her mother meant well, it would be wrong to let her think there was something going on between her and Ewan. 'We're just friends, Mum, and that's all we'll ever be, too. So if you're holding out any hopes of a romance, forget it. Ewan isn't interested in me that way and I don't blame him.'

'What do you mean?'

Becky sighed, realising that she had boxed herself into a corner. Although her mother knew that she and Ewan had come close to dating in the past, Becky had never told her the full story. 'To put it in a nutshell, he asked me out but I chose to stay with Steve.'

'Really!' Ros exclaimed. 'I knew you'd been close when you were working at the same hospital but I hadn't realised you'd had a relationship.'

'We didn't...well, not really.' Becky flushed. 'I called a halt before things got too heavy.'

'I see.' Ros shrugged. 'It was a long time ago though, darling, wasn't it? And Ewan doesn't strike me as the sort to hold a grudge.'

'No, he isn't. But he's bound to be wary.' Becky felt a lump come to her throat, which was silly really. However, admitting how stupidly she had behaved seemed to make it all so much worse.

Ros patted her hand. 'I'm sure you only did what you thought was best.'

'I did. Ewan was a real flirt. He made no secret of the fact that he wasn't interested in settling down. He was keen to travel as well and I knew it wasn't what I wanted to do. It seemed better to not start anything with him then end up making us both miserable.'

'Then I'd say it was the right decision for both of you,' Ros said firmly. 'And I'm sure that Ewan thinks that too.'

'Maybe. But that doesn't mean we're going to get together now.'

'It's early days yet, darling, and I understand that you're still grieving, but the time will come when you feel ready to move on. All I'm saying is don't let Ewan slip through your fingers a second time, will you?'

Becky shook her head. 'It isn't going to happen, Mum. Even if Ewan wanted me back—which he doesn't—it wouldn't be fair.'

'Fair?' Ros put her cup down and looked at Becky in surprise. 'What do you mean by that?'

'Oh, nothing. Forget it.' Becky could have bitten off her tongue for making such a slip. She knew her mother wouldn't rest until she found out what was behind the comment.

'How can I forget it? What did you mean, Becky? Why wouldn't it be fair if you and Ewan got together?' Ros demanded.

Becky hesitated but all of a sudden the desire to tell her mother the truth was too strong to resist. 'Because Ewan will probably want a family of his own some day.'

'So why is that a problem? Are you saying that you don't want any more children?' Ros sounded perplexed, as well she might. Becky knew that she had to explain it all properly.

'No. I'd love to have more children but it isn't possible. You know that I sustained some really serious internal injuries in the crash?' She carried on when Ros nodded. 'Well, unfortunately, I had to have a hysterectomy. The fact is that I can't have any more children, Mum. I could never give Ewan a child, so it wouldn't be fair if we got together, would it?'

'Oh, darling, I am *so* sorry!' Ros got up and hugged her. 'Why didn't you tell your father and me what had happened? It must have been awful for you, having to go through something like that on your own.'

'I couldn't tell you, Mum. I don't know why but it

was just too much to deal with on top of everything else.' Becky gulped. 'I suppose in a way I thought if I didn't talk about it, it might not be true, but it is. I'll never have another child, but I have Millie, so I'm very fortunate, aren't I?'

'You are indeed.' Ros kissed her on the forehead. 'Millie is a real sweetheart. Your father and I adore her, as you know. Anyone would, which is why I'm begging you not to rule out the idea of falling in love again.'

'I can't imagine it happening,' Becky said, wondering why the claim didn't ring true. She hurried on, not wanting to dwell on it right then. 'Although I haven't completely ruled it out.'

'Good.' Ros smiled at her. 'Ewan is wonderful with Millie, isn't he? And she seems to have really taken to him, too.'

Becky sighed. 'Stop it, Mum. I've already explained that Ewan and I aren't going to get back together so let's leave it at that, shall we?'

'If that's what you want, darling.' Ros stood up and gathered up the tea things. 'I'd better go and see if your father's awake. He's in the study, supposedly writing a report about the accident, but actually having a snooze. He'll need to get showered and changed before we set off for this evening's celebrations. We may as well walk down to The Ship if that's all right with you.'

'Fine,' Becky agreed.

She got up as soon as her mother left and went into the en suite bathroom, turning the shower to full blast so that the water bounced down onto the tiles. She stepped under the jets, hoping that the hot water would wash away all the thoughts that kept invading her mind, thoughts of her and Ewan and what they could and couldn't be to one another. She knew how it had to be, knew that they could never be together and why, but it didn't stop her wishing that things could have been different.

Ewan cast a quick glance into the mirror then picked up his car keys, wishing with all his heart that he had refused Tom and Hannah's invitation. He had never felt less like celebrating in his life, if he was honest. Maybe it was a knock-on effect from being so tired but his spirits were at an all-time low. He didn't want to spend the evening with Becky, knowing that she would have preferred to be with anyone but him. It would only rub salt into an already raw wound.

The fact that he still felt anything about what had happened all those years ago was unsettling. Ewan did his best to put it out of his mind as he drove to Bride's Bay. They were eating early because of the children and it was still light when he turned into pub's car park. Ewan felt his breath catch when he saw Becky heading into the pub. She was wearing a slim-fitting dress in a very deep blue—possibly sapphire or maybe azure—he wasn't that well versed in colours and couldn't be sure. However, what he could say was that it did all the things it should have done, highlighting the golden gleam of her hair and the trimness of her figure.

She was wearing high-heeled sandals with it and he groaned as he caught a glimpse of her shapely calves before she disappeared inside. Tonight promised to be even more of an ordeal than he'd feared. He knew that Becky really didn't want him there. That was hard enough to contend with. However, the fact that he was doomed to spend the evening lusting after her would make it so much worse!

CHAPTER TEN

'YOURS IS THE chicken, isn't it, Becky?'

'Yes, that's right. Thank you.'

Becky took the plate that Marie offered her, relieved that they hadn't had to wait very long for their meal. With a bit of luck she should be able to make her escape as soon as dinner was over. They had already toasted Tom and Hannah, so nobody would think it rude if she left. After all, she did have the perfect excuse of needing to put Millie to bed, so give it another hour and she should be on her way home, thankfully.

'Salt?'

Ewan touched her arm and she jumped. Summoning a smile, she turned to him. It had been taken for granted that she and Ewan would want to sit together and the strain was starting to tell. Every time she moved, her arm brushed his arm or her thigh came into contact with his. Quite frankly, her nerves were in shreds and it was all she could do not to let him know how on edge she was feeling.

'No, I'm fine, thanks.'

Ewan put the salt cellar down. 'The food's always been good here, hasn't it? Thank heavens that Mitch and Marie haven't gone down the "fine dining" route.'

He drew imaginary speech marks round the words and Becky flinched as his shoulder brushed against hers. She murmured something, but she could feel her skin tingling from the contact. What on earth was the matter with her? Was she really so starved of sex that all it took was the lightest touch to arouse her?

The thought sent a rush of colour to her cheeks and out of the corner of her eyes she saw Ewan frown. She knew he was going to say something and hurriedly forestalled him. Turning, she smiled at Millie. 'Let Mummy help you with those peas, sweetheart.'

Picking up a spoon, she went to help Millie scoop up her peas but the little girl was having none of it. She pushed Becky's hand away, her lower lip jutting ominously. 'Me, me.'

'She's a determined little madam, isn't she?' Ewan laughed as Millie picked up a handful of peas and shovelled them into her mouth. 'Oh, well done, poppet. Clever girl for working out the best way to eat them.'

Millie beamed at him and Hannah, who was sitting opposite them, laughed. 'Looks like you've made a conquest there, Ewan.'

'What can I say?' He adopted a suitably modest expression. 'You've either got it or you haven't. Obviously, I'm a big hit with females under the age of two!'

Everyone laughed. Even Becky managed to dredge up a smile, knowing it was expected. It was clear that everyone believed she and Ewan were a couple and short of announcing that they weren't, she had no choice other than to go along with it.

'You should practise your technique and see if you can have the same effect on their mothers,' she suggested, setting off another round of laughter.

'Good idea.' Ewan grinned at her but his eyes were cool. 'I might just try that.'

The others all thought they were joking, of course, but Becky knew differently. She applied herself to her dinner but although the food was excellent, it tasted like sawdust. Ewan hadn't welcomed her advice and why should he have done? He didn't need her to tell him how to woo a woman. He could manage it perfectly well by himself!

The thought of all the women that he had wooed and won was even harder to swallow than her dinner. It was a relief when everyone finished and she could make her excuses and leave.

'I hate to be a party pooper but I really should take Millie home now,' she said, standing up. 'She had a really late night last night and I don't want her getting overtired.'

'Do you want me to walk back home with you, darling?' her mother offered.

'No, you stay and finish your wine.' Becky smiled around the table, deliberately avoiding Ewan's eyes. Although she knew she had no rights where he was concerned, it still hurt to think about Ewan and all those other women. 'I'll see you very soon, I expect.'

'Too right you will,' Tom put in with a grin. 'Tomorrow morning at the surgery, bright and early.'

Becky drummed up a laugh as she lifted Millie out of the high chair. 'It hardly seems worth going to bed, does it?'

'Oh, I don't know.' Tom glanced at Hannah, making it clear why he disagreed with that sentiment.

Becky smiled, although her heart was aching in the most peculiar fashion. So what if Tom and Hannah intended to celebrate their engagement in time-honoured fashion? It shouldn't bother her. 'I don't think I'll ask what you meant by that!' she replied, adopting a deliberately upbeat tone.

She picked up her bag then glanced round in surprise when she realised that Ewan had stood up as well. He smiled at her but his eyes were still rather chilly.

'I'll walk you home.'

'There's no need,' she began, but he didn't let her finish.

'I have to leave, anyway, and I'd prefer to know that you and Millie had got home safely.'

Becky's mouth thinned when she saw the approval on everyone's faces. It was obvious that they thought it only right that Ewan should see her home and, short of making a scene, there was nothing she could do. She popped Millie into her pushchair then led the way across the restaurant, nodding her thanks when Ewan opened the door for her because she didn't trust herself to speak. Didn't he realise that he was only making the situation worse by fostering the idea that they were a couple? She waited until they were safely out of earshot before she rounded on him.

'What are you playing at, Ewan? The last thing we need is people thinking we're an item!'

'They're going to think it no matter what we do.' He shrugged, his broad shoulders moving lightly under the thin cotton shirt he was wearing.

Becky felt her mouth go dry as she saw his muscles ripple, and looked away. She didn't need this, didn't need any more reminders of how attractive he was. Ewan had always been fit but his body had matured in the past few years. Now there didn't appear to be

an ounce of spare flesh on him. All of a sudden she
found herself imagining how he would feel if she ran
her hands over him: smooth warm skin, hard, toned
muscles, a dusting of crisp dark hair...

She drove the images from her mind. She wasn't
going to think about things like that! Taking a firmer
grip on the pushchair, she headed across the car park,
aware that Ewan was keeping pace with her. Even
though she *really* didn't want him walking her home,
she knew there was no point objecting. Once Ewan
made up his mind, it was impossible to change it.

They walked back to the house in silence. Millie fell
asleep almost immediately, worn out by her adventures.
Becky unlocked the door then bent down and undid
the harness. With a bit of luck she might be able to get
Millie into bed without waking her, she thought as she
carefully lifted her out of the pushchair.

'I'll fetch the pushchair in.'

Becky barely glanced at Ewan as he lifted it over the
step. He could do whatever he liked—she didn't care
anymore. She carried Millie upstairs and laid her on
the changing mat, quickly stripping off her dress before popping on a clean nappy and a pair of pale green
cotton pyjamas with bunnies on them. The little girl
didn't stir as she settled her in the cot and covered her
with a blanket.

'Night-night, darling,' she murmured, stroking the
child's soft little cheek. It was at moments like this that
she realised how lucky she was. Millie meant everything to her; she was her reason for living, the one thing
that had kept her going after the accident when life had
seemed so grim. So long as Millie was safe and happy,

nothing else mattered, not what people thought about her and Ewan, or how she felt about him...

Her heart gave a painful little jolt. How *did* she feel about Ewan? There was no doubt that she liked and admired him. That she found him physically attractive as well wasn't in question either if tonight was anything to go by. So what did it all add up to? Was it possible that she was falling in love with him again?

Becky left the bedroom and went and sat on the top step, her legs suddenly too weak to support her. She didn't want to fall in love with Ewan. It would be a mistake for all sorts of reasons. However, she couldn't put her hand on her heart and swear it wouldn't happen, could she?

Ewan glanced at his watch and frowned. Becky seemed to be taking an inordinately long time putting Millie to bed. Maybe he should check if everything was all right....

And maybe he shouldn't.

He sighed when it struck him that Becky was probably doing it deliberately, spinning things out in the hope that he would get fed up and leave. Well, if that was the case then he didn't intend to disappoint her!

Opening the back door, he went to step out, then hesitated. Maybe it was silly, but he hated to think that they were parting on bad terms, especially when he knew it was mainly his fault. After all, Becky was bound to be sensitive about people misinterpreting their friendship. It was barely a year since she'd been widowed and it was only natural that she wouldn't want everyone to think that she had forgotten her husband.

Ewan went back inside. He made his way along the

hall, pausing when he reached the stairs. Should he go and find Becky and apologise? Or would it be better if he left her a note? He didn't want to add to her distress so it was hard to decide. It was only when he happened to glance up and saw her sitting on the stairs that he made up his mind.

'Are you all right?' he asked as he went to join her. He sat down on the step below so that they were on eye level, his heart contracting when he saw the anguish on her face. It was obvious that she was torturing herself, unnecessarily, too.

'I'm really sorry, Becky,' he said, taking hold of her hand. Her fingers felt so small and cold and his hand tightened, wanting to instil some warmth into her flesh. 'I never meant to upset you.'

'Upset me?'

'Yes.' He sighed. 'I understand now why you don't want folk thinking we're an item. I mean, it's barely a year since you lost your husband, isn't it?'

'Yes.' She bit her lip and Ewan felt even more wretched. To know that he had caused her all this heart-ache was very hard.

'I promise you that I'll make sure everyone knows the truth. In fact, I'll phone Tom tomorrow and set him straight, and ask him to tell everyone else.'

'If that's what you want, then fine,' she said flatly.

Ewan frowned. 'It's what you want, isn't it? I mean, that's why you're upset, because you hate the idea of people thinking that you're over Steve?'

She shrugged. 'I don't care what they think.'

'Really?' He bent closer. 'So if it isn't that which has upset you, what is it?'

'Nothing. I'm just tired, that's all.'

Ewan knew it was a lie and he wasn't prepared to let her get away with it. 'I don't believe you, Becky. Something's wrong and I want to know what it is.' He dredged up a smile. 'That's what friends are for, to share problems and give you a boost when you need it.'

'Do you think we can stick to being friends, Ewan?' She looked at him and Ewan felt his pulse leap when he saw the awareness in her eyes. It took every scrap of willpower not to respond but he'd caused enough damage for one evening.

'If it's what we both want, then, yes, I do.' He hesitated but he had to ask even though he knew it was a mistake. 'Why? Don't you think we can?'

'I don't know. I want to, but...'

She tailed off and Ewan realised that whatever he did next was going to determine which direction their relationship took. His head began to spin as thoughts raced this way and that. Did he want them to be solely friends or did he want them to be more than that? Could he face the thought of falling in love with her again after what had happened the last time? On the other hand, was he strong enough to stop it happening?

It felt as though a lifetime had passed while he churned it all over in his head, but in truth it was mere seconds. For every question there was an answer, the same answer repeated time after time: Yes. Yes. Yes! He was already reaching for her before the last yes faded, already sure that he was doing the right thing. He wanted her so much, wanted to be her friend, her lover, plus everything beyond and in between.

Their mouths met and it was as though they had never been apart. It was like finding a part of himself that had been missing, Ewan realised in wonder. He may have kissed a lot of women since he'd last kissed Becky but not one of them had made this impact on him. When they finally broke apart, he could tell that Becky was as stunned by what had happened as he was. She hadn't expected this reaction either and now it was up to him to ensure that she didn't end up feeling guilty.

'Wow! That was some kiss,' he said, adopting a deliberately teasing tone.

'I…erm…yes, it was,' she agreed huskily.

Ewan felt the tiny hairs all over his body stand to attention. Had she any idea how deliciously sexy she sounded? he wondered, before he ruthlessly erased the thought. He mustn't get too far ahead of himself, mustn't try to lead her down a path she might not want to take. Maybe Becky had enjoyed the kiss but it didn't mean she wanted to make love with him.

He took her hand, overwhelmed by a sudden need to protect her. Making love with her was what he wanted— desperately!—but his needs had to come second to hers. 'It seems that the old feelings aren't dead after all. The question is where do we go from here? If we stop now, we may still be able to remain friends, but if we move things up a notch, that won't be possible.'

'I realise that.' She looked into his eyes and he could see the uncertainty in hers. 'I don't know, Ewan—that's the honest answer. Part of me knows it would be wrong to pick up where we left off but the other part…'

She shrugged, leaving him to fill in the rest, which he did with alacrity. Bending, he kissed her again, just lightly and with infinite tenderness. 'I feel the same, Becky. Part of me feels it would be madness if we got involved, but another part can't think of anything I want more.'

'Then maybe we should take time to think about it,' she suggested.

She looked at him and Ewan felt his breath catch when he saw the desire in her eyes. It was all he could do not to haul her back into his arms and kiss her until neither of them could think straight, but he had to be sensible, had to make sure it was what they both truly wanted. There was too much at stake and it would be far too easy to end up getting hurt.

'I think it's a good idea,' he said quietly, feeling the first stirrings of alarm. When they had decided against getting involved before, he had felt hurt but not devastated. His feelings had been tempered by relief because his plans to travel wouldn't need to be changed, but it was different now. Something warned him that it would be far worse to lose Becky this time round. 'We don't want to rush into anything and regret it, do we?'

'No, we don't.' Her fingers closed around his. 'The last thing I want is either of us getting hurt, Ewan.'

'I don't want that either.' He squeezed her hand then glanced round when he heard the back door opening. 'It sounds as though your parents are home.' He stood up, not wanting to cause her any embarrassment by having Ros and Simon find them in such a compromising position. 'I'd better go. I'm due in work early tomorrow but I'll phone you in the evening, if that's okay?'

'Fine.'

She stood up as well, smoothing down her dress. Ewan turned and ran down the stairs, trying not to think about how he would have loved to help her out of it. He could just imagine inching down the zip a fraction at a time while he laid a trail of kisses down her spine....

'Ah, just off, are you, Ewan?' Simon appeared from

the direction of the kitchen and Ewan hastily rid himself of such tantalising thoughts.

'Yes. I'm in work early tomorrow,' he explained, glancing round when Becky appeared. Heat roared through his veins as the image of her standing in front of him, half-naked, came flooding back. Her skin would be so soft and so smooth, like the finest satin. He could imagine how it would feel beneath his hands and his lips....

'No rest for the wicked, eh?' Simon said cheerfully.

Ewan started, afraid that he'd said something revealing before he realised that Simon was referring to his early start. 'So they say,' he agreed with as much aplomb as he could muster. 'Right, I'll be off then. I'll speak to you tomorrow, Becky.'

'Fine.'

She gave him a quick smile and he couldn't help feeling disappointed even though he knew it was ridiculous to expect anything more with her father standing there. He said goodnight to Ros on his way out and walked back to The Ship Inn to collect his car, calling himself a whole load of unflattering names.

He was an idiot if he imagined that Becky was going to declare her feelings for him in front of her parents! If truth be told, she wasn't sure how she felt and neither was he. Oh, that kiss had been magical; there was no doubt about that. However, it didn't prove she loved him now any more than it had proved she'd loved him eight years ago.

Ewan slammed the car door, aware that he was doing the one thing he had sworn he wouldn't do. He was on the verge of falling in love with Becky all over again.

CHAPTER ELEVEN

'THIS IS THE last time you'll need to come in to the surgery, Mrs Rose. Your leg has healed beautifully and it won't need dressing anymore.'

Becky smiled at the old lady, doing her best to set aside her own problems, but it wasn't easy. She'd spent the night thinking about her and Ewan and what she should do. Would it be right to have a relationship with him when she knew it couldn't lead anywhere? Her head said no but her heart said just the opposite. If her heart had its way then she and Ewan would be the couple everyone believed them to be very soon.

She cleared her throat, trying not to think about all that it entailed. Thinking about making love with Ewan certainly wouldn't help her reach a measured decision. 'You'll need to be careful, of course. The new skin is still very delicate and you don't want to damage it. But all things considered, you've done remarkably well.'

'That's good to hear, my dear.' Mrs Rose beamed at her. 'It's all down to your excellent care, of course. I really appreciate the trouble you've taken.'

'It's been no trouble,' Becky declared truthfully. She put the soiled dressing into the hazardous waste bin and peeled off her gloves, popping them in as well. 'You've been a model patient. I only wish there were more people like you.'

Mrs Rose laughed. 'Some folk can be a little troublesome, I imagine. I must confess that I'm not looking forward to taking care of my son once he's discharged from hospital. Geoffrey isn't what you would call an easy person to help.'

'I didn't know your son was ill!' Becky exclaimed. 'I'm so sorry.'

'Oh, it was his own fault. He was the driver of the car that collided with that coach at the weekend.' Mrs Rose looked disapproving. 'It appears he was using his mobile phone at the time. Geoffrey has denied it, of course, but the police have applied for a copy of his phone records and no doubt they will prove he was on the phone at the time.'

'Oh, dear.' Becky grimaced. 'It sounds as though he may be charged with dangerous driving.'

'It will serve him right,' Mrs Rose said sternly. 'It's only by the grace of God that no one was killed.'

Becky nodded, knowing it was true. She added a note to Mrs Rose's file to the effect that she was discharging her and smiled. 'That's it, then. I shall miss our little chats now that you won't need to pop in to see me.'

'So will I.' Mrs Rose sighed as she stood up. 'It gets rather lonely, living on your own, especially since Emily moved away.'

'Oh, so you and Emily were friends, were you?' Becky asked, not wanting to hurry the old lady after what she'd said.

'Friends and neighbours, actually. Emily rented the cottage next to mine and I really miss not having her and little Theo around.' Mrs Rose shook her head. 'The agents are thinking of letting it out as a holiday rental but it won't be the same. I mean, you can't get to know people if they're only there for a couple of weeks.'

'Would they consider another long-term let?' Becky asked slowly, wondering if this might be the answer to her problems. If she could afford the rent then she and Millie would have a home of their own again.

'Oh, yes. They'd prefer it, in fact. Why? Are you interested in renting it, my dear?' Mrs Rose had perked up at the thought.

Becky nodded. 'Yes, I am. My parents have been marvellous but I really would like to find a place of our own for me and Millie.'

'The cottage would be ideal!' Mrs Rose assured her. 'Emily got it looking really nice inside. And although the garden is small, it's all fenced in so you wouldn't have to worry about your little girl getting out.'

'It sounds perfect.'

Becky wrote down the details of the agents who were handling the property then saw Mrs Rose out. She went back to her room, buoyed up by the thought of having a home of her own again. Much as she loved her parents, it was what she wanted, to be independent while she raised Millie. Maybe it hadn't been her goal a few years ago but things had changed since then. She was never going to be a happily married mum, looking after her brood, but a single parent with a child to raise. She frowned. Maybe she should make sure that Ewan understood that before they went any further?

'You look shattered. What did you get up to at the weekend, or shouldn't I ask?'

Ewan grinned when Cathy Morrison accosted him

in the staffroom. 'Oh, you can ask all right, although you'll be disappointed by the answer. I ended up helping out at that coach crash. It kind of ruined my peaceful day off.'

'Really?' Cathy grimaced as she switched on the kettle. 'I'd say that was above and beyond the call of duty. What did you do—follow the ambulances to see where they were going?'

'No way!' Ewan laughed. 'I gave up ambulance chasing a while back. I leave that to the insurance people these days. No, I just happened to be around when the call came through and went along to help. A couple of doctors from Bride's Bay Surgery were having a party and they invited me along,' he added by way of explanation.

'Oh, hard luck. Still, it'll teach you to hobnob with other medics during off-duty hours.' Cathy grinned as she spooned instant coffee into a couple of mugs. 'You should do what I do and make sure that all your friends are strictly non-medical!'

'I shall bear it in mind,' Ewan agreed with a grin as he accepted the mug of coffee.

Cathy took her coffee back to the desk, leaving him alone with his thoughts. He sighed as he sank down onto a chair. The call-out was only partially to blame for his weariness. The real culprit was lack of sleep. He'd spent the night tossing and turning while the same thought had whizzed around his head: was he completely mad to consider getting involved with Becky?

A week ago—less, even—he would have agreed wholeheartedly with that sentiment but not any longer. The thought of a future without Becky was impossible to imagine and that's what worried him most of all. He had gone from not wanting to get involved with her to needing to know she would be part of his life in what seemed like the blink of an eye. If that wasn't a sign he was crazy then heaven knew what was!

Ewan got up and tipped the rest of the coffee down the sink. He couldn't bear to sit there, churning it all over again. He went back to the unit, lifting the next patient's notes out of the tray. It would be better if he kept himself busy, although he would have to decide what he was going to do soon. Becky was expecting him to phone her that night and he needed to know what tone the call should take. Light and friendly? Or something deeper?

He grimaced. He knew what he really wanted to do, but it didn't mean it was right.

It was almost eight before the telephone rang. Becky shot to her feet, smiling sheepishly when her mother looked at her in surprise. 'I'd better get that before it wakes Millie,' she said, hurrying out of the room.

Snatching up the receiver, she pressed it to her ear, wondering why she felt so nervous. It was just a phone call. Nothing to get excited about. However, the fact that it might be Ewan phoning gave it a whole new significance. 'Dr Harper's residence. Becky speaking.'

'Becky, it's Ewan. Hi!'

He sounded so light and breezy, a world away from the nervous wreck she'd turned into, that Becky couldn't help feeling a little irritated. 'Oh, hello, Ewan. I'd forgotten you said you'd ring tonight. How are you?'

'Tired but that's nothing new.' He gave a short laugh and she heard the edge it held. He obviously hadn't appreciated her comment but hard luck. While she'd been worrying herself to death, he'd been swanning about without a care in the world, apparently. She hardened her heart. 'Are you phoning about something special or just for a chat?'

'Both, actually. But if you're busy, it will keep until another time. Enjoy your evening.'

'Wait!' Becky realised that he was going to hang up and knew that she couldn't bear to be left wondering. She needed to know what he had decided, come what may. 'I'm not doing anything important,' she admitted, swallowing her pride.

'Well, if you're sure...' There was a hint, the merest trace of laughter in his voice, and she glared at the receiver even though he couldn't possibly see her.

'Of course I'm sure!'

'Good.' His voice softened, flowing down the line like warm honey, and her irritation melted away. 'I've been thinking about you all day. That's why I was so late in calling you. I couldn't decide what I was going to say.'

'I understand.' She sighed. 'It isn't easy, is it? I mean, we didn't expect this to happen, did we?'

'No. If I'm honest it was the last thing I wanted but I won't lie to you, Becky. I still have feelings for you and I think you still have them for me, too.'

'I do.' She bit her lip, unwilling to say anything else. They were still on fairly safe ground at the moment, still able to step back, but once they moved their relationship onto a physical level that wouldn't be possible. The thought made her shudder with sudden apprehension.

'So what are we going to do?' he said softly. 'I may as well admit that I still haven't made up my mind. Have you?'

'No. Part of me wants us to remain friends because it would be so much simpler that way…'

'And another part wants us to be more than friends,' he said, finishing the sentence. 'It's the same for me, if it's any consolation.'

'So what do you suggest?'

'I suppose the sensible thing is to take it slowly and not rush into anything. At the moment we're still in shock and it would be stupid to let ourselves get carried away. Maybe in a week or so's time we'll have a clearer idea of what we want.'

'That sounds like a good idea to me.'

'Does it?' He laughed. 'Miracle of miracles. I'm actually making sense even though it feels as though my head is spinning!'

Becky laughed as well. 'Mine too. So how do you want to play this? Shall we see one another, purely on a friendly basis, of course?'

'I don't think we'll ever work this out if we don't,' he said wryly. 'I'm on earlies all week but I'm off on Saturday so do you fancy doing something then, maybe take Millie to the beach if the weather's fine?'

'That would be lovely…oh, the thing is, I've arranged to view a cottage on Saturday morning. Emily used to live there and it sounds ideal.'

'I'll come with you,' he offered at once and she laughed.

'Would you? That would be great.'

They arranged what time he would pick her and Millie up before they hung up. Becky went back to the sitting room, hoping that she hadn't made a mistake. She didn't want to hurt Ewan but there was no guarantee it wouldn't happen if they got close again. At the end

of the day she mustn't forget that she could never give
Ewan the family he would want one day.

'Who was that, darling?' Ros looked up as she went
back into the room and Becky did her best to put on a
cheerful face.

'Ewan. We've arranged to meet on Saturday.' Becky
took a quick breath, deciding that it would be better to
get it all over with in one fell swoop. She'd been trying
to work out the best way to broach the subject but there
was really only one way. 'Actually, I'm going to look
at a house that's for rent. It's Emily's old home and it
sounds perfect for me and Millie.'

'I thought you'd want to find a place of your own
once you got settled,' Ros said calmly.

'You don't mind? Don't think I'm ungrateful, will
you? You and Dad have been marvellous but it would
be good to have my own space,' Becky explained anxiously.

'I understand, darling. Really I do.' Ros smiled at her.
'You're a grown woman with a child of your own—it
would be strange if you didn't want your own home.'

'Thank you.' Becky went and gave her mother a hug.

'There's nothing to thank me for. Your father and I
only want what's best for you.' Ros frowned. 'Are you
sure you know what you're doing with regard to Ewan,
though? Don't get me wrong, I'd be over the moon if
you two got together but I got the impression that it was
never going to happen.'

'It isn't. I like Ewan, more than just like him, if I'm
honest. But I won't ruin his life, Mum.'

'He may not see it like that,' Ros pointed out.

'Maybe not but it's a risk I'm not willing to take.'

Becky shrugged. 'Ewan needs someone who can give him a family eventually. And that's something I can't do.'

'I'm so sorry, darling.'

Becky smiled sadly. 'Me too.'

Ros changed the subject. She obviously didn't want to upset her, although Becky knew that talking about the issue wouldn't make it any worse. She couldn't have another child and that was final. No amount of discussion would solve the problem, although it didn't mean she intended to tell Ewan. Knowing Ewan, he would probably claim it didn't matter but she knew that it did. She had no intention of ruining his chances of having a family of his own one day.

Saturday dawned bright and clear. Ewan was up before six despite the fact that he and Becky weren't due to meet until mid-morning. He took a shower, whistling to himself as the water pounded down on his head. He felt all bright-eyed and bushy-tailed and it was all down to Becky. The thought of spending the day with her was a definite boost to his spirits. How marvellous it would be if he could spend the rest of his life with her.

The thought stayed with him while he ate his breakfast. The main reason he had come back to England was to settle down. Although he had enjoyed seeing something of the world and wouldn't have missed it for anything, he had realised recently that he wanted more. It was time to put down roots, find the woman he wanted to spend his life with and start a family. Now that he'd met Becky again, it seemed that all the boxes had been ticked. He couldn't think of anything better than having Becky as his wife and the mother of his children.

Ewan put his dishes in the sink and picked up his car

keys. Even though it was way too early to set off, he needed to see Becky and find out if she felt the same as him. Maybe they had agreed to take things slowly but he couldn't bear the thought of waiting. He needed to know if there was a chance that Becky loved him!

Becky had just finished getting Millie dressed when she heard a car pull up. Hurrying to the window, she gasped when she saw Ewan getting out. What on earth was he doing here at this time of the morning? She ran downstairs to let him in.

'I know, I know. I'm horribly early.' He grinned at her, his blue eyes alight with laughter and something else, something that made her pulse race. 'I'll understand if you tell me to take a hike.'

'Of course not.' Becky dredged up a smile but her heart was pounding away as though it was trying for a new world record. To have Ewan look at her with all that desire in his eyes wasn't easy to deal with. She cleared her throat. 'Mum and Dad are still in bed but Millie's up. Go on through to the kitchen while I fetch her.'

She ran back upstairs and picked Millie up then paused while she tried to calm herself down. She had to remember that they were taking things slowly....

Ewan didn't seem to be setting too much store by that idea, though, did he?

Becky shook her head to dislodge that insidious thought and carried Millie downstairs. Ewan had the kettle on and he looked round when she went in.

'Tea or coffee?'

'Tea, please.' Becky popped Millie into her highchair. Although the little girl had already eaten her breakfast, she peeled a banana and gave it to her, then sat down.

'Here you go.' Ewan placed a mug in front of her. Bending over, he pretended to take a bite of Millie's banana. 'Yummy, scrummy. That looks delicious.'

Millie chuckled as she tried to ram the fruit into his mouth and he laughed. Taking a handkerchief out of his pocket, he wiped away the mashed banana smeared all round his mouth. 'Thank you, sweetheart. It's really kind of you to give me a taste.'

Becky sighed as she watched the interplay between them. Ewan was so good with Millie, seeming to know exactly how to treat her. He had a natural affinity with children and would make the most wonderful father. Pain ripped through her and she glanced down at her tea, not wanting him to suspect anything was wrong. She had made up her mind that she wasn't going to tell Ewan about her not being able to have any more children and she must stick to it.

'So what time are you meeting the agents?'

She looked up when he spoke, adopting a deliberately upbeat tone. 'Ten-thirty.'

'Have you told your parents what you're planning?' he asked, pulling out a chair. He was wearing fawn chinos and Becky felt her pulse race even faster as she saw the fabric tauten across his muscular thighs.

'Yes, and they're fine about it,' she said huskily. 'They understand that I need my own space.'

'I didn't think it would be a problem.' He grinned at her. 'Fingers crossed that the cottage turns out to be suitable.'

'Ditto.' Becky made a great production of crossing her fingers. She had to be sensible, had to remember that no matter how much she wanted Ewan, they didn't have a future together. She stood up, unable to deal with the thought right then. 'I'll make a start on our picnic. Cheese and ham sandwiches all right with you?'

'Perfect.' He captured her hand as she came around the table. 'I've been looking forward to today, Becky.'

'Me too.'

She gave him a quick smile before she freed herself. Taking the bread out of the bread bin, she set to work and in a very short time had assembled their picnic. It was easier when she had something to do, less stressful. When Ewan offered his help, she declined, deeming it safer to leave him sitting in the chair rather than run the risk of them bumping into one another.

She gulped because she knew where that would lead. The thought of making love with Ewan both scared and thrilled her. Their relationship had never reached that point eight years ago; she had broken it off before they had got that far. However, she knew that once it happened, it would be even harder to do the right thing. And the right thing meant walking away. Again.

CHAPTER TWELVE

THE COTTAGE WAS perfect. Ewan could tell that Becky was going to take it even before the agent had finished showing them round. Once everything was agreed and the agent had left, they took a last look around the garden. Becky couldn't hide her delight as she lifted Millie onto a junior-sized swing that Emily had left behind.

'This is going to be our new home, sweetheart. You'll love living here, won't you?'

Ewan laughed. 'I'm not sure Millie understands you.'

'Of course she does! She's a very intelligent little girl—can't you tell?'

'Oh, I can.' He smiled back, relieved that she seemed to have got over whatever had been troubling her earlier. He'd had the distinct impression when they were in the kitchen that she'd been keeping her distance, although he wasn't sure why. 'She's very like her mother in that respect,' he declared, deciding not to say anything. It was only natural that Becky should have reservations about them, after all.

'I shall take that as a compliment, thank you.' Becky lifted Millie off the swing, shaking her head when she started to wail. 'We have to go now, darling, but we can come back again very soon.'

Millie refused to be mollified, however. She
screamed even louder as they made their way down
the path. Ewan bent and looked into her angry little face.

'What a racket! You're making so much noise that
you're frightening the birds.'

Millie stopped screaming and looked at him in surprise. He took her from Becky, holding her up so she
could see the flock of sparrows nesting in the bushes
that ran alongside the path. 'See, there they are. If you
keep very quiet you'll hear them singing.'

Mille stared at them in wide-eyed wonder and Becky
laughed. 'You seem to be a dab hand at this. How come
you know so much about entertaining young children?'

'One of the benefits of being an uncle to so many
little nieces and nephews,' he replied wryly. 'You have
to find ways to distract them if you hope to survive!'

'Really?' Becky frowned. 'But surely you haven't
seen that much of your family with working abroad?'

'More than you'd think.' He swung Millie onto his
shoulders and gave her a piggyback to the car. 'Anna
lives in France so I spent a lot of time with her and her
family while I was working there. And Fiona has moved
to Spain—Marbella, which is a great place for holidays
as I discovered. Then there's Shona—I think I told you
that I stayed with her on my way back here.'

'You did. You said she was expecting another child—
has she had it yet?'

'Yes. Another little girl.' He grinned as he unlocked
the car. 'Ryan's girlfriend is expecting too so I'll have
to get a move on if I hope to compete with the rest of
my family!'

'You certainly will.'

Becky gave him a quick smile but Ewan was aware

that some of the sparkle had gone out of it. What had he said? he wondered as he handed Millie over so Becky could strap her into her seat. He had no idea but it seemed that he had touched a nerve.

He drove them straight to Pringle's Cove after they left the cottage. Although the beach there was much smaller than the one at nearby Denton's Cove, there were lots of rock pools, which he knew Millie would enjoy exploring. Drawing up close to the top of the foot-path, he switched off the engine.

'I'll fetch our bits and bobs while you carry Millie.'

'Are you sure you can manage?' Becky asked as she got out of the car. She looked dubiously into the boot. 'We seem to have an awful lot of stuff in there.'

'I'll just bring the essentials for now and come back for the rest as and when it's needed,' he assured her.

'Oh, right. Good idea.'

She set off down the path while Ewan gathered to-gether what they needed. The picnic basket and the rug were essentials, as were a child-sized bucket and spade. He piled everything on the ground then reached for the parasol he'd discovered at the back of a cup-board, stopping when he heard a scream from below. Hurrying to the top of the path, he peered down, his heart turning over when he saw Becky lying sprawled on the ground. He ran down to her, skidding to a halt when he reached her.

'Are you all right?'

'I think so.' She went to stand up, no easy task when she still had hold of Millie.

'Let me take her.' Ewan took the little girl off her, putting his hand under Becky's elbow as he helped her to her feet.

'Thanks. My foot caught on a stone and down I went. Is Millie all right?' she asked anxiously.

'She's fine, aren't you, poppet?' Ewan gave the child a cuddle then took a firmer grip on Becky's arm. 'Let's get you down safely before I go back for our things.'

Becky didn't protest as he helped her down the rest of the path. Ewan guessed that the fall had shaken her up but he didn't say anything. Becky wouldn't appreciate him fussing over her. She wasn't the sort of woman who demanded attention, although maybe he should have paid her more attention eight years ago and then she might not have married Steve. He sighed as he left her and Millie sitting on a piece of driftwood and went back for their things. It was pointless thinking like that. Becky had married Steve and nothing would change that fact. All he could do was hope that she would get over losing her husband in time.

Despite its inauspicious start, the afternoon turned out perfectly. Ewan was patience itself as he helped Millie make dozens of sand pies. He even dug a trench so the sea could form a moat around them, much to Millie's delight. As Becky listened to her daughter's squeals of joy as the water flowed along the channel, she couldn't help feeling sad. If things had been different then Millie could have been the luckiest little girl in the world. She could have had Ewan around to love and care for her while she was growing up.

'I…am…pooped!' Ewan deposited a decidedly sandy Millie onto the rug and flopped down beside her. 'This little lady has worn me out.'

'I thought you said you were an expert at looking after little ones,' Becky retorted, determined not to let him know how she was feeling. She knew the score, understood that Ewan could never take on the role of Millie's father, and there was no point torturing herself.

'Hmm, obviously I had a rather rosy view of my prowess.' He raked back his hair and grinned wickedly at her. 'Remind me not to make any false claims in the future, will you?'

Even though ostensibly they were discussing his claim to be an expert childminder, Becky blushed. She busied herself with unpacking the picnic, trying not to think about what else Ewan might claim to be an expert at. So what if he was a wonderful lover? There was no guarantee that they were compatible, was there?

The thought nagged away at her as they ate. She had lost all interest in sex in recent years and it was worrying to wonder how she would react if she and Ewan made love, especially in view of what Steve had said. She couldn't bear to think that he had been right and that she was frigid.

Millie fell asleep as soon as she had finished her lunch. Becky laid her down on the rug, frowning as she looked round for something to use as a sunshade. The sun was quite strong now and she didn't want Millie getting burnt.

'Use this.' Ewan produced a battered-looking parasol. He dug it into the sand, angling it so that Millie was sheltered from the sun's rays.

'That's great. Where on earth did you get it, though?'

'I found it in the back of a cupboard. The previous tenants must have left it behind when they moved out of the flat.' Ewan sat down again, resting his forearms across his up-bent knees as he stared out to sea. 'It's so peaceful here. It's hard to believe that only a few miles away there are people rushing about.'

'It must make a pleasant change after working in ED all week,' Becky observed, leaning back on her elbows. She tilted her face to the sun, enjoying its warmth. It seemed ages since she'd had time to relax like this and she intended to make the most of it.

'True. Although, I must admit that I love the job.' He shrugged. 'I must be a bit of masochist, I suppose.'

'You always wanted to work in emergency medicine,' she pointed out, turning to look at him.

'I did.' He smiled at her. 'I guess I'm one of the lucky ones. Not everyone gets to do a job they love. Oh, that reminds me, did I tell you that I called in to see Sandra Fielding?'

'The lady who fractured her femur in the coach crash?'

'That's the one. She's doing very well, you'll be glad to hear, although whether that's down to the excellent nursing care she's received or because her friend—Edward, isn't it?—cancelled his flight home to Canada so he could be with her, I'm not sure.' He laughed. 'They say that love is the best medicine of all and they could be right.'

'Really? Oh, how lovely!' Becky exclaimed.

'Isn't it?' His voice dropped, sounding deeper than ever, and she shivered. 'I think it proves that time doesn't always destroy people's feelings.'

He leant sideways and Becky knew that he was going to kiss her. Just for a moment panic assailed her as she wondered if it was right to let their relationship take this direction. But then Ewan's lips found hers and all her doubts fled. She wanted his kiss, wanted it so much that she couldn't bear to wait another second.

Their mouths met with a small jolt and she heard him sigh, knew that he understood how desperate she felt because he felt the same. Ewan was as eager for this kiss as she was. Their mouths clung then parted. Becky closed her eyes when she felt his lips skim over her face, scattering butterfly-soft kisses along the way. She could feel the sun on her skin, see its glow through her closed eyelids, and it felt as though she was suddenly enveloped in warmth and light. Ewan's mouth was so hot, his lips burning as they travelled over her skin. Everywhere they touched it felt as though a flame had ignited. Would it always be this way? she wondered dizzily. Or would her delight in his kisses fade with time?

'I didn't think it could ever be as good between us as it was before.' Ewan drew back and Becky shuddered when she saw the desire in his eyes.

'And is it?' she asked huskily.

'No.' He dropped a kiss on her mouth, letting his lips linger, and she knew it was because he couldn't bear to break the contact. When he finally pulled away his face was set, the tense line of his jaw hinting at the struggle he'd had. 'It's even better.'

He eased her down onto the rug and kissed her again, his mouth demanding a response that she was more than willing to give. Becky could feel desire roaring through her veins, feel her blood heating and her heart racing. Ewan was right, she thought, it was better now: more passionate, more sensual, more...*everything*!

They were both breathless when they broke apart, both trembling as though they had a fever. Becky could feel little flurries of heat rippling beneath her skin and knew they had nothing to do with the weather. It was Ewan who had set her alight; his kisses had reawoken her passion and proved that she wasn't frigid.

'Although I hate to say this, we should stop.' He ran his thumb over her swollen lips and she felt him shudder and shuddered too. He had to breathe in and out before he could continue. 'It's not exactly private here, is it? I'd hate it if someone came along and found us in what could only be called a compromising position.'

Becky blushed as her mind conjured up the scene. The thought of making love with Ewan right here on the beach was so tempting but she knew he was right to call a halt. Even if they had the cove to themselves there was Millie to consider: she could wake up at any moment.

'You're right. I'd hate it too. It would make it seem so cheap and tawdry...'

'Which it isn't.' He kissed her softly and with infinite tenderness. 'There's nothing cheap or tawdry about what we're doing, Becky.'

'I know that.'

'Good. I'd hate to think that you felt it was wrong in any way.'

She saw the question in his eyes and shook her head. 'I don't think that, Ewan. Really, I don't.'

'So long as you're sure it's what you want?' He gave her a moment to reconsider then shrugged. 'At least we're clear on that point. Now we have to decide how to handle this. I understand if you don't want to go public so maybe we should keep this to ourselves until you're comfortable with the idea of us being a couple.'

'I don't think we need to worry unduly about that,' she said, her heart sinking. She took a quick breath but she had to make it clear that no matter what happened, they weren't going down the happily-ever-after route. It would be wrong to mislead him, wrong and cruel to offer him something she couldn't deliver. 'I imagine folk will get the message eventually. Once the expected announcements—engagement, wedding—don't materialise, they'll give up.'

'I'm sure they will.'

Ewan's tone was bland. If he was upset by what she'd said, it didn't show. Becky couldn't help feeling hurt even though she knew how selfish it was. She should be glad that he didn't consider their relationship to be a long-term arrangement. At least this way he wouldn't get hurt.

He stood up, brushing the sand off his legs, and she forced herself to smile even though it felt as though her heart had split wide open. 'So we're agreed, then. We shall be discreet and leave everyone to watch and wonder.'

'Sounds good to me.' He glanced towards the sea, shading his eyes against the glare so that it was impossible to read his expression. 'Right, I think I'll go for a swim. With a bit of luck the sun will have taken some of the chill off the water by now.'

He stripped off his T-shirt and dropped it onto the sand. His trousers quickly followed, leaving him clad only in a pair of black swimming shorts. Becky gulped as she was treated to a glimpse of his hard, tanned body before he jogged towards the water. He plunged into the waves, swimming strongly towards the mouth of the bay.

Becky watched him until her eyes blurred, until she was unable to distinguish the sea from the sky. Lying back on the rug, she tried to console herself with the thought that she had done the right thing, but it didn't help. She might want Ewan even though she knew she couldn't have him, but it was obvious that he didn't want her. Oh, he might be happy to have a relationship with her, would certainly enjoy making love to her, but he didn't see her as part of his future. It made her wonder if he had his own agenda for taking up with her. Was he trying to get even with her for the way she had rejected him? It was possible. Anything was possible. Ewan could be playing her for a fool....

Only she didn't really believe that, did she? It wasn't Ewan's way to be deceitful. He was far too honest to play those sorts of games. Which meant that she'd been right in the first place. Ewan considered her to be a temporary addition to his life, a pleasant distraction. Nothing more and nothing less.

Ewan swam until his lungs burned and his arms felt as though they had turned to lead. Rolling over onto his back, he let the waves carry him back towards the shore. It was lucky the tide was coming in as he doubted he had the strength to get back there under his own steam.

He swore roundly, cursing his own stupidity and the fact that he had allowed his emotions to strip away his common sense. So what if Becky didn't want to spend her life with him? It was hardly a surprise. She'd had her chance eight years ago and decided against it. It wasn't as though he had spent those years pining for her either. He'd had a lot of fun, lived life to the fullest, and enjoyed himself both with and without a female companion in tow. Maybe Becky did seem to press an awful lot of buttons but he would meet someone else who pressed even more. The law of averages made that a certainty.

Out of all the women in all the world, Becky couldn't be the only one he'd fall in love with...

Could she?

Ewan ditched that thought before it could grow wings. Rolling over, he forced his tired limbs into a rapid crawl that soon had him back at the beach. He stood up and shook himself, watching the droplets of water leave pockmarks in the smooth damp sand. Not so long ago it had felt as though everything he had ever wished for was within his reach but now that idea was pockmarked with doubts, like the sand under his feet. Becky might be happy to have a relationship with him but she was never going to make a lifetime's commitment to them as a couple.

Millie was awake when he went back. He towelled himself dry and dragged on his clothes. Becky had packed up the remains of their picnic and he took it as a sign that she was ready to leave. Maybe she'd realised that they'd had the best out of the day and that it was all downhill from this point on.

The thought was depressing. It was an effort to appear upbeat as he picked up Millie. 'I'll carry Millie up the path. I wouldn't want you to slip again.'

'Thanks.'

Becky sounded unusually subdued but he refused to speculate about the reason for it. If she didn't want to share her life with him then she definitely wouldn't want to share her thoughts. He set off up the path, singing a rousing version of 'Baa Baa Black Sheep' to amuse Millie as well as distract himself. There were too many dark thoughts whizzing around his head, thoughts he wouldn't want to share with Becky either. He sighed.

Maybe they were equally at fault. He was just as determined to keep his counsel as she was hers, it seemed.

He handed Millie over then went back to collect their things. By the time he had stowed everything in the boot, the sun had disappeared behind a bank of ominously black clouds. He grimaced as he started the engine.

'Looks like we're leaving at the right time. There's a storm brewing.'

The words were barely out of his mouth when the first raindrops fell from the sky. Ewan turned on the windscreen wipers as he looked for somewhere to turn the car around. The lane leading to Pringle's Cove was extremely narrow, which was one of the reasons why very few visitors made it there. It also made reversing a problem.

'There's a gateway further down the road. You should be able to turn round there,' Becky suggested, leaning forward to point through the windscreen.

Ewan flinched when her arm brushed against his. He gritted his teeth as he drove towards where she'd indicated. He needed to reassess the situation, decide what he wanted to do and not simply be led by his emotions. He turned the car around and headed back to Bride's Bay. What it all came down to was simple: could he handle having a relationship with Becky that was based on sex and nothing more?

CHAPTER THIRTEEN

A WEEK PASSED, then a second, and still Becky didn't hear a word from Ewan. She found herself lingering by the telephone each evening like a lovesick teenager but couldn't help it. She missed him. Missed hearing his voice, missed seeing his smile, just missed him. In a few short weeks he had become an important part of her life and every day she didn't see or speak to him felt emptier because of it.

She knew that at some point she would have to face up to the reason why she felt this way, but not just yet. It was too much, too soon; she wasn't ready. She couldn't handle the fact, either, that no matter how she felt, she could never tell Ewan. She had to protect him even though it appeared he might not need protecting after all. Ewan's feelings seemed to be far more prosaic than hers were.

The start of the new month loomed and Becky got ready to move into the cottage. Her parents had been typically generous and insisted on buying her some furniture. She had sold her old furniture before she'd come back to England, not wanting it as a reminder of her former life. She would have had next to nothing to furnish her new home if her parents hadn't bought her a table and chairs, a bed and a sofa as well as giving her the new nursery furniture, and Becky was suitably grateful.

Thankfully, it was a dry day when she moved in. Her father had hired a van and Tom and Hannah had offered their help as well. Her mother had insisted on looking after Millie and Charlie so the four of them were able to concentrate on getting everything sorted out. By six o'clock that evening, the house was ready.

'I can't believe we've got everything done!' Becky exclaimed, looking around the sitting room. The new sofa with its pale green covers and heap of colourful cushions looked even better than she'd hoped and she smiled in delight. 'It looks absolutely lovely in here. Thank you all so much. You've been brilliant.'

'Our pleasure.' Hannah gave her a hug. 'I take it that Ewan was working today and that's why he couldn't be here to help?'

'I…erm…that's right.' Becky knew it was silly but she simply couldn't bring herself to admit that she hadn't seen Ewan in weeks. Hannah would want to know why and she couldn't face the thought of having to explain the situation to her.

'He probably volunteered to work overtime so he could avoid it,' Tom observed cheerfully. He glanced at his watch, mercifully sparing Becky from having to reply. 'We're going to have to cut and run, I'm afraid. Charlie's usually in bed by seven and it's better if we don't upset his routine.' He kissed Becky's cheek. 'I hope you'll be very happy here, Becky. You deserve to be.'

Becky felt tears rush to her eyes. 'Thanks, Tom.'

She kissed Hannah and her father and thanked them

again then went back to the sitting room and sat down.
Millie was spending the night with her parents as Becky
had decided it would be less unsettling for her if the
house was ready when Millie moved in. She hadn't expected to get everything finished so quickly and now
the evening stretched before her. She wasn't sure what
she was going to do with the time. The only thing left
was to make herself some supper and watch television.

Becky went into the kitchen and set to work, cut-
ting up some chicken for a stir-fry even though she really wasn't hungry. Still, it stopped her thinking about
Ewan and the fact that he obviously didn't care a jot
about her. How could he do when he hadn't even bothered to phone and wish her well?

Her knife flew as she chopped a mound of vegetables. There was far too much for one person but so
what? What did an extra bit of broccoli matter in the
great scheme of things? The man she loved didn't love
her—that was what mattered.

It was only when that thought sank in that Becky
stopped what she was doing. She loved Ewan. It wasn't
a question but a statement. She loved him. How it had
happened she had no idea but she had fallen in love with
him all over again, always assuming that she had fallen
out of love with him in the first place, and she was no
longer sure about that. She had opted for security, for
the kind of life she had dreamed of having when she
had chosen to stay with Steve, but she had never loved
him the way she loved Ewan. Her love for Ewan would
last a lifetime—her lifetime, not his.

Ewan stopped the car and switched off the engine. Night
was falling and the light from the cottage cast a puddle

of yellow across the path. He had spent the day wrestling with himself and lost. He knew it was a mistake to come here but he had to see Becky even if it was only to wish her well. Reaching over to the back seat, he picked up the bouquet he'd bought that afternoon. He'd opted for gerberas rather than roses because roses could have given out the wrong message. He was a friend wishing her well in her new home, not a lover come to court her.

His footsteps rang as hollowly as his thoughts as he walked up the path. He knocked on the door, just one light rap of his knuckles on the wood so that he wouldn't wake Millie. He could hear movements inside and imagined Becky getting up, wondering who it was, wondering if she should answer. Would she be more inclined to open the door if she knew it was him or less? He had no idea.

The door opened and there she was. Ewan felt his heart swell, felt it fill with so many emotions that he couldn't speak. He had missed her so much. Missed her more than he'd believed it possible to miss anyone. And it was then that it hit him that he loved her. Then when he felt at his most vulnerable. He loved her and there was nothing he could do about it, the same as there was nothing he could about the fact that she didn't love him.

'Ewan!'

He heard the surprise in her voice and rallied. Holding out the bouquet, he smiled at her. 'I brought you these to welcome you to your new home.'

'Thank you. They're lovely.' She took them off him, burying her face in the brightly coloured petals. It was a delaying tactic, he realised sadly, because they gave off very little scent. Becky had no idea what to say to him so maybe he should put them both out of their misery.

'I'm sure you must have loads to do so I won't keep you. I just wanted to give you the flowers and wish you well. I hope you'll be very happy here, Becky. You deserve to be.'

'That's what Tom said.' There was a catch in her voice that tugged at his heartstrings but he had to be strong.

'Tom gave you a hand to move in, did he? Great.'

'He and Hannah were brilliant. I wouldn't have managed half as well without their help.'

'That's good to hear.' He managed another smile even though his heart felt as though it was dangling round his heels. He should have been here to help her. He would have been, too, if he'd stuck to his plan to be her friend and nothing more. It was too late for regrets, however, so he had to make the best of it. He gave a tiny shrug, the weight of his heart weighing him down like a lump of lead. 'Anyhow, as I said, I don't want to hold you up...'

'You aren't.'

Colour ran up her cheeks when she realised how vehement she had sounded and Ewan couldn't help being intrigued. It appeared that Becky wasn't as eager for him to leave as he'd thought. He raised a brow, leaving her to elucidate, which she did in a breathy tone that completely destroyed his resolve to behave sensibly. How could he walk away when it appeared she wanted him to stay and wanted it badly, too?

'Everything's sorted out, amazingly enough.' She gave a tinkly little laugh that wouldn't have convinced the least perceptive person that she hadn't a care in the world. It certainly didn't convince him. 'There's nothing left to do.'

'As you say, that's amazing,' Ewan agreed, wondering if he was misreading the signals. Maybe he had it all wrong and Becky wasn't really trying to find a reason to detain him?

'Would you like to come in and have a look?' She opened the door and his heart gave an almighty bounce as it reclaimed its rightful place in his chest when he saw the plea in her eyes. 'After all, you helped me find this place, Ewan, so it seems only right that you should see the finished result.'

'I'd love to. Thank you.'

Ewan stepped into the tiny hall, ignoring the taunting little voice in his head that seemed rather keen to remind him that he'd had very little to do with her decision to rent the cottage. The truth was all well and good, but sometimes it was better dispensed with! He followed her into the sitting room, and looked around in genuine amazement. There were pictures on the walls, knick-knacks on the coffee table and cushions piled invitingly on the sofa.

'Good lord! It looks as though you've been living here for ages. I wish my flat looked half as cosy as this does.'

'It's lovely, isn't it?' Becky agreed, looking around with satisfaction. 'I can't believe how well everything has come together.' She plumped up a purple silk cushion and placed it back on the sofa. 'I'm really thrilled.'

'No wonder. You've worked miracles to get it all done in a day.' Ewan hesitated but he knew it had to be said. 'I'm sorry I wasn't here to help.'

'That's okay.' She gave a little shrug but he saw the hurt that crossed her face, and sighed.

'It isn't though, is it?' He touched her arm, felt the

flash of awareness that arced through his body, and moved his hand away. 'I should have been here to help you, Becky.'

'Don't worry about it. I expect you were busy. Now, how about a cup of tea? I'm afraid I don't have anything stronger so I can't even offer you a glass of wine.'

'No, thank you.' Ewan felt frustration bubble up inside him. She seemed determined to gloss over his inadequacies and it wasn't right. Maybe she hadn't missed him but he had missed her!

He spun round on his heel, knowing that he was on a very slippery slope. For the past two, very long, weeks he had done his best to be sensible. Every time he'd been tempted to phone her, he had reminded himself of the reason why it would be the wrong thing to do. Until he had decided if he could cope with them having a purely sexual relationship, he had to stay away from her and that meant no phone calls, no visits, nothing that might influence him one way or the other.

It was too important that he get it right. Too dangerous if he made a mistake. He had to be sure of what he wanted, one hundred per cent certain. If there was even the tiniest margin of doubt then it could all go horribly wrong and he could find his life in tatters.

'Don't go.'

The words were softly spoken yet they stopped him in his tracks. Ewan felt tension grip him as he stood there, half in and half out of the door. There was a roaring in his ears that seemed to grow louder with every second and yet he heard each word with perfect clarity as Becky continued.

'Please stay, Ewan. It's what I want more than anything.'

'Why?' His own voice sounded remarkably level given the fact that her answer was mind-bogglingly important to him.

'Because I missed you. Because the past two weeks have been so empty without you.' She paused and he realised that he was holding his breath. 'Because I need you in my life even if it's not going to be forever.'

Pain ripped through him. Nothing could have been clearer than that, could it? He turned around slowly, his heart aching when he saw the strain on her face. If this was hard for him, it was no less hard for her. The thought cut through all the clouds of uncertainty that had curdled his thoughts. Becky might not need him forever but she needed him now.

Two steps and she was in his arms, that was all it took. Ewan held her against his heart and knew she could feel it racing. It didn't matter; nothing mattered apart from the fact that she needed him. He bent and kissed her, softly and with a tenderness that stemmed from his love for her. Maybe she only wanted the comfort of sex from him but he would make sure that their lovemaking was as perfect as it could possibly be. It would be his gift to her, hopefully something she would remember with pleasure in the years to come.

The thought of the future sent a chill through him but he refused to allow it to spoil things. Lifting his hands, he cupped her face, tilting her head so that he could deepen the kiss, his tongue sliding into the warm sweetness of her mouth with an ease that made him shudder. Becky wanted him. She wanted his kisses, his caresses; she wanted him as her lover. It might not be all he wanted from her but it was enough.

He swung her up into his arms and carried her to the

sofa, pushing aside the cushions as he laid her down. Her eyes were half-closed, their hazel depths darkened with passion, and he kissed her again with an urgency that made her tremble. Reaching up, she took his face between her hands.

'This is what I want, Ewan. I'm sure about that.'

She drew his head down, her mouth opening under his, and he responded immediately. As he plundered her lips, any doubts he still had melted away. This was what he wanted too. He was sure.

He ran his hands down her body, following the curve of her breasts, the dip of her waist, the swell of her hips. They had never reached this point in the past; all they had shared had been that single mind-blowing kiss, and it was doubly exciting to have been given the licence to explore the soft, lush curves of her body.

His hands found the buttons down the front of her checked shirt and he carefully worked them free then hesitated before he drew it apart, wanting to take his time and savour the moment. His breath caught as he parted the folds of cotton and drank in the beauty of her body. Her skin was lightly tanned where the sun had touched it, pearly white beneath the black lace of her bra. Ewan slid the straps of her bra down her arms and lifted her breasts free, his heart pounding when he felt their weight nestle into his palms. Her nipples were already standing proud and erect yet they peaked even more when he drew them into his mouth. Becky wanted him and her body was telling him that too.

The thought was just too much. Ewan groaned as he claimed her mouth once more and kissed her, hotly, urgently, and with a hunger he couldn't disguise, and she responded with equal ardour. Grasping the hem of his

T-shirt, she pulled it over his head, their mouths parting just long enough to complete the action. Ewan was trembling as he allowed his weight to settle over her. He could feel her warmth seeping into his skin, feel her softness moulding itself to his shape.

Although he had made love to other women, nothing had prepared him for how he felt right then with Becky in his arms. It felt like the very first time he had ever made love, he realised in awe. There was a freshness about it, a thrill of discovery that made every touch, each caress seem untried, untested. Making love to Becky was unlike anything he had experienced before.

The room was dark, the moon that had been shining through the window while they were making love now hidden behind a cloud. Becky lay curled up on her side, watching Ewan while he slept. Although she couldn't see his face clearly, every feature was etched on her mind. The thick curl of his lashes lying on his cheeks, the slope of his nose—slightly crooked thanks to a skirmish on the rugby field— and the long mobile curve of his mouth, a mouth that had kissed every inch of her body.

A shiver ran through her at the thought. Making love with Ewan tonight had been a revelation. She had never experienced anything like it before. She let her mind drift, recalling the heat of his skin burning into hers, the feel of his hands caressing her, the strength and power of his erection as he had entered her. Was it the fact that it had been such a long time since she had made love that had made it all seem so much more intense? She wasn't sure. All she knew was that she had never experienced the range and depth of emotions she had discovered tonight in Ewan's arms.

'Can I move or do you plan on lying there, watching me, for a bit longer?'

The laughter in his voice made her smile and she grinned at him. 'I'm not sure. Give me a couple more minutes to decide, will you?'

'No way!' Rolling over, he scooped her into his arms with a speed that made her gasp. His lips were hot when they found hers, hot and hungry, and Becky sighed with pleasure. It seemed that Ewan hadn't tired of her just yet.

They made love again and once again it was so wonderful that Becky could scarcely believe what was happening. How could the simple touch of his hand on her breast make her feel as though she was flying? How could a kiss fill her with such intense pleasure? By the time their bodies joined in the most intimate act of all, her senses were awash. The deliciously male scent of Ewan's skin filled her nostrils, the touch of his fingers dancing over the soft inner skin of her thigh made her shudder, whilst the salty taste of perspiration when she touched his neck with the tip of her tongue was an aphrodisiac in itself.

Opening her eyes, she watched the dark shadow of his body looming over her and felt safe, secure, protected, listened to him breathing and knew that no matter what happened in the future, she would never regret what was happening now. Ewan had given her back something that had been missing for far too long. He had made her feel like a woman again and she would always be grateful to him for that, would always love him. It seemed only fitting that he should be the one to restore her femininity.

They fell asleep soon afterwards, their limbs entwined, their bodies spooned together. When they awoke the next morning, they were still holding onto each other. Ewan smiled as he turned her round and dropped a kiss on the tip of her nose.

'I couldn't bear to let you go.'

'Me too, or should that be neither?' Becky murmured. Had he any idea how sexy he looked lying there with his chest bare and his hair all rumpled? she wondered. Probably. After all, she wasn't the first woman Ewan had slept with, was she?

The thought was like a douse of cold water. Becky bit her lip as she tossed back the quilt. It was stupid to feel possessive, stupid and selfish too. She wanted Ewan to meet someone else, wanted him to have a wife and a family in time. She couldn't keep him to herself even if she wanted to because it wouldn't be right.

'What's the matter?'

He caught her hand and pulled her back down onto the bed. Becky shook her head because there was no way that she could tell him how she felt. How would lead to why and she couldn't take that risk, wouldn't risk having him tell her that it didn't matter if she could never give him a child, that he wanted her anyway. It would be far too easy to believe him.

'Nothing. It's just time I got up. Dad will be here soon with the furniture for Millie's bedroom,' she explained, relieved to have a valid excuse.

'In that case, I'd better get up as well.' He tossed back the quilt and she gulped as she was treated to an unobstructed view of his naked body as he got out of the bed. 'I'll give your father a hand to get everything upstairs…unless you'd rather I left, of course,' he added as an afterthought.

'I…no, of course not. Dad will be glad of your help.'

'It doesn't bother you, then? I mean, it will be pretty clear that I've spent the night if I'm here at this time of the morning.'

'It's fine. Really.' She shrugged. 'As we've said before, folk will believe what they choose to believe whatever we do.'

'Fair enough.' He gave her a quick grin and Becky told herself she had imagined the fleeting sadness in his eyes. 'Right, last one in the shower has to make breakfast!'

He headed for the door and after a moment's hesitation Becky ran after him. They reached the bathroom at the same time and had a playful tussle in the doorway before Ewan solved the problem of who was going first by carrying her inside. He deposited her in the shower stall and turned on the tap, ignoring her squeals as cold water rained down on her head. Stepping in beside her, he picked up the soap and smiled wickedly.

'Here's the deal. Obviously I won the challenge but I'm prepared to be generous. I'll make breakfast if I can scrub your back.'

Becky pouted. 'What about the dishes?'

He rolled his eyes. 'Talk about driving a hard bargain! Okay. I'll make breakfast *and* do the dishes. Deal?'

Becky held out her hand. 'Deal!'

Ewan caught hold of her hand and pulled her to him so that their bodies collided, wet skin sliding slickly against wet skin. His voice sounded more like a growl, rumbling beneath the gushing of the water. 'I'll get round to the back scrubbing in a moment.'

Becky sighed as he bent and kissed her. She closed her eyes, savouring the coolness of the water, such a contrast to the heat of Ewan's mouth. If only they could freeze time life would be perfect but it wasn't going to happen.

At some point in the not too distant future she had to call a halt, even though the thought filled her with dread. Having Ewan back in her life had made such a difference. He'd brought sunshine and laughter, warmth and fun plus a whole lot more, but they couldn't carry on like this. Not when it could mean him missing out on something as important as a family. He would only regret it and, worse still, probably end up blaming her, and she couldn't bear it if that happened.

Wrapping her arms around his neck, she kissed him back, aware of just how precious this time was. It could be weeks or even months but at some point they would have to part. And this time it would be forever.

CHAPTER FOURTEEN

'I DON'T KNOW what you're on but can I have some, please? Nobody should look as cheerful as you do after the day we've had!'

Ewan laughed as Cathy followed him into the staff-room. It was three weeks since that first night he and Becky had spent together and, quite frankly, it felt as though life couldn't get much better. They spent as much time as possible together and the amazing thing was that they seemed to be remarkably in accord. They enjoyed doing the same things, laughed at the same jokes, even watched the same television programmes—with one or two exceptions, he amended ruefully, re-calling Becky's love of reality shows, which he loathed. It was little wonder that he breezed through even the busiest days without it getting him down.

'I'm not sure if it will work for you,' he told Cathy with a grin.

'Try me.' She rolled her eyes. 'I'm open to any sug-gestions, believe me. My feet are killing me, my back aches, and as for the rest—well, booking myself into the knacker's yard could be my best option!'

'Sounds a bit extreme.' Ewan grabbed his jacket out of the locker. He was meeting Becky in town as they were planning on having dinner together. Her mother had offered to mind Millie so she was also spending the night at his flat. His heart, as well as various other bits of his anatomy, leapt at the thought. It was little wonder that he sounded a little strained as he offered Cathy some friendly advice. 'Why don't you book some time off? A break would do you the world of good.'

'And when do you think I'll be able to get any time off?' Cathy snorted. 'We're another nurse down since Laura left, so that makes three vacancies we're carrying. It's overtime for me, not a holiday, which is why I want to know what you're on that makes you so cheerful. Come on, Ewan, spill the beans!'

Ewan looked over his shoulder as though making sure the coast was clear. He bent closer to Cathy and lowered his voice. 'Love.'

'Pardon?' Cathy reared back and stared at him.

Ewan grinned. 'You wanted to know why I'm feeling so cheerful—well, it's all down to love.'

'Ah, I see. Pity. I thought it'd be something more prosaic, like some new drug you're testing or a super-duper new drink guaranteed to give you a boost.' She shook her head. 'Much as I love my husband, the days when the thought of seeing him put wings on my feet are long gone!'

Cathy took her bag out of the locker and left. Ewan chuckled as he followed her along the corridor. Maybe love did become less exciting with time but he couldn't imagine it, not if his feelings for Becky were anything to go by. As far as he was concerned, he would still find her exciting and sexy when they were both ninety!

The thought struck a chord, one he didn't want to think about. He headed into town, trying to ignore the tiny inner voice that was doing its best to have its say. So what if Becky hadn't said anything to indicate that she had changed her mind about them having a purely temporary relationship? He hadn't said anything either so he could hardly read anything into it. No, Becky needed to be sure about what she was doing after what had happened to her and he understood that. He was prepared to wait, however long it took.

She was already waiting outside the restaurant when he arrived. Ewan didn't hesitate as he took her in his arms. He would never get tired of kissing her, he thought, never, ever become complacent about their relationship. He had lost her once before and he was going to do his utmost not to lose her again.

'Hi,' he said softly as he reluctantly let her go. His gaze skimmed over her, drinking in the picture she made. She'd opted for cream trousers that night made from some sort of silky fabric that just hinted at the curves beneath. With them she was wearing a sleeveless top in a deep honey colour that made her hazel eyes look more gold than green and set off the light tan of her skin. She looked so beautiful that he felt his breath catch. He loved her so much and tonight he intended to tell her that too.

'Hi, yourself.' She laughed up at him, her nose wrinkling adorably. 'Do I take it from that very enthusiastic greeting that you missed me?'

'I did indeed.' Ewan grinned wickedly as he put his arm around her. 'I'd be more than happy to show you just how much, too. Why don't we skip dinner and go straight back to the flat?'

'No way!' She scooted out of his grasp and smiled

up at him. 'I'm absolutely starving, so unless you want to risk me passing out, I need to eat.'

Ewan didn't try to change her mind. Opening the restaurant's door, he ushered her inside. A couple of times he'd sensed that she'd been pulling back, but he understood. Becky didn't want them to go too fast. Neither did he really, only sometimes—like now—it was hard to remember that. He took a deep breath as he followed her inside. He had to be patient, give her time to adjust to the idea of them being together. If he pushed her he could end up losing her and that was the last thing he wanted.

The evening was perfect, but it always was when she was with Ewan. Becky spooned up the last of her raspberry mousse, determined not to let anything spoil the evening. She knew it couldn't last and that at some point they would have to break up, but not tonight. Tonight she was going to be with Ewan.

The thought sent heat flowing through her veins and she picked up her glass and took a sip of the wine. Their lovemaking had continued to be incredible. Although it seemed impossible, each time they made love it simply got better. She'd read that phrase about two people becoming one and dismissed it; now she knew it could and did happen. She couldn't imagine how she was going to feel when Ewan was no longer part of her life.

'That was delicious.' Putting down her glass, she smiled at him, refusing to go down that path. It was the here and now that mattered, not what happened in the future. 'How did you find this place? You never said.'

'One of the nurses recommended it.' Ewan sat back

in his chair and groaned. 'I am *so* full I think I might burst!'

'Oh, I see. She's got good taste, obviously,' Becky replied, trying to keep the edge out of her voice. Feeling jealous at the thought of the nurse recommending the restaurant to him was ridiculous. Ewan was free to talk to whomever he liked.

'He.' He smiled but there was a glint in his eyes that told her he'd picked up on her feelings. 'It was Rob who recommended the place to me. He's one of the charge nurses on the unit and a great guy too.'

'My mistake.' Becky attempted to brush it off but Ewan wasn't prepared to let it go.

'I'm not seeing anyone else, Becky, firstly because I don't want to and secondly because it wouldn't be right when I'm seeing you.'

'I didn't meant to imply that you were,' she said shortly, and he sighed.

'Maybe not, but you're bound to have doubts after what Steve did.' He shrugged. 'I know I had a reputation for playing the field in the past and that it was probably justified too. But I'm strictly a one-woman-at-a-time kind of a guy.'

'I know.' Becky smiled, putting every scrap of effort into making it appear genuine; however, his reassurances had done little to comfort her. Ewan might not choose to date more than one woman at a time but he hadn't claimed that he'd be eternally faithful to her, had he?

As that was the last thing she wanted, Becky realised how ridiculous she was being. She put it out of her mind as Ewan paid the bill. They walked back to his flat hand in hand because they both needed the contact. Ewan let them in, then took her in his arms as he kicked the door shut.

'Got you to myself at last,' he growled in a tone that was meant to be humorous but somehow fell short of the mark.

Becky closed her eyes as he kissed her, letting herself be carried away by the feel of his mouth and the promise of his touch. He was as eager for her as she was for him and that was all that mattered. As he led her into his bedroom, she knew that no matter what happened in the future, she would always have this. Ewan made her feel whole again, complete. Nobody else could have done this, only him. He made her feel like a real woman and she loved him all the more because of it.

Their lovemaking seemed to reach new heights that night, as though they both needed to prove to themselves as well as to each other how deep their feelings were. As Becky lay in his arms later, she knew that nothing could ever be as profound as what they had just shared. If this wasn't love then what was? The thought filled her with dread. She couldn't allow Ewan to fall in love with her!

'I love you.'

The words were so softly spoken that for a moment Becky thought they had escaped from her head, but then she realised that Ewan was looking at her and her heart seemed to freeze.

'No. Please don't say that.'

'Why not when it's true?' He brushed her mouth with his knuckles and a spasm passed through her, compounded partly of fear and partly of desire. 'I love you, Becky, and not saying it won't change how I feel.'

'I don't want you to love me, though!' The words slid out before she could stop them and she saw him wince.

'Because you still love Steve?' He shrugged, deliberately trying to downplay the hurt she could see in his eyes. 'I understand, Becky. Really I do.'

Becky knew that she could leave it there, that he would accept it and not push her, but it seemed wrong to let him believe a lie. 'It isn't that.'

'No? Then what is it?' He laid his hand against her cheek. 'Tell me, sweetheart. I don't want there to be any secrets between us even if the truth is far more painful.'

'I...' She stopped, afraid to go on yet unable to mislead him. She loved him too but that wasn't the issue. It was bigger than that, far, far bigger. She took a steadying breath. 'One day you'll want to have a family, won't you, Ewan?'

His hand lowered as he stared at her in confusion. 'Probably, yes. But what's that got to do with it?' He paused for a moment then said slowly, 'Are you saying that you don't want any more children, Becky?'

Becky knew she could use that as her excuse but it would be wrong. Ewan deserved the truth, nothing less. 'No. I would love to have more children but it isn't possible. I had a hysterectomy following the accident. The fact is that I can't have any more children—now do you understand?'

He did. He understood perfectly. All of a sudden Ewan couldn't speak, couldn't move, could barely breathe as the enormity of what she'd said hit him: Becky couldn't have any more children. She could never have *his* child.

'I'm so sorry, Ewan. This is exactly what I was trying to avoid. I never wanted to hurt you.'

Tears clogged her voice and the feeling came rushing back to his limbs. Reaching out, he pulled her into his arms, praying that he could find a way to comfort her. If he was hurting, how much worse must it be for her? 'It's all right, my love. Don't cry. It isn't your fault. None of it is your fault.'

His voice broke at that point, the tears he'd been struggling to hold back streaming down his face, and it was her turn to offer comfort. Wrapping her arms around him, she held him to her and he could feel her love pouring out of her and into him. It was almost too painful to realise how much she loved him at this most desperately sad moment.

They clung to one another for a long time before Ewan gently set her away from him. Although it was a blow to discover that they could never have a child, it didn't change how he felt about her. He loved her with all his heart, needed her in his life, couldn't imagine a future without her. Now all he had to do was convince her that their relationship could work.

'I wish it could have been different, Becky, really I do, but it doesn't alter how I feel about you. I love you and the fact that we can't have a family doesn't change anything.'

'Maybe not at the moment it doesn't but it could do in the future.' Her tone was bleak. 'The time will come when you realise just how much you are missing by not having a family of your own. I know how fond you are of your nephews and nieces and it's only natural that you'd want a child of your own one day. I can never give you a child, Ewan, and I couldn't bear it if you ended up hating me for denying you something so important.'

'I could never hate you!' He went to take her in his

arms again, appalled that she could think such a thing, but she pushed him away.

'You don't know how you'll feel in a few years' time and it's a risk I'm not prepared to take.'

'So you think it's better that we split up?' he said harshly, scarcely able to believe what was happening. To plummet from the heights of euphoria to the depths of despair in mere minutes was just too much to take in.

'Yes, I do. I won't be responsible for ruining your life, Ewan.'

'You could never do that.' He captured her hands and held them tightly, willing her to understand that he meant every word. 'I need you, Becky. I know we can be happy even if we can't have a child together. We'll have Millie, don't forget, and she's such a joy.'

'She is but she isn't your flesh and blood, Ewan.'

'I don't care about that— really I don't!' He gripped her hands harder, desperate to convince her. 'I love her and I can't think of anything I'd like more than to be a proper father to her.'

'And you'd be a wonderful father too. I know that, Ewan, but it doesn't change how I feel. It wouldn't be fair to allow you to sacrifice your chances of having a child of your own for me and Millie.'

She gently freed herself and tossed back the quilt. Ewan lay quite still, his head reeling, his heart in turmoil. He could try again to change her mind but he knew it would be a waste of time. Becky had made her decision and nothing he said would change it.

Despair washed over him in a huge grey tide. He couldn't bear to imagine how empty his life was going to be without her. When Becky came back and climbed into bed beside him, he drew her into his arms, drinking in the scent of her skin, the warmth of her body, the very essence of her being.

'I love you, Becky. Always remember that,' he said, his voice grating.

'And I love you too.'

The words should have been the sweetest in the world but they filled him with pain. Ewan closed his eyes, praying that sleep would offer some relief from the agony, although he knew it would be only temporary. Nothing was going to change. Tomorrow he would have to learn to live without her and he wasn't sure if he could do it.

It was raining when Becky got up the next morning. Surprisingly, she had slept heavily, her mind too filled with pain to dream. She made coffee and took a mug through to the bedroom for Ewan. He was wide awake, staring at the ceiling, and she didn't need to ask what he was thinking. It was obvious from his expression how devastated he felt.

'Don't.' She put the mug on the bedside table and sat down on the edge of the bed. 'I don't want you torturing yourself, Ewan. You have to accept that you and I are going nowhere and get on with your life. It's as simple as that.'

'Is it?' His smile was forced. 'Then why do I feel like this? If it's so simple, I should know that you've made the right decision.'

'It's been a shock. Once you're thinking clearly, you'll see that it would be a mistake if we got back together properly.'

'Properly? So the last few weeks don't really count?' His laughter was harsh and she flinched. 'Thanks a bunch, sweetheart. You really know how to cheer a guy up.'

'I didn't say that. Of course they count. They've been wonderful, the most wonderful time of my life, in fact.' She shook her head when he went to speak. 'But that was before we faced the facts and the fact is that if we stay together, we can't have a family. I can't give you a child, Ewan. Not ever.'

She stood up, unable to go over it all again. Picking up her clothes, she went into the bathroom and took a shower, trying not to think about the times Ewan had joined her there. There was no point thinking about what had happened and certainly no point thinking about what might have been. Their relationship had to end. And she had to make sure it did, no matter what Ewan said.

He was in the kitchen when she went to find him. He looked round and her heart ached when she saw the anguish in his eyes. He was hurting badly and what made it worse was knowing that she was responsible.

'I have to go. I'm sorry about what's happened but I hope we can still be friends.'

'So we can meet up for coffee?' He shrugged. 'I can't see that happening, Becky, can you? It's probably best if we make a clean break.'

'If that's what you want,' she said, wondering how she could bear the thought of not seeing him again.

'It isn't what I want. It's what you want, apparently.'

Tears stung her eyes when she heard the censure in his voice. 'I'm simply doing what I believe is right, Ewan. If you're honest then you know it would be madness to carry on. You'd end up hating me for not being able to give you a child and that isn't what either of us wants.'

She turned away before he could reply, afraid that if she didn't leave then, she wouldn't find the strength to do so. Ewan didn't try to stop her as she let herself out and that in itself seemed to prove her point. In his heart, he knew she was right, knew that no matter how much they loved one another, their relationship was doomed.

It was barely seven when she let herself into the cottage. She changed into her uniform then drove to the surgery. Hannah had just arrived as well and she grinned when she saw Becky.

'Another early bird. Charlie had us up at five so that's my explanation for such an early arrival. What's yours?'

'Oh, I woke up early too,' Becky said shortly, feeling her eyes fill with foolish tears once more.

'Hey, what's up? Have you and Ewan had a row?' Hannah grimaced when Becky looked at her. 'Ros happened to mention that you were staying over at his flat last night. Sorry. I didn't mean to pry.'

'That's okay.' Becky tried to smile but her mouth wouldn't seem to obey her.

'Come along.' Hannah took her arm and steered her through the surgery doors, quickly dispensing with the alarm before it started ringing. 'I think a cup of tea is called for, don't you?'

Hannah briskly led her to the staffroom, ignoring her protests that she was fine. Becky sank down on a chair while Hannah made the tea, wondering what she was going to do. There weren't that many options. She and Ewan had to go their separate ways, so she would just have to learn to live without him. Tears streamed down her cheeks and Hannah pressed a cup of tea into her hands.

'Here you are. Drink this and tell me all about it.'

Becky did as she was told, letting the whole sorry story come tumbling out. Hannah sighed when she had finished. 'Oh, Becky, I don't know what to say. It's so awful for both of you. Are you sure that you and Ewan can't find a way around the problem? I mean, you could adopt or even try to find a surrogate. It's perfectly acceptable these days.'

'But why should Ewan have to go through all that to have children? There's nothing wrong with him. It's me who can't give him a child.' She shook her head. 'No. He needs to find someone else, someone who can give him a family.'

'And who's to say that if he does find someone else, she can have kids? Or even if Ewan himself can have them? I mean, nobody really knows if they can until they try. Imagine how you'd both feel if that happened.'

'Don't!' Becky shivered. 'The only thing that's keeping me going is the thought of Ewan being a father one day. I can't bear to imagine it all going wrong.'

'I'm sorry. I don't mean to upset you, but you need to think about this. You love Ewan and he loves you. That's an awful lot to give up for something that might never happen anyway. Plus there's Millie. Anyone can see that Ewan thinks the world of her. Maybe she isn't his biological child but Ewan loves her just as Tom loves my Charlie.'

Hannah gave her an encouraging smile before she left the staffroom. Becky finished her tea, wondering if Hannah was right. Was it wrong to give up their love for something that wasn't a guaranteed certainty?

She sighed. She was looking for reasons for her and Ewan to stay together because she loved him so much. However, at the end of the day, she knew it wouldn't be fair to let him make such a huge sacrifice. She had to let him go no matter how much it hurt.

CHAPTER FIFTEEN

A WEEK PASSED, the longest, most agonising week of Ewan's life. Although he had been upset when Becky had left him eight years ago, it had been nothing to compared to this. Fortunately, life in ED continued to be hectic so everyone was far too busy to notice his downbeat mood, even the ever-perceptive Cathy. Ewan knew that he couldn't have explained what was wrong. It was far too painful to talk about why his heart was broken.

Saturday night arrived and he volunteered to work overtime when the agency registrar failed to turn up. Rob Blessing, the senior charge nurse who'd recommended that restaurant he'd visited with Becky that fateful night, was on duty. He grinned when he saw Ewan making his way to the desk.

'Here comes the cavalry.' He peered past Ewan, a look of mock surprise on his face. Rob was happily gay and very involved in amateur dramatics. 'Don't tell me you're riding solo tonight, cowboy.'

'Yep. There's just me and my trusty steed, only I think he's deserted me too and gone back to his stable.' Ewan made a determined effort and smiled. 'It's just you and me, pardner. Think we can handle it?'

'No sweat! We'll soon sort out the bad guys.'

The phone rang at that point so Rob passed him a file and answered it. Ewan made his way to the cubicles. His patient was a child, a boy aged ten who had come off his bike and injured his arm. His mother was with him and Ewan had to spend a few minutes calming her down before he could examine the boy.

'Right, then, Ethan, let's see what damage you've done to yourself.'

He carefully removed the sling the paramedics had used to support the boy's arm and discovered that his shoulder was dislocated. It was a forward and downward displacement, typical of a fall onto an outstretched hand.

'Hmm, looks like you've popped your shoulder out of its socket,' he told the boy in a deliberately upbeat tone that was at odds with his mood. Could he live out the rest of his life without Becky? Could he see himself growing old with someone else, because that's what it would mean? If he didn't find someone else and have a family then it would make a mockery of their sacrifice, yet he couldn't imagine it happening. How could he make love to another woman when it was Becky he loved, Becky he wanted, Becky he needed?

'I told you something like this would happen!' Ethan's mother's voice was shrill as she rounded on her son. Ewan hurriedly collected his thoughts.

'It's a fairly common injury,' he said soothingly. 'All it takes is a fall and—bingo—out it pops. We'll soon get it sorted out, so don't worry that Ethan's done himself any permanent damage. Give it a couple of weeks and his shoulder will be as good as new.'

'It should never have happened in the first place,' Mrs Jones declared. 'I told him he wasn't to go on that new BMX track but he took no notice.' She turned to the boy. 'Well, it's the last time this is going to happen, my lad. As soon as we get home, I'm going to put your bike up for sale!'

Ethan started to cry and Ewan frowned. The child had been extremely brave and it didn't seem fair that he should be treated so harshly. 'That seems a little harsh, if you don't mind my saying so. Your son could have popped his shoulder if he'd tripped over in the street.'

'But he didn't, did he? He came off his bike and it's not going to happen again.' Mrs Jones glared at him. 'It's obvious that you don't have any kids, Doctor, but when you do, you'll realise that you can't give them an inch or you'll regret it.'

Ewan forbore saying anything, afraid that anything he said would be unprofessional. He wrote out an instruction for the boy's shoulder and arm to be X-rayed as a fall like this often caused damage to the humerus and left the cubicle. If he and Becky got married then he would never get the chance to be a father, except to Millie, of course. Would he come to feel that he had missed out, as Becky believed, or would it be enough that he had her and Millie to love and care for? Pictures suddenly flashed through his head, pictures of the fun he'd had playing with Millie that day at the beach. He wouldn't have enjoyed it any more if Millie had been his *biological* daughter.

The thought was a much-needed boost to his spirits. As he made his way to the desk, he decided that he wasn't going to give up. Somehow he had to make Becky see that they could be happy together despite everything. He obviously looked more cheerful because Rob grimaced when he saw him.

'You aren't going to look nearly as happy when you hear what I have to tell you.'

'Why? What's happened?'

'It seems there's been a fight at one of the caravan parks. A gang of youths have knocked seven bells out of each other.' Rob sighed. 'The police are ferrying them in so we can patch them up.'

'Great.' Ewan glanced at the queue of people waiting to be seen. 'Looks like there's going to be a bit of a backlog. Any chance of drafting in some reinforcements to help?'

'What do you think?' Rob replied tartly.

The first police van arrived just then so Ewan went out to meet it. There were three young men inside, not much more than teenagers really, and they all had cuts and bruises.

'Right, you lot,' he said, knowing that they needed to know who was in charge. 'I shall make this clear: anyone who doesn't behave himself won't be treated. So no swearing at the staff and no causing a nuisance to the other patients. You're to sit quietly until your name is called. Understand?'

There was a bit of muttering but no real objections. Ewan led them inside and sat them down. The police had to go back to collect some more of the wounded but they left an officer behind to keep an eye on things. Ewan took the first youth into a cubicle, using glue to close the cut over his eye before he sent him on his way. If the police wanted to interview him, they would have to take him to the station. He was more concerned about clearing the decks before the next influx.

They worked as a team. He and Rob dealt with the worst cases while Moira and Trish saw to the rest. In a

very short time most of the youths had been seen. Rob
nodded towards the waiting room, which was packed.

'I'll see to the last of this little lot if you'll make a
start on the rest.'

'Will do.' Ewan picked up the next patient's notes.
'Amanda Lewis. Can you follow me, please?'

He led the woman into a cubicle. She'd twisted her
ankle and as it looked very swollen he decided to send
her for an X-ray to make sure it wasn't broken. Rob was
in the next cubicle and he could hear voices being raised
as he wrote out the slip and handed it to her. 'Along the
corridor on your right. Just knock on the door and someone will come out to you. Do you need a wheelchair?'

'No, my boyfriend can help me,' Amanda told him.
She grimaced when there was a crash from next door.
'I'll be glad to get away from here.'

Ewan hurried out of the cubicle and into the neigh-
bouring one, taking in the scene that greeted him. Rob
was trying to calm down his patient, who had over-
turned the trolley containing supplies. 'Everything okay
in here?' he asked, neutrally.

'Fine.' Rob grinned. 'Jez here isn't too keen on having an injection, it appears. We had a difference of opinion, shall we say?'

'Too right we did.' The teenager rounded on Ewan,
his face contorted into an ugly expression. 'I'm not having the likes of him putting needles in me. I might catch
something!'

It was a direct reference to Rob's sexuality and Ewan
couldn't let it pass. 'You were warned that if you didn't
behave yourself you wouldn't be treated. I think you'd
better leave.' He flipped back the curtain and waited
but the youth didn't move. 'The police are outside. Do

you really want me to call them in? You're in enough trouble as it is.'

Jez glowered at him. 'Do what you like but he's not putting his hands on me.'

Ewan had heard quite enough. Stepping forward, he took hold of the boy's arm. 'Come on, don't make this worse for yourself than it already is.'

He went to lead him towards the corridor, stopping when he felt something punch him hard in the chest. He looked down in surprise when he saw a knife sticking out of his body. Where had that come from? he wondered before everything started to go dark. There was a rushing in his head, the feeling that he was falling, down and down, and then nothing.

Becky was in her room when Tom came to find her. It was Monday morning and she'd just done a BP check on one of his patients and assumed he was eager for the results.

'You were right, her BP is rather low,' she told him, picking up the notes. 'One hundred over fifty so it will need checking again.'

'Thanks. I'll get Lizzie to make another appointment for her.' Tom paused as though he wasn't sure what to say next and Becky laughed.

'Come on, spit it out. If you want me to fit someone else into my list then I promise not to bite your head off.'

'It's not that.' He took a deep breath. 'I've just been speaking to a friend of mine at Pinscombe General. He told me that Ewan's on the cardiac unit.'

'Is he? How odd. He loves working in ED so I wonder why he's changed specialities?' Becky tried to keep her tone even, although after a week of not seeing Ewan it was hard to hold back her tears. She missed him so much and couldn't bear to imagine a future without him, even though she knew it was the right thing to do.

'He hasn't. He's a patient.' Tom's tone was gentle. 'It appears he was stabbed on Saturday night. The knife went straight into his heart.'

'Stabbed!' Becky exclaimed in horror.

'Yes.' Tom came around the desk and sat her down. 'It's bad, Becky. You need to know that, but he is alive.' He squeezed her hands. 'Hannah told me about you two splitting up because you can't have children, but I thought you'd want to know.'

'Of course.' Becky took a deep breath, trying desperately to clear her head. Ewan was hurt and she needed to be with him; nothing else mattered except that. She jumped up and grabbed her bag out of the drawer. 'Can you tell Lizzie that I have to go out? I don't know what she's going to do about my appointments...'

'We'll work something out,' Tom assured her. He followed her into the corridor. 'Are you sure you're fit to drive? I can phone for a taxi if you want.'

'No. I just need to get to the hospital and see Ewan.'

'Of course. Give him our love, won't you?' Tom told her and she nodded, afraid to admit how scared she was that it might not be possible. If Ewan died she wouldn't be able to give him her colleagues' love or her own.

Tears blurred her eyes as she hurried out to her car but she blinked them away. It seemed to take forever to get to the hospital and then there was all the hassle of finding a parking space. In the end she parked on double yellow lines. The car wasn't in the way and she didn't care if she got a ticket. It took her another few minutes to find the cardio unit and when she arrived, she was told that Ewan had been moved to ICU. His condition had worsened in the last hour and it had been decided that he needed specialised nursing care.

Becky could barely contain her anguish as she made her way to ICU and went through the rigmarole of explaining who she was. Fortunately, Ewan's parents were there and they vouched for her but it all took time. Then she had to wait while the consultant finished examining him but finally she was allowed in to see him.

She made her way to the bed, trying to ignore all the tubes and monitors he was attached to. She knew they were essential but it was a shock to see him like this, so still, so pale, so very vulnerable. Ewan had always been very fit, always been strong in mind as well as body, and it hurt to see him lying there like that. Sitting down beside the bed, she covered his hand with hers, mindful of the wires leading from it.

'Ewan, it's me, Becky. I'm sorry I didn't come sooner. I didn't know what had happened, you see, but I'm here now and I'm going to stay until you're better. I love you so much, my darling. You have to try really hard to fight this because I need you.'

A sob welled to her throat and she stopped, not wanting him to hear her crying. He couldn't die. Not when she needed him so much. Maybe she couldn't give him a family but she could love him with all her heart and that had to count for a lot.

'I love you,' she repeated. 'I love you so much, Ewan. Please don't leave me.'

Consciousness came back in a rush. One minute there was nothing but blankness and the next he could feel and hear. Someone was talking to him, a voice he recognised, although for a second he couldn't place it. And then he realised it was Becky and sighed. Everything would be all right now that Becky was here.

He turned towards her, forcing his eyelids to open, but they wouldn't move. He tried again but they seemed to be stuck together... He flinched when the tape was removed, taking one of his eyelashes with it. However, at least he could see and that was a relief. His gaze rested on her as a rush of emotions hit him. He loved her so much, far too much to let her go. Maybe they could never have a family but they could have each other and that was more than enough. He would devote his life to loving her and Millie, and be happy.

'Ewan, can you hear me?' She bent over him, her hazel eyes filled with worry, and his heart wept for what he must have put her through.

'Yes,' he whispered because his throat was raw from having had a tube down it. Unlike all those scenes in the movies when the unconscious patient awoke and had no idea what had happened, he remembered everything: the pain in his chest, the darkness, followed by nothing....

He shuddered, not wanting to think about that. He was alive and Becky was here with him—that was all that mattered. 'I love you,' he said hoarsely, praying that she understood what he was trying to say.

Her face lit up so it appeared that she did. 'I love you too, so very much.' She kissed him with exquisite gentleness and he groaned in frustration. He didn't want kid-glove treatment—he wanted passion!

'Did I hurt you?' The anxiety in her voice made him smile because it was so totally misplaced.

'Nope. I'd just prefer it if you kissed me with a bit more enthusiasm, shall we say?'

She chuckled as she glanced over her shoulder. 'I shall once we dispense with our audience.'

Ewan peered past her and only then realised that his parents were standing outside the glass wall of the cubicle. That they had heard what he'd said was only too apparent from the expression on his mother's face. Ewan bit back a chuckle as he promised himself that when Millie grew up, he would accept that she was an adult and had needs.

The fact that he was picturing himself playing a major role in Millie's future suddenly filled him with doubts. What if Becky didn't agree? What if she still insisted that they had to split up? He had to make her understand how wrong it would be. He needed her. She needed him. And they both needed Millie.

'I don't want us to part, Becky,' he said urgently. 'I understand why you think it's the right thing to do but I can't bear it.'

'I don't want it either, so long as you're sure, Ewan.' She looked into his eyes, searching for the truth, and smiled when she found it. 'Thank you. That you're willing to give up so much for me makes me realise how lucky I am.'

'I'm the lucky one. I get to have you and Millie in my life long term.' He smiled back, unashamed of the tears in his eyes. 'I love you both. You're my heart, my soul and my family.'

They kissed then, not the light touch of lips their audience expected but a kiss of passion and commitment, of promise and desire. Ewan felt Becky's lips on his and could feel the strength flowing back into his body. Becky had done this. She had given him the best reason in the world to get better. She had promised him herself and her love, and her daughter. He had to be the luckiest man alive.

Two years later...

'It's a boy! Here you go, mum. Meet your new son.'

Becky felt her heart overflow with happiness as she took the towel-wrapped bundle from the midwife. She stared down at the tiny, puckered face in wonder. The baby had Ewan's nose and his eyes. His hair was dark like Ewan's too and she knew it would stay that way. This little chap was going to be the image of his father when he grew up.

'I can't believe how much he looks like you.' Ewan gently parted the folds of towel and stared at his son in amazement. 'He's the image of you, Becky!'

Becky laughed. 'I was just thinking how much he favoured you. Look at his eyes and the shape of his nose. If that's not a MacLeod nose, I don't know what is!'

'I see we shall have to agree to differ.' Ewan hugged her. 'Well, whomever he favours, he's gorgeous and I can't wait to show him off to everyone.'

'Neither can I. I just want to thank Shona again for all she's done.'

'Me too.'

They went over to the bed. All three of Ewan's sisters had offered to act as a surrogate for them but in the end Shona had won. She and her family had moved back to Devon, so that had made the process a lot simpler. Becky's eggs had been fertilised by Ewan's sperm and Shona had, as she put it, acted as the incubator.

Amazingly, it had taken just one attempt for her to get pregnant and they were holding the result in their arms. Becky bent and kissed her sister-in-law on the cheek.

'Thank you from the very bottom of my heart. I can't tell you what this means to us.'

'I think I can guess.' Shona smiled as she held her husband's hand tightly. He'd been behind her every step of the way, which had made it feel even more right. 'Now go and show off your new son to his adoring fans. There'll be a riot out there if they don't get a glimpse of him soon!'

Becky laughed as she followed Ewan to the delivery room door. They were all there, waiting to meet the new arrival: her family, her mother holding tight to Millie's hand; her father and brother, both looking uncharacteristically anxious; Ewan's family, complete with various nieces and nephews. Tom and Hannah had brought along the latest addition to their family, six-week-old Olivia, as well as Charlie, while Ben, Emily and Theo had flown over from France especially for this moment. Turning so that they could all see the precious little bundle she held, Becky said the words she had never thought she would be able to say.

'We would like you all to meet James Ewan MacLeod. Our son.'

* * * * *

A sneaky peek at next month...

Medical Romance™

CAPTIVATING MEDICAL DRAMA—WITH HEART

My wish list for next month's titles...

In stores from 2nd August 2013:

☐ The Maverick Doctor and Miss Prim

& About That Night... — Scarlet Wilson

☐ Miracle on Kaimotu Island — Marion Lennox

& Always the Hero — Alison Roberts

☐ Daring to Date Dr Celebrity — Emily Forbes

& Resisting the New Doc In Town - Lucy Clark

Available at WHSmith, Tesco, Asda, Eason, Amazon and Apple

Just can't wait?

Where will *you* read this summer?

#TeamSun

Join your team this summer.

www.millsandboon.co.uk/sunvshade